# THE COURT-MARTIAL OF
# BENEDICT ARNOLD

## RICHARD MCMAHON

IRONWOODS
PRESS

THE COURT-MARTIAL OF BENEDICT ARNOLD by Richard McMahon

First Edition, August 2015

Published by Ironwoods Press

Copyright © 2015 Richard McMahon

Author Services by Pedernales Publishing, LLC.
www.pedernalespublishing.com

Cover by Pedernales Publishing, LLC.

Library of Congress Control Number: 2015947159

ISBN:    978-0-9961568-5-1 Paperback Edition
         978-0-9961568-4-4 Hardcover Edition
         978-0-9961568-3-7 Digital Edition
         978-0-9961568-2-0 Audiobook Edition

Printed in the United States of America

# BOOKS BY RICHARD MCMAHON

# THE COURT-MARTIAL OF BENEDICT ARNOLD: WHAT IF—?

BENEDICT ARNOLD was the most notorious traitor in American history. Entrusted with the defense of West Point by George Washington during the Revolutionary War, he attempted to surrender it to the British. The conspiracy, had it succeeded, would probably have been the death knell for the American cause. Fortunately, his treachery was discovered at the last moment. Warned of the plot's failure, Arnold just barely evaded capture and escaped to British lines.

But what if Arnold *had* been captured by the Americans and tried by court-martial for treason? What would his defense have been? Would we have learned what prompted this man, a true hero of the war's early days, to suddenly turn on his country?

A novel that blends fact and fiction can be confusing to readers trying to determine which is which. With a few exceptions, all events depicted in this book actually occurred. Past events referred to during the trial are historically accurate, including military campaigns, and details of Arnold's life and military service. Most characters appearing in the book are real, with the exception of those listed as "Actors" at the end of the book. Actions and statements by real persons outside the context of the court-martial are accurately recorded. When the real characters assume actor's roles, I have tried to make them act and speak as I believe they would have done.

Letters and other documents reproduced in the text are genuine, except the news story from *The New England Courant* in Chapter 2, and André's letter to Clinton in Chapter 26. These papers can be found in various archives, libraries, and collections.

# CAST OF CHARACTERS

## American Army

General George Washington, Commander in Chief, Army of the
United States of America

Major General Benedict Arnold, Commander, Fortress West Point
& Highlands Department

Major General The Marquis de Lafayette, Corps commander,
Continental Army

Major General (Inactive) Phillip Schuyler, Member of Congress
from New York

Brigadier General Henry Knox, Chief of Artillery, Continental
Army

Brigadier General Anthony Wayne, Division commander,
Continental Army

Colonel John Laurance, Judge Advocate General, Continental
Army

Colonel John Lamb, Resident Commandant, Fortress West Point

Colonel Ebenezer Thatcher, Commander, Wayne's Reserve
Regiment

Lieutenant Colonel Alexander Hamilton, Aide to General
Washington

Lieutenant Colonel John Jameson, Commander, 2nd Continental
Dragoons

Lieutenant Colonel Eleazar Oswald, former secretary to General
Arnold

Lieutenant Colonel Richard Varick, secretary to General Arnold
Major Benjamin Tallmadge, Second in Command, 2nd Continental
  Dragoons
Major David Franks, Aide to General Arnold
Lieutenant Solomon Allen, 2nd Continental Dragoons
Private John Paulding, irregular militiaman

**British Army**

Lieutenant General Sir Henry Clinton, Commander in Chief,
  British Army in North America
Lieutenant General James C. Robertson, Military Governor, New
  York City
Colonel Beverly Robinson, Commander, Loyal American
  Regiment, British Army
Major John André, Adjutant General, British Army
Captain George Beckwith, temporary successor to Major André
Captain Caleb Fowler, Commander, Loyal American Rangers
Lieutenant John Sutherland, Captain, HMS *Vulture*

**Civilians**

Amelia Martin, schoolmistress, and sometime barmaid
Joshua Hett Smith, special agent, assisting General Arnold
Pierre Eugene du Simitière, friend of Major André
Margaret (Peggy) Shippen Arnold, wife to General Arnold
Thaddeus Stewart, surgeon, Continental Army headquarters
Mary Burns, friend of Amelia Martin

**Members of the Court-Martial**

President:  Major General Nathanael Greene
Members:  Major General Lord Stirling [William Alexander]
          Major General Robert Howe
          Major General Arthur St. Clair

Major General The Baron Friedrich von Steuben
Brigadier General James Clinton
Brigadier General John Glover
Brigadier General Edward Hand
Brigadier General Jedediah Huntington
Brigadier General Alexander McDougall
Brigadier General Samuel E. Parsons
Brigadier General John Paterson
Brigadier General John Stark

## Counsel

For the United States: Lieutenant Colonel Thomas Edwards,
    JAG Corps
For the Defense: Major Joshua Thorne, JAG Corps

# CHAPTER ONE

*Along the Peekskill-Fishkill Road, New York*
*September 25, 1780*

GEORGE WASHINGTON WAS enjoying the morning. The Hudson Valley had just begun to display its fall colors, and the brisk, invigorating air of autumn temporarily took his mind off the dire conditions that faced his army. His inspection trip was going well, and he looked forward to a visit with his best fighting general, Benedict Arnold, and his beautiful and vivacious wife, Peggy. He would be joining them for a late breakfast at Robinson's House, Arnold's residence, now less than a thirty-minute ride away. He also looked forward to a thorough tour of Fortress West Point, which Arnold now commanded, and which was the finest fortification constructed by the Americans since the start of the war. It needed to be. Its loss would probably end the war for American independence.

Farther to the east, a weary messenger with an urgent packet of documents rode to intercept the commander in chief of the Continental Army. He had been dispatched the day before, expecting to reach Washington at Danbury, where he was scheduled to stay that night. However, Washington's party met the French ambassador on the road, and had turned back for discussions, lodging the night at Fishkill instead. Not finding Washington in Danbury, the messenger spent the night, then started early the next morning for the general's next stop, West Point.

Slightly farther to the south, another messenger was riding to West Point, with an equally urgent message for Benedict Arnold. Although it was unknown to any of the participants at the time, history would turn on which messenger reached his destination first.

Robinson's House was an unusual location for the residence of the commander of West Point. It lay on the opposite side of the North River from the fortress, almost two miles downstream, and only accessible to it by barge. However, the spacious, two-story wood and brick mansion was well within American lines, and had also been the residence of the previous commander, General Howe. Once owned by Beverly Robinson as part of his 8,000-acre estate, it had been confiscated by the Americans when Robinson declared his loyalty to Great Britain and joined the British to fight against the rebellion.

As Washington's party turned off the main road for the final mile to Robinson's House, the messenger caught up with them. He recognized General Henry Knox riding in the rear, and reined so hard his horse reared.

"An urgent packet for General Washington!"

Knox, the army's chief of artillery, opened it at once. A moment later he dug in his spurs and raced toward Washington, who rode at the head of the column.

Meanwhile, General Arnold and his wife relaxed over tea, waiting for Washington to join them. With them were Lieutenant Colonel Alexander Hamilton, and two other aides to Washington, who had arrived in advance of their chief. When word came that the commander in chief and his party were approaching, General Arnold rose from the table. Limping noticeably, as a result of two severe wounds suffered at Quebec and Saratoga, he took his wife's hand. Together, they made their way to the doorway of the large house, where they waited to greet Washington, who was not only Arnold's commander, but his friend and mentor. The others joined them, standing just behind the general and his lady.

The sound of hooves approaching at a gallop, rather than the expected leisurely trot, was the first indication that something was amiss. Thundering up to the doorway, accompanied by a half-dozen of his blue-and-white-uniformed Life Guards, Washington reined up in front of the astounded couple, spraying gravel at their feet.

"Seize this man!" Washington shouted to his guards. There was an instant of dead silence as the guards hesitated. They recognized Arnold and were as dumbfounded by the order as Arnold appeared to be.

"Seize him I said!" Washington sprang from his horse, drew his sword and pointed it only inches from Arnold's face.

The guards now scrambled to obey their commander. Leaping from their horses, they advanced on Arnold from both sides and pinioned his arms behind his back.

"Sir...Your Excellency...." Arnold was having difficulty speaking. "What is the meaning of this?"

For an answer, Washington brandished a document close enough for Arnold to read. "What is the meaning of *this*?" he demanded. "It is a pass found in the possession of a British officer, captured attempting to cross from our lines south to New York."

Arnold flushed, his eyes widening. "I...I don't understand—"

Washington shoved the document closer to his restrained subordinate. "Is this not your signature?"

"It...it appears so, but—"

"And this?" Washington raised another document at Arnold. "It is a detailed analysis of the strength and armaments of Fortress West Point. It was also found in his possession, and it is also in your hand." Washington was furious now, his countenance a deep red, his steel-gray eyes blazing. "There is more here, much more," he said, shaking the papers in Arnold's face. "All of it shows a clear intent to betray West Point to the enemy, and all of it has your mark upon it."

Thoroughly shaken, his countenance pale, Arnold struggled to reply. "Your Excellency, I..."

"Choose your words carefully, general. Your life is at stake."

"Sir," Arnold stammered, "I cannot understand any of this. I...I need time to investigate..."

"You shall have time, sir, but it is I who will do the investigating." Washington turned to Hamilton, who was standing behind Arnold, his eyes wide with shock. "Take General Arnold under guard to the fortress and have him placed under closest arrest. Have him put in chains, if necessary."

Arnold's face reddened. "General...I must protest," he pleaded. "I am innocent of any intrigue, I assure you."

"The evidence says otherwise, sir." Washington turned aside, motioning to Lafayette and General Knox, who hastened to his side. "In any case, I have urgent matters to attend." He dismissed Arnold with a wave. As Hamilton attempted to brush past her, Peggy Arnold fainted in his arms.

After Arnold was led off, a hasty conference between Washington and his staff sent aides and messengers rushing in several directions. General Knox raced to Robinson's Landing, where he overtook the barge taking Hamilton and Arnold to West Point—his mission, to order the garrison to full battle alert. He was also to ascertain if the garrison commander, Colonel John Lamb, an old friend of Arnold's, had any part in the conspiracy, and if the treachery went any further than Arnold himself. A courier galloped south to the main army at Tappan with orders to General Nathanael Greene to send a brigade to reinforce West Point immediately, in case a British attack was imminent. Others rode eastward, alerting veteran regiments in Connecticut and Massachusetts to be prepared to move quickly against the flank of any British attack upon the Highlands. Pickets were posted south along the River Road to warn of the approach of any enemy force that might be intent upon capturing the commander in chief of the American Army and his staff.

In the midst of this activity, a tired, dusty lieutenant arrived at Robinson's House. He bore a letter to General Arnold from Colonel John Jameson, commander of the 2nd Continental Dragoons at North Castle, the same officer who had also sent the documents seized from the British officer to Washington. Hearing of Arnold's fate, the lieutenant presented the letter to the commander in chief. It informed Arnold that Lieutenant Solomon Allen was delivering "a certain John Anderson, taken going in to New York," along with papers he possessed which seemed "of a very dangerous tendency." The letter ended by informing Arnold that the papers had been sent directly to Washington.

Washington tossed the letter onto the table. "If the other messenger had not reached me first, Arnold would have escaped." He glanced up sharply at Lieutenant Allen. "The letter says you are delivering John Anderson. Where is he?"

Allen was young and had never been in the presence of Washington, but he was tired enough not to be intimidated by his rank or his stern manner. "Sir, shortly after I departed North Castle, I was overtaken by a messenger from Colonel Jameson warning me that there were reports of enemy patrols operating between North Castle and West Point. To avoid losing our prisoner, I was directed to take him to our outpost at South Salem, and leave him under heavy guard. I was then to proceed with the delivery of the letter to General Arnold."

"A providential change," Washington mused. "If not for that detour, Arnold would have been warned." He knew of no British patrols operating anywhere in the area, and suspected that the reason for the change in plan lay elsewhere, and had not been revealed to Lieutenant Allen. He would ascertain the true cause later. He dismissed the young officer to his breakfast, and returned to conferring with his staff.

After everything possible had been done to react to the emergency, Washington finally allowed himself to reflect on the events of a day which had sent his world careening. Slowly, the immensity of the betrayal began to register. He left the confines of the house and sank onto a wooden bench in the front garden, where he retreated into a gloomy silence. The two aides who had arrived with Hamilton kept the commander in chief under their observation, but from a safe and respectful distance.

"He takes it hard," observed the junior of the two.

"It's to be expected," replied the other. "The man was like a younger brother to him. Only Lafayette holds more affection in his heart." He looked up to a window on the second floor of the mansion, where the curtains were tightly drawn. "'Tis her I feel pity for, the young wife. She's been here less than a month, poor woman, and with a young babe. Colonel Hamilton says she's distracted to the point of madness."

Both officers continued to regard Washington with guarded concern. Although at the moment it seemed that all his spirit had deserted him, they knew that this usually most courteous of commanders, when sufficiently provoked, was capable of towering rage.

Perhaps they recalled how it was unleashed upon General Charles Lee at the battle of Monmouth. Lee, never fully convinced that American soldiery would ever be a match for British regulars, had ordered a retreat from the battle, when there seemed no military reason to do so. Confronted by a storm of profanity from the commander in chief, Lee claimed that his men were not able to stand against the redcoats. George Washington had replied with icy fury, "Sir, they *are* able, and by God they *shall* do it!" He then proceeded to turn the retreating troops around, and form defensive positions, narrowly averting disaster. General Lee had faced a court-martial for his action, and was found guilty. Suspended from command for one year, he was later dismissed from the army.

Or they may have remembered Kip's Bay, earlier in the war, when Washington's troops had broken and run before the British regulars landing on Manhattan Island. He had fumed, shouted and cursed them, riding among the fleeing ranks, striking right and left with the flat of his sword, demanding that they stand fast. But the panic-stricken men could not be rallied. "Are these the men with whom I am to defend America?" he roared, enraged at such cowardice. Now, with the American cause at its lowest ebb since those grim days of 1776, this new disaster might well be its death knell. Who could tell his reaction when he finally roused from his present mood?

A horse and rider appeared on the road, from the direction of Robinson's Landing. It was Hamilton, returning from West Point, where he had accompanied General Knox. Dismounting, he walked quickly up to where Washington sat.

"Sir, General Knox wishes to report that he is convinced Colonel Lamb is innocent of any knowledge of this conspiracy. Lamb has placed General Arnold under 24-hour guard in a cell at Fort Putnam to await further instructions."

At the words, Washington slowly roused as if from sleep. Color returned to his face and clarity to his eyes. "Inform Colonel Lamb that he is to take no instructions pertaining to General Arnold except those from me." Aware of Arnold's popularity among the rank and file of the army, and his long-standing friendship with Lamb, he added. "I shall hold him personally responsible if the prisoner escapes, or is freed from imprisonment by any means." He then rose from the bench, the paleness of his features gradually giving way to the dull red of anger. When he spoke again, even the sentries at their removed posts at the mansion's doorway cringed at the sound.

"By God, I will not rest until we have hanged that traitorous swine!"

# CHAPTER TWO

*THE NEW-YORK PACKET*
*Fishkill, September 26, 1780*

## A MOST HEINOUS BETRAYAL
### Treason at West Point!

### General Arnold Implicated!
### Imprisoned at the Fortress!

A CATASTROPHE OF great magnitude was narrowly averted yesterday, when a plot was uncovered to surrender Fortress West Point to British forces. By a stroke of good Fortune, a party of patriot irregulars captured a British officer disguised in civilian clothes who had in his possession detailed plans of the Fortress, as well as information pertaining to the strength of the garrison, its stores and weapons, and other information of great value to a potential attacker. Included among the documents, which were found in the officer's boot, was information of a secret nature from a recent Council of War between General Washington and his staff. But even more shocking was the fact that this officer also carried a pass made out by General Benedict Arnold, Commander of Fortress West Point and of all the Highlands Department.

The captured British officer was turned over to the commander of Continental Army forces in North Castle, who placed him in arrest and forwarded the suspicious documents to General Washington, who by coincidence, was in the vicinity to make an inspection visit to West Point. Upon receiving and reading the documents, General Washington hastened with all speed to General Arnold's quarters, where he was expected for breakfast, and confronted him with the incriminating papers. Unable to give an explanation to his commander, General Arnold was placed under arrest and imprisoned within the fortress.

It is said that at first General Washington could scarcely believe this act of treachery from one of his most trusted associates. Finally, however, accepting the reality of this infamous act, he assembled his staff. "General Arnold has betrayed us," he announced, a tear running down his cheek. "Whom can we trust now?"

Recovering quickly from the emotional scene, His Excellency ordered an immediate reinforcement of the West Point garrison, and other security measures to thwart a surprise enemy attack. He also set in motion and investigation to determine if this vile conspiracy has permeated deeper into the ranks of the Army. Meanwhile, the British officer captured with the fateful documents remains under heavy guard at an undisclosed location.

What is there to be made of such a woeful event? How can it be that the Conqueror of Montreal and the Hero of Saratoga stoops to lowly treason? In truth, we may never know. But we can be assured of one thing. As announced yesterday in a proclamation to the Army on behalf of the Commander in Chief, the timely discovery of this "treason of the blackest dye affords the most convincing proof that the liberties of America are the object of Divine protection."

# CHAPTER THREE

*Headquarters, British Army of North America, New York City*
*September 26, 1780*

GENERAL SIR HENRY Clinton paced the length of his office to his large window and then back again. Normally, the commander in chief of His Majesty's army in the American colonies felt at ease in his spacious headquarters at One Broadway, with its large, airy rooms and sweeping views. The immense parlor, more than 50 feet in length, lent a particular grandeur to the mansion, even though it was now occupied by various members of his staff, and cluttered with their desks and files. Built in 1750 by Archibald Kennedy, a retired Royal Navy captain and one of the greatest landholders in New York, it was easily the finest home in the city. But Clinton was far from at ease on this day. News of the capture of Major John André, adjutant general of the command, had come as a brutal shock.

Clinton had been back in New York a little more than three months, returning from his resounding victory over rebel forces in South Carolina. The fall of Charleston, and the surrender of its defending army of more than 5,000 Americans, was the greatest British military achievement of the war, and had dealt a crushing blow to the rebel cause. The capture of West Point, with its strategic position on the North River, would sever New England from the rest of the colonies, and almost certainly end the war, assuring the commander in chief a position in history perhaps equal to that of the Duke of Marlborough. But now that would not happen.

The general, who had been raised in Manhattan, was comfortable in this friendly city, where many residents remained loyal to the Crown. His father, an admiral in the Royal Navy, had been governor of New York, and it was with some reluctance that young Henry had left for schooling in England at the age of 19. Now, many years later, his service as second in command to General Sir William Howe had returned him to New York. However, the assignment had involved a series of frustrations, with Howe consistently ignoring his suggestions and recommendations. In desperation, Clinton had seriously considered resigning. In the end, however, it was Howe who resigned, following the disaster of Burgoyne's defeat at Saratoga, and Clinton had assumed the command.

Clinton knew that he was not popular in the army, or in Whitehall, where he had only lukewarm support from the ministers of His Majesty's government. He realized that he did not possess a natural gift for command; his forte was planning. Even his detractors admitted that his plan for the battle of Long Island, making a wide envelopment of the American left wing, had led to a brilliant victory. Now, more than two years later, with the victory at Charleston in the south, he felt that his strategy for winning the war had been vindicated. He had hoped to follow through with a similar blow in the north, and end the rebellion. The opportunity to seize the heavily defended fortress of West Point would have been the perfect realization of his plan, a plan which had now been dashed.

Three men entered his office in silence. Clinton's secretary, Captain Smith, seemed unperturbed, awaiting instructions, but Colonel Beverly Robinson, commander of the Loyal American Regiment, and Lieutenant Andrew Sutherland, captain of HMS *Vulture*, were clearly ill at ease. Both officers had accompanied André on the *Vulture* en route to his appointment with General Arnold, and they had returned without him. As Clinton continued his pacing, they knew there was little they could offer that would reduce their general's agitation. It was well known that the commander in chief was exceptionally fond of his handsome and talented adjutant general, so fond, in fact, that eyebrows were sometimes raised.

For Robinson, the situation was particularly unsettling. In approving the West Point operation, Clinton had initially refused André permission to meet with Arnold, specifying that Robinson would be the officer to do so. It was only after weeks of pleading by his impetuous and ambitious young subordinate that Clinton agreed to allow him a role. But it was clear that, although André would meet with Arnold, Robinson would be in charge. He knew Clinton would hold him responsible, and for that reason he was not looking forward to this meeting.

Finally, Clinton ceased his pacing, and motioned the men to be seated. It was to Robinson that he directed his first words.

"How did this sorry situation come to pass, colonel? As the senior and more experienced officer, I expected you would insure success of the mission. Instead, it has unraveled completely, and one of my most promising young officers is a prisoner, accused by the enemy of being a spy."

Robinson cleared his throat, trying to dispel the dryness that would impede his speech. "Sir, I sincerely wish I could explain events to your satisfaction, but I am in the dark about much which transpired." The words came scratchy and hoarse, and he cleared his throat again.

"Be kind enough, then, to tell me what you *do* know."

"Yes, sir." Robinson cleared his throat for the third time. "As planned, Major André came aboard the *Vulture* at about 7 pm on Wednesday, the 20th. By previous arrangement with Arnold, we were to expect his agent, Smith, to arrive at the ship under cover of dark early the following morning. In that, we were disappointed, for Smith failed to appear. It was especially disheartening for Major André, since, as you know, it was his second failed attempt to meet Arnold. The major had developed a severe grippe overnight, and decided to rest another day before returning to New York."

Although he said nothing, Clinton knew more than Robinson did regarding André's prolonged stay. The young officer had written his chief early Thursday morning, explaining that he had feigned illness in order to remain aboard ship and give Arnold one more chance to consummate the meeting.

"That night Smith finally appeared," Robinson continued. "It was near to midnight. He stated he was to take Major André to a meeting onshore with Arnold."

"And you let him go alone?"

Expecting the question, Robinson replied at once. "It was unavoidable, Sir Henry. Smith had a pass for only himself, two boatmen, and Mr. John Anderson, André's cover name. He brought nothing that mentioned my name or André's and mine together. Considering this, Major André thought it was best for him to go alone, since it was he that Arnold wished to see. I therefore submitted to be left behind. Major André left the ship between twelve and one o'clock Thursday night, and that was the last we saw or heard of him."

Clinton allowed a moment to digest Robinson's information. "And it was clear to him that when the business was done he was to return to the ship?"

"Completely clear, sir. There was a small complication, but—"

"What kind of complication?"

"Well, as you know, Arnold's first letter to me stated he wished the *Vulture* to continue her station at Taller's Point for a few days—"

"So that she would be there when André returned," Clinton finished. "What happened?"

It was Captain Sutherland who replied. "Sir, at daybreak on Friday morning we were fired upon from Taller's Point by a six-pounder and a howitzer. They placed a very hot fire upon us for two hours. Six shot hulled us, one between wind and water, others striking the sails and rigging. Since the tide was slack, with no wind, it was only with great difficulty that we launched our boats and towed the ship out of range. Fortunately we sustained no major casualties—"

"Except for Major André," Clinton interrupted, glaring at Sutherland.

"Sir Henry, we did not leave the area. I dropped down river just far enough to avoid more damage to the ship. We still could be seen from the spot where Major André went ashore. Our move would not have interfered had he returned there."

"It would have interfered had he tried to return at the time of the cannonade," Clinton pointed out. He turned to Robinson. "How do you account for the firing on the ship, in light of Arnold's request that she remain on station?"

"I'm at a loss to account for it, Sir Henry. I can't believe it was by Arnold's order. It would have endangered the whole enterprise."

"As it did." Clinton spent a moment in silent reflection. Perhaps it was the initiative of some local commander, he thought. He was aware that the Americans were notorious for acting on their own authority, and Arnold could hardly give an order not to fire upon a British warship. "In any event," he finally resumed, "what's done is done. We must now do our utmost to protect Major André from the spying charge, and secure his release. I'm preparing a letter for immediate dispatch to Washington. Colonel Robinson, I would appreciate a letter from you for inclusion with mine, dating from yesterday aboard the *Vulture*, stating whatever facts you can muster showing that André was not acting in the capacity of a spy." He then dismissed both officers, indicating that his secretary should remain.

When the two men had left, Clinton turned to Captain Smith.

"Did I not forbid him to go behind enemy lines, or to carry any compromising letters or documents?"

His secretary nodded. "Indeed, you did, sir."

"And did I not require him to wear his uniform at all times and tell him not to disguise himself?"

"I remember quite clearly, sir, that you did."

"Then why, in God's name, did Johnny violate his instructions?" Clinton sighed and slowly put his head in his hands. "I fear he has put a noose 'round his neck."

# CHAPTER FOUR

*Rear Echelon, Continental Army, Tappan, New York*
*September 26, 1780*

"THOMAS, WE HAVE a lot to do and little time in which to do it." Colonel John Laurance, Judge Advocate General of the Continental Army, waved his deputy to a seat beside him at a small oak table. Laid out before him on the cramped desk were several packets of loose documents, a sheaf of lined foolscap, several quills, and two ink bottles. "You've heard why I summoned you?"

Lieutenant Colonel Thomas Edwards gave a bemused nod as he sat down. "I'm finding it difficult to believe, though. General Arnold a traitor?"

"There seems to be little doubt of it. Washington is furious, and he's demanding immediate action." Laurance selected the largest packet of papers on the table and pushed them toward Edwards. "These arrived in Washington's hands yesterday afternoon. Look them over. You'll soon understand why Arnold is to be tried. While you're doing that, I'm going to prepare a proposed list of members of the court."

Laurance combined his office and quarters in a small but neat house off Main Street, belonging to a widow whose son was serving in the Army. Surrendering her son's room to Laurance, she had offered to move in with her sister down the street, but Laurance had insisted she remain in her room in her own home. It had turned out to be a comfortable arrangement. Not only did the lady keep the house in spotless order, she brewed the colonel's tea and even cooked many of his meals. She was not here this evening, however, allowing the officers to work in privacy.

Although both men were the same age, just over thirty, Laurance appeared the elder of the two. A rounded face, heavily lidded eyes, full lips, and a slight double chin, all suggested laziness, but actually masked an energetic personality and a sharp intellect. Though a comfortable girth betrayed a tendency to enjoy his food and drink, he was not much overweight. Edwards stood in sharp contrast to his chief. Thinner, and nearly a head taller, he was reserved, where Laurance was gregarious. Edwards had been born in Boston, while Laurance came from Falmouth, England, and emigrated to New York when he was seventeen. For someone not acquainted with them, Laurance might be taken for an innkeeper or a prosperous merchant. Edwards appeared to be exactly what he was, a committed and competent lawyer.

As Edwards took up the packet, Laurance returned to his work. The Articles of War required that a general court-martial consist of thirteen officers, and custom required that as many as possible be senior to the accused. He had found it difficult to locate thirteen senior officers available on such short notice. Fortunately, Nathanael Greene was nearby, in command of the main army, and could serve as president of the court. The only other officer on active service senior to Arnold was Horatio Gates, and he was in South Carolina. He would be a poor choice in any event. There had been bad blood between Gates and Arnold since Saratoga. At this moment, Anthony Wayne was rushing his troops to reinforce the defenses of West Point, so he would not be available. Benjamin Lincoln was at his home in Massachusetts, but he had been taken prisoner in the disaster at Charleston, and had been paroled by the British, with a stipulation that he would remain out of service for one year. If at all possible, Laurance wanted the court to consist only of general officers. Combing a list of their assignments and current locations, he saw that he would just barely make it. Arnold would outrank all of them except Greene, but there was no help for it.

With Laurance preoccupied, Edwards read the top document his chief had given him. It was a letter addressed to Washington from Major John André, adjutant general to the British Army, in which he admitted that he had used the name "John Anderson," and attempted to explain the circumstances of his presence behind American lines. Edwards then read a pass permitting John Anderson to move between the lines, signed by Benedict Arnold. He held it up.

"Is this in Arnold's handwriting?"

"According to Washington, it is," Laurance confirmed. "And the signature is also Arnold's. Even more incriminating, is that some of the other documents are also in Arnold's hand."

Edwards next read what appeared to be a copy of the military situation that Washington had given to his staff at a recent council of war. The remaining documents all pertained to West Point. There was an estimate of the number of men necessary to man the works, a breakdown of the actual strength of the garrison, an artillery order showing disposition of the guns in the event of an alarm, and a complete inventory of all 120 artillery pieces at the fortress. Most damaging was a two-page report on the construction and condition of the four forts and nine redoubts which made up the fortress complex, indicating points of weakness most suitable for an attack by an assaulting force.

"My God!" Edwards turned to his chief in astonishment.

"There's more," Laurance announced. "There are papers found in Arnold's office, consisting of letters and ciphers, which seem to show a treasonous correspondence. There are also some papers belonging to Arnold's wife. It seems she became hysterical upon her husband's arrest. She refused to recognize Washington, screaming that he was someone come to kill her baby. While they were attempting to calm her, Lieutenant Colonel Varick, Arnold's secretary, removed her personal letters from her desk and gave them to Washington, who still has them."

"Is there any possibility that the lady is involved."

"Washington refuses to entertain any thought of it. Lafayette and Hamilton, who also witnessed her breakdown, are likewise convinced of her innocence. Washington has also received a letter from Arnold, protesting that he is innocent."

"Innocent?" Edwards held up the packet of documents. "With all this?"

Laurance allowed himself a thin smile. "Apparently, he claims he's the victim of an elaborate plot to discredit him." He put his work aside and leaned back in his chair. "Because of the unique nature of this case and the seriousness of the charge against one of the most senior generals in the army, I've obtained Washington's permission to make a change in the conduct of this trial. Instead of the Judge Advocate serving all three functions of prosecutor, legal adviser to the court, and friend to the accused, I intend to appoint a separate counsel for the defense, to come from our department. Do you foresee a problem with that?"

"On the contrary," Edwards replied, after only a slight pause, "it eliminates a conflict of interest that has always concerned me. Perhaps we could make the change permanent?"

"Perhaps we could, if someone would kindly double the size of the department. Of course, Arnold would be free to decline the offer."

"Wouldn't that be rather unlikely?"

"Not as unlikely as you might think. At his prior court-martial at Morristown, Arnold did a masterful job in his own defense."

In June of 1778, upon the British withdrawal from Philadelphia, Washington had appointed Arnold military commander of the city and its surrounding area, giving Arnold a respite from active field service while his wounded leg healed. Arnold's lavish life style, his social association with leading families suspected of loyalist sympathies, and his possible illegal use of his office for personal gain, aroused the suspicion and ire of the Pennsylvania civilian authorities, and especially their leader, Congressman Joseph Reed. By February 1779, Reed had amassed sufficient information to publish eight charges against Arnold. Pressured heavily by the Pennsylvania

Congressional delegation, and after months of investigations and inquiries, Congress finally ordered Washington to court-martial Arnold on four of the charges.

The court finally convened in December, and Arnold was convicted of two of the offenses: Issuing a pass to a merchant ship when he lacked authority to do so, and the improper use of government wagons for his own private use. He was sentenced to be reprimanded by the commander in chief. Although Washington issued the reprimand in writing, and published it in General Orders, it had not affected Arnold's reputation or status in the army, or the high opinion of him held by Washington himself.

"From my observation of his performance during that trial," Laurance continued, "I expect that Arnold might choose to present his own case again, and to do so with the most dramatic flourish possible."

As Laurance prepared to return to his work, Edwards decided to ask one more question. "I take it from this meeting that I am not to defend Arnold."

Laurance nodded. "Normally, as the next senior JAG officer, I'd select you to do so. However, with Washington breathing down my neck demanding immediate action, I need your assistance in preparing the case. We've got lots to do, piece the facts together, assemble all the necessary elements of proof, and prepare a list of witnesses."

Edwards rose, removed his coat, and hung it on the deer antler at the door that served as a coat hook. "Who will defend Arnold?" he asked.

Laurance sighed and leaned back in his chair. With only 15 officers in the entire Judge Advocate General Department, he was hard pressed to keep up with the present trial load. Food and clothing were scarce in the ranks, and with no soldier or officer having received his pay in five months, desertions were high. Acts of thievery against the civilian populace were on the rise, as desperate soldiers took by force the food that their government could not provide them. There were also courts-martial for refusal to obey orders, disrespect to superiors, and even isolated cases of mutiny. In fact, only four months ago, two entire regiments of the Connecticut line had mutinied, claiming they hadn't been paid and were starving. With his small force of lawyers spread from Rhode Island to South Carolina, Laurance was helpless to prevent a growing backlog of cases.

"I'm thinking of Joshua Thorne," Laurance said finally, watching his deputy from the corner of his eye.

Edwards looked up at once. "Thorne? Are you sure?"

"I would have preferred Ainsworth, but he's with Gates in Carolina. No one else is available."

"How about Kingman? He could certainly handle it."

Laurance thought for a moment, but then shook his head. "I won't do that to Thorne. Kingman is much junior to him. Besides, Thorne is a good advocate."

Edwards knew he would have to proceed carefully. He suspected that Laurance had a soft spot for Joshua Thorne. "There is his rather close association with John Barleycorn."

"True, but it's never affected his duties."

"Also, he makes no secret of the fact that he believes Congress should have accepted the terms of the Carlisle Commission and returned the colonies to the British Crown."

"There are others who feel the same way," Laurance reminded him, "especially now that things appear so grim."

In June 1778, the British government had sent a peace commission to America, which had agreed to all the demands of the colonists, including self-rule, denying only complete independence from Great Britain. The commission's misfortune had been to arrive just after the American victory at Saratoga, and when the treaty with France was about to be signed.

"If they arrived today," Laurance continued, "they'd likely be received with open arms. At any rate, such feelings enhance Thorne's qualifications for defending Arnold, don't you think?"

Edwards made a noncommittal nod. He and Thorne had both graduated from Harvard College and read the law at the same

Philadelphia firm, but at different times. Although he agreed with his chief that Thorne was a good lawyer, Edwards was not so willing to overlook Thorne's Loyalist leanings. Also, in his view, Thorne *had* reached the point where alcohol was affecting his duties. However, there was a favorable side to Thorne's appointment, at least as far as Edwards was concerned. It meant that he and Laurance would face a weak opponent in the court room, and for this reason he was not inclined to argue further against his selection. With this in mind, he did not want to appear hostile toward Thorne.

"What is it, Thomas? You seem concerned."

"It's just that...well...Thorne has become affected by his role in prosecuting men for what he considers offenses brought about by forces beyond their control. He might even come to think that way about Arnold. Defending a case like this, where a conviction is certain...it's like throwing him to the wolves."

"Nothing is certain, Thomas. And be thankful that I need you on the government side, or it's you I would be throwing to the wolves."

# CHAPTER FIVE

*Mabie's House, Tappan, New York*
*September 26, 1780*

"MAJOR THORNE, DO I understand that you rest the government's case?" The president of the court looked sharply toward the judge advocate's table.

Joshua Thorne was sweating heavily, even though the room was far from warm. The dull ache in his forehead had grown worse, and his stomach rumbled. Yet he rose steadily from his chair. "Yes, sir, I do."

The president's gaze hardened. "Then tell me, sir, why have we no extract of the company morning muster?"

Thorne closed his eyes. Good God, how could he have forgotten that?

"We have a man accused of desertion," the president continued, "which is defined as being absent from his unit for more than thirty days." It was a lecture and a rebuke, a fact so obvious it did not need stating. "How, pray, are we to determine how long this man has been absent, without the morning muster on the date he was discovered missing?"

"I...I'm sorry, sir. I'm afraid I overlooked it."

"You *overlooked* it?" The president seemed truly astonished.

"Uh...due to many pressing duties—"

"Major, we all have pressing duties, and you increase ours by your failure to properly prepare your case. I adjourn this court until you obtain the pertinent muster extract."

Later that day, Joshua Thorne sat at the small bar in Mabie's, contemplating the morning's fiasco. Despondent, he saw himself moving one more rung downward on a descending ladder. He would like to believe that overlooking the morning muster report was due to an unconscious sympathy for the accused soldier. But he was not that self-delusional—at least not yet. He was becoming increasingly more careless and forgetful. And he knew why. But at least his headache was gone, fading under the influence of several mugs of beer. As usual, he marveled that the cause of his distress could also be its cure.

He and the young woman behind the small bar were the only persons in Mabie's common room, but that would soon change. For the past eight months Mabie's had been popular with senior officers of the rear echelon of Washington's headquarters, and now the full staff was converging on the small town. Some of the officers had already arrived, and the commander in chief himself was due to ride in tomorrow. The usual scramble and negotiation for billets was made easier because Washington had headquartered here only a month before, and many of the various segments of the staff would settle into the same quarters they had previously occupied.

"May I have another beer, please, Amy."

Amelia Martin eyed Thorne critically, as she had so many times before. She was at a loss to understand her attraction to him. Although he basically had good features, his face was lined and showed a weariness beyond his age. Even when he smiled, which was seldom, his eyes remained solemn, as if they had seen much they didn't like. A body once muscular, was turning soft, and his shoulders slouched, as if reflecting the disillusionment with his assignment, which was becoming increasingly obvious. And on top of it all, he drank too much. Her first experience with love had been a disaster, and her affair with Joshua Thorne promised no better.

23

"Don't you think you've had enough, Josh?"

Thorne met her gaze amiably. "Is there ever enough in times like these?"

"In times like these a Continental officer might want to keep a clear head on his shoulders."

Her remark brought a hint of a smile. "Beer creates just the right balance between clarity and oblivion. And besides, doesn't Benjamin Franklin say that beer is proof that God loves us and wants us to be happy?"

"Doctor Franklin also says that drink does not drown care, but waters it and makes it grow faster."

"Did he really say that? Well, I suppose a school mistress should know." Amelia Martin was both mistress and sole teacher at the local schoolhouse, the only one in all of Rockland County. When the army's rear echelon arrived, Mabie had hired her part-time to help with the increase in his business. With classes now suspended until the harvest was in, she was able to work on a full-time basis. "But then," Thorne continued, "Franklin hasn't had the opportunity to try your beer, or he might make an exception. In fact, one more tankard could hardly make my cares grow any faster. There's no room for any more growth."

"I can't help but be reminded of the doctor's warning that he that drinks fast pays slow."

"Well, not having been paid in five months, I suppose I must agree with him." Thorne reached across the bar with his arm and brought her toward him, trying for a kiss. "If I don't have any money, at least I have you."

Amelia Martin twisted from his grasp. She preferred to avoid any public indication of their relationship, and she did not like being taken for granted. "You don't *have* me, and you shan't ever, if you can't pay your bills. Casparus Mabie is getting tired of hearing my excuses for you."

Thorne sat back on his stool and appeared deep in thought. "I have it," he announced. "Tell him to send the bill to Congress." He motioned to his empty tankard, his expression half pleading and half teasing. For a moment, she seemed ready to refuse, but then with a sigh, she refilled it.

Shortly after Casparus Mabie built his stone house on Main Street in 1753, the town board of supervisors began using it to hold their monthly meetings. Mabie, an enterprising merchant, soon started offering refreshments to the group. Over the years the house became known as a meeting place for county and town officials, for both pleasure as well as business, and he put a small bar and several tables in the largest room, making it a convivial place to gather. As the winds of revolution began to blow, Mabie's house became the center of much of the patriot activity in the region. Whenever military units passed through or were quartered in the town, Casparus Mabie always extended his hospitality to the senior officers of the army.

A large field spider suddenly peered over the end of the bar. Attracted either by the light or the warmth, it crawled onto the bar top and made its way slowly toward a candle. Midway, it stopped, perhaps confused by its surroundings. Just then the cook came from the kitchen to speak to Amy. He saw her and Thorne both staring quietly at the spider. When neither of them reacted, he finally asked, "Is anybody gonna do somethin' about that thing?"

For an answer, Thorne picked up a large bowl and popped it over the spider. He then slid a flat plate under it, turned the whole thing over and carried the covered bowl outside, where he released the spider. When he returned, he found the cook staring at him. Shaking his head, the man returned to his kitchen, muttering.

The incident reminded Amy of the time Joshua told her about a day on the family farm when he was a young boy. He had been watching a line of large, brown ants marching single file across the yard, fascinated by their disciplined and seemingly intelligent behavior. When his father appeared and casually eradicated the entire column with his foot, it had horrified him.

"My father wasn't a cruel man," Joshua had explained. "Seeing how upset I was, he said, 'Son, those ants could take down a whole corn stalk overnight.' I knew right then that I'd never be able to kill any of the farm animals, and I think my father knew it too. I think that's why he allowed me to leave the farm and go to college." It was one of the things that Amy found attractive about him. Engaged in a war and surrounded by death, Joshua Thorne took pains to spare the life of a spider.

Thorne took a long swallow from his tankard, and then leaned over his drink so that he was only inches from Amy. "You know, if I were in civilian practice, I would be coming into a large fee." Amy eyed him quizzically, but said nothing. "I have a new client, a famous one. But since we're both in the Army, I can take no fee, and he likely has no more ready money than I."

"This nonsense about a fee can only mean that you are about to—" She stopped in mid sentence, her eyes growing wide. "Josh! No!"

He rose stiffly in his seat, assuming a feigned air of importance. "I am to represent General Benedict Arnold. I'm riding up to West Point tomorrow to interview him." It took him a moment to notice how disturbed she was.

"Oh, Joshua, why you?" Her voice had taken on an almost desperate note. Thorne was too astounded to reply. "You must refuse," she announced.

"Refuse? I'm in the Army, Amy. I don't have the option to refuse."

"Ask them to find someone else, then."

"There *is* no one else. Why are you so upset?"

"I don't want you to be the one to defend that traitor." It wasn't only because she thought Arnold deserved to hang, although that was certainly how she felt. She was concerned about the effect the trial would have on Josh. She knew he was tormented by the type of cases he was required to prosecute. "Stealing a farmer's pig to avoid starvation is a tragedy, not a crime," he told her once. "The crime is committed not by the soldier, but by Congress in failing to provide him with his needs." With Arnold claiming he was innocent and the victim of a British plot, she could visualize Josh being taken in, only to be badly disillusioned later, when his guilt was proven.

"I won't be defending him in the true sense," Thorne explained, "I will represent him."

"Even so, he's now the most hated man in America. Everyone's demanding his head."

"That's all the more reason he needs representation."

"But why does it have to be you? You'll be pilloried along with him."

"Why *not* me? No man is guilty until proven so, Amy."

"That man is." She spoke with such intensity that he held back any answer. "He's worse than Judas. Judas betrayed one man. Arnold betrayed an entire nation. Joshua, they're even saying he did it not out of principle, but for money."

Thorne knew he would have to proceed carefully. She had called him "Joshua," rather than "Josh." It was a sure sign that she was upset with him. He was not sure what his true feelings were for Amelia Martin, but their relationship was what had kept him going in the months that army's rear echelon had been located at Tappan. She was pretty, intelligent, and affectionate, and for some reason she favored him. She tended to discourage his attentions when in the presence of others, but that was because of her position as schoolmistress of the county's lone school. He once chided her good-naturedly about that, wondering why the town gentry would frown upon her association with a Continental Army officer, yet have no complaint with her tending a bar. Her answer was to the point. The town elders recognized that she had difficulty living on the wages they paid her, and were happy that she was able to supplement her income. Association with an army officer, on the other hand, offered nothing but abject poverty.

Joshua reached over the bar again, put his arm across her shoulder, and slowly caressed her neck. Surprising him, she did not resist, but her expression remained pained.

"Mistress Martin," he said softly, "you of all people recognize that one of the principles of our new nation is that everyone is entitled to a fair trial. Even the most despicable murderer has his day in court. Shall we deny that to one of our most illustrious generals?"

He hugged her closer, the bar between them making the pose awkward, yet, somehow intimate. She seemed somewhat mollified, and leaned in toward him.

"Promise me you will not try to prove him innocent."

"Amy, it's not my duty to prove him innocent. It's to see that he is not unfairly proven guilty. From what Laurance tells me, at his last court-martial General Arnold proved to be a sharp advocate in his own defense."

"Let him defend himself, then. I don't want your name forever associated with that of a traitor."

It was a sobering thought. If Arnold was found guilty, which seemed almost a certainty, how would he, Joshua Thorne, be perceived by posterity?

# CHAPTER SIX

*Fort Putnam, West Point, New York*
*September 27, 1780*

JOSHUA THORNE WAITED nervously in a small room in Fort Putnam's barracks, a two-story wooden building that seemed totally inadequate to house the 300-man garrison which was the fort's designed complement. He had started before dawn that morning from Tappan, and ridden the 38 miles directly to Fort Arnold, West Point's main bastion, making the ride in fine weather. The first splashes of orange and red were appearing in the green hills, but along the river it was more brown than usual this early in the fall. The Highlands were in the grip of a severe season of drought, and the landscape was littered with dead oak and chestnut leaves.

The previous night, made restless by the day's events, Joshua had been unable to sleep. Even Amy, normally quiet throughout the night, had tossed uneasily by his side. The pleasure of having Amy in his bed began only about a month ago, when after months of flirtation and banter, they had finally become lovers. At first, she had been reluctant to move in with him. She lived in a small house belonging to an older widow, and shared the single bedroom and bed with her. Although a one-room loft above a stable, Joshua's billet was spacious and decently furnished. Finally, that, and the comfort of being closer to Josh, overrode her concern that their affair would almost certainly become known, but she did not give up her arrangement with Mary Burns.

Immediately after his arrival at West Point, Joshua had presented himself to Colonel John Lamb, the garrison commander, informed him of his appointment to represent General Arnold, and requested to see the prisoner. Over a late lunch, one of the first things Lamb told him, as if to confirm Benedict Arnold's fall from grace, was that the name of Fort Arnold had been changed to Fort Clinton, renamed for George Clinton, the governor of New York. Following lunch, Lamb accompanied Joshua to Fort Putnam, and had asked him to wait in the cramped room.

Joshua was shocked at the condition of Putnam, which had been completed only two years ago to protect the approaches to Fort Arnold and the great iron chain across the North River. Much of the stone wall on its east side had collapsed, and the earth-and-wood rampart on the south side had fallen in at several places. He wondered if this had been Arnold's doing. Although more than one hundred men were now busy repairing the damage, it was obvious that the work had only recently begun.

He shifted uncomfortably in the plain wooden chair. Another chair and a small campaign table were the only other furnishings in the room, its tiny window providing the dimmest of light. For the first time in his three years as a judge advocate, Joshua found himself ill at ease with the prospect of meeting an accused. He wondered if it was Arnold's previous reputation or the charge against him. Probably a combination of both, he decided. He found himself checking his appearance, brushing off his frayed lapels, smoothing his breeches, and making sure no mud clung to his boots. With no mirror in the room, he ran both hands through his hair, hoping for the best.

At last the door to the room opened, and Colonel Lamb entered, followed by two guards, escorting another figure between them. Joshua rose from his chair. The man in the middle was taller than the guards. His black hair, flecked with gray, had not been brushed or combed, and a dark stubble covered his cheeks. Joshua quickly took in his features. A prominent, hawk-like nose, well-defined chin, and ruddy complexion gave the face an attractive ruggedness, which was enhanced by powerful shoulders and a stocky build. Even in his present position the man reflected an air of authority, and there was a presence about him that Joshua could feel emanating from his intense, light-blue eyes. As they adjusted to the dim light in the room, these eyes locked on Joshua.

"My guards will leave you alone with the prisoner," Lamb announced. "They will lock the door after them and remain outside. When you've finished, knock, and they'll open the door." Lamb then left the room with his guards, without ever having glanced at Arnold. After a pause, the general limped over to the second chair and sat down, his injured leg protruding stiffly in front of him, staring silently at Joshua. When it seemed apparent that Arnold did not intend to speak, Joshua broke the silence.

"General Arnold, I am Major Joshua Thorne of the Judge Advocate General Department. I have been appointed to assist in your defense at your trial."

His gaze never leaving Joshua, Arnold finally spoke. 'Thank you, major, but I do not believe I have requested such assistance. It was not offered at my previous court-martial, and I see no need for it now." The words were spoken evenly and without emotion, yet the power of the man's personality came clearly through.

'I realize that, sir, but the seriousness of the offense, and your own importance, convinced General Washington that such representation is desirable."

"Ah, I see." Arnold accepted the information with a wry smile. "His Excellency wishes to appear concerned and fair. Are you aware of my letter to him?"

"I am, sir."

"Then you know that I have been falsely accused and viciously slandered by an enemy plot."

"I only know, sir, that is what you state in your letter."

Arnold's eyes narrowed. "Then you do not believe what I have said?"

"What I believe, general, has no bearing upon the issue. I'm here to protect your interests."

"I see. Well, major, if you have concern for my interests I ask that you petition General Washington for better treatment for an old comrade. Have you seen my cell? It is underground, for God's sake—more like a dungeon than a prison. And I wear the clothes I was taken in, and have not been permitted to bathe or have a razor. Enemy prisoners of war are treated better than I am. I would be grateful if you would do something about this."

"I will try my best, sir. Meanwhile, may we discuss your case?"

"What is there to discuss? I am innocent of these foul charges."

"Apparently General Washington does not think so, hence your present situation." As Arnold seemed to be about to interrupt, Joshua went on quickly. "You claim that you're the victim of a British plot to implicate you in a treasonous act in order to damage our cause?"

"It is not a claim, major. It is God's truth."

"You are aware, general, that there are documents seized from a British officer bearing your name and in your hand?"

"They are forgeries."

"Even to the handwriting, which several reliable witnesses identify as yours?"

"Surely there are clever imitators of handwriting if they possess sufficient accurate samples. And I have initiated much correspondence these past years."

"There is correspondence, seized from your own files at Robinson's House, which indicate a treasonous communication between you and the headquarters of the British army in New York."

Arnold waved his hand. "More forgeries, placed there to further the plot."

"I see, sir. Do you have evidence to support any of this?"

"My evidence I will introduce myself to the court. For the rest, I shall rely upon my honor and my word as an officer." Arnold then changed the subject. "You have mentioned the correspondence in my files. I shall need those files to prepare my defense."

"They are currently being reviewed by Colonel Laurance. When he's selected those he will use in court, I will have the rest returned to you. Perhaps we could go over them together."

The general leaned back in his chair, repositioning his injured leg, which seemed to be causing him pain. He studied Joshua for a moment before speaking. "Major Thorne, you are a member of the Judge Advocate General Department, and, as such, a part of the organization that is prosecuting me. If you were more acquainted with the persecutions I have endured from this government, you might understand why I am not impressed with any offer of assistance from it. Also, you have made it clear that you do not believe my word. I will not entrust you with my defense."

To Joshua, Arnold's speech sounded like an oration and a decision, but he pressed on. "Will you allow me to at least try to protect your interests, to see that you receive a fair trial?"

Arnold allowed himself a wry smile. "I have too long endured the ungratefulness of this government to have faith that even a small measure of fairness will be afforded me. There are those in the Congress and in the Army, who are jealous of my accomplishments, and are always eager to believe the worst slanders about me. Even General Washington, had he truly wished to be fair, would have permitted me to remain free and assist him in getting to the bottom of this conspiracy."

More oratory. Did he always talk like this? But Joshua thought he detected a change in attitude on the part of Arnold, who now seemed willing, even anxious to talk. He remained silent, hoping the general would continue.

"While we speak of fairness, major, may I ask you when you were last paid?"

"It has been about five months, sir."

"I have not received one dollar in pay in the five *years* I have served this nation, receiving only sporadic allowances and advances for expenses. I have neglected my business, and exhausted my personal fortune in the support of my family, and to feed and supply my soldiers when Congress failed to do so. Although I have been called the 'Hannibal of North America' for the invasion of Canada, I have been constantly viewed with hostility and suspicion by certain members of Congress ever since that time."

Joshua was aware of Arnold's problems with Congress, as were many other officers in Washington's headquarters. Most of them took Arnold's side. "Congress has refused to settle my accounts for the Canadian campaign," Arnold continued, "insisting that I provide receipts for expenses down to the penny—receipts which were either impossible to obtain, lost on overturned bateaux in the rapids of the Kennebec, or in the sinking of the *Liberty* at Valcour Island. It is generally acknowledged that at the battle of Lake Champlain, my defense saved Albany from almost certain British occupation. Yet, when Congress issued a list of promotions to major general, my name was not on it, although I was the senior brigadier general in the service. Thus, five officers junior to me in rank—and if I may say so—in accomplishment, were promoted over me. A strange way to reward a victorious officer, wouldn't you agree?"

Despite the general's bombast, Joshua had to agree with him. The news that Arnold had been passed over for promotion had caused a stir in the army and upset Washington, who protested to Congress over the slight to his best fighting general. In response, Congress hemmed and hawed. Some members took umbrage, asserting the right of civilian authority over all things military, and John Adams expressed exasperation with military officers who "quarrel like cats and dogs...scrambling for rank and pay like apes for nuts." Finally, Congress justified its position by citing its "Baltimore resolution," which stated that in considering general officers for promotion, regard should be given, not only to date of rank and merit, but also to the quota of troops raised by each state. Since Connecticut, Arnold's home state, already had two major generals, it was deemed to have its fair quota. The fact that this resolution had been passed on the same day the promotion list was published, led more than one officer to conclude that it had been aimed specifically at Arnold.

But there was another side to the story, as Joshua knew. Although Arnold had high-placed friends in the army—Washington, Greene, Schuyler, and even Gates, prior to Saratoga—he had also made enemies, men who were determined to bring him down. Chief among them were Lieutenant Colonel John Brown and Joseph Reed, of the Pennsylvania Congressional delegation. It was in Canada that Arnold earned Brown's undying hatred. Arnold had advised Congress against promoting Brown to colonel, pointing out that Brown had been publicly impeached with plundering the baggage of British officers who had surrendered. Furious, and thirsting for revenge, Brown commenced a series of assaults on Arnold's integrity. He accused him of stealing goods from Montreal merchants, and later presented General Gates with a demand for Arnold's arrest on 13 charges, most of which proved to be absurd and the rest doubtful. Gates refused to arrest Arnold, but on Brown's insistence, forwarded the charges to Congress. Despite repeated efforts by Brown, Congress failed to act on them. But the barrage of complaints and accusations could not fail to have an effect, and certain delegates began to view Arnold with caution, if not outright suspicion.

One problem for Arnold was that John Brown was a capable and respected officer. Much like Arnold himself, he was brave, proud, and sensitive of his honor. Fortunately for Arnold, Brown's vindictive and strident one-man war against him eventually caused Congress to turn a deaf ear to his appeals. Discouraged, Brown temporarily resigned from the army, and as a civilian published a paper maligning the general. In its conclusion, it stated, "Money is this man's god, and to get enough of it he would sacrifice his country." Later, when Arnold was military commandant of Philadelphia, Joseph Reed would bring charges against him that would give these words a ring of prophecy.

Arnold had lapsed into silence, allowing Joshua to think over what he had said so far, but now he continued his narrative. "Had it not been for the plea of General Washington, I would have resigned my commission. In fact I wrote him at the time stating that I thought that in denying my promotion Congress was employing a very civil way of requesting my resignation, and I was more than ready to give it to them. But Washington urged me to allow time for him to intercede for my promotion."

"And you were subsequently promoted," Joshua pointed out.

"Oh, I was promoted, but it was not Washington's doing. It was my action against Tryon's raid on Danbury that shamed Congress into a belated promotion. Even then, they failed to restore my seniority in rank. It took Saratoga to do that." Arnold lapsed into silence again, apparently brooding over a wound to his pride which had never healed. If Arnold had indeed committed treason, Joshua thought, its origin was almost certainly here.

"Sir, are you aware that during this last half hour you have outlined good reasons for your disaffection?" Arnold seemed taken aback by the statement. Joshua continued. "This is exactly why I should represent you, to prevent you from making statements like this, and to guard other interests."

"Major, I have already suggested how you can serve my interests right now, by getting me better treatment. I am the third-ranking general in the Continental Army, other than Washington. There are Greene, Gates, and then myself. I have yet to be charged with anything, have been convicted of nothing, yet I am imprisoned under worse conditions than the foulest criminal. Improve my conditions, major, and if you can do so, then perhaps we will discuss your further services." With that, the general rose from his chair, limped across the room, and pounded on the door.

As Joshua left the building, he was joined by Lamb, who had been inspecting the repair work on the fort's walls. Together, they rode back to Fort Clinton.

"I was with him at Quebec." John Lamb said as they rode. "My men were dragging a brass six-pounder on a sled. When it skidded into a snow bank, we kept on without it. On a scaling ladder, trying to get over the walls, that's where I lost my eye." He had lost more than an eye, Joshua had already observed. Nearly half of the colonel's face had been shot away. "There was no braver man in the army or one that I would have been prouder to follow."

Joshua could think of no appropriate response, and they rode the rest of the way in silence. Since he was spending the night at West Point, Lamb invited him to dine with him that evening. With a few hours free, he took the opportunity to tour the fortress. Joshua well understood the strategic importance of West Point. If the British were to seize it, they would gain control of the North River and the entire water route from Canada to the Bay of New York, thus separating New England from the rest of the newly formed American states. It would make continuation of the war for independence virtually impossible. The British had tried this maneuver once before, but had been stopped at the battle of Saratoga, largely by the heroic actions of Benedict Arnold. But if the execution of the plan had failed, the strategy remained sound. It was highly likely that the British would try again, and that was why Washington was turning West Point into an American Gibraltar.

Almost three years of effort had gone into building its system of forts and redoubts. Its main bastion, Fort Arnold (now Fort Clinton), overlooked a sharp bend in the North River. Protected by the fort's guns, a huge iron chain weighing more than 150 tons stretched 500 yards to the opposite bank of the river, barring all passage by ship. Joshua was aware that most of the river was actually a tidal estuary. The influence of the ocean tides were felt as far north as the city of Albany, nearly 200 miles upstream from New York Bay. In recognition of this, the original inhabitants of the area, the Mohican Indians, had named the river *Muh-he-kun-ne-tuk*, "the river that flows both ways." Now the river had a possible third christening in store. Settlers of English origin were starting to call it the *Hudson*, even though the British navigator had been in the employ of the Dutch when he explored the river in 1609.

But it was a land attack upon the fortress that presented the most danger, Joshua knew. After observing the condition of Fort Putnam, he was further disturbed by what his tour revealed. Fort Clinton seemed in reasonably good shape, although part of it had been destroyed by fire and was being rebuilt. But there were high hills to the west, which, if seized by an enemy, would dominate the surrounding terrain, and enable artillery to fire directly on Fort Clinton. To prevent this, Colonel Thaddeus Kosciusko, a Polish engineer and volunteer to the American cause, had designed a series of interlocking defenses, of which Fort Putnam was one. The most critical of these, in Joshua's view, was Redoubt 4 on Rocky Hill, the highest peak in the area. Yet Rocky Hill seemed to him completely exposed from the rear, and if the British were able to bring cannon to bear from its heights they could neutralize nearby redoubts, including Putnam, and Fort Clinton would be at their mercy.

At the end of his ride, Joshua had questions he wanted to ask Lamb about all of this, but realized it would be improper to do so. Lamb was one of the witnesses summoned to testify in Arnold's trial, and it was certain that these matters would be raised in court.

Arriving at Colonel Lamb's quarters, Joshua found another guest present, Lieutenant Colonel Eleazer Oswald, who had also served under Arnold in the Quebec campaign. He was among Arnold's closest friends, and for a time had served as his secretary. The dinner conversation was subdued. Neither of the other officers seemed anxious to discuss Arnold in Joshua's presence, despite his appointment as defense counsel. At the end of the meal, Lamb rose and selected a bottle and three glasses from a sideboard.

"Madeira," he said in an apologetic tone. "Port is hard to come by these days."

"And expensive," added Oswald. Madeira was smuggled directly from the Portuguese island, much of it evading the British embargo, and was rapidly taking the place of port throughout the colonies. In addition to its lower cost, the wine was one that actually improved in shipping, unlike port and other wines from Europe, which often spoiled during the long weeks at sea.

The trio began discussing mundane subjects, comparing shared acquaintances and reminiscing over prior campaigns. When Lamb produced another bottle of Madeira, Oswald finally raised the topic they had avoided all evening.

"It's a sad irony. The first time the British tried to cut the colonies in half they were stopped by Arnold. The second time they tried it, he apparently helped them." He shook his head and his expression darkened. "He was everywhere at Saratoga, riding up and down the line, encouraging his men, charging the works again and again, always out in front. Even the British gave him credit for the victory. I'd like to have seen the look on the face of 'Granny'

Gates when Burgoyne told him Arnold had been responsible for the British defeat."

"It was the same at Quebec," Lamb said, staring into his glass, and talking to himself as much as anyone in the room. "If Arnold hadn't been wounded that day, we'd have taken the city. He was the soul of the army, rallying the troops, urging them forward. But when he fell, Dan Morgan took over, and he let his officers persuade him to hold up and wait for more men to come up before assaulting the last barricade. That let the British bring up reinforcements. Arnold would have charged immediately, while they were weak and demoralized by our attack. And we would have succeeded."

Lamb rose, fetched a third bottle, and refilled the glasses. "They're saying now that he would do anything for money," he continued. "I was taken prisoner at Quebec, along with most of the attacking party that wasn't killed. When the British let Meigs go on parole back to our camp for our luggage, Arnold stripped himself of almost all his personal cash, so that Meigs could distribute it to us. And when I was released, I tried to raise an artillery battalion and get back into the fight, but Congress, with its usual incompetence, didn't come up with the money. And although he was hard-pressed himself, Arnold lent me a thousand pounds for the purpose."

"He's been supporting Joe Warren's four children these many months," Oswald added. "Just recently, in spite of his strained finances, he sent another check for 500 pounds." Warren, a friend and mentor of Arnold's, had been killed at Bunker Hill, and for three years Congress had neglected to act on a request for a general's pension for his orphans.

As a fourth bottle found its way to the table, Arnold's two old friends grew morose. "I wish he had died at Saratoga," Oswald said, his voice mournful rather than bitter. "He would then have finished his career in glory."

"It was his wish, too" Lamb added. "At least at the time it was. Henry Dearborn was with him when he fell, and asked him where he was hit. 'In the same leg,' he answered, 'I wish it had been my heart.'"

When the conversation drifted off into silence again, Joshua rose to excuse himself. He would be rising again before dawn for the ride back to Tappan. As they shook hands at parting, Lamb's grip held for a moment, his lone eye staring intently at Joshua.

"I would look hard and carefully at that young, pretty wife, if I were you."

# CHAPTER SEVEN

*New-York, Sept. 26, 1780*

*His Excellency General WASHINGTON.*

*S I R:*

Being informed that the King's Adjutant General in America has been stopped, under Major General Arnold's passports, and is detained a prisoner in your Excellency's army, I have the honour to inform you, Sir, that I permitted Major André to go to General Arnold, at the particular request of that general officer. You will perceive, Sir, by the enclosed paper, that a flag of truce was sent to receive Major André, and passports granted for his return, I therefore can have no doubt but your Excellency will immediately direct, that this officer has permission to return to my orders at New-York.

*I have the honour to be, your Excellency'*
*Most obedient and most humble servt.*
H. CLINTON.

# RICHARD McMAHON

*Vulture, off Sinsinck, Sept. 25, 1780*

*His Excellency General WASHINGTON.*

*S I R,*

I AM at this moment informed that Major André, Adjutant General of his Majesty's army in America, is detained as a prisoner, by the army under your command. It is therefore incumbent upon me to inform you of the manner of his falling into your hands : He went up with a flag at the request of General Arnold, on public business with him, and had his permit to return by land to New-York : Under these circumstances Major André cannot be detained by you, without the greatest violation of flags, and contrary to the custom and usage of all nations; and as I imagine you will feel this matter in the same point of view as I do, I must desire you order him to be set at liberty and allowed to return immediately : Every step Major André took was by the advice and direction of General Arnold, even that of taking a feigned name, and of course not liable to censure for it.

*I am, Sir, not forgetting our former acquaintance,*
    *Your very humble servant,*

        BEV. ROBINSON, Col.
        Loyl. Americ.

# CHAPTER EIGHT

*Tappan, New York*
*September 28, 1780*

WHEN JOSHUA THORNE entered his room the next night after the long ride from West Point, Amy was already in bed. He lit the stub of a bedside candle, undressed, and lay down by her side. As he did so, Amy shifted, turning toward him, laying an arm across his waist. Aroused by her sudden nearness, and thinking her awake, he drew closer. But her regular breathing told him she was still asleep, and he decided to let her remain so.

Joshua recognized that his feelings for Amy were conflicted. Although he considered her the most important person in his life, someone who helped him bear a difficult situation, his only other serious affair had left him traumatized and guilt-ridden, and he did not want that to happen again.

In his final year at Harvard, he had fallen into a relationship with a young milliner's apprentice. She was all he could ask for as a bed mate, but as time went on, he saw that they had little else in common. Just before graduation, he broke off the relationship. Three days later, her body was found in the Charles River. Although the death was classified as an accident, Joshua knew that for the rest of his life he would never be sure.

When the rear echelon of the Continental Army moved to Tappan in January of 1780, Joshua soon made the acquaintance of Amelia Martin. Although strongly attracted to her, he was ever mindful of his first relationship, and he proceeded slowly. Finding her to be both intelligent and witty, he soon spent almost all his evenings at Mabie's, and gradually, she responded to him. Believing that it was the sexual relationship he valued most, Joshua still sensed that he would miss more than that if Amy were to suddenly vanish from his life. To prevent that, he sometimes considered marriage, but he usually convinced himself that the times were too unsettled. Besides, he wasn't sure how he would react if she were to turn him down.

He had not put out the candle, and he became aware that Amy was now awake, gazing at him with eyes still languorous with sleep. She stretched, and her body arched toward him.

"How did it go?" she asked, blinking the sleep from her eyes.

Although her nearness made conversation the least attractive activity that came to mind, Joshua recognized that at this moment her curiosity took priority. "I have met the ogre," he announced.

"And?" She cradled her head in her hand, propped up by her elbow, facing him squarely. She was almost on top of him, and he could feel her breath on his cheek. The candle sputtered and finally died, but he made no move to light another.

"We talked for some time, and he made it clear that he does not want my services."

"Good, then you're free of him."

"Not quite yet. I've just come from Laurance. He insists that I continue until the court convenes. If Arnold wants to reject me, he must do so officially before the court." He then went on to describe his meeting with Arnold, mentioning his many complaints. Amy, ignoring his hand which he placed in her lap, took immediate issue.

"Does he think he's the only one in the army who's had to make sacrifices?" To his disappointment, she rose, lit another candle, and sat on the side of the bed, rather than lie down again beside him. "We both know officers who have lost their fortunes and neglected their affairs in the service of their country, yet he is the only one who chose to turn his coat."

"I doubt if there's another officer in the army who hasn't been paid in more than five years though." Joshua could see she was becoming angry, as she mostly did whenever Arnold's name came up. Not wishing to continue the argument, he changed the subject. "He did ask me to perform a service." He explained how Arnold had asked for better treatment. "Laurance took the matter to Washington, and he agreed, although reluctantly. He warned Laurance that if Arnold should somehow escape, those responsible will take his place on the gallows. He's well aware that Arnold still has friends in the army."

"I find it difficult to believe he has any at all, after what's happened."

"There still seems to be some disbelief that Arnold is capable of such treason." His hand was now slowly caressing her thigh.

"In spite of all the evidence?"

"He claims it is all forged, a British plot to discredit him."

"Do you believe that?"

"Not at the present time, no."

Amy eyed him with suspicion. "Josh, is he beginning to beguile you?"

"No, but I must admit feeling that in some ways he has been poorly treated." He explained the circumstances of Arnold's being passed over for promotion and Congress's later failure to adjust his date of rank. He could see she was unmoved. "Amy, if an officer is passed over in favor of those more junior to him, it is taken as a lack of confidence in his ability, or a punishment for some perceived offense. If you have a dozen or more major generals, there is no way to determine who is senior—who may give orders to whom—except by the dates they were promoted."

"Does ability count for nothing then?"

"Of course it does," he replied. "And that's what made Arnold's treatment by Congress so difficult to understand. He wasn't only the most senior, but also the most capable. Washington said so, and made his views known. It was Washington who kept fighting for him, who kept insisting to Congress that he be promoted, and when they finally acquiesced, it was Washington who kept after them to adjust his date of rank so that his seniority would be restored."

Amy sighed heavily. "You know, Josh, I'm very glad that General Arnold rejected your services. You're far too good an advocate for him already, and the trial is yet to begin."

She allowed him to gently ease her back into the bed. As sometimes happened as they were about to make love, an involuntary memory flash of her only previous relationship intruded on the moment. During her first teaching assignment, she had drifted into an affair with a young associate at the same school. After almost two years, realizing that his promises of marriage were empty, she had ended it. She abruptly resigned her job, and to get away, had taken a lower-paying position as school mistress in Tappan. Even though years had passed, the experience had left her disillusioned and wary. She wasn't going to be wounded again. But Josh was wounded too, although in a different way. As he moved closer, she pushed her thoughts aside. When he put his arms around her, she relaxed and surrendered to his embrace.

Afterward, as Joshua was reaching to put out the candle, Amy was not ready for sleep.

"They brought Major André here late this afternoon," she told him.

"Oh?"

She could tell he had little interest in either conversation or the incident, but she continued anyway. "He's being held in the back room of Mabie's, under very heavy guard. He's to appear before a board of inquiry tomorrow, and I hear that every general officer in the headquarters, except for Washington, will be a member." She paused for a response, but realized he was drifting off. "I delivered him a supper this evening," she persisted. "General Washington sent it over from his own table. I must say, he is very personable, and has a charm not expected in younger men."

This prompted a response, although a sleepy one. "Perhaps that's because British officers don't have as hard a life as their Continental counterparts."

"Or drink as much."

"Now, Amy, you know that I can hold my drink"

"The problem is that you hold it too well. If you were able to hold it less you would drink less, and that would be a good thing." She expected a reply, but received none. She still wanted to talk. "You know, Major Tallmadge, who is one of his guards, says that he's an accomplished poet, and he does fine sketch work." An acquiescent mumble told her she was still losing him. "What do you think will happen to Major André?" she continued.

She finally received another sleepy reply. "He'll probably be declared a spy and hanged. Why are you so concerned for André?" It was an afterthought, rather than a true question, and he began to doze again.

"I just feel sorry for him, that's all. I wouldn't be surprised if Arnold planned the whole thing, luring Major André into the scheme."

"The hearing tomorrow will decide things like that. Why don't we wait to see how it comes out?"

It was an appeal for sleep, rather than a question, and she recognized it. Sighing, she let him go. But sleep would not come for her as easily as it did for him. She wished she could be as comfortable with their relationship as he seemed to be. She wished she understood her feelings for him better than she did. Josh was often moody and depressed, he had no money or prospects, and he drank too much. Yet, here he was, beside her in bed, and deeply involved in her life. Was she out of her mind? But there was another side to Joshua Thorne, gentle, humane, deeply concerned for the neglected soldiers of the army, and overwhelmed by his inability to do anything about it. Was that it? Did she simply feel sorry for him, sorry enough to want to comfort him in ways only a woman could? Unlike her previous lover, Joshua had never mentioned marriage. Most times she was glad he didn't. She wasn't sure how she would react to such a proposal. For all his likeable qualities, Joshua was unhappy and adrift. Did she really want to assume his problems? She was reasonably happy with the current arrangement. Yet, she knew that someday the army would leave Tappan, and Joshua Thorne with it. And that prospect filled her with dread.

# CHAPTER NINE

*Old Dutch Church, Tappan, New York*
*September 29, 1780*

THE REFORMED CHURCH of Tappan was the second to occupy
the site, replacing the original, erected in 1694. It was a square, stone
structure, its roof in the shape of a pyramid without an apex. In its
place, a small belfry rose, housing a single bell and topped by a wind
vane. It stood on Main Street, just north of Mabie's house, and facing
the small village green. On the opposite side of the green and at a
farther distance, was the parsonage, the largest dwelling in town.
The war for independence had not been kind to the interior of the
church, which, since 1778 had been pressed into war service. For
a time it had also served as a prison, and, unlike most houses of
worship, it contained a small room to the left of the altar, which had
been added during its use as a military hospital.

In preparation for the board of inquiry meeting, the wooden
pews in the front part of the church had been removed and replaced
by several tables standing end to end, creating one long bank.
Behind it sat fourteen general officers of the Continental Army.
Facing them in a chair about ten feet away was Major John André,
Adjutant General of the British Army, who had been escorted in by
two American officers, and had just taken his seat. One other officer
was in the room, seated alone at a small campaign table at the end of
the larger one, and situated so he faced both the generals and André.

The arrangement was such that the major was facing the church's simple altar, with the generals facing toward the entrance. Sentries were posted at the entrance. There were no other persons in the church, and none would be admitted.

When his escorts had departed to the rear of the church, and it appeared that Major André was comfortable, the officer at the center of the table spoke.

"Major André, I am Major General Nathanael Greene, president of a board of general officers convened by order of General Washington to examine the circumstances of your presence and capture behind our lines on September 23rd this instant. The other members of the board are as follows: On my right are Major Generals Lord Stirling, The Marquis de Lafayette, The Baron Friedrich von Steuben, and Brigadier Generals James Clinton, Jonathon Glover, Edward Hand, and John Stark. On my left are Major Generals Arthur St. Clair, Robert Howe, and Brigadier Generals Samuel Parsons, Henry Knox, John Paterson, and Jedediah Huntington. The officer at the small table to my right is Colonel John Laurance, Judge Advocate General of the Continental Army."

At the end of the introductions, Major André rose and made a slight bow. "I am honored, gentlemen."

"Major André," Greene resumed, "I will now read to you the letter of instructions from General Washington to this board."

*The Board of General Officers*
*Convened at Tappan*

Gentlemen,

Major André, Adjutant General to the British army, will be brought before you for your examination. He came within our lines in the night, on an interview with Major General Arnold, and in an assumed character; and was taken within our lines, in a disguised habit, with a pass under a feigned name, and with the enclosed papers concealed upon him. After a careful examination, you will be pleased, as speedily as possible, to report the precise state of his case, together with your opinion of the light in which he ought to be considered, and the punishment that ought to be inflicted. The Judge Advocate will attend to assist in the examination, who has sundry other papers relative to this matter, which he will lay before the Board.

*I have the honour to be,*
*Gentlemen,*
*Your most obedient and humble servant,*
G. WASHINGTON

Greene placed the letter down on the table and turned to his right. "Colonel Laurance, will you now present the documents you have brought from General Washington to Major André?"

"Yes, sir." Laurance rose, carrying several papers as he walked toward the center of the room. He placed the documents on the table in front of Greene, and then turned. "Major André, the board has already seen and read these documents in closed session before your appearance here. My purpose now is to determine whether you acknowledge them, and to ask you certain questions regarding them."

André nodded. "I understand, sir."

Laurance picked up the first paper and handed it to André. "This is a letter addressed to General Washington and signed 'John André.' Do you acknowledge that this letter was indeed written by you?"

André gave the letter only a short perusal. "I do, sir. It is my letter."

"If I may summarize only those portions of the letter which pertain to your activities ashore, then." Laurance began reading from the letter. "You state that you came ashore from the *HMS Vulture* and met with a person who was to give you intelligence.

51

The approach of daylight prevented you returning to the ship until the following night, and against your intention you were conducted within one of our posts, and against your will you were subsequently directed to return to your lines by land. As I understand it, because of the duress of your situation, you considered yourself become a prisoner of war, with a duty to escape. You therefore quitted your uniform. On your second full night ashore, you were passed without our posts to neutral ground, and you then proceeded to ride for New York, but were captured at Tarry Town by a group of volunteers." The judge advocate replaced the letter on the table. "Major, is that a fair summarization of your activities as you have described them in your letter?"

"It is, sir. I would only like to emphasize that it was without my knowledge beforehand, and against my intention, that I was conducted within your lines."

"So noted, major. Now, before accepting the facts of this letter, the board would like to afford you the opportunity to clarify, add, or withdraw any information, if you feel it in your interest to do so."

"That is most generous, sir, but there is no need. The facts are accurate and truthfully expressed, as much as it is in my power to know them."

"Very well. The final documents I would like to show you are those purported to have been found on your person at the time of your capture." Retrieving the documents from the table, Laurance handed them to André one by one. He showed him the pass signed by Arnold, the estimate of the force at West Point, the estimate of the men necessary to man the works, the Artillery Orders of September 5th, the report on the condition of the fortress and its redoubts, the inventory of artillery, and finally, a copy of Washington's council of war on September 6th. "Are these the documents that were taken from you at the time of your capture?"

André spent some time reviewing the documents, but he finally nodded. "They are the same," he said.

"And they were found in your boot?"

"Excepting the pass, yes."

Laurance put all the papers aside. "Now, major, I would like to put certain questions to you. In giving your answers, you must weigh the situation in which you were taken, and that in which you now find yourself. Your very life may depend upon your answers, and you are under no obligation to incriminate yourself, or to answer at all if doing so would be detrimental to your interests."

"I thank you for your consideration, colonel, but I assure you that my answers will be honest and truthful, as is required by my honor as a gentleman and my position as an officer in His Majesty's Army. My personal safety is only a secondary consideration to the first."

"That's well said, sir." Laurance could see that other members of the court were also impressed by the young officer's statement. "We appreciate your forthright intentions." He then turned toward Greene. "Sir, may I proceed?"

Greene nodded. "Please do so."

"Major André, the pass you had in your possession was made out for a John Anderson. Can you explain that?"

"It was a name I had assumed for the purposes of my mission."

"So the pass was actually for your use?"

"It was."

"You stated in your letter to General Washington that you were to meet with a person who was to give you intelligence. Will you tell us please, who was this person?"

André shifted uncomfortably in his chair. "Sir, I feel honor-bound not to implicate others in my own misfortune. I prefer not to answer the question."

"But you carried a pass signed by General Arnold, and other documents in your possession were in his handwriting."

"Be that as it may, sir, I still prefer not to answer."

"Major," Greene interrupted, "While your intent is commendable, there is little point in trying to protect General Arnold in light of the documents you were carrying. By doing so, you could well damage your own case before this board, which might look upon your position as unnecessarily obstructive. It will do you no good to refuse to answer the question, nor will it help General Arnold. I ask you to reconsider your answer."

"If I answer the question sir," André replied after considerable thought, "may I be excused from naming any other parties to the affair, and may I also be excused from going into the details of my meeting with the person in question, since I feel this would be more appropriately done in an inquiry of that individual?"

Greene could not have asked for a better arrangement. He knew that most of the officers at the table would also be members of the court-martial convened to try Arnold. By eliminating a detailed investigation into Arnold's actions at this time, he could prevent court members from hearing prejudicial information prior to Arnold's trial.

"Fair enough, sir," Greene responded, happy that the young major had unknowingly solved a significant problem for him.

"Then to answer the question, I came ashore to see General Arnold."

"Was this meeting at his request?" Laurance pursued. André shot a quick glance in Greene's direction.

"Colonel Laurance," Greene interrupted, "I believe my ruling prevents further questioning along this line. May we move on?"

"As you wish, sir." Laurance turned back to André "Now, major, are you willing to tell us what transpired after you came ashore from the *Vulture*, up until the time of your capture?"

"I would be happy to sir, although there is not much I can add to what has already been revealed by the letter you just read in this room." André then leaned back. "I came ashore on the night of the 21$^{st}$, accompanied by a guide who would take me to meet General Arnold. It was understood that I would return to the ship that same night."

"Did you come ashore carrying a flag of truce?" asked Greene. It was a critical question. In the closed session prior to the hearing, the board had read the two letters Washington had received from General Clinton and Colonel Robinson. Both had insisted that André had come ashore under a flag of truce, and therefore could not be considered a spy, and must be released. These letters had not been made known to André, who wasted no time in replying.

"No, sir, I did not." He seemed not to notice the quick glances between several members of the board. "I was, however, wearing my regimentals, with a surtout over them. I met General Arnold on the shore, and had an interview with him. Our meeting lasted longer than expected, and with the advent of daylight, it was determined that I should be brought to a place of safety and concealed until nightfall, when I would return to the ship. Unfortunately, the ship came under fire later that morning, and was forced to slip downstream. My escorts then decided that I must return via a land route and I was given the pass you have seen. Although I protested vigorously, it had no effect.

"Having no choice in the matter, and being completely under the control of my escort, as soon as darkness came, we began the journey. After about four hours, due to the reported activity of irregulars, my escort decided to stop at a farmhouse, rather than risk encountering them on the road. In the morning, he accompanied me to a point near Pine Bridge, where he said that, since American patrols did not cross the Croton, I would now be safe. My escort left me there, and I had crossed the bridge and was well on my way to the White Plains when I was taken by a party of volunteers."

There was a moment of silence while the board members digested this information. "Major, André," Laurance then continued, "When did you enter within our lines?"

It was a direct question and a dangerous one, which André might be expected to refuse to answer. However, the young officer spoke promptly. "The first I became aware I might have come within your lines was on the first night, when our party was challenged by a sentry."

"And where was this?"

"I am not certain, sir. Probably it was somewhere between Haverstraw and Stony Point."

"May I ask when it was that you departed our lines?"

André shook his head. "You will understand, Colonel, that I am not familiar with the location of your lines or pickets. I did pass your posts at Stony Point and Verplanck's Point on the night of the 22$^{nd}$."

"Were you in your regimentals at the time?"

It was another dangerous question, but again André disregarded caution in favor of truth.

"I was not; I was in my present dress, which was procured for me after I left the *Vulture*."

"Then you changed your dress when you were within our lines."

"I presume so, but as I mentioned, I was not certain as to the location of your lines."

Laurance then prepared to change the subject. "You have admitted that your purpose in coming within our lines—"

Greene interrupted once more. "I am not sure that the major has stated positively that he *had* come within our lines, whereas he *has* stated that it was not his intent to do so."

At this point Laurance realized that he was being unnecessarily prosecutorial toward the young major, who seemed so determined to tell the truth without regard for his own safety. "You are correct, sir." He then turned again to André, his voice lower and more relaxed. "Major André, you have admitted coming ashore from a warship to obtain intelligence, and that you were in possession of such information when you were apprehended, is that correct?"

"Yes, sir."

"Information which could cause great damage to the American cause."

"Sir, it is within the duty of any officer to procure an advantage over the enemy by obtaining information of intelligence value."

"But there are specific rules to which uniformed officers must adhere. They must not, for example, appear behind enemy lines in civilian dress, or assume a false identity. Such is the manner of spies."

For the first time, André seemed concerned about his situation. "I have stated that after I was conducted behind your lines without my consent I considered myself to be a prisoner of war, with an obligation to escape. Both the civilian dress and the false identity would further that effort. I had hoped, sir, that this explanation would be given credence by the board. Apparently, that is not to be the case."

"Major André," Greene interjected, "I assure you it is our attention to give your actions every consideration, so long as they conform to the accepted standards of warfare."

"Thank you, sir." André seemed somewhat relieved."I can only hope that your interpretation and my own are not too far apart."

Even the crusty von Steuben smiled at the remark, and it was clear that there was a good deal of sympathy for André among the members of the board. Laurance turned once more to Greene. "I have no further questions, sir."

"Does any member of the board have any questions?" Greene asked, turning from one side of the table to the other.

Jonathon Glover leaned forward. "Major, when and where was it that you removed your uniform and substituted your present dress?"

"It was toward evening of the 22nd, my second day ashore, at the home of Mr...of my escort. He informed me that return to the *Vulture* was no longer possible, and that I could not proceed on land in a British Army uniform. As mentioned, I protested vigorously, but it had no effect."

John Stark posed the next question. "If you considered yourself a prisoner of war, why did you not take any active measures to escape?"

"You surely understand sir, that so long as events were moving in a direction that would secure my return to British control, there was no point in resisting. There was no way I could force my return to the *Vulture*, which would have been the only other preferred course."

When it appeared that there were no more questions from the board, Greene turned once again to the young British officer. "Major André, do you have anything further to say on your own behalf or regarding the facts presented to the board?"

"Only that I leave them to operate with the board, sir."

Greene nodded. "The board will now consider the evidence and prepare a recommendation. Major André, you will please wait upon our deliberation in the small room." The court had earlier determined that their voices could not be heard from inside that room once the door was closed.

After André had been conducted from the room, Laurance outlined the elements of proof to be considered in determining the young officer's status.

"Major André admitted that he came ashore in a private and secret manner," he summarized. "He changed out of his uniform while within our lines, and under a false name and disguised habit he passed our lines at King's Ferry. When captured, he had in his possession documents which contained intelligence for the enemy. These are all the actions of a spy."

Greene pursued the assertions in the letters from General Clinton and Colonel Robinson. "What are we to make of the claims of these officers that André came under Arnold's orders while within our lines, and therefore could not be considered a spy?"

"Very little," Laurance replied. "There is no code of war that requires an officer to obey an enemy's orders, and to assert that André was under Arnold's orders while his mission was to suborn treason is ludicrous. Nor should we give credence to the major's claim that because he was 'conveyed' behind our lines, he thus became a prisoner of war and obliged to make his escape. At all times he was operating as an agent of his government, and subject to no physical restraint. The fact that he was required to return to his own lines by a method other than he planned for does not constitute force or restraint. That he quitted his uniform for that reason is not an excuse for doing so."

"I have concern about the matter of *die fahne*...the flag," von Steuben announced.

"I think we all have the same concerns," Edward Hand added.

"It is an awkward situation," agreed William Alexander, who preferred the title "Lord Stirling," despite the fact that the House of Lords had consistently refused to recognize him as such. "Clinton and Robinson claim André came ashore under a flag, yet André himself denies it." John Paterson put into words what they all thought. "They are obviously trying to save him, and he, not being aware of their letters, is ignorant of their strategy."

"Normally, we should give serious consideration to the statements of these two officers," Laurance advised. "However, the overriding weight must go to André's statement that he did *not* come ashore under the sanction of a flag. After all, had he done so, why would he deny it? It could save his life. And I remind the court that flags of truce do not cover subornation of treason."

"It concerns me that the life of this fine young officer can be lost over this issue," Lafayette said, clearly troubled. "Can we give him one more chance, to, shall we say, 'clarify' the issue?"

"I'm not sure it would help, "Greene replied. "The major is either too ingenuous or too honorable to dissemble. Whichever is the case, I don't think it will change his answer."

"Nevertheless, can we not give him a final chance?"

Major André was once more escorted in to face the board. If he was aware of the somber attitude of the generals facing him, he gave no indication. Greene wasted no time.

"Major André, we would like to return to the matter of a flag. You earlier stated that you did not come ashore under that sanction."

"That is correct, sir."

"You are quite sure about that?"

"Sir, it is impossible to suppose that I came ashore under such a sanction. Had I done so, I certainly would have returned under it."

A heavy silence descended on the room, which Greene finally broke. "Thank you, major. May I ask you to once more wait upon us?"

When André had left the room again, it seemed that no one wanted to speak. Finally, it was von Steuben who ended the gloomy silence. "We gave him every chance to save himself," the old general sighed. "He refused to take it."

Greene gazed around the table. "Gentlemen, do we need more discussion?" No one spoke. "Then I suggest we vote."

Once more André faced the board. This time he stood, his posture one of rigid attention.

The members of the board were clearly ill at ease. Some of them avoided looking at André, staring instead down at the table.

"Major André," Greene announced, "I shall now read to you the unanimous findings of the board and its unanimous recommendation to General Washington." Clearing his throat, he began.

"The Board having considered the letter from His Excellency General Washington respecting Major André, Adjutant General to the British army, the letter of Major André to General Washington, the documents found on Major André's person, and the testimony of Major André before this Board, report to His Excellency, the Commander in Chief that, having maturely considered these facts, the Board concludes that Major André, Adjutant General to the British army, ought to be considered as a spy from the enemy, and agreeable to the law and usage of nations, it is their opinion, he ought to suffer death."

For a long moment André continued to stand motionless, staring straight ahead. Then his eye blinked rapidly several times, and his shoulders drooped slightly as his eyes turned downward. He rallied quickly, however, and once more he raised his gaze to meet the board.

"So you condemn me, gentlemen."

Greene's voice was edged with regret as he replied. "By your candor, sir, you have condemned yourself."

On the following day, Washington approved the recommendation of the board and sentenced Major John André to death.

# CHAPTER TEN

*DeWint House, Tappan, New York*
*Head Quarters, Sept. 30, 1780*

*T O: His Excellency Sir Henry Clinton*

*S I R,*

IN answer to your Excellency's letter of the 26th instant, which I had the Honour to receive, I am to inform you that Major André was taken under such Circumstances as would have justified the most summary Proceedings against him. I determined, however, to refer his Case to the Examination and Decision of a Board of General Officers; who have reported on his free and voluntary Confession and Letters: 1st that he came on shore from the Vulture sloop of war in the night of the twenty first of September instant on an Interview with General Arnold in a private and secret Manner.

2dly that he changed his Dress within our Lines and under a feigned Name, and in a disguised Habit passed our Works at Stoney & Verplancks Points, the Evening of the twenty second of September instant, and was taken the morning of the twenty third of September instant at Tarry Town in a disguised Habit, being then on his way to New York, and when taken he had in his Possession several Papers which contained Intelligence for the Enemy.

From these proceedings it is evident Major André was employed in the Execution of Measures very foreign to the Objects of Flags of Truce, and such as they were never meant to authorize or countenance in the most distant Degree; and this Gentleman confessed, with the greatest Candor, in the Course of his Examination, That it was "impossible for him to suppose he came on Shore, under the Sanction of a Flag."

*I have the honour to be your Excellency's*
*Most obedient and most humble servant,*
G. WASHINGTON.

*New-York, Sept. 30. 1780*

*T O: His Excellency General Washington*

*S I R:* FROM your Excellency's letter of this date, I am persuaded the Board of General Officers, to whom you referred the Case of Major André, can't have been rightly informed of all the Circumstances on which a Judgement ought to be formed. I think it of the highest Moment to Humanity, that your Excellency should be perfectly apprized of the State of this Matter before your proceed to put that Judgement in Execution.

For this reason, I shall send His Excellency Lieut. General Robertson, and two other Gentlemen, to give you a true State of Facts, and to declare to you my Sentiments and Resolutions. They will set out to morrow as early as the Wind and Tide will permit, and wait near Dobb's Ferry for your Permission and safe Conduct, to meet your Excellency, or such Persons as you may appoint, to converse with them on this Subject.

*I have the honour to be, your Excellency's*
        *Most obedient and most humble servant,*
                H. CLINTON

# CHAPTER ELEVEN

*DeWint House, Tappan, New York*
*October 1, 1780*

UPON RECEIVING CLINTON'S second letter, Washington appointed Nathanael Greene to represent him at the meeting with General Robertson. In the late afternoon Greene returned to report. Washington was in the middle of a discussion with Colonel Laurance, his judge advocate general, but he interrupted it, indicating Laurance should remain to hear what Greene had to say.

It was the second time George Washington had made his headquarters in the small brick house of Dutch origin and design. As one of the few remaining structures in lower New York with the flaring roof truss common to Dutch architecture, it stood out clearly from the other homes in the town. Although it contained only two rooms on the ground floor, they were large, and separated by a center hall, which enabled the commander in chief to use one for his office and the other as a private room where he relaxed and slept. The town was now crowded with troops, and a contingent of his Life Guards were encamped around the house and its attached wood-frame kitchen.

"When the boat pulled up," Greene began, "Robertson had with him Andrew Elliot, the lieutenant governor of New York, and William Smith, the chief justice. I did not permit either of them to land. We have enough problems with Congress without the suspicion that the army is dealing with enemy civilian officials." Washington nodded in agreement, but said nothing.

"Robertson had nothing new to offer," Greene continued. "The same claim of a flag of truce, that André came ashore under the protection of the general who commanded the district, and that everything he did while ashore was by the direction of Arnold. He was clearly upset that I did not allow Smith to come ashore. He said he had hoped that the chief justice, with his knowledge of the laws of war and nations, might be allowed to express an opinion on the matter. It was also obvious that Robertson considers André a close friend, and is distressed by his sentence. When he saw that I was not moved by his argument, he chose another approach, pointing out that Clinton holds André in high esteem, and would be infinitely obliged by his liberation."

"Sir Henry might be encouraged if he knew how many members of my own staff would also be obliged by that same action," Washington said. "He has managed to find his way to the hearts of all of them." His visage then firmed. "But charming young gentleman or not, the man has been fairly judged a spy. Had his mission succeeded, it may well have destroyed this nation. He must pay the price."

"I hope you will give consideration to my previous suggestion," Laurance said, referring to their interrupted conference. "I think it wise to wait André's execution upon Arnold's fate."

Washington rolled his eyes toward the ceiling, feigning exasperation. "He has not seduced you too, has he, colonel?"

"Not at all, sir. I believe, as you do, that he should hang. However, I feel it would be more appropriate to withhold announcing the date of execution until after Arnold's trial is over."

"You don't feel his act stands on its own?"

"I do, but as you are well aware, there is a lot of sympathy for him, high and low. Arnold's trial will bring out the depth of the treachery and the calamity it would have caused. It will link André to Arnold as a co-conspirator, and make the execution more understandable, even to his admirers."

Washington pondered for a moment. "When will you begin the trial?"

"I think we should be ready in about a week."

"A week!" This time the exasperation was not feigned. "It has already been a week." Washington shook his head firmly. "It must be sooner." He consulted a calendar on his desk. "No later than this coming Wednesday," he announced.

Laurance raised his eyebrows, but gave a slight bow. "I will do my best, sir."

Considering the date settled, Washington turned to details. "I had hoped to set the court at West Point, a fitting place for this treachery to be avenged. However, I cannot have all my generals so far from the main army. I plan to convene it here instead. The church where André's inquiry was held, is it suitable for the court?"

"I'm afraid it's too small," Laurance replied, "especially the room where we would need to hold the witnesses prior to their testimony. However, I've arranged to use the parsonage across the green from the church. It's referred to locally as the Manse. It has a floor plan similar to your accommodation here, two rooms separated by a center hall, but the rooms are much larger."

"And is there a secure place for Arnold to be confined during the trial?"

Laurance thought for a moment. "There's a stable just off Main Street which has a loft above. It was used as a storeroom for a time, so the windows are barred. It then became servants quarters for the main house. I know of it because one of my officers is billeted there now. Putting Arnold in his place should also spare us further complaints about his treatment."

"We can bivouac a company on the property," Greene added, "which would provide both guards and perimeter security."

"It's done, then," said Washington. "Please arrange for Arnold's transfer."

As the two officers prepared to leave, Washington asked Laurance to remain. He indicated a small stack of letters on his desk. "This is Mrs. Arnold's correspondence which Colonel Varick gave to me. I have glanced through it and am satisfied that none of it has any bearing on this case. However, there is a letter from Major André referring to an acquaintance before her marriage, and a copy of a letter from her in reply, which would cause Mrs. Arnold embarrassment if they were revealed, especially at this time."

Laurance raised his eyebrows. "I can understand why they would."

"I am acquainted with the Shippens, Colonel Laurance," Washington said. "They are an old, established family. The judge himself has not quite decided on which side his loyalty should lie, and tries to steer a neutral path. His daughters are incurable coquettes, but otherwise fine young ladies. Any association with British officers while their army occupied Philadelphia I am sure was nothing more than innocent flirtation. I plan to return the correspondence to Mrs. Arnold, and we can consider the matter closed."

"Sir, may I see the letters?" Laurance knew it was a dangerous request. Washington did not like his decisions questioned. However, after a brief pause, he reached for two letters set apart from the rest, indicating he had anticipated such a request. He slid the envelopes across the desk to Laurance. When the judge advocate finished reading, he looked up to find Washington staring at him.

"General, with the greatest respect for your concern about the lady's privacy, I feel I must be able to examine these letters in more detail. They may be perfectly innocent, and it is clear they were exchanged well before the conspiracy began, but there are certain indications—"

"You may have the letters," Washington interrupted, "if you think they may point you toward finding additional evidence. But you will not introduce them in the trial, and you will not contact Mrs. Arnold regarding them."

As Laurance made a slight bow and turned to leave, Washington added, "I accept your suggestion to withhold setting the date of André's execution." He then added, "I do not expect it to be much of a delay."

# CHAPTER TWELVE

*Widow Morrison's House, Tappan, New York*
*October 1, 1780*

AFTER LEAVING WASHINGTON, Laurance called an immediate conference with his deputies. Mrs. Morrison had fortuitously prepared a succulent hotchpot, which was ample to feed the extra guests on short notice. It featured squirrel, and included carrots, turnips, sweet potatoes, and parsnips. Since the elderly widow was an unlikely hunter, Joshua guessed that a friend had presented her with several of the small animals. After she had cleaned up the dishes, she left for her daughter's house, leaving the officers to their business.

Laurance began by announcing the date for the court-martial. Both Edwards and Joshua protested that they needed more preparation, but Laurance waived their objections aside.

"Washington will not be swayed on this, so we must go with what we have. With two more days to work, I believe it's enough. If we find that we need to explore further avenues of evidence, we can seek adjournments." He knew how Washington would view any attempt at delay, but he wanted to offer his colleagues some hope. "I'm afraid Washington views the trial as another André hearing, to be concluded in a day or two."

Edwards cocked an eyebrow. "And you did not disabuse him of that?"

"He was in no mood to be disabused."

"Is he aware that Arnold's court at Morristown took more than a month?" Joshua asked.

"With adjournments," Laurance corrected. "I'm sure he is, but no matter. We begin on Wednesday. Joshua, a messenger has been dispatched to Colonel Lamb to send Arnold here at once. Interview him tomorrow and urge him once more to accept your assistance. He needs to establish some sort of a rational defense. His claim of a British plot is far-fetched, and seems unsupportable."

'I'll do what I can," Joshua promised. "Perhaps I have some credit with him now that my plea for better treatment was successful." Joshua was only too aware of Arnold's expected arrival. He had been told to vacate his quarters for the general, and had moved into a room with another officer. His nightly pleasure of sleeping with Amy was over until the end of the trial.

Laurance then placed two single sheets before each of his assistants, one, a list of the members of the court, and another showing the names of the witnesses he intended to call. Since the judge advocate at a trial normally represented both the government and the accused, it was not unusual for Joshua to be present at the meeting. His new role as defense counsel, established for this trial only, did not suggest an adversarial relationship between the two parties, such as might be the case in a civil trial. It was incumbent upon the judge advocate to protect the rights of the accused as well as present the evidence against him, and in this trial, Joshua personified that protection. The two parties would not conceal evidence or information from each other, and would cooperate when the situation required it.

After a brief perusal of the lists, Joshua held up the one containing the members of the court. "I'm concerned that these are the same officers who examined Major André, heard his testimony, and passed judgment upon him."

"I share your concern to some degree," Laurance conceded, "however, there are two points I would ask you to consider. First, there is the honor of the officers themselves. No matter what they may have heard as testimony from André, and no matter what personal feelings this testimony may have produced, these officers will judge Arnold fairly and without prejudice.

"Secondly, the matter is moot. The Articles of War require that there be thirteen officers on the court, and Arnold's rank requires that they be the most senior we can find. Even as it is, only one officer outranks Arnold, the president, General Greene. Would you have Arnold tried by a motley assortment of colonels? Do you think he himself would want that?"

Joshua shook his head. He had to acknowledge the points Laurance had made. These men all knew Arnold as a brave and effective soldier. He was one of them. They would treat him fairly.

"Arnold must have guessed the approximate composition of the members of the court," Laurance continued. "Has he raised the issue with you?"

"No."

"Then let's see if he does so tomorrow."

Laurance was anxious to move on. "Here is a list of the witnesses I intend to call. There could be more as the trial develops. Major André still refuses to testify. I suppose he feels there would be no point, merely tighten the noose around his own neck."

"And Arnold's," Edwards added. "Couldn't we suggest to Washington that we offer André a lighter sentence in exchange for his testimony?"

Laurance shook his head with a wry smile. "I made that very suggestion and he almost threw me out of his office. He is adamant that both André and Arnold must hang." He paused, mulling over the issue for a moment, and then continued. "I think we might as well remove André's name from the witness list, since there is virtually no hope of his testifying."

"May I suggest that we keep his name on the list just the same?" Edwards said. "We have nothing to lose."

"Nothing to gain either, I'm afraid. However..." Laurance's shrug of his shoulders indicated his acceptance of the suggestion.

"Who is Joshua Hett Smith?" Joshua asked, looking up from the witness list.

"A squire who lives nearby West Point," Laurance replied. "He apparently assisted Arnold in the André affair, but claims he was duped by Arnold into believing they were engaged in a secret intelligence mission. I only got the opportunity to talk to him yesterday. He is under arrest, pending further investigation. With André not testifying, he's a strong witness to place both André and Arnold together."

"If he can be believed," Edwards said.

"Yes." Laurance then turned to Joshua. "Are there any witnesses General Arnold wishes to call?"

"As far as I know, he has no witnesses of his own," Joshua replied, "but plans extensive examination of prosecution witnesses."

"The final item I would like to discuss," Laurance continued, "is the evidence. Congress has seized all Arnold's papers left behind in his Philadelphia office, and they are being thoroughly scrutinized. Sam Huntington has informed Washington it already appears that some of them may point to corruption on the part of Arnold in his dealings with commercial interests, but they need more time to sort it all out. If we had more time, we could add more charges to the list."

"What would be the point?" Joshua asked. "The evidence is more appropriate for his previous trial than this one. And treason is by far a more serious charge than corruption."

"But it shows turpitude and reflects on his character. Also, it suggests a need for money, which might lead him to sell out his country. But the point is moot. We must go to trial Wednesday."

Laurance then passed out another list, this one thicker than the previous two. "I have divided the evidence against General Arnold into categories which correspond to the three specifications of the charge against him. In the first category are copies of four letters retrieved from Arnold's files addressed to Major André. They are in Arnold's hand, and show a chain of communication of a treasonable nature between Arnold and André. They show that Arnold had been passing intelligence information to the enemy, and that he was betraying his country for money—a very large sum. The second category is the packet of documents taken from André, which show Arnold's intent to surrender West Point. Finally, in the third category is a single letter from Arnold to André informing him of Washington's location on September 17$^{th}$," showing that he intended to betray Washington to the enemy."

Laurance leaned back in his chair and began strumming his fingers idly on the desk. "We have a problem, obviously," he continued. "Coding and cipher materials were found in Arnold's office. Of itself, this isn't unusual, since it can be assumed that he encoded important messages to his command, in case a messenger was intercepted. Since the four letters we have here were still in Arnold's files, we can assume he wrote them out, encoded them, and sent the encoded copies to André. But without André's testimony, we have no proof that he received them, or even that they were sent at all."

"But they are in his hand," Edwards pointed out again. "Why would he write such things, unless he was contemplating treason?"

"Why, indeed," Laurance agreed, "and I hope the court will think the same way."

"Without corroboration from André," Joshua countered, "I have serious reservations about these letters standing up in court, and if they are introduced, I plan to challenge them." He was particularly concerned about the letter giving Washington's location. If it could be proven genuine, it was an infamous betrayal, but even if not, it would still linger in the minds of all who heard it. Joshua felt the main purpose of the charge was to inflame the court.

To Joshua's surprise, Laurance concurred. "I agree that without André there is some doubt that the letters will stand on their own. And with Arnold's contention that he is the victim of a plot, we can expect him to claim the letters are forgeries and were planted in his files. We could withdraw the letters and drop both specifications. The charge of betraying West Point is supported by strong evidence and by itself is enough to hang him."

"I think we should let things stand as they are," Edwards said. "The correspondence will condemn Arnold if it can be substantiated. Who knows what may happen as the trial unfolds?"Laurance appeared unconvinced. "I'm reluctant to burden the court with papers that will amount to nothing."

Edwards remained insistent. "We can always withdraw the charges later. Arnold's files from Philadelphia may arrive any day. They could provide more information."

"We've already concluded that any corrupt activities in Philadelphia have no place in this trial," Joshua said.

"Colonel," Edwards continued, ignoring Joshua, "we must not discard now what may prove to be good evidence later. What do we gain by doing so?"

"Well, if you feel so strongly about it, Thomas...." Laurance turned to Thorne. "Joshua?"

Joshua shrugged. "Whatever you wish. But I will still challenge them." It was settled. The letters would remain part of the prosecution's case.

"How about the correspondence Varick took from Mrs. Arnold's file?" Edwards then asked.

Laurance produced the letter from André to Peggy Arnold, and the copy of her reply. "Washington has read the correspondence, and these are the only letters he thinks have any significance." In the interest of time, he then read them aloud.

*Head-Quarters, New York,*
*the 16th Aug. 1779*

Madame. Major Giles is so good as to take charge of this letter, which is meant to solicit your remembrance, and to assure you that my respect for you, and the fair circle in which I had the honour of becoming acquainted with you, remains unimpaired by distance or political broils. It would make me very happy to become useful to you here. You know the Mesquianza made me a complete milliner. Should you not have received supplies for your fullest equipment for that department, I shall be glad to enter into the whole detail of capwire, needles, gauze,

&c., and, to the best of my abilities, render you in these trifles services from which I hope you would infer a zeal to be further employed. I beg you would present my best respects to your sisters, to the Miss Chews, and to Mrs. Shippen and Mrs. Chew.

I have the honour to be, with the greatest regard, Madam, your most obedient and most humble servant,

John André

Captain André

Mrs. Arnold presents her best respects to Capt. André, and is much obliged to him for his very polite and friendly offer of being serviceable to her. Major Giles was so obliging as to promise to procure what trifles Mrs. Arnold wanted in the millinery way, or she would have with pleasure accepted of it. Mrs. Arnold begs leave to assure Capt. André that her friendship and esteem for him is not impaired by time or accident. The Ladies to whom Capt André wishes to be remembered are well, and present their Compliments to him.

Philadelphia, October 13th 1779

As soon as he had finished, Edwards spoke. "Colonel, we must introduce these letters in court."

Laurance shook his head. "Washington has denied us that option. He feels they contain nothing that would justify embarrassing Mrs. Arnold by doing so."

"But sir, showing a connection between Arnold's wife and the man Arnold approached to offer the surrender of West Point is damning evidence."

"Not really," Joshua broke in. He was concerned about what

might turn up by delving into the letter, remembering John Lamb's admonition about the "pretty young wife." It would be best to keep the letters suppressed. "It could be a coincidence."

"Coincidence? You can't be serious. Why would André re-establish communication with Peggy Arnold after all this time? Merely to offer her assistance obtaining sewing supplies? In time of war, has he nothing better to do? Are we to believe that all this talk of needles, capwire, and gauze doesn't hide another purpose?"

"That's only a matter of conjecture," Laurance replied. "We must accept that Washington has a deep affection for Peggy Arnold and believes her innocent in this affair. That, and his natural chivalry, make him reluctant to involve a woman in a matter such as this."

Edwards raised his eyebrows. "Sometimes chivalry can go too far. The letters contain much possible double meaning."

"Only if you are determined to find it," Joshua said. "The lady is clearly rejecting his offer."

"Not clearly at all. There is a strong indication of other meanings."

"I don't think we should pursue this," Joshua said. "The letter is of little value as evidence unless it can be identified in court by Mrs. Arnold, and a wife may not be forced to testify against her husband."

"I disagree," Edwards persisted. "We have a firm chain of custody. The letter was part of Mrs. Arnold's correspondence taken from her desk by Colonel Varick and personally delivered to General Washington. It will stand by itself. And if it should turn out that she is involved—"

Laurance held up his hand for silence. "Gentlemen, all this talk is pointless. General Washington is thoroughly familiar with spy craft, and I'm sure he sees all the possibilities for deception in the correspondence that you do, Thomas. But he apparently does not see the evidence as firm enough, or necessary enough, to embarrass Mrs. Arnold." Laurance then turned to Joshua, changing the subject with finality. "Does Arnold have any evidence to produce?"

"If he does, he's not made me aware of it. I expect him to rely heavily on his reputation and his honor."

"Which have nothing to do with the current charge," Edwards said, still miffed by the rejection of his views.

"True, and I have informed him so."

Laurance then handed Joshua a large box containing Arnold's correspondence, indicating he had taken what he needed and the rest could be returned to Arnold. "Regarding his defense," Laurance said, addressing himself to Joshua, "I've had a private word with General Greene about keeping you on the court, even if in only an advisory capacity to Arnold. I hope, that as the trial proceeds, Arnold will allow you to participate more fully. His defense is a weak one, but if he permits it, you must do everything you can to assist him and find evidence to support his claim of a conspiracy against him. Regardless of the seriousness of the charge, Arnold is one of the great patriots of our nation. He must be given every opportunity to clear his name, if it's possible to do so. Joshua, we won't meet again in this manner. It wouldn't be appropriate once the court convenes. Future conferences between prosecution and defense must take place under the umbrella of the court."

Laurance then turned to Edwards. "Thomas, we have much to prepare." He looked from one of his officers to the other, in an unspoken invitation to offer something more. Neither did. "I have nothing further," he announced, picking up his papers. "The court will convene at 10 A.M. on Wednesday."

# CHAPTER THIRTEEN

*Tappan, New York*
*October 2, 1780*

ALTHOUGH THE MESSENGER had ridden to West Point through the night, it was not until late afternoon that Arnold arrived at Tappan. He had been escorted by an entire cavalry troop. In deference to his injured leg, he had been placed in a wagon, rather than on horseback, his hands tied, and two armed troopers riding in the wagon with him. He was in a foul mood when he arrived, but, expecting a cell, the relative comfort of his quarters somewhat improved his disposition. After a decent meal, also unexpected, his state of mind was even better, and he agreed to see Joshua.

"Ah, Major Thorne, good evening." Arnold gestured to his surroundings. "Do I have you to thank for this...luxury?"

In more ways than one, Joshua thought, but did not voice. "I hope that your situation at West Point was similarly improved, general."

"Nothing as grand as this. It was still a cell, but at least it was above ground, and I could enjoy the light of day. The meals improved also, and my old friend John Lamb even allowed me a half-bottle of Madeira at supper. You will also note that I have been given a change of clothes and permitted to shave."

Joshua then delivered the correspondence files that Arnold had requested earlier, and which Laurance had just released, apologizing for the short time remaining before the trial. Arnold did not seem to mind, taking the box without comment.

"Sir, your court-martial will begin the day after tomorrow," Joshua said, getting right to the point. "In thirty-six hours you will be on trial for your life. To my knowledge, your defense is totally unprepared. You have no witnesses, you have assembled no proofs—"

"On the contrary, major, I have all that I need," Arnold replied, indicating the box of files. "My other proofs are my record and my honor. My witnesses are the very ones who will be brought forward to testify against me."

"If you will permit me, sir, your past record, while most distinguished, will not protect you from the present charges against you, and your honor is no more than is to be expected of any other gentleman of your rank and position. As for the prosecution witnesses, I fail to see how they can in any way aid your case."

"If you had been present at my prior court-martial, you would understand. My examination of them demolished their testimony and exposed their lies. This case will be no different."

Joshua was aware that Arnold had been convicted of two of the eight charges against him, proving that his "demolishment" was not quite complete, but he felt that continuing in this line would prove fruitless. He then showed Arnold the list of witnesses and court members. The general stretched out on the bed as he read the papers. Joshua could not help visualizing the scene of a much more attractive occupant on that same bed only a few nights ago.

"André's name is here," Arnold said. "You told me he would not testify."

"He still refuses," Joshua assured him. "Not everyone on the witness list will be called. For example, the three men who captured André are on the list, but I expect Colonel Laurance to call only one of them. And both Colonel Jameson and Major Tallmadge from North Castle are there, but I don't expect Tallmadge to be called. You might say the list is inflated to cover any contingencies."

"Such as André changing his mind?"

"I don't see that as much of a possibility, do you?"

Arnold did not reply, turning his attention to the members of the court. "I am uneasy with General Howe," he said, reading the document. "He was president of the court at my prior trial."

"Do you believe that prejudices him against you?"

"He found me guilty of two of the charges. How does any man feel when trying the same person again for another offense? I probably should seek his removal."

"To do so you would have to claim he is prejudiced," Joshua informed him. "There is no provision for peremptorily challenging a member of the court."

"I challenged three of the members of my previous court peremptorily, and Howe allowed it," Arnold retorted. Joshua had not been aware that Arnold had successfully secured the removal of these officers solely because they were Pennsylvanians, whom he suspected would not judge him impartially.

"Perhaps I should leave Howe on the court after all," Arnold now conceded. After the British had taken Savannah, Howe himself had suffered a court-martial of his own on charges similar to those against Arnold in his first trial, and had been acquitted. There was at least a chance that he would view Arnold with sympathy, and many in the army felt that was why Washington had appointed him president of Arnold's previous court-martial.

"Sir, it is by General Washington's insistence that you come to trial on Wednesday. But, if you feel that you need more time, we can petition the court for a delay."

Arnold shook his head emphatically. "No. In this, General Washington and I are in accord. We must strike and kill this snake now. I am ready. But if you wish to be of service, I want to see my family. Colonel Lamb was kind enough to forward a letter from me through General Washington to my wife, but I have heard nothing in return. Do you have any idea where they are?" In making this inquiry, Arnold was referring to his second marriage. His first wife had died in 1775, and his three sons by that marriage were being cared for by his sister, Hannah, back in New Haven, who was also tending to his business interests.

"The last I heard, sir, your wife has been allowed to remain at Robinson's House until she decides her plans for the future."

"Then, surely, there is no danger in her being allowed to visit me here, even if the court is in progress."

"I will forward your request. Meanwhile, general, if you should change your mind about my assistance, my office is just down the street, and my quarters are equally close by. Please consider me at your disposal."

"Oh, one more thing, major," Arnold added, as Joshua rose to leave. "As I am to stand trial before a court of general officers, I must present myself in my dress uniform. Colonel Lamb has arranged to retrieve it from Robinson's House and is sending it here, along with my sword. I would be grateful if you would look out for them."

"I will be happy to, general, and will insure that the uniform is delivered to you upon arrival. I doubt, however, that you will be permitted to have your sword."

# CHAPTER FOURTEEN

*Headquarters, British Army in North America, New York City*
*October 2, 1780*

LIEUTENANT GENERAL JAMES C. Robertson sat quietly in General Clinton's office, awaiting the commander in chief's arrival. As royal governor of New York City, he had no official connection with the army staff, yet it was well-known that he was one of Sir Henry's most trusted advisers. At least he had been, until, following his meeting with the rebel General Greene, he had informed Clinton that in his opinion André was safe from execution. Then, yesterday they had learned that Washington had approved the death sentence, which could be carried out at any time. Robertson had asked for this meeting at once, hoping to gain Clinton's approval for a bold plan.

Upon his arrival, Robertson had been told that Clinton was breakfasting privately, and was ushered into his office to wait. Already in attendance were two officers whose presence Robertson had requested, Colonel Beverly Robinson, commander of the Loyal American Regiment, and Captain George Beckwith, officially assigned as aide to General Kynphausen, but now involved in the command's undercover operations. Beckwith was temporarily performing Major André's duties.

When Clinton arrived, Robertson was shocked by his appearance. The general seemed to have aged overnight. His shoulders sagged, his eyes appeared dull and unfocused, and his manner listless. Moving slowly across the room, he slumped into the chair behind his desk.

"Sir Henry," Robertson began immediately, foregoing formalities, "I have asked these gentlemen to join me this morning as I would like to propose that we devise a plan to rescue Major André from the rebels." He saw a flicker of interest in Clinton's expression as he continued. "Colonel Robinson's Loyal Americans know the Highlands better than any other troops, and would be the ideal force to effect a rescue." It was true. Robinson, in creating his regiment, had recruited many of his own tenants and overseers from his large holdings in the Hudson Valley. Somewhere in this fertile valley, through which the North River flowed to New York City, André was imprisoned.

"Do we know where Johnny is being held?" Clinton asked, his interest now definitely aroused.

"That's why I asked Captain Beckwith to be here. His operatives have been working constantly to discover his whereabouts." He nodded to Beckwith, who took over the conversation.

"What we know so far, sir, is that Major André was captured near Tarry Town and taken to a rebel post at South Salem. There, he spent a night, and was then taken to Colonel Robinson's house."

"That's just across the river from West Point," Clinton observed, frowning. "If they've imprisoned him in the fortress, it will be virtually impossible to rescue him."

"We have reason to believe that may not be the case, though, Sir Henry. We have an unconfirmed report the he was seen being placed upon a guarded barge, which proceeded down river. We are using every resource to pick up the trail from there."

"Also," Robertson added, "we know that André was examined by a board of general officers, of which Greene informed me he was one. And the speed with which Greene's representative was able to meet with me near Dobb's Ferry on Sunday, and the speed with which I received Washington's response to my arguments, indicate that the rebel headquarters lies not more than five to ten miles inland from the west bank of the river. I think it highly unlikely that Washington would have dispatched a significant number of his generals so far north as West Point to examine André."

"Then you think Johnny might be being held at the rebel headquarters?" Clinton asked, his hopes rising.

"I think it highly likely. And since Washington's letter to you was dated from Tappan, there is a good chance that is where the headquarters may be."

"All of our assets are concentrated on that area, Sir Henry," Beckwith added. "I will know something by tomorrow. I feel confident that we will know very quickly where the rebel headquarters is located, and if Major André is being held there."

"Meanwhile," added Robertson, "with your approval, Colonel Robinson can begin planning a rescue mission."

"By all means, by all means." Clinton turned to Robinson. "How soon can you furnish a plan?"

Robinson was alarmed at the thought of attempting a rescue effort in the middle of the rebel encampment, which he thought had little chance of success. However, he felt partly responsible for André's capture, and also, he did not want to dampen Clinton's sudden improvement in mood. He would discuss it with his staff and his commanders to see if together they could come up with something feasible.

"I can have a rough outline by tomorrow, and depending on firm information from Captain Beckwith's agents, we can then proceed with a detailed plan."

"Time is critical of course," Clinton warned. "Those barbarians have threatened to execute Johnny at any moment."

"We may have some leeway there," Robertson said. "It would be unusual for them to execute him before Arnold is tried."

As the mood in the room improved as a result of the discussion, Robinson thought it appropriate to inject a warning. "We should all be aware that, depending upon how well he is being guarded, a rescue mission could cost Major André his life."

The silence which followed the remark was finally broken by Clinton. "His life is forfeit in any event, is it not?"

# CHAPTER FIFTEEN

*Tappan, New York*
*October 3, 1780*

THOMAS EDWARDS WAS unhappy. He had reread the letters on his desk half a dozen times, and each time he became more frustrated. There was no doubt in his mind that they were far from an innocent exchange of pleasantries. The idea that André was renewing acquaintance with a woman who was now the wife of an enemy general merely to provide her with millinery supplies was ludicrous. He was convinced that the "cap-wire, needles, gauze, &c." in André's letter referred to things more sinister. And the reference to "Major Giles" in both letters strongly suggested the services of an accomplice serving as an intermediary. Although Peggy Arnold's reply to André seemed innocuous, it could be read as "all is well and proceeding according to plan." The dates were a problem, though, a full year before the beginning of the conspiracy— unless it had started much earlier than they knew.

Laurance seemed to feel that they had an air-tight case, but Edwards was not that sure. He was less confident than he had previously indicated regarding the correspondence from Arnold's files. Thorne would challenge it, and there was a chance the documents would not stand. Although he agreed with Laurance that the rest of the case was strong, he had read the transcript of Arnold's previous trial, and Laurance was correct; Arnold had defended himself with skill and passion. Who could tell what might transpire during the course of the trial? They needed every advantage available. *He had to find a way to use those letters!*

It was the day before the trial, and although Laurance and Edwards would be busy, Joshua found himself with little to do. Arnold insisted he was ready to go to trial, and had refused to allow him into his confidence. Even so, Joshua intended to see him later in the morning, with a final offer of assistance. He decided to breakfast at Mabie's, where Amy made them an Indian meal pudding. Consisting of Indian corn meal, eggs, generous portions of butter, sugar, and flavored with mace, nutmeg and Madeira, it was one of Joshua's favorite dishes. As they were finishing, Amy voiced her disapproval that the public would not be permitted to attend the trial.

"A man like that should be tried publicly, so we can all see how evil he is," she complained.

"The other night Laurance called Arnold one of the great patriots of our nation," Joshua countered.

"That may be true today, but after the trial he will be its greatest scoundrel." She glanced over her shoulder at the door to the room where André was being held. "And that poor boy is going to his death."

"Poor *boy*? He's my age, Amy."

"Really? He looks so much younger."

"Thank you."

She ignored his sarcasm. "I brought him his breakfast just before you came. Washington sent it over again, just as he has every morning. I saw a self-portrait which he sketched after hearing his death sentence." Her voice became pensive and slightly tremulous. "He shows himself sitting at a small, circular table, with a quill and ink pot. The sweet melancholy of his face was so composed, and yet so poignant." She ended with a sigh.

"Interesting," Joshua replied. "A poetic, artistic spy, although I imagine it will be difficult for him to portray himself on the gibbet."

"Very funny."

"Why are you so concerned about André? He's every bit as culpable as Arnold."

"It's just...well...he seems like such a gentleman, compared to a rogue like Arnold."

"Oh, come now. Arnold is a fighting man. André seems little more than a headquarters dandy. Until now, Arnold has performed valuable service for our country, André has worked from the beginning to undermine it." He found it difficult to understand her sympathy for an enemy spy.

"I'm sure Arnold is the instigator of this whole thing, and John—"

"John?"

She reddened slightly. "Major André...was lured into the plot. Don't you think that's possible, Josh?"

Joshua drained his cider tankard and rose to leave. "I suppose it's possible, but it doesn't make any difference." He gave her his most evil smile. "He'll hang anyway." Amy's interest in André irritated him. And it made him uneasy that the woman in his life was nurturing an infatuation for a dead man.

As Amy watched him stride purposefully for the door, she wondered if he was jealous. She frowned, but was not displeased by the thought. Josh was being entirely too flippant about André's fate. Major Tallmadge, Colonel Hamilton, and every officer who had come in contact with the young major was highly impressed with him, yet Josh disliked him without even meeting him. Well, if he was going to champion Arnold, she could certainly support poor John André.

Joshua's visit to Arnold was even briefer than he had expected. The general greeted him at the door with a question.

"Is there word on my family being allowed to visit me?"

"Not yet, sir."

"What is causing the delay?" Arnold's voice rose as he limped to a chair, where he began to rub his bad leg irritably.

"It's been less than a full day—"

"It has been more than enough time." Arnold sat forward, leaning awkwardly over his outstretched leg. He looked directly into Joshua's eyes. "You may think me powerless in this situation, major, but I assure you I am not. Unless I have a positive response by tomorrow morning, you shall see that for yourself."

# CHAPTER SIXTEEN

*The Manse, Tappan*
*Wednesday, October 4, 1780*

THE WIND SWEPT a cold rain through Main Street as the members of the court made their way into the parsonage. A lead-gray sky gave warning that the bad weather would likely continue. As there was no provision for hanging them, the officers piled their wet greatcoats and cloaks in the wide hallway. Rising from the wet clothing, a characteristic odor wafted slowly through the room. Joshua Thorne always thought of it as the smell of the army, a blend of wet wool, leather, sweat of men and horses, campfire smoke, and gunpowder. It was usually present in some degree, more pronounced in the forward camps, less so in the rear. But even here it could be detected in the uniforms of the assembled generals. To Joshua, it was not an unpleasant smell. He was comfortable with it, as evoking comradeship, organization, and a sense of belonging to something larger than himself. Unfortunately, the army produced other odors that were anything but comforting, as anyone downwind from the field latrines could attest.

General Greene had decided that his court would meet in one daily sitting, commencing at 10 A.M. and ending at four, with no recess for lunch. The late start and early recess did not indicate a leisurely approach to the trial, but rather that the members of the court had other responsibilities that needed attending on a daily basis.

The war did not cease for General Arnold's court-martial, nor did General Greene's many duties as Washington's second in command. The configuration of the court was similar to André's hearing, and the only new requirement was the addition of a table for the court recorder. Witnesses waiting to testify would be accommodated in the second large room across the hall. If the court needed to confer in closed session, Arnold could be temporarily removed to the kitchen in the basement.

By 10 A.M. all members of the court were in their seats. Laurance and Edwards were at their table, and Joshua at the one he would share with Arnold. The court recorder was poised over his quills and lined foolscap. General Greene rapped his gavel.

"The court will come to order. The guards will bring in the prisoner."

The door to the small room opened, and Arnold appeared, escorted by two armed guards. In his blue and buff uniform, with its two stars on the epaulettes, he appeared every inch a major general. In lieu of his sword, he wore the gold sword knot presented to him by Washington after Saratoga. As he limped across the room, assisted by a polished cane, Joshua marveled at the man's demeanor. He appeared to be simply attending a staff meeting, rather than on trial for his life. He smiled warmly at Greene and at the other members of the court, saluted the president, and took his seat. If he sensed any hostility in the room, as Joshua did, he did not show it.

"Are all parties to the trial present?" Greene asked.

"They are, sir," Laurance replied.

"The court will be sworn."

The members of the court rose and raised their right hands. Laurance did the same and administered the oath.

"You, members of this court, do swear that you shall well and truly try and determine, according to the evidence, the matter now before you, between the United States of America, and the prisoner to be tried. So help you God."

Greene then administered an abbreviated oath to Laurance, Edwards, and Joshua, in which they swore not to divulge the sentence of the court, or the vote or opinion of any of its members. As Joshua sat back down, Arnold leaned over and asked in a low voice, "Is there any word on my family visiting me?"

Joshua shook his head. "Not yet," he whispered. Arnold sat back, his lips pressed in a grim line.

"Is the prosecution ready?" Greene asked.

"It is, sir," Laurance answered.

"Is the defense ready?"

Before Joshua could reply, Arnold intervened. "If I may, gentlemen," he began, struggling slowly to his feet, assisted by his cane, "I wish to represent myself before this court. Therefore, Major Thorne's presence is not necessary."

Forewarned by Laurance, Greene was prepared for the issue. "General Arnold, I must advise you in the strongest terms to accept the services of Major Thorne to assist in your defense. It is in your own interest that I advise this. There are complicated legal matters which may arise."

"I appreciate your concern, sir," Arnold replied, "but as you are aware, I have endured such a procedure previously, wherein I defended myself, and I have no reason to regret my action. Although not completely happy with that result, the outcome could not have been altered by the services of a legal representative, thanks to the prejudices of certain members of the court against me."

"May I point out, general, that this court involves a far more serious matter than your former trial?"

"Indeed it does, sir, which is precisely the reason I wish to represent myself. There is no advocate I could have that is more interested in my fate, and none more qualified to conduct my defense."

Greene took some time to mull over the matter. "If I allow you to represent yourself, will you allow me, in the interest of a smooth and uninterrupted procedure, to place Major Thorne at your table to provide you with such legal advice as you may need, and to insure that proper legal procedures are maintained?"

"And he will be under my direction?"

"He will."

"Then I accept."

"Very well, then, you may represent yourself."

Arnold bowed slightly. "Thank you, sir." He slowly sat down, again, using his cane for assistance, with a bit more stagecraft than was necessary, Joshua thought.

Greene nodded to Laurance. "You may proceed."

Laurance rose. "I shall now read the charges against the accused." Before he could begin, Arnold interrupted again.

"If you will permit me." He again went through the ritual of rising to his feet. "I must object to Colonel Laurance as the trial judge advocate in my case."

The statement brought stares of surprise from Laurance, and from Greene. "You are objecting to the Judge Advocate General presenting the case for the government?" Greene asked, a tinge of irritation in his voice.

"I am."

"On what grounds, sir?"

"Colonel Laurance represented the prosecution at my last court. I feel that the possibility of prejudice from that experience will work to my detriment in the present trial."

"General Arnold," Laurance interposed, "I am charged by Congress, General Washington, and the Articles of War to prosecute trials of persons by general courts-martial. There is no provision for challenging me from performing this responsibility."

"Nevertheless, I must do so," Arnold replied. "I did not find you particularly friendly at my previous court, and I have no cause to believe I would fare better in this one. You will recall sir, that the court found me guilty of two of the charges preferred. Since you were instrumental in achieving that finding, I cannot but feel that your service on this court would be tainted by the former result."

Laurance bristled. "General, I think that finding was most generous to you. Of the eight charges originally brought, four were dismissed, you were found not guilty of two, and guilty of only two minor offenses."

"Offenses for which the court recommended I be reprimanded by the commander in chief—"

"Gentlemen," Greene interrupted, "This is no place for discussion of the previous trial. General Arnold, I am not much inclined to remove the Judge Advocate General from this case."

"Then I am not much inclined to submit to the authority of this court."

"Sir," Laurance began, speaking to Arnold, in a conciliatory tone, "I assure you that I have no ill feeling toward you, but if I had it would make no difference in the prosecution of this case. The judge advocate is required to present all available evidence against you, be he your friend or foe. Such evidence cannot be embellished or mitigated. Were I to step down, it would not change the presentation of the government's case one iota."

"Then what is your objection to stepping down, Colonel?"

Joshua Thorne saw an impasse looming, and rose to his feet. "If it will be of help, sir," he said, addressing Greene, "Section XIV, Article 3, of the Articles of War states that the judge advocate general, *or some person deputed by him,* shall prosecute in the name of the United States."

Greene nodded his acknowledgment of Joshua's statement, but he felt that Arnold's position was completely without justification, and was inclined to rule to that effect. Yet this trial was so sensitive that he knew he needed to proceed carefully. This was a new army and a new military justice system. Precedents, once established, would be difficult to reverse. Before making a ruling, he would have to consult Washington. Fortunately, he was in his office, and with his desire for a speedy trial, would almost certainly render a quick decision.

"Gentlemen," he announced, "it seems that this matter will not be settled without further study and consultation. I propose to adjourn the court until 1 P.M. this afternoon."

As Laurance was leaving the church, Joshua approached him. "Colonel, may I have a moment?" He informed Laurance of his conversation with Arnold regarding permission to see his family, and his veiled threat if it were not granted.

"And you think he is being deliberately disruptive?" Laurance asked.

"I'm sure of it. And unless he gets his way, his next step will be to challenge General Howe from the court for cause, which will require a further delay until another officer can be seated. And after that, he will find further obstructions."

Laurance grimaced. He and Greene were on their way to see Washington. "He is not going to be happy as it is. I almost hate to mention this new development. It smells too much of blackmail, and, considering how he feels about Arnold, it will probably infuriate him." He looked hard at his assistant. "You're certain this is the game he's playing?"

"I am," Joshua confirmed.

Laurance sighed. "Then I suppose Washington must be told."

"We must settle this business quickly," Washington announced. Greene and Laurance were standing in front of his desk. "The army and the country talk of little else. Already there is sentiment that I've acted too rashly, condemning Arnold prior to a trial. We can brook no more delays." He turned to Laurance. "What are the consequences of replacing you as prosecutor?"

"Well, the Articles do allow me to appoint someone else, especially with your concurrence. But the seriousness of the charge, and the rank of the accused—"

Washington waved him into silence. "We must be done with it. Whom would you select?"

Laurance did not hesitate. "My deputy, Lieutenant Colonel Thomas Edwards."

"You have confidence in him?"

"Complete confidence. He is a graduate of Harvard College, has been certified in law by a fine Philadelphia firm, and is well versed in its military aspects. In addition, he's tried many cases before general courts, although none, obviously, at this level."

"Get on with it then. This poison must be removed from our system before it festers further."

Washington took the news of Arnold's obstruction more calmly than Greene or Laurance had expected, but they could tell it rankled him. "I have merely been waiting to hear the lady's wishes, and only this morning received her reply. She desires to see him. You may tell him that his wife and child will soon be on their way."

As Laurance bowed and turned to leave, Washington's voice stopped him.

"Colonel, do you have any doubts about obtaining a conviction?"

"None whatever, sir."

"You've read his letter to me?"

"I have. A flight of fancy. A desperate grab at straws no one will credit and no evidence will support."

The commander in chief's eyes turned to steel as they bored into his judge advocate. "I want him to hang, Colonel Laurance."

Laurance's gaze did not waver. "He will hang, General."

# CHAPTER SEVENTEEN

GREENE TAPPED HIS gavel once, lightly. "The court will come to order."

"All parties to the trial who were present when the court recessed are again present," Laurance stated.

Greene then announced the replacement of Laurance by Edwards, at which Laurance rose, saluted Greene, and withdrew from the room. Arnold leaned toward Joshua, speaking in a low voice.

"I am surprised that Laurance was unaware of the Article allowing him to delegate his authority to Edwards until you announced it."

"You can be sure he was aware of it, sir," Joshua replied. "And you may be equally sure that I did not endear myself to him by mentioning it. This will probably be the most important trial of the war. He did not want to step down."

Joshua had informed Arnold that Peggy Arnold and their six-month-old son, Edward, would be coming to Tappan, escorted by Arnold's former aide, Major David Franks. Joshua was keeping his fingers crossed that General Howe would now remain on the court.

"The prosecution will now read the charges against the accused," Greene announced. Arnold and Joshua rose, and Edwards began to read from a single sheet of paper.

"<u>Charge</u> - Treason

Specification 1: That on or before the 7th day of June, A. D. 1780, and on divers other days between that day and the 25th day of September, A. D. 1780, Major General Benedict Arnold did maliciously, unlawfully, and traitorously on numerous occasions provide to the enemy intelligence information regarding the order of battle of the Army of the United States of America, to include strength, location, movements, disposition, and status of military organizations, together with their supplies, fortifications, and weaponry.

Specification 2: That on or before the 15th day of July, A. D. 1780, and on divers other days between that day and the 25th of September, A. D. 1780, Major General Benedict Arnold did maliciously, unlawfully, and traitorously conspire to surrender to the enemy the Fortress of West Point, together with its garrison, stores, and armaments.

Specification 3: That on or about the 15th day of September, A. D. 1780, Major General Benedict Arnold did maliciously, unlawfully, shamefully, and traitorously attempt to deliver into enemy hands, his superior officer, General George Washington, Commander in Chief, Army of the United States of America."

At the reading of the final specification, there was an audible stir in the courtroom. It was clear that the members were caught by surprise at this particularly heinous charge. Joshua thought he could actually feel a chill descend over the court, and he could clearly see the visages of several members harden. Laurance and Edwards had achieved their objective. The inflammatory nature of the accusation had done its work. But if Arnold was aware of any of this, he gave no sign.

Edwards placed the charges in front of Greene. "General Arnold, how do you plead?"

"To the charge and all specifications, not guilty, "Arnold answered. "I shall show that this entire affair is a plot engineered by the enemy to discredit me and damage our army."

"A simple 'not guilty' will suffice, general," Greene responded, "and will be so entered in the record."

"The prosecution waives opening argument," Edwards then announced. The statement did not surprise Joshua. He knew his colleague as a man who avoided rhetoric, and who counted on the facts in the case to achieve the intended result. He also knew that Edwards was a master at presenting those facts.

"General Arnold." Greene nodded toward the defense table.

Slowly, Arnold rose to his feet, and limped from behind the table, standing directly in front of it, facing the members of the court. Considering the condition of his leg, he could have been expected to remain seated to make his opening statement. That he did not do so added intentional drama to the proceedings.

"Mr. President and gentlemen of this honorable court: I appear before you to answer the most heinous charge that can be leveled against a soldier—treason. I am accused of conspiring to betray my country and my comrades, with providing intelligence to the enemy, and attempting to deliver my commander into enemy hands. I assure you, gentlemen, if I am guilty of even one of these ignominious offenses, then I stand before you as the vilest of men, stigmatized with the indelible disgrace of abuse of an appointment of high trust and importance. If any of these charges are true, then I must be publically hanged from the highest gibbet in the land."

The silence that had descended on the court room was total. Every eye was fixed on Arnold, and breathing seemed to stop, waiting for him to continue. "When one is charged with practices which his soul abhors and which conscious innocence tells him he has not committed, honest indignation may easily turn to rage at those who accuse him of such nefarious crimes. I beg you, therefore, should I, despite my efforts, become intemperate during these proceedings, you will allow for it, and be considerate of the circumstances." Arnold paused and shifted his weight, moving his injured leg to a different position. Normally, Greene would have suggested he ease himself by resuming his seat, but like the others, he was so intent on Arnold's words that it did not occur to him.

"All of you know me, and some of you know me well. We have fought side by side in a just and noble cause. Most of you are aware that I was one of the first to appear in the field. When this war commenced, I was in easy circumstances and enjoyed a fair prospect of improving them. I was happy in domestic connections and blessed with a rising family. But the liberties of my country were in danger, the voice of my country called, and with cheerfulness I obeyed the call. I sacrificed domestic ease and happiness to the service of my country, and in her service I have sacrificed a great part of a handsome fortune. I have also sacrificed my health, receiving two grievous wounds, which have left one leg shorter than the other, and which cause me constant pain. Having made every sacrifice of ease, family, fortune and blood, and become a cripple in the service of my country, is it probable that I should suddenly sink to a course of conduct so vile and so unworthy of a soldier and patriot?"

Arnold stopped, to let the question hang in the room. Joshua marveled at the oratory, delivered without benefit of notes. It was formal and at times florid, yet it made its point. Could such a man be guilty of treason? Arnold then took several documents from a sheaf of papers on the table, then turned once more to the court. "Gentlemen, I ask your indulgence to be permitted to read several citations and letters attesting to the service I have performed for my country these past five years."

The previous evening, after much discussion, Joshua had convinced Arnold that such testimonials to past conduct were not evidence in his current trial. However, the general still insisted that they somehow be put before the court. They had finally agreed that he would read them during his opening statement. Leaning on his cane with one hand, holding a document in the other, Arnold spent the next hour quoting letters of praise dating as far back as his Canadian campaign, including commendations from Washington and Congress. He concluded his readings with an article from the

*Royal Gazette*, a Loyalist New York newspaper, praising him for being more distinguished for valor and perseverance than any other American officer, including Washington. Continuing to quote from the newspaper, he read,

> General Arnold heretofore has been styled another Hannibal, but losing a leg in the service of Congress, the latter, considering him unfit for any further exercise of his military talents, permit him thus to fall into the unmerciful fangs of the Executive Council of Pennsylvania, Mr. Joseph Reed, President.

"It seems to me both ironic and tragic, gentlemen," Arnold said, laying the newspaper aside, "that it is an *enemy* newspaper which recognizes my talents and my persecutions, while my own government does not." Arnold was now finished reading, and he returned the last of the documents to his table. There was a stirring of relief in the court, its members glad that the long recitation had come to an end. But Arnold was not finished.

"Unfortunately, although favored by the goodwill of gentlemen such as generals Washington, Schuyler, Spencer, Mifflin, the fallen Warren and Montgomery, and even General Gates, prior to Saratoga," (this last comment elicited a slight smile and barely perceptible nod from Greene), "I have had the misfortune to have implacable enemies who have done all in their power to undermine my standing within the Army and the Congress. Whether prompted by jealousy or other low motives, I have no way of knowing, but they have done me grave damage. As John Adams, the delegate to Congress from Massachusetts said of me, 'Although he fought like Julius Caesar, he has been basely slandered and libeled.' Perhaps, as another member of Congress, Richard Henry Lee of Virginia stated, 'There is a plan afoot to assassinate the characters of the friends of America in every place and by every means,' and who then pointed out that 'An audacious attempt of this kind was being made in Congress against the brave General Arnold.'

"In the past, I have always been able to weather the slings and arrows of my enemies, confident in my own rectitude and the support of my friends. However, since the disclosure of this infamous plot against me, I no longer seem to have friends, only enemies. I am seized in front of my family and thrown into prison. I am permitted to make no explanation, allowed to take no action to clear my name. General Washington, my commander, my mentor, friend to my small family, refuses to even hear me, shutting himself off from me as if I were a leper." Arnold paused to let the words sink in. Every eye in the court room was glued to him when he continued.

"My sole consolation is to have this opportunity to be tried by gentlemen whose delicate and refined sensations of honor will lead them to entertain similar sentiments concerning those who stand unjustly accused. My conduct from the earliest period of the war to the present time has been steady and uniform. Conscious of my own innocence, I look forward to these proceedings, in which, by the judgment of my fellow soldiers I shall stand honorably acquitted of all the charges brought against me, and shall soon again share with them the glory and danger of this just war."

As Arnold limped stiffly to his seat, Joshua had to admit it had been a practically flawless performance. All members of the court seemed impressed. Only the long reading of citations had been tedious, yet it had reinforced Arnold's opening remarks which, taken together, made it seem almost inconceivable that he could be guilty of treason.

"Colonel Edwards," Greene said, finally breaking the silence, "we have less than thirty minutes until the time of adjournment. In the interest of not interrupting the testimony of your first witness, I suggest we stop now."

Edwards offered no objection, and neither did Arnold. Greene then announced an adjournment until ten o'clock the following morning.

As they were leaving the church, Joshua realized that Laurance had been right. Arnold had begun his defense brilliantly. He had brought his military achievements and reputation to the fore, where they would linger in the minds of the court throughout the trial. Claiming that he had dangerous enemies, he showed that a member of Congress agreed, and sided with him against them. Finally, he had set the stage for his main line of defense by quoting another member of Congress speaking of character assassination plots against senior American officials. After listening to him today, Joshua was convinced that Arnold was either innocent, or one of the most magnificent liars in history.

"He's beginning to convince you. I can tell." Amy was upset as she listened to Joshua relate the day's events. "And the trial is only a day old."

"He hasn't convinced me," Joshua replied. "We've only heard Arnold's story, which he was very good at telling. There are almost a dozen witnesses to be heard against him. They will certainly make a difference."

"I know you, Joshua. You've been for the underdog for so long I fear you will begin to work to set him free." She could see him becoming emotionally involved in Arnold's defense— another example, in his view, of evil circumstances forcing a good man to do bad things. The trial's outcome could be the thing that would finally destroy him.

"He won't give me any opportunity to work to set him free, as you call it, although I would be happier if he did."

"Why? His treason could have undone us. It's put him beyond pity or redemption. Can't you see that?"

"All I see is a great patriot, accused, but not yet convicted of a heinous crime." It was not quite true. Deep down, he still felt Arnold was guilty, but he was annoyed with Amy's unwillingness to see him granted even the basic legal safeguards.

"Josh, I have a sense that this trial is going to come between us."

He was alarmed by her tone, which suggested it already had. "But we needn't let it, Amy," he pleaded, taking her hand in his. "And we mustn't let it. Besides, Arnold is more determined than ever to handle everything himself. I will be little more than an observer to this trial."

"Observers, too, can be swayed."

"You can be sure I will not be swayed, unless there are facts to sway me."

She looked directly into his eyes. "Why does that not give me ease?"

# CHAPTER EIGHTEEN

*British Army Headquarters, New York*
*October 4, 1780*

"WE HAVE ESTABLISHED that Major André is being held in the town of Tappan." Captain Beckwith pointed to the location on a map spread out on the commander in chief's desk. Generals Clinton, Robertson, and Colonel Robinson, hunched over the map, peering closely. "It is also the headquarters of the rebel army, as General Robertson correctly surmised."

"Do we know precisely where Johnny is being held?" Clinton asked.

"We do, sir. He is secured in a room in a house that appears to serve as a small tavern. It is protected by a captain, five subalterns, and forty rank and file. From this force Major André is guarded 'round the clock by six sentries, with two officers always present in the room with him."

Clinton seemed depressed by the news. "That seems a formidable guard, especially since the location is already within the rebel lines."

"I wouldn't take that as a certainty, sir," Beckwith said. "The rebels are often lax where guard duty is concerned, especially after it becomes routine."

Beckwith produced a rough drawing of the floor plan of Mabie's, pointing out André's room and the public area and bar at the opposite end of the building. "Interestingly, the house continues to provide service to a small number of senior headquarters staff officers. Even more interesting, Benedict Arnold is also being held nearby, under close guard by a company of foot. Our source informs me that his court-martial is under way."

"Which does not give us much time," Clinton said, in a worried tone.

"What is the rebel strength in the area?" Robertson wanted to know.

"They have a regiment of foot deployed in blocking positions east of the town, and another to the south. There seem to be only light patrols to the west and north, as they expect no threat from that direction."

Clinton turned to Robinson. "Colonel, what can you do?"

Robinson, previously informed of the situation by Beckwith, had already conceived a rough plan. "Any attempt to rescue André alive must rely on surprise and deception. Mounting a conventional operation will take too long to prepare and would not succeed. The enemy would simply move him out of our range. The crossing of a rescue force at Dobb's Ferry, the closest point to the rebel camp and the most direct approach, will be detected quickly and would have the same result."

Robinson unrolled a large map, which the others bent over. "I shall move my regiment, with only its light artillery, under cover of dark by boat from Kingsbridge to Fort Lee. Because the area is sparsely settled and well removed from rebel lines, the crossing should not be detected. Even if it were, its purpose and objective would be unclear. It is fourteen miles south of Tappan, and such a small force would not be expected to attack the well defended rebel headquarters. The first battalion to cross will secure the area and block the roads, to prevent any warning reaching rebel forces to the north. My second and third battalions of foot will make a night march upon Tappan by the most direct route. The first battalion will follow, dropping off detachments at critical points, again to block any attempt to alert the rebels of our movement. My dragoons will make a wide sweep to the west, approaching the town from its unprotected west side.

"Once in position, just before dawn, but still under cover of dark, my Rangers will infiltrate the town by stealth, seize the inn and take André under their protection. At dawn, I will launch a holding attack against the two rebel regiments, using a battalion against each. The purpose will be to engage them and keep them in place. Then, once the rebel regiments are fully engaged and occupied with our battalions, my dragoons will sweep in from the west, relieve the Rangers of André, and withdraw the way they came. I will then slowly withdraw my battalions, using them as a rear guard to block any enemy attempt to intercept or overtake the rescue force."

Robinson's presentation was followed by silence, as each officer evaluated what he had heard. It was Robertson who finally spoke. "It is a good plan, but I'm concerned about the western approach for the dragoons. Are we certain it is open?"

"We are, sir," Beckwith answered. "We know the location of all rebel forces in the area. One entire brigade has been sent to reinforce West Point. The local regiments are protecting the most likely avenues of approach, from the east and south. Our sources scouted the area on the west thoroughly. They observed only occasional light patrols. There are no rebel forces either encamped or occupying positions west of town, only a strong picket post just before the town itself."

"Which my dragoons will trample in the dust." Robinson was confident that his dragoons, more heavily armed than regular cavalry, would make quick work of even the strongest picket post.

"How about the presence of Benedict Arnold?" Robertson asked. "Will that weigh against us?"

"It may," Robinson conceded, "but it is more likely to operate to our advantage. When our attack begins, I expect the rebels to do all in their power to prevent Arnold from being freed. That should help take their attention away from André."

"How soon can you move?" Clinton asked.

"I can begin ferrying my units across North River at dark on Saturday night, the 7th. We will be at Tappan and commence operations before first light the morning of the 8<sup>th</sup>. We may gain some advantage from it being Sunday."

"I like this plan," Clinton announced, his mood obviously improved. "For the first time since this sorry affair began, I have some hope that Johnny will be spared a gruesome fate."

Robinson said nothing. He, too, liked the plan. But he was well aware that many plans look good—until the fog of war descends.

# CHAPTER NINETEEN

*The Manse, Tappan, New York*
*Thursday, October 5, 1780*

"YOU MAY CALL your first witness," Greene directed Edwards, after opening the court.

"I call volunteer militiaman John Paulding." Edwards announced. The orderly exited the court room and returned ushering a balding, giant of a man, with a weather-beaten face, dressed in plain homespun. Appearing somewhat unsure of what to do, he finally faced the president of the court and saluted.

Greene returned the salute. "Please face the trial counselor and be sworn."

Paulding turned to faced Edwards, and both raised their right hands.

"You swear that evidence you shall give in the case now in hearing shall be the truth, the whole truth, and nothing but the truth. So help you God."

"I swear."

Edwards then directed him to the witness chair. "Mr. Paulding, on September 23$^{rd}$ last, did you have occasion to stop and arrest a horseman on the Tarry Town Road?"

"I did, sir."

"Please describe the circumstances of that event."

Paulding settled back in the chair, which seemed too small for his extra tall frame. "Myself, Isaac Van Wart, and David Williams was lyin' by the side of the road about half a mile above Tarry Town, between nine and ten o'clock in the morning, when we saw a gentlemanlike-looking man riding toward us, well dressed, with boots on. I got up and presented my firelock at the breast of the person and told him to stand, and then asked him which way he was going. "Gentlemen," said he, "I hope you belong to our party.' I asked him what party was that, and he said, 'The Lower Party.' Upon that I told him I did. Then he said, 'I am a British officer out of the country on particular business, and I hope you will not detain me a minute.' And to show me that he was a British officer he pulled out his watch. I then told him to dismount. It seemed he realized his mistake then, because he then said, 'My God, I must do anything to get along.' He made kind of a laugh of it, and pulled out General Arnold's pass, which—"

"Sir," Arnold broke in, addressing Greene, "there has been nothing introduced to show that I issued a pass to anyone."

"If the court will permit me," Edwards picked up a document from his desk and approached the witness. "Is this the pass you referred to?"

Paulding took the document and studied it briefly. "Yes, this is it. Colonel Jameson told me to make my mark on it after I delivered it to him, and here it is, in the right corner."

"Will you please read the document to the court?" Edwards could have read the document to the court himself, but he needed to establish that Paulding could read.

The witness took the hand-written document and read:

Head Quarters Robinsons House
*Sept: 22 . 1780*


Permit Mr. John Anderson to pass the
Guards to the White Plains, or below
if he Chuses. He being on Public
Business by my Direction
B. Arnold MGenl

"I introduce this document and request it be accepted into evidence as Government Exhibit Number One," Edwards said, taking the pass from Paulding and walking it across to the defense table. Arnold reached for it.

"It is a forgery," he announced. "I never wrote any such document. I object to it being accepted into evidence."

"The document is being introduced as one having been seized by competent authority from a suspected enemy spy," Edwards countered, handing it now to Greene. "Whether it is genuine or not is up to the court to determine as may be established by this and subsequent testimony and evidence."

It did not take Greene long to rule. "Subject to objection by any member of the court, the document will be accepted into evidence, and marked for identification as 'Pass *purported* to have been issued by General Benedict Arnold.'"

Seeing that Arnold was obviously unhappy with the ruling, Joshua rose. "Sir, may we pause a moment so that I may confer with the accused?"

"You may do so," Greene responded.

"General Arnold," Joshua began in a low voice, "Colonel Edwards will introduce the remaining documents taken from André. If you wish to obtain the good will of the court, you must not object to each one. His action is legal and proper. Your objections will accomplish nothing except to convince the court that you are being deliberately obstructive."

Arnold thought the matter over. "Very well, but I will rely on you to insure that these forgeries are labeled exactly as this one was."

"Thank you, sir." Joshua then turned toward Greene. "Sir, we are ready to proceed."

Greene nodded toward Edwards. "You may continue with your witness."

At a cue from Edwards, Paulding went on with his account. "Well, as I said, after I told him to dismount and he pulled out General Arnold's—uh, the pass—he said, 'Gentlemen, you had best let me go, or you will bring yourselves into trouble, for your stopping me will detain the general's business.' He said he was going to Dobb's Ferry to meet a person there and get intelligence for General Arnold. Upon that, I told him I hoped he wouldn't be offended, that we did not mean to take anything from him, and I told him there were many bad people who were going along the road, and I didn't know but perhaps he might be one.

"We then took him into the bushes, and ordered him to pull off his clothes. After we took off his boots Dave Williams found some papers between his stockings and his feet, and he passed them to me. When I read them, I knew we had stopped a spy. We told him to get dressed, and when he had, he offered us a very large sum if we would take him to the nearest British post. I told him if he would give us ten thousand guineas it would make no difference, he would not stir one step. We then took him to North Castle, where I turned him over to Colonel Jameson." When it was apparent that Paulding was finished, Edwards asked, "At any time did you ask this person his name?"

'I did. He said he was John Anderson."

Edwards then picked up several papers. "I will now show you several more documents, which I will ask you to identify, if you can." He first showed the papers to Arnold, who gave them only the briefest glance before pushing them aside.

"More forgeries," he announced.

Edwards reclaimed the papers and approached Paulding. "First, I show you a paper estimating the forces at Fortress West Point and its dependencies, dated September 13, 1780. Next is an estimate of the men necessary to man the works at the fortress. Then, an inventory of ordnance at West Point, showing the number of artillery pieces at the fortress as of September, 1780. Next is a two-page report showing the construction and condition of the fortress and its redoubts. Finally, I show you a copy of matters laid before a council of war by General Washington, held September 6th, 1780. Can you identify these documents?"

Paulding took his time, examining each document carefully, before replying. "Yes, sir, these are papers we took from John Anderson. Each page has my mark on it, as ordered by Colonel Jameson."

Edwards then placed the documents before the court, and they were entered into evidence with the same stipulation that the pass had been, without objection by Arnold or Joshua. "I have nothing further for this witness," Edwards announced.

As Arnold started to rise, Joshua leaned quickly toward him. "Sir, I advise you not to question this witness. There is nothing to be gained. He has testified only to the capture of André and to the identity of the documents."

But Arnold ignored him, stood, and braced himself against the table with both arms. "Mr. Paulding, I am General Arnold. Are you familiar with my signature?"

"No, sir."

"Then you did not know whether the signature on the pass was indeed mine?"

"I did not, no, sir."

"Could this be the reason that you did not permit this John Anderson to pass, that you suspected the pass was a forgery?"

"No, sir, the pass looked official enough. When he showed it to me, I would've let him go, except him tellin' me earlier he was a British officer."

It was not the answer Arnold sought. Joshua could see the displeasure in his eyes.

"Mr. Paulding, what was your status when you and your companions stopped John Anderson?"

Paulding appeared puzzled. "Status, sir?"

"Were you soldiers in the Continental Army? Militiamen? Sheriff's deputies?"

"You might say we was volunteer militiamen. We would go out to a post at nights to guard the area and stop infiltration along the road of suspicious persons."

"You belonged to no regular military unit?"

"Nossir."

"What prompted you to perform such...er...service?"

"Doin' our duty for the cause, sir."

"And perhaps enriching yourselves as well?"

111

"We didn't receive no pay."

"You received nothing for delivering your prisoner to North Castle?"

"We was allowed to keep his horse and saddle as prize."

"So, you go out to stop travelers on the road, hoping to make off with their property. It would appear you are little more than brigands."

Edwards started to rise, but Greene waved him down. "Whatever you might choose to call them, General Arnold, these men may well have saved the country that morning." He turned to the court recorder. "You will strike General Arnold's last remark from the record." Glaring at Arnold, he asked, "Do you have anything more for this witness?"

"I do not," Arnold replied, resuming his seat. Joshua could not help feeling concerned. By attacking the character of the men who had captured André, Arnold had risked alienating the court. When he informed him in a whisper what he had done, the general refused to listen. "Brigands, that's all they are," he repeated to Joshua, resolutely ignoring the damage he had caused himself. It did not bode well for the rest of the trial.

"Does any member of the court wish to question this witness?" Greene asked. When none did, he announced that the witness was excused, and Paulding saluted and left the room. Edwards next called Privates David Williams and Isaac Van Wart, Paulding's two companions, who had assisted in André's capture. They corroborated Paulding's testimony, contributing nothing new. Accepting Joshua's recommendation this time, Arnold declined to question them.

Edwards then called Lieutenant Colonel John Jameson, commander of the 2$^{nd}$ Continental Dragoons at North Castle, the officer who received the André documents from Paulding and sent them on to Washington. Joshua noted that Jameson seemed nervous and ill at ease. There were rumors that Washington had severely reprimanded him for alerting Arnold of André's capture at the same time he had informed Washington. But the officer still held his command and wore his rank, which said something. Edwards took the witness through receipt of the André documents from Paulding, and, as he had with Paulding, had him identify the documents one by one. At this point Jameson's nervousness seemed to have disappeared.

Edwards collected the documents, then returned the pass to Jameson. "Your command at North Castle comes directly under General Arnold, does it not?"

"It does. General Arnold is—was my commanding officer."

"As such, I assume you can recognize General Arnold's signature?" he asked.

"I can," Jameson replied.

"And is that his signature on this pass?"

"It is."

"Do you recognize General Arnold's writing when you see it?"

"I do."

"Is the rest of the writing on this pass also in General Arnold's hand."

"Yes, it is."

Edwards then returned a second document to Jameson. "This document which provides details of the redoubts at Fortress West Point, is it in General Arnold's hand also?"

"It is."

"Both pages?"

"Yes."

Edwards collected the papers and returned to his desk. "Referring to the name 'John Anderson' had you occasion to hear it before?"

"Yes, I had. On September 11 General Arnold sent instructions that we watch for a John Anderson, a person the general was expecting to arrive from New York. If he appeared, we were to furnish him an escort to General Arnold's headquarters."

In calling Jameson to the stand, Edwards's main purpose had been to identify and establish the evidence chain for the André papers, verify Arnold's signature and handwriting, and to bring out the previous association of the name 'John Anderson' with Andre.

That had now been done. However, he was aware that subsequent events had not been handled by Jameson as well as might be expected. Rather than put the witness to the risk of hostile examination by Arnold, he felt it best to allow the officer to tell his own story.

"Colonel, will you please tell the court what occurred after 'John Anderson' was delivered to your headquarters."

Jameson glanced at the court, then wet his lips. "After Paulding and his party had left, I questioned 'John Anderson' in detail. He was most persuasive in his claim that he was on General Arnold's business, and now that he had been delivered to competent authority, he felt certain I would free him to go about his important mission. He seemed completely at ease, showing none of the nervousness one might expect from someone suspected of being a spy. In fact, I am more ill at ease here than he was that day."

There were some sympathetic chuckles from the court, but it was clear that Jameson remained uncomfortable. "There were two problems with his story, of course," he went on. "One was that I was led to expect 'John Anderson' to arrive *from* New York, and he was traveling in the opposite direction. The other, far more damaging, was the nature of the documents he was carrying hidden on his person."

"Did these documents lead you to suspect that General Arnold might be involved in treasonous activity?"

"They did, but the idea was so incredible I couldn't accept it. I thought perhaps they had some secret intelligence purpose that only 'Anderson' and the general were privy to. I was, frankly, in a quandary. I was under orders to escort 'Anderson' to General Arnold, yet the papers were of such a dangerous tendency that I hesitated to send them with him. Finally, I decided to compromise by sending 'Anderson' under guard to General Arnold, while dispatching the papers to General Washington.

"Some time after both parties had left, my second in command, Major Benjamin Tallmadge returned from an inspection. He took a far more serious view of General Arnold's involvement, and urged that I recall 'Anderson.' I told him I couldn't possibly do so without being guilty of grave insubordination. After thinking about it, he came up with a scheme." Here Jameson paused, seeming reluctant to proceed. Swallowing and mopping his brow, he continued. "We would pretend we heard rumors of enemy patrols in the area, and would inform General Arnold that we recalled 'Anderson' for his own safety. I dispatched a messenger informing Lieutenant Allen, who was escorting 'Anderson,' that because of enemy activity, he was to divert his prisoner to South Salem, where he would be safe from capture, and then he, Allen, was to continue on to West Point to deliver my letter to General Arnold and explain why 'Anderson' was not with him."

Despite the coolness of the room, Jameson's forehead was now damp with perspiration. He seemed to be debating whether to say any more. Finally, he continued. "I have been criticized severely for my action in alerting General Arnold—from the very highest level." There was some good-natured laughter from the court. A few of its members had also been, at one time or another, on the receiving end of Washington's wrath. "But General Arnold was my commanding officer. I don't see how I could have failed to notify him of the capture of 'Anderson' without being accused of failing to obey his instructions. That he was in the act of committing treason was impossible to believe. Also, I'm not proud of my act of deceiving him in regard to recalling the prisoner, but under the circumstances, by holding 'Anderson,' sending the papers to General Washington, and informing General Arnold of my actions, I believe I made the best choice I could."

As Jameson fell silent, it was obvious to all that this was a man still in the throes of wrestling with his conscience.

"I have nothing further for this witness," Edwards said.

Joshua could see no good reason for Arnold to question Jameson, and told him so. However, Arnold rose. He stared quietly at his former subordinate for a long moment, the other man returning his gaze, but obviously uncomfortable.

"Colonel Jameson, you mentioned that in deciding whether or not to send the documents to me, along with 'John Anderson,' you thought that perhaps they had some secret intelligence purpose that only 'Anderson' and I were privy to, is that correct."

"That's what I said, yes, sir."

"Well, if you thought that, why did you not send them to me? Why send such unsupported documents to General Washington, which could only cause confusion and misunderstanding?"

Jameson had a large Adam's apple, and when he swallowed, it bobbed noticeably. "I can only say, sir, that the documents seemed extremely dangerous. By sending them to General Washington, if they turned out to be harmless, they would soon be returned to their intended purpose."

"Had it ever occurred to you, prior to this time that I might be contemplating treason against my country?"

"No, sir, nothing could have been further from my mind."

Arnold shifted his weight, indicating his bad leg was bothering him. "Colonel Jameson, I put it to you that had you sent 'Anderson' to me, together with the papers, I would have been able to investigate the matter and discover its purpose. Had you sent both 'Anderson' and the papers to me, as you should have done, we would not be meeting here today."

"General Arnold," Greene broke in, "please do not presume to lecture the witness about how he should have acted. What you think he should have done has no bearing here."

"To the contrary, sir, it is of the highest importance. By failing to follow my orders, Colonel Jameson has done me grave damage, precipitating an arrest and a court-martial that never should have occurred. That fact must be pointed out to the court, and made a matter of record"

"Colonel Jameson is not on trial here."

"But *I am*, sir. I am not focusing on Colonel Jameson, but rather on the result of his actions, as they affect me and the case against me. Later on, I shall be making further reference to this matter."

At this point, General Clinton leaned over and whispered something in Greene's ear. Greene nodded and rapped his gavel. "The court will be closed to take the matter under consideration."

Except for the members of the court, the room quickly emptied. Edwards, Jameson, the recorder and the orderly exited to the porch to wait outside. Arnold was taken under guard to the basement kitchen, where Joshua joined him. He was rubbing his injured leg, and Joshua did not think it was for effect.

"How do you think they will rule?" Arnold asked.

"In your favor," Joshua responded. "I believe General Greene wants to give you as much leeway as possible. I was watching Edwards. He made no attempt to argue, so I think he also senses the sentiment of the court."

Arnold seemed satisfied, but then his features hardened. "If I were able, I would court-martial Jameson for not obeying my orders."

Joshua smiled. "And General Washington would like to court-martial him because he *did* obey them."

The remark seemed to irritate Arnold. "Don't you think he should have obeyed my instructions?"

"Let's look at it this way, sir. If you are guilty—I say *if*," Joshua hastened to add, seeing Arnold bristle, "following your orders could have cost us the war. Surely, sir, you must see the predicament he was in. He did what he thought best, and he notified you of what he had done. And the men who stopped André—"

"They were brigands, I tell you. I know what goes on in that no-man's-land they operate in. I can assure you they were there not to check André's status. They were there to rob him."

"Even if they were, they uncovered a dangerous plot, and if this plot is, as you say, a British attempt to destroy you, you should be grateful to them." Joshua surprised himself with the candid manner he had adopted with Arnold this morning, but Arnold did not seem to mind. He therefore continued. "So far, you are not making any friends on the court by your hostile examination of these two witnesses."

"My objective is not to make friends, but to reveal the truth," Arnold responded.

At that point the orderly entered the basement and announced that the court was ready. After everyone had filed back into the room,

Greene called the court to order. "The court rules in favor of General Arnold. His remarks will stand in the record." He then turned to Arnold. "You may resume your questioning of the witness."

Arnold rose, leaning more heavily on the table than he had before. "Colonel Jameson, you stated earlier that you are able to recognize my signature and my handwriting?"

"Yes, sir."

"Based on orders and documents seen while you were under my command?"

"Yes."

"Tell me, how long have you been in command of the 2$^{nd}$ Dragoons?"

"I...I assumed command on...September 15$^{th}$." Heads turned on the court at his answer.

"Eight days before 'Anderson' was brought to you. How many communications did you receive from me during that period?"

Jameson's Adam's apple bobbed again. "Well, none, but there was your order of September 11$^{th}$ directing that 'Anderson' be sent to you. I compared this instruction with the pass and other documents taken from Anderson, and saw they were also in the same hand."

"So on the sole basis of comparing several questionable documents and finding them in the same hand, you claim to be able to recognize my writing. I suggest, sir, that you had no way of knowing that these documents were actually written by me, or even that the handwriting was mine. All you really knew was that all of them seemed to be in the same hand, is that not true?" The sheen had reappeared on Jameson's forehead, and he wiped at it with a hand-held kerchief. "I...I suppose that...that is true, yes."

"Then, considering your previous answer to the question asked by Colonel Edwards, I ask you that question again: Are you able to recognize my handwriting."

"No, I am not." Jameson had paused only a moment before replying, and now he seemed relieved.

Arnold nodded with satisfaction. "I have nothing further."

As Jameson left the witness chair, Edwards reflected on the

impact his witness had on the court. It was a plus for Arnold, he had to admit. But he did not blame himself. Although he wished he had known that Jameson had been in command only a little more than a week, there had been no opportunity to properly vet all the witnesses in the limited time allotted before the trial. As he gazed across the room, he noted that Arnold appeared pleased with himself. It rankled him, but he felt confident that pleasure would not last long.

"I call Lieutenant Colonel Alexander Hamilton."

Joshua watched with interest as the witness entered the room. Hamilton was something of a legend at army headquarters. At the start of the war, he had raised his own artillery company, and although only twenty years old, had led it with distinction from the beginning through the battles of Trenton and Princeton, where he had caught Washington's eye. He was soon selected by the commander in chief to be his aide de camp, a position he had held ever since. Hamilton was known to be brilliant, energetic, eloquent, and after more than three years, thoroughly tired of processing the unending paperwork that crossed his chief's desk. He longed for a field assignment again, but Washington could not spare him. Frustrated in his ambition, Hamilton at times became critical and acerbic, even quarreling on occasion with Washington himself. That the general treated these occasions with forbearance testified to his fondness for his young aide, recognition of his talents, and need for his services. And Hamilton, born and raised in the West Indies, spoke fluent French, making him an even more valuable asset to the headquarters staff.

As the young officer took the witness chair, Joshua observed a man of average height, but rather slight build. Dark-blue eyes contrasting with a ruddy complexion and a shock of reddish-brown hair, gave his face a distinctive, arresting appearance.

Once Hamilton had stated his name, rank, and military position, Edwards got right to the point. "Colonel, as General Washington's aide, have you had occasion to process communications from General Benedict Arnold to the commander in chief and other members of the staff?"

"I have."

"Can you tell us how many such documents you have seen?"

"I have no exact count, but during the last three years there must have been four or five dozen."

"Then you are familiar with General Arnold's hand?"

"Thoroughly."

Edwards then handed him several papers. "These documents all pertain to Fortress West Point. Will you tell the court if any of them are in General Arnold's hand?"

After a quick perusal, Hamilton held up one of them. "This document is in the general's hand, the other two are not."

Taking the document first to Arnold, Edwards then showed it to Greene. "I ask that the record show that the witness selected 'Details of the Redoubts of Fortress West Point,' purported to be in General Arnold's hand, and previously admitted into evidence as taken from the person arrested as John Anderson."

"The record will so state," Greene replied, passing the document to the other members of the court.

Edwards then showed Hamilton the pass made out for 'John Anderson.' "Is this document in General Arnold's hand?"

Hamilton studied it briefly. "It is."

"And is that his signature on the document?"

"Yes."

"You are certain?"

"Completely. I have seen it many times."

The prosecutor picked up another paper and showed it to Arnold, who read it with interest and returned it without comment. "Colonel Hamilton, can you identify this document?"

Hamilton did so quickly. "It is a letter written by Major John André to General Washington."

"How did you happen to become familiar with the letter?"

"It was part of the packet of documents delivered to General Washington on his way to General Arnold's headquarters, which included those seized from Major André. It was written from South Salem, where André had been taken for confinement. Since the messenger bringing the seized documents to Washington had overnighted in South Salem, and was on his way to deliver them, it was added to the packet."

"Will you please read the two portions of the letter I have marked?"

Hamilton then read the first marked passage, which was the beginning paragraph of the letter.

> "S I R,
>
> What I have yet said concerning myself, was in the justifiable attempt to be extricated; I am too little accustomed to duplicity to have succeeded."

He then read the second excerpt.

> "The person in your possession is Major John André, Adjutant General to the British Army."

"Finally, sir, is it clear from this letter that the person previously identifying himself as John Anderson, is now admitting that he is Major John André?"

"It is."

"Thank you, I have no further questions."

Arnold spoke without rising. "Colonel Hamilton, how can you be so certain that the signature on the pass in André's possession was mine?"

"Because, sir, I have seen it often enough these past three years."

"Is it not possible that someone copied my hand and forged these documents?"

"If you mean that someone was able to mimic your handwriting, I do not find that at all credible. A signature might be traced, although I found no indication of that on the pass I was shown. But I do not believe that anyone could replicate another person's handwriting consistently throughout a two-page document such as the one shown me."

"Are you stating that such a feat would be impossible?"

"Within my knowledge and experience, yes."

Arnold rose from his chair, and stared intently at Hamilton. "In your capacity as General Washington's aide, have you ever written any letters on his behalf?"

"Many times."

"And have you signed his name to those letters?"

Hamilton's eyes flickered for an instant. "I have."

"Tell me, are you aware that many recipients of these letters have stated that the signature is indistinguishable from Washington's own?"

Hamilton shifted in his chair. "I am aware of that, yes."

"I have heard it said in the headquarters that you are even able to write complete letters which mimic perfectly the general's hand. Is that true?"

"I don't know how perfectly, but I can do so."

"But, sir, how can that be? You have just stated that such a feat would be impossible."

"I...I have had much practice over three years and with hundreds of documents." Hamilton was now obviously ill at ease. Arnold had gained the upper hand.

"You are telling us, then, that with practice you can accomplish the impossible?"

There was a ripple of laughter in the court room, and Hamilton reddened. Greene tapped his gavel. "General Arnold, the court can do without sarcasm. Please modify your questioning."

"There is no need, sir," Arnold replied. "I have nothing more for this witness."

Joshua was impressed. After a bad start with Paulding, Arnold had, to use his own term, 'demolished' one witness, and neutralized another.

Greene then called a twenty-minute recess.

"I could use a breath of fresh air," Arnold told Joshua. Accompanied by the guards, they stepped outside on to the porch which faced the church. The large lawn between the parsonage and the town green was partly occupied by pens of sheep and pigs, their blended odors hanging in the damp air. The rain had ceased, but the sky was still threatening. Despite the smell of the animals, Arnold breathed deeply of the early autumn air.

"There is nothing as precious as freedom after it has been taken from you." He let his gaze roam over the distant hills to the west, already beginning to change from green to shades of yellow and red. "I think it is going well, don't you?" he asked.

Joshua nodded. "So far, better than I expected, but we have a long way to go."

Arnold shrugged, dismissing the issue. He gestured toward the guards. "You know, major, I am a general officer in the Continental Army. Surely my professional and personal honor are sufficient to guarantee that I will not flee from custody. Can we not dispense with the guards?"

"If you will permit me, sir, General Washington believes it highly likely that you have committed treason, and...well...it is not exactly an honorable act." He had been about to say, and therefore he is not likely to trust your honor, but he knew by now how sensitive Arnold was to any attack on his honor. What he had dared to say was provocative enough. To cut off any angry reaction from the general, he added quickly, "But, if you wish, I will raise the question."

"I only ask because I am concerned about the effect it will have upon my wife. The sight of her husband under armed guard..." He let the words trail off, and his eyes once more gazed into the distance. Joshua could see a deep longing in those eyes, enhanced by a furrowed brow and anxious expression. For the first time, he thought he was seeing Arnold with his guard down. This was a man who was in true anguish over the separation from his family. There was no acting here.

"I will do my best," Joshua promised. A few minutes later the orderly announced that the court was ready to go back in session.

# CHAPTER TWENTY

"I CALL MAJOR General Philip Schuyler." Edwards announced as soon as the court opened. A tall, courtly figure in civilian dress entered the room. Schuyler was descended from one of the great Dutch patroon families of New York, and possessed the easy air of self assurance that came with landed wealth and importance in the community. He was one of the richest men in America, and a warm, personal friend of George Washington's ever since they served together as delegates to the Second Continental Congress. Schuyler was one of the original four major generals appointed by Congress to serve under Washington in the Continental Army, and he had commanded the Highlands Department during the critical days of the Canadian campaign.

In the fall of 1776, a British army under General Guy Carleton invaded northern New York with the object of seizing Albany. Benedict Arnold, then under Schuyler's command, hastily constructed a small fleet on Lake Champlain, opposing the British advance. Although Arnold's fleet was eventually destroyed, the delay it caused the invaders forced Carleton to abandon his plans and to return to Canada before the onset of winter. As a result, Arnold was credited with saving New York from invasion. He became a protégé of Schuyler's, and a genuine affection soon developed between the two men. After Schuyler was relieved of his command by Congress just before the battle of Saratoga, Arnold's continued friendship with his former commander was an important reason for the poor relationship that eventually developed between him and Horatio Gates, the general who replaced Schuyler. Schuyler had left the Army in 1777, and was now a delegate to Congress from New York.

After being sworn, Schuyler took the witness chair without a glance toward Arnold.

"General Schuyler," Edwards began, "may I ask you to turn your memory back to late May of this year? Did you receive a letter from General Benedict Arnold during that time?"

"Yes, I did."

"Please relate to the court the purpose and contents of that letter."

"If you will permit me, I would like to refer first to the incidents which prompted the letter, so that the court may have a better understanding of it."

Edwards nodded. "Please do so, sir."

Schuyler settled back in the chair. "Last April I was selected chairman of a committee to confer with General Washington on reorganization of staff departments of the Army. Before leaving for the headquarters at Morristown, I visited with General Arnold and his family in their residence in Philadelphia. During this visit, General Arnold made known to me that he wished to leave his appointment as military commander of Philadelphia and return to more active service. He stated that although he wished for a field command, his wound still made it difficult and painful for him to walk or ride, and that he hoped General Washington would find a suitable assignment for him in an important stationary command."

"Did General Arnold name any specific location?"

"He did. He requested that I intercede with General Washington to secure him the command of Fortress West Point."

"Thank you, please continue."

"I promised I would discuss his request with General Washington, and did so. It is my opinion that General Washington was favorably disposed toward General Arnold's request, and that he was prepared to offer him the choice of either a field command or another important post. I informed General Arnold of this result in a letter written on May 11<sup>th</sup>, but that letter has apparently gone astray and was never received by General Arnold. He therefore wrote to me on May 25<sup>th</sup> asking about the situation, and that is the letter about which you spoke."

"In this May 25<sup>th</sup> letter from General Arnold, did he once more mention a desire to command West Point?"

"He did."

Edwards selected a document from his table and showed it to Arnold, who quickly waved it aside, and then handed it to Schuyler. "Is this that letter? And if so, will you please relate how it came into my possession?"

Schuyler looked at it only briefly before replying. "Yes, it is. During our meeting at Morristown, General Washington asked to see the letter, and I left it with him, neglecting to pick it up later. After the...the attempted betrayal of West Point, he wrote to inform me that he was turning the letter over to the Judge Advocate General for possible use in General Arnold's trial."

"Sir, at any time, either during your conversation with him in Philadelphia, or in his letter of May 25<sup>th</sup>, did General Arnold indicate that he was willing to take any important post that might be offered to him, or did he exclusively mention West Point?"

Schuyler considered the question at length before finally answering. "He never mentioned any other location or command. I am convinced his mind was set on West Point."

"Do you think he would have accepted another similar type of command, had it been offered?"

Joshua rose and addressed the president of the court. "Sir, the question calls for speculation on the part of the witness."

"So it does," Greene agreed.

Joshua had acted on instinct, forgetting that he was merely an adviser to Arnold, and glanced at him anxiously. But the general seemed to accept his intrusion. He was also surprised that Edwards would ask such an obviously challengeable question, but then he realized that Edwards had been testing Arnold's knowledge of the law. By interrupting unexpectedly, as he had, Joshua had thwarted his purpose.

"I have nothing further for General Schuyler," Edwards announced.

Arnold rose slowly. Rather than lean on it, as he had done in previous questioning, he moved to the front of the table, where he proceeded to lean back against it in a half sitting position. It placed him closer to the witness, and established a more intimate setting. Until now, Schuyler had not acknowledged the presence of Arnold in the courtroom, and he still avoided eye contact with his former protégé.

"General Schuyler, our relationship in this war goes back a long way, does it not?"

"It does," Schuyler answered, his voice non-committal.

"To the Canadian campaign, the defense of the New York Highlands, right until just before the Battle of Saratoga. And we have been close friends since then, is that not so?"

Schuyler was showing signs of discomfort. "Up until now, yes."

Arnold then changed direction. "General, you yourself faced a court-martial in October 1778, if my memory is correct about the date."

Edwards rose, addressing Greene, "Sir, the question is inappropriate and not material to the issue. "General Schuyler's military record is a most honorable one."

"Indeed it is," said Arnold, before Greene could rule, "and my question is most material to the issue. I intend to show that General Schuyler, *because* of a fine record, was made the target of plots to discredit him by parties who wished to damage our Army, much as has been the situation in my own case. Before ruling on this matter, I request that the court determine from the gentleman himself, whether he objects to this line of questioning."

Greene turned to the witness. "General Schuyler?"

"I have no objection whatsoever." In fact, Schuyler seemed anxious to proceed. After a brief aside with Alexander and St. Clair, Greene allowed the line of questioning, and Arnold continued.

"Sir, prior to the time of your court-martial, were you aware of any attempts to discredit you or attack your military record?"

For the first time, Schuyler allowed himself to make eye contact with Arnold. "There were several. The first came after Carleton's attempt to invade New York. I had concluded that Crown Point was too weak to be held, and ordered its evacuation. Even though the British invasion had by now been turned back, I was accused of leaving Lake Champlain unprotected and opening New England to the possibility of invasion. It took a demand by me for a court of inquiry and a threatened resignation before Congress sent me assurances of its confidence and appreciation. Later, in the spring of 1777, several members of Congress sought my removal from command, based upon trivial and unfounded charges. It required a trip to Philadelphia on my part to clear my name and have the allegations withdrawn."

There was a stir in the court at this information. Although most of its members were already aware of Schuyler's difficulties, they could not help noting the similarity between his experience and Arnold's opening remarks about character assassination, which had even reached the halls of Congress.

"It was the loss of Ticonderoga that finally gave my enemies the victory they sought," Schuyler continued. "I had visited the fort in the late spring and found it in poor condition. Its garrison was miserably clad and armed, with many men barefoot and in rags. Much of the interior structure of the fort had been torn up and used for firewood the previous winter. I wrote to General Washington informing him of the dismal outlook for its defense, then did the best I could to insure resupply of the most urgent necessities, spending my own funds in the process. What followed is well known. When Burgoyne arrived before the fort with a force more than twice the strength of our garrison, its commander decided to evacuate it, rather than put up a fight."

Everyone in the room knew that the commander referred to was St. Clair, who was now sitting on the court. There was complete silence as they waited for Schuyler to go on. "Although I was caught by surprise by the abandonment of the fort without a struggle, I believe that the decision to do so was a sound one. The British had placed artillery upon Sugar Loaf Hill, where their guns could fire directly down into the fort, which would quickly reduce it to rubble. Our own guns could not be elevated high enough to return fire. The choice was either to remain in the surrounded fort, under constant bombardment, without hope of resupply or reinforcement and with the surrender of 3,000 troops inevitable, or save the army to fight another day."

"Sir, if Sugar Loaf was such a critical position, why was it left undefended?" Arnold asked.

"Most of our military experts considered it impossible for an enemy to haul heavy guns up its steep and forested slope." Schuyler neglected to mention that both he and St. Clair were among those "military experts." Here, he turned to look directly at Arnold. "You, however, were an exception. When you reconnoitered the position, and climbed to the top despite your wounded leg, you warned that the feat could be achieved. But by then it was too late. We had neither the resources nor the manpower to fortify another location. As it turned out, the British did exactly what you said they would do, winching their guns up from tree to tree, until they were looking down the throats of our garrison."

Schuyler paused momentarily, staring off into space, as if wishing for the opportunity to go back and do things differently. "With the fall of Ticonderoga," he resumed, "I devoted all my efforts to slowing Burgoyne's advance, while continuing to build up my own forces and supplies. I can say, with some degree of pride, that although he had advanced 150 miles from Canada to Skenesborough in less than a month, it took Burgoyne a full month to advance only a few miles against my delaying operation. Also during this period, we delivered two sharp reversals to the enemy, one by General Sharp near Bennington, and the other, led by yourself, which relieved the siege of Fort Stanwix, and sent St. Leger fleeing back to Canada. By the end of July, I was readying plans and organizing forces to actively engage Burgoyne. But then, on

August 4, I was relieved of my command by Congress, and replaced by General Gates."

A brief silence ensued before Arnold spoke. "And only two months later, General Burgoyne surrendered his army at Saratoga. Would it be correct to say that your planning and provisioning of the army in the months preceding Saratoga were instrumental in achieving the greatest American victory of the war?"

"I need not say it. It has been said for me by others." Several members of the court turned sideward glances toward the president. It was common knowledge that Nathanael Greene had been against Schuyler's removal from command. When Gates accepted the British surrender, Greene had remarked that "the foundation of all northern successes was laid long before his arrival there. He enjoyed the laurels of those who preceded him." And more recently, following the debacle at Camden, Greene said that although Gates did not deserve credit for the nation's greatest victory, he had earned full credit for one of its worst defeats.

"I must also add," Schuyler continued, looking directly at Arnold, "that your own actions in that battle were undoubtedly the single most important reason for our victory. Even General Burgoyne said as much himself, when I spoke to him after the surrender."

Uncharacteristically, Arnold seemed flustered by the compliment. "Thank you, sir," he managed finally. "It's good of you to say so, under the circumstances." After a brief pause, he continued. "So, then, despite the fact that you set the stage for the greatest victory of American arms during this war, Congress relieved you of your command before you could gain the fruits of that victory. I am sure every member of this court will support me when I say this act gave offense to many officers of all ranks within the Army. And, as you know, General Washington was so distressed that he refused to name your successor. I ask you then, sir, does it seem far-fetched to say that in light of what you have told us here today, you have been the victim of a plot to discredit you, and thus do damage to our Army and our cause?"

Schuyler considered the question carefully before answering. "I know I have been the victim of repeated attacks upon my character and my conduct of the war. I was charged with neglect of duty over the loss of Ticonderoga. I have been accused of certain minor irregularities which have been proven false. Whether or not this all fits into the specific design you suggest, I am not prepared to state."

"But is it possible?"

Schuyler hesitated, but finally said, "Yes, I suppose it is possible."

Arnold nodded with satisfaction. "Before I change to another subject, the record should state that the court-martial I mentioned earlier, which took place on October 1, 1778, was convened at the insistence of General Schuyler himself, and that he was found innocent of all charges, and acquitted with honor."

"The record will so note," Greene responded.

"General Schuyler, I would now like to turn to a more personal and subjective area of questioning, if I may." Schuyler, who now gave Arnold his full attention, regarded his former protégé with a mixture of puzzlement and disappointment. Yet, there was also a hint of receptiveness, a willingness to hear an explanation for an almost unbelievable event. "Sir, in all the time that I served under your command, have you ever known me to seek safe and comfortable assignments, and avoid difficult and dangerous ones?"

"On the contrary, I always found the reverse to be true. When I asked for a volunteer among my brigadiers to lead the Fort Stanwix relief effort, and none came forward, you offered to take the command, even though it did not call for the rank of major general. And the delaying action against Burgoyne, where you commanded one division of the Army and I the other, was a difficult and taxing mission, which you performed cheerfully and with enthusiasm."

"And, sir, when I asked you to help me obtain the command of Fortress West Point, did you suspect that it might be for the purpose of surrendering it to the enemy?"

"At the time that would have been totally inconceivable."

"And now, sir?" Arnold asked softly.

Schuyler's countenance slowly changed, and color seemed to

drain from his face. "Even now," he said, staring directly into Arnold's eyes, "I find it hard to believe."

"Would you find it inconceivable that this is a plot on the part of the enemy to discredit me and to undermine our cause?"

Edwards rose, and addressed Greene. He had enough of this line of defense. "Sir, this is conjecture and calls for speculation by the witness. There is no evidence to be obtained here."

Greene thought for a long moment before he ruled. "Considering that his life stands in possible forfeit, it shall be the policy of this court to afford the accused wide latitude in the conduct of his defense. Inasmuch as General Arnold has indicated that his line of defense will be based on the supposition he has just posed, the witness may answer." Edwards bowed slightly and resumed his seat, as Greene continued. "General Arnold, will you please repeat the question."

"Thank you, sir. General Schuyler, I ask you again, do you find it inconceivable that this whole scenario could be a plot by the enemy to discredit me?"

"I do not find it inconceivable. In fact, it seems more believable than the alternative."

Arnold knew when he was ahead. "Thank you, general. I have nothing further."

Joshua marveled at Arnold's performance. So far, he was making good his statement that the prosecution witnesses would be his best defense. And with each raising of the issue, his claim to be the victim of an enemy plot seemed more believable. Also important, he seemed to be gaining the sympathy of the court.

As Arnold slowly eased his way into his seat, Edwards rose. "If I may address the witness again?" He selected several documents from his table and handed one of them to Schuyler. "General, I am going to show you two documents taken from Major André, the British spy, when he was captured. May I ask you to read this document?" As Schuyler did so, his eyes widened, but he said nothing. "As you can see, it is a pass in General Arnold's handwriting"

Joshua rose. "If it please the court, at this point we may only say that the document *appears* to be in General Arnold's hand." He had gotten away with it again. Arnold accepted his action without reaction. Perhaps he was glad to stay off his leg for a time.

Edwards appeared annoyed. "Very well, then. Sir, you have testified that you have maintained correspondence with General Arnold. Does the document appear to be in his hand?"

"It does."

He handed Schuyler a second document. "This document gives details of the construction of the redoubts at West Point. Does it also appear to be in General Arnold's hand?"

"Yes." Schuyler's reply was just above a hoarse whisper.

"Will you please peruse the document to your satisfaction?" When he had done so, Schuyler returned the document to Edwards, his face paler than before. "Do you still feel it inconceivable that General Arnold attempted to betray Fortress West Point to the enemy?"

When Schuyler spoke, his voice was flat and tired. The tone was that of a man who had lost something of great value. "If these papers are genuine...if they were indeed authored by General Arnold...then I must conclude...I must conclude that...." Schuyler's voice broke and he lowered his head in despair. Edwards did not press him.

"I have nothing further," he announced. By showing the documents to Schuyler, he had counter-attacked Arnold's attempt to get the witness on the side of his "plot" defense. It would prove useful from now on, if Arnold employed the same tactic again. He was gratified to see that the self-satisfied smile Arnold had showed at the result of his cross examination had vanished.

After Schuyler left the stand, Greene called an adjournment for the day.

# CHAPTER TWENTY-ONE

JOSHUA THORNE ACCOMPANIED Benedict Arnold as his guards escorted him from the court. Once back in his confinement room, Joshua attempted to discuss strategy for tomorrow's court session. The next scheduled witness was the Marquis de Lafayette, whom, as far as Joshua knew, had little contact with Arnold, and he wondered why the prosecution would call him. He hoped to probe Arnold for a possible reason. The general, however, was preoccupied by the coming visit of his family. He asked Joshua if he could obtain fresh linen for his bed, and arrange for the laundering of some personal clothing. He fussed about the room, rearranging the few items of furniture, and eyed the chest of drawers, wondering aloud if its bottom drawer could serve as a bed for his baby son. He did appear to be looking forward to questioning Lafayette, but would not discuss it with Joshua. Frustrated, Joshua left, and arranged for Arnold's requests, not quite sure why he had gradually accepted the role of the general's lackey.

It was evening before he was able to visit Mabie's. It was an important visit. He had not seen Amy since breakfast yesterday, and now regretted leaving her with the flippant remark about André "hanging anyway." Fortunately, the common room was empty, and he found her sitting at the bar, her back toward him, reading. She looked up as he entered.

"Thomas Malory's *Le Morte d'Arthur*," she announced, holding up the book. "School begins in ten days, and I'm starting my upper level students with it." It was a good sign. She was not holding a grudge. He walked over and kissed her warmly on the neck. "I'm afraid it may be a little advanced for them, though," she said, ignoring, but not rejecting his caress. "What do you think?"

"I'm sure they'll be capable of anything with you as their teacher," he answered, circling his arms round her waist.

"You don't think it's too difficult for them then?"

"Not at all."

"You haven't even read the book, have you?"

"No," he admitted, nuzzling closer, "but I have complete confidence in you."

She eased gently from his grasp and went behind the bar to pour him a tankard of beer. "You really should read it someday, Josh. It's one of the finest pieces of prose in our language." She poured herself a small cider and sat down across from him.

"Why read about something gloomy, like the death of King Arthur? Now, if it were about his life, I'd be interested."

"It *is* about his life. The title is taken from its last chapter."

Trapped by his own words, Joshua picked up the book and gazed at it without enthusiasm. "Hmm, well, do you think you can get me a copy?"

"Only if you truly want to read it."

"Perhaps after the trial is over."

"Or perhaps when the war is over." They both laughed, and Joshua breathed easier.

"Tell me what happened in court today," she asked.

He summarized the day's testimony, concentrating on that of Schuyler, emphasizing the strong bond that existed at one time between Arnold and his former commander. "I was very impressed with Schuyler. If we become an independent nation some day, he'll certainly be one of our leaders."

"Not General Washington?"

"Of course Washington. If we prevail, Washington will certainly lead the country, whether it be king, prime minister, or whatever title is chosen for the head of the new state. But Schuyler will either assist him or succeed him." For some reason, his mood had turned reflective. "Ironically, Arnold would have been a strong contender to assume the mantle when either of them stepped down. And I think men like Greene and Hamilton will also play major roles. Our military leaders will probably run the country for many years."

"How about the members of Congress?

Joshua snorted. "Congress has proven itself completely incompetent. If we win this war, it will be in spite of Congress. Men like Adams, Laurens, Madison, and Jefferson will disappear from history. They won't play any part in the formation of our new nation."

"I hope you're wrong," Amy said. "I don't feel comfortable with the idea of military men running the country."

"We're not talking about professional military officers, Amy. These men were civilians before they donned the uniform, and they'll be civilians again. But they've proven themselves in adversity, while the politicians have achieved nothing more than establishing a powerless debating society."

Amy sighed. "Tell me more about Schuyler, then, since you seem to think he'll be running the country some day."

He told her what he knew of Schuyler's background as a descendent of one of the great Dutch patroon families of New York, his position in the New York political aristocracy, and his contributions to the revolutionary cause. "He has a sincere affection for Arnold, and was obviously crushed when Edwards showed him the documents taken from André. It was an emotional scene. And, to give you an idea of his character, Edwards told me after court today that during the Saratoga campaign the British burned Schuyler's country manor to the ground. Yet, after Burgoyne's surrender, Schuyler invited him to his home, provided a sumptuous dinner, and treated him with the utmost courtesy."

"You mark me," Amy warned, "the British will burn down Washington's home in Virginia before this war is done, and Jefferson's as well."

"I doubt that. Both homes are too far from the area of operations."

"Then they'll do it with a raiding party, like the one that captured General Lee."

"No, that would appear as an act of terror or banditry, outside the code of war."

"Then they'll get a band of Tories to do it."

"You make it sound as though Loyalists are nothing but lawless marauders." He didn't like the way the conversation was going, but he felt her position was too extreme.

"Well, they're not much better. They should all be driven out of the country and their property taken from them."

"It's not that simple, Amy, not just a matter of black and white— or red and blue, if you prefer. Take the Fairfaxes of Virginia, for example. A fine family, in America for generations. They're General Washington's neighbors and closest friends. They prefer to remain loyal to the Crown, but they are Americans too. Should they have their property taken from them?"

"From what you've told me, General Schuyler's family has been here even longer, yet he is a patriot. Why should they be treated equally? How can we treat anyone equally who is fighting against us? Even Benjamin Franklin disowned his own son when he remained a Loyalist."

"As much respect as I have for the good doctor, I can't condone the way he's treated his son." Franklin had allowed his son to be thrown into prison, even interfering when Washington tried to have him released. "One of the evil things about this war is the way it has split friends and family."

"So our cause is evil then?" She knew she should stop. She was helping to fulfill her own stated misgiving. But she could not allow Joshua to say such things without rebutting them.

"I'm not saying that, but it *is* harming our society, pitting father against son, brother against bro—"

"My God, Joshua, by defending a traitor, are you becoming one yourself?

Her insinuation was unfair. He could feel his temper warming. "Only the outcome of this war will determine who the traitors are,

Amy. But we were talking about confiscation of property. Do people like the Fairfaxes deserve to have their property confiscated?"

"That's exactly what would happen to patriot families if we lose."

"That's not true. The Carlisle Commission proposed a return to pre-war status, without reprisals, retaliation, or confiscations. It agreed to every demand we made earlier, including self rule, as long as we gave up the idea of complete separation from Great Britain."

"And you trust the lobster-backs?"

"Come, Amy, this would have been a treaty. It would have been respected. The British are not barbarians."

"You sound as though you wish we had accepted it."

"I have to think we would be better off today if Congress *had* accepted it. The British offered self government and reconciliation. Our side seems to offer confiscation and vengeance. This is my country, Amy. No matter how I feel about this war, or who wins it, no one is going to take it from me." Noticing how angry she had become, he added, "If Carlisle had been accepted, at least I would be able to pay my bar bill." He smiled, but she was not mollified. "It was a very generous offer, Amy."

Amy shook her head in exasperation. "I can't believe I'm sitting here arguing with a Tory." She stood up, gathering her shawl.

"Tory?" Joshua was now truly angry. He put both hands on his uniform. "Does this coat look red to you?"

"It looks like you don't belong in it," she snapped. With that, she rounded the bar, headed for the door, and left the building without looking back at him.

For a short while Joshua remained at the bar, allowing his anger to seethe. But as it cooled, and his emotions returned to normal, he could only ask himself one question. Why had an evening that started so well ended so badly?

# CHAPTER TWENTY-TWO

AS THE DAY waned, the sun made a belated appearance in the west, turning the sky red beneath the retreating rain clouds. At the headquarters mess, Laurance read the day's court transcript, while Edwards munched on a cold turkey leg. As was customary, while in garrison the mess served the main meal of the day at noon, providing only a small repast in the evening. As a result, Laurance was satisfied, Edwards was hungry. It was difficult adjusting to General Greene's court schedule. Laurance had been called away the previous afternoon, and was now catching up on the first two days of court. He looked up from his reading.

"Much of Arnold's opening remarks is a restating of those at his first trial. Some of it is word for word."

"Well, perhaps that's not so unusual," offered Edwards, "if he considers them good words. And," he added with a smile, "he may have sought your removal from the court to spare you hearing them again."

"I wouldn't have wanted to sit through the reading of all those citations again, I assure you." Laurance continued to read while Edwards poked without enthusiasm at a large boiled potato on his plate. "Arnold asked Hamilton if he was an expert in the field of handwriting?" Laurance shook his head. "Can you imagine what a trial would be like if both sides were to bring in "experts" to testify to the yeas and nays of an issue? How could a jury possibly be expected to decide what to believe?"

After both men finished the light meal, Edwards reviewed for Laurance what he considered to be his achievements. So far, he had established the legitimacy of the papers taken from André, and the fact that two of them were in Arnold's handwriting. Arnold's defense that his handwriting was forged, seemed preposterous to him, and Laurance agreed, but there was no way to know how it would be regarded by the court. He had established that André and Anderson were the same person. And, with Schuyler's testimony, he had shown that Arnold had actively sought the command of West Point.

"And the negatives?" Laurance asked.

Edwards thought it over. "I should not have called Jameson, and perhaps I shouldn't have called Schuyler either. We gained little from their testimony, and Arnold gained much. If we'd had more time...."

Laurance shook his head. "If we hadn't called Schuyler, Arnold would have."

"He's certainly making good on his claim that the prosecution witnesses would be his best defense."

"He'll probably derive some benefit from many of the prosecution witnesses. It can't be helped." Laurance changed the subject. "How is Arnold coming across to the court?"

"Hard to say. He's egocentric and sometimes abrasive, but I think he's sowing some measure of doubt in the court. There wasn't a man in the room unaffected by his opening speech, including myself."

"What do you plan for tomorrow?"

"Finish up with showing Arnold's attempts to secure the command of West Point, and then begin connecting him with the conspiracy. If there's time, I'll make the connection with André, through Smith. Without André, Smith will be our most important witness."

"At some point, you're going to have to introduce the letters found in Arnold's office," Laurance said. "Either that or withdraw Specification 1. As we agreed previously, without André to authenticate the letters, they remain the weakest part of our case, and probably won't stand with the court."

"I have a plan which will change that," Edwards said, but I need time."

"André will not testify," Laurance reminded him.

"Not in the present situation."

The judge advocate general eyed his assistant sharply. "You think he can somehow be convinced to do so?"

"I do." And Edwards laid out his plan.

# CHAPTER TWENTY-THREE

*The Manse, Tappan, New York*
*Friday, October 6, 1780*

"I CALL THE Marquis de Lafayette," Edwards announced. The orderly exited the court room and returned ushering a thin, lanky figure in uniform, whose youthful appearance almost belied the insignia of rank upon his shoulders. As usual, after being sworn and taking the witness chair, he was asked to state his name, rank, and position.

"Marie Joseph Paul Yves Roch Gilbert du Motier, Marquis de Lafayette, Major General, of the Continental Army of the United States of America."

Before Edwards could proceed, Sergeant Porter, the court recorder, rose, and addressed Greene. "Sir, may I have some assistance in the spelling of all the general's names?"

Even Lafayette joined in the good-natured laughter, which seemed to relieve some of the tension accompanying the opening of the third day of the proceedings. Joshua was struck by the serious countenance of the young Frenchman. His pale, uncreased skin, his lustrous, sandy hair, and his alert hazel eyes proclaimed youth, yet those same eyes suggested experience far beyond his twenty-two years. And Joshua had never seen a profile quite like Lafayette's. His forehead sloped nearly 45 degrees from the hairline, and this angle continued uninterrupted along the bridge of his nose, ending at a sharp point. Seen from the front, it gave the young marquis an inquisitive air, as though he were constantly questioning something.

When he had first presented himself to Congress more than three years ago, there was little to suggest that the nineteen-year-old aristocrat had much to offer the American cause. A title, a fortune, and a captaincy in the French army seemed little justification for the rank of major general that Lafayette requested. But Congress must have sensed some special qualities in the young man, and when he offered to serve without pay, and agreed not to press for command of a division, Congress accepted his application and granted him that rank.

And Joshua knew that in the years that had intervened, their confidence had been more than rewarded. Beloved by Washington, admired by his peers, and liked by all who knew him, Lafayette had proven fanatically courageous in battle, and skilled in troop deployment and tactics. Older and more senior officers had willingly served under his command, and during the frequent periods when Congress failed to provide pay or supplies for the army, Lafayette had used his own private funds to feed and clothe his men.

With the recorder satisfied, Edwards directed his attention once more to Lafayette. "If I may, General, I would like to call your attention to the date of Monday, July 31st of this year. Did you have occasion to witness a meeting and conversation between General George Washington and Major General Benedict Arnold, the accused in this case?"

"Yes, I did."

"Will you please describe that conversation to the court?"

'It was the day that our army cross the North River near Stony Point. A French army had made landing at Newport, and we learn that the British Army in New York was sailing north to engage them. As counter measure, General Washington decide to attack New York. General Washington, a small staff and myself watch from a hill as the boats cross the river. We were not there long when General Arnold arrived, and he and General Washington engage in conversation. I remember that General Arnold ask His Excellency if he had decided upon a position for him. His Excellency made a big smile and said yes, that he was to command the left wing of the Army."

Joshua was impressed with the young marquis' command of English. Although accented, his vocabulary was broad, and except for a tendency to drop past tense "-ed" endings, his diction was clear and understandable.

"And how did General Arnold react to that news?"

"Only way I can describe is to say that it was like General Washington had slap him in the face. I was most astonished. It was a post of great honor. He would be third in command of the Continental Army. But General Arnold only stare at the ground. He did not thank General Washington, or say anything. His Excellency was greatly affronted. He then told General Arnold to go to headquarters and wait for him."

"Did you see them together again that day?

"I did. I return with General Washington to his headquarters, where General Arnold was waiting. Immediately, General Arnold approached His Excellency and ask him to reconsider his decision, and to give him command of West Point instead. He was much upset, and limped back and forth on his bad leg. He complained that he cannot serve in the field or on horseback for such a long period in an active campaign. Only in a post command, like West Point could he continue to serve his country, which he swore he most wanted to do. His Excellency treated him with kindness, trying to convince him by saying that, I remember almost exactly his words, 'an important position of command would restore his spirit and self-esteem. It would enhance his reputation in the army, in Congress, and with his countrymen.' But it was no use. General Arnold insist that only in command of West Point could he perform his duty. I could see it was a great disappointment to General Washington. Finally, His Excellency announce that he would not make a decision at that time, but would think it over."

Edwards paused to let the court digest the words of the witness. "General Lafayette, what impression did General Arnold's statements have on you?"

"I was surprised that such a brave and talented officer, one of the best fighting generals in our army, would refuse the position of honor. I could only assume his leg wound was much worse than I thought."

"Can you tell us now what happened afterward?"

"The next day, August 1st, general orders were issued, placing General Arnold in command of the left wing. From that time his leg became much worse. It seem as though the news of his assignment had a bad affect on it."

"I object most strongly to that remark, sir," Arnold said, rising to his feet. "Do you accuse me of malingering?"

Before Lafayette could answer, Greene interrupted. "General Arnold, please direct any objection you may have to the court and not to the witness." He then turned to Lafayette. "Sir, I believe your comment about General Arnold's leg borders on insinuation. Subject to objection by any member of the court, it shall be stricken from the record." There was no objection, and Greene instructed the court reporter to remove Lafayette's last sentence. He then turned to Edwards. "You may resume."

"General, what was the result of the publication of that order?"

"On August 3rd General Washington amend the order, stating that General Arnold would take command of West Point."

"Do you know why this decision was made?"

Lafayette hesitated, and his gaze flicked momentarily at Arnold's leg, which stuck out stiffly from his chair. "We had learn that General Clinton abandoned his plan to attack the French in Rhode Island, and was returning to New York. General Washington called a council of war, and it was determine we had not the strength to attack him there. Since there would now be no active campaign, it was easier for His Excellency to give to General Arnold his desire."

Edwards then turned toward the defense table."I have nothing further for General Lafayette."

As the young officer turned to face Arnold, Joshua noted that his profile accentuated the sharpness of his features, the receding forehead, and his strangely pointed nose. Leaning on the table, and favoring his good leg, Arnold addressed Lafayette. "Sir, we have known each other for some time, is that not so?"

Lafayette nodded. "More than three years."

"Until now, have you ever known me to attempt to avoid battle or responsibility due to health, injury, or any other such reason?"

"No, General, I have not, and I wish to apologize for my earlier inference."

At that, Arnold's voice lost its tone of stridency. "No apology is needed, General."

"In fact," Lafayette continued, "I would say just the reverse is true. For example, it is well known that at Saratoga, although your leg wound from Quebec had not yet healed, you led the charge which brought victory, receiving another bad wound in same leg."

Arnold now seemed completely mollified, and he adopted a more friendly tone. "From the time of my conversation with General Washington near Stony Point on July 31st until the unfortunate events of September 25th last, did it ever occur to you that the reason for my request to command West Point might possibly be to turn it over to the enemy?"

"Never. I could not conceive it."

"Finally, sir, would it seem unreasonable to believe that this whole scenario is a plot by the enemy to discredit me and thus create havoc and dissension in our army?"

When he answered, Lafayette stared intently into Arnold's eyes. "With all my heart, general, I pray that it might be so."

For a moment the two generals stood as if frozen in time, one young and sincere, the other graying and proud, holding in common the comradeship of war. Then Arnold, nodded his head slightly. "Thank you, General." As he turned away, he announced he had nothing further. Greene established that no member of the court desired to question the witness, and Lafayette was excused. As Edwards was preparing to call his next witness, the orderly handed a message to Joshua, who read it, then passed it immediately to Arnold. As soon as he read it, Arnold rose and addressed Greene.

"Sir, I have been informed that my wife and latest born child will be arriving here at about noon today. I have not seen my family since the day I was brutally torn from my wife's arms and placed under arrest. Knowing her tender nature and sensitive character, I am certain that she has been in a state of utmost anxiety and despair ever since then. I ask the court's indulgence to allow me to meet with my wife, comfort her, and allay her fears. Having confidence in the understanding and humanity of its members, I request a recess until tomorrow."

Although Greene knew it would be highly unusual to recess the court for such a purpose, he could not help but feel some sympathy for Peggy Arnold in this situation, and even for her husband. He also felt that other members of the court probably shared the same sympathy. Yet he knew only too well that Washington wanted a speedy trial. They had already been slowed by one adjournment, and now Arnold was asking for another. As president of the court, Washington would hold him responsible for any delays. Still, he was reluctant to act arbitrarily. He turned to Edwards, a hopeful tone in his voice. "Colonel Edwards?"

But Edwards had felt a surge of excitement at Arnold's request. An adjournment would be a godsend, coming at a perfect time for his purpose. "I have no objection, sir."

"Does any member of the court wish to address the issue?' Greene asked.

John Glover was the first to speak. "I am in favor of granting the request."

"So am I," seconded Clinton. It was clear that despite the charges against him, Arnold was able to benefit from being a member of the fraternity of men who were sitting in judgment of him.

Anticipating the court's mood, Greene went ahead anyway. "May I see a show of hands of those in favor?" There was some hesitation, some slower than others, but eventually every hand was raised. Greene sighed, and leaned back in his chair. He thought about recessing and discussing the matter with Washington, who, after all, was just down the street. It would relieve him of the responsibility, but it would also thwart the wishes of the court if Washington disapproved Arnold's request. And he, Nathanael Greene, was president of the court. It was his decision to make. He rapped his gavel.

"The court will adjourn until ten o'clock tomorrow."

Shortly before one o'clock that afternoon, less than two hours after the court had adjourned, Joshua Thorne was summoned to Washington's headquarters. He had just finished informing Arnold that the request to have his guards removed had been denied. The general accepted the decision without comment, as if he had expected it. When Joshua arrived at the DeWint house, he found Washington and Margaret Arnold on a sofa in the reception room, finishing cups of tea. The Arnold's infant son resided in a bassinet on the floor. The commander in chief introduced him to Mrs. Arnold, with the request that she be taken to General Arnold's quarters. Joshua noted that he used the term "quarters" with a straight face.

Margaret Arnold, known to her friends as Peggy, was a beautiful woman, and she knew it. She was the daughter of Edward Shippen, a well-known judge and member of one of the wealthier families of Philadelphia. Although his brother, William, was surgeon general of the Continental Army, Edward maintained a neutrality which caused many to suspect him of Loyalist leanings. During the British occupation of Philadelphia, Peggy Shippen had enjoyed a gay and heady swirl of activity centered on the social affairs sponsored by the headquarters of General Sir William Howe, then commander in chief of the British Army in North America. Her near constant companion at these soirees was a dashing British captain, who, in addition to his military duties, wrote and produced plays for the enjoyment of the commander and his guests, and possessed a flair for poetry and sketching. His name was John André.

André was a frequent visitor at the Shippen house, and once made a sketch of Peggy wearing a headdress he had designed for her. He also drew the pattern for a costume she was to wear to a ball, which her father prohibited her to wear, due to what he considered its scandalous nature. The former association between the wife of

Benedict Arnold and the convicted British spy was now becoming generally known, and caused speculation as to her possible role in the West Point conspiracy.

Peggy and Benedict Arnold had met after the British evacuation of Philadelphia, during the general's term as military commander of the city. He had quickly fallen in love with the vivacious, charming young girl, and she had apparently returned his affection. After a six-month courtship, they were married in September, 1778. He was 38 years old and she was not yet 19.

Although she had a reputation as a flirt, there was nothing flirtatious about Peggy Arnold as she rode beside Joshua on the way to Arnold's detention room. When the invitation from Washington had arrived at Robinson's House, rather than wait until morning, she had left at once, and ridden through the night in a small army wagon to be with her husband. And now, it was obvious that there was nothing on her mind but a reunion with him. Joshua respected her for that, and it even made him think better of Arnold.

There was an awkward silence as they rode together in the small cart toward Joshua's former quarters. It was Peggy who finally broke it. "General Washington informed me that you are defending my husband. I'm grateful to you."

"Madam, at present he is determined to defend himself. I'm merely his legal adviser."

She seemed satisfied with this, but after a pause she spoke again. "You do believe he is innocent of these heinous charges?"

Joshua took his time before replying. He did not want to upset her, which made him recognize that he was already affected by her charm. "In due honesty, I'm afraid I can't say that at this time. The evidence against him is most persuasive."

"If you knew him, you would know that my husband could never be a traitor to our cause. He is an honorable man and one of our greatest patriots. He has done much, and lost much in the service of our country, and would never do anything to betray it." He was struck by her sincerity. Whether it was due to conviction, or came from loyalty and devotion to her husband, he could not tell.

"All I ask," she continued, "is that you keep an open mind, and do your best for him."

"You have my promise, ma'm." As she turned from him fixing her gaze on the road, he could not help glancing across at her again. If he were ever to find himself in the general's position, he would be fortunate to have a wife like Peggy Arnold.

As they approached the door to the room where Arnold was confined, the sentries discreetly stood aside. Joshua knocked, and after a moment, Arnold opened the door. Upon seeing his wife, Arnold took a slight step backward, and his eyes brimmed with tears. Attempting a weak smile, he extended both his arms, and Peggy cradling her child at one side, rushed into them.

"My darling girl...my darling, darling girl," Tears spilled down Arnold's face as he pressed his wife and child into a fierce embrace. "Ah, Neddy...Neddy," he said, turning back the blanket covering the child's face. "My sweet little boy...." Joshua could hear Peggy's broken sobbing as he turned from the scene.

# CHAPTER TWENTY-FOUR

*Mabie's House*
*October 6, 1780*

WHEN ALEXANDER HAMILTON, the officer detailed to guard André that day, ushered Lieutenant Colonel Thomas Edwards into Major André's room, the young officer was sitting by the lone window, apparently sketching the outdoor scene. Hamilton had agreed to wait outside until the completion of Edwards' interview, while the sentries would remain at their station outside the door. As the young officer rose, he noticed Edwards gaze briefly at the sketchbook he had just put down.

"That might be appropriately titled, 'My Last View from a Window,'" he said, with a wry smile.

Edwards introduced himself, and they then sat facing each other at a small table. "I presume you are aware from your...uh... companions...that General Arnold's court-martial is under way?"

"I am, sir." André's tone was amiable and non-committal, as if the matter did not concern him in any way.

"His line of defense is that he is innocent, and that the whole affair is a British plot designed to discredit him and thus damage our cause."

"I have been made aware of that also."

Edwards was not surprised. Arnold's claim was now well known within the headquarters, and André was on good enough terms with his American "chaperones" to keep him up to date. "Yet you do not feel it necessary to deny that was your purpose? It is an acceptable practice of war to attempt to turn an enemy general, but quite another to deliberately smear his reputation with false charges. And that is what he claims you have done." Edwards noticed the trace of a frown cross the young officer's brow, and it took André a long moment to reply.

"General Arnold is on trial for his life. He is obliged to try to save himself."

"By impugning to you a dishonorable purpose? Did *you* try to save yourself by false inventions when you were brought before the board of inquiry Friday last?"

André's lips formed a tight, grim smile. "You will not trick me into speaking either for or against Arnold, colonel. My honor impels me in a certain direction, others may choose a different one. If my life was too easily forfeit, you will have to work for General Arnold's. I will not assist you."

But Edwards pushed on, not wanting to give André any pause for reflection. "There are others who are under the cloud of suspicion, his aide, Major Franks, his secretary, Lieutenant Colonel Varick."

"If it's a fair court, their guilt or innocence will be established."

"And what of Mrs. Arnold?" How will her guilt or innocence play out?"

"Sir, I will not speculate upon the relations between a husband and wife."

"You may be certain, sir, it will be speculated upon in the court room, with or without your presence. The lady has been summoned and she is here now in this very encampment." He could see the shock and surprise in André's eyes. Edwards went on. "We are well aware of your relationship with the former Miss Peggy Shippen."

André now appeared truly troubled. "It was nothing more than an innocent flirtation. You have no right—"

"An innocent flirtation in which upon your departure from Philadelphia you gave her a lock of your hair, which rumor has it she still carries. We are in possession of a packet of letters taken from her on the day of her husband's arrest." Edwards felt confident that André had no way of knowing that Washington had precluded their use. He continued relentlessly. "There is damaging correspondence between you and the lady, from which it is easy to infer—"

André rose, his fist striking the table. "Colonel, you go too far. I swear to you there was nothing untoward between us. God forbid that poor girl should be shamed or implicated in this because of me."

Edwards leaned forward. "By appearing under oath in court you could prevent that. If you testify, I would have no need to introduce the letters." He could not offer André his life in exchange for his testimony, but he was counting on the young officer's sense of honor to come to the rescue of Peggy Arnold.

The young major strode to the window, staring across the common, deep in thought. He seemed in no haste to reply. Edwards decided to turn the screw. "We also know of your acquaintance with another Philadelphia woman, Miss Margaret Chew."

André whirled around. "What kind of false scenario are you trying to create here? Miss Chew has absolutely nothing to do with any of this."

"I believe that is a matter for the court to decide."

Once again, André turned to gaze out the window. Edwards did not disturb his thoughts. Without turning, André finally spoke. "And if I testify, you will not introduce any correspondence concerning Mrs. Arnold or Miss Chew?"

"I will not."

"Nor will any reference be made to either lady in my examination before the court?"

"You have my word." Edwards held his breath.

André left the window and his eyes fixed directly on Edwards. Finally, he sighed and sat back down.

"Appearing in court against General Arnold is out of the question without the consent of General Clinton. If the matter is to be pursued, I must have permission to write him a letter."

Edwards hoped he was able to conceal the flush of victory he felt. "I'm sure General Washington will not object. But time is of the essence. I will be happy to wait upon your writing of the letter, and deliver it at once to General Washington for his approval."

Without further ado, André sat down and wrote the letter, which he then gave to Edwards.

Tapaan, October 6th 1780

His Excellency, Sir Henry Clinton K. B
Sir,

I have been approached to testify in the case against General Arnold. Although I have refused to do so previously, I now believe my testimony is required in order to eliminate innocent parties from suspicion of involvement in the matter. I ask your advice and instructions, sir, having full confidence in your sound and sensible judgement in this affair. Please be assured that I will fully abide by any decision you shall make. I have been offered no amelioration of the doom which has been imposed upon me in exchange for such testimony, and in the unlikely event it should be offered, please also rest confidently that I will take no action, nor make any statement, even though my life be at stake, that might be construed in any way as to reflect upon the honour of British Arms or the Crown. If I must die to protect such honour, then I shall die happily, secure in the knowledge that I have served my King and Country to the best of my conscience and ability.

Please be aware, sir, of my utmost regard, and heartfelt thanks for the many kindnesses you have shown me whilst in your service.

I have the honour to be with the most respectful Attachment

Your Excellencys Most obedient and
  Most humble Servant
    John André  Adj Gen

After excusing himself from André, Edwards went immediately to DeWint House, where he learned that Washington had left for an inspection of some redoubts along the river. It was critical that the letter be dispatched at once. With André testifying, the whole presentation of his case changed. The treasonous correspondence, weak evidence when standing alone, would now become more credible if supported by André. Learning that Nathanael Greene was acting in Washington's absence, Edwards quickly found him. Greene did not quite understand the judge advocate's need to get the document on its way at once. But, fortunately for Edwards, Greene also had an interest in moving the letter without delay—Washington's demand for a speedy trial. After weighing Edwards's argument, he authorized the letter, and within minutes it was on its way to Dobb's Ferry under a flag of truce.

# CHAPTER TWENTY-FIVE

MUCH LATER THAT day, as the evening sky was darkening, Joshua made his way to Mabie's. As he entered, he noticed three members of the court and another officer seated at one of the common tables. Being served by Amy were four brigadier generals, Clinton, Huntington, and Paterson, all court members, plus Anthony Wayne. Of the four, only Wayne was familiar to Joshua. He had a reputation in the army similar to Arnold's. He was a natural leader, admired by his men, and fearless in battle, although some said "reckless" might be a better term. His most notable feat had been an assault upon Stony Point, in which the fort had been overrun in less than a half-hour, capturing more than 500 British prisoners, 15 cannon, and valuable military stores. When the West Point plot was revealed, Wayne, leaving his tents still standing at Tappan, had raced his division to its defense with such speed that he received Washington's personal praise. His mission to defend the fortress and the highlands was the reason Laurance had left him off the court.

Seeing that Amy would be occupied for several minutes, Joshua wandered into the kitchen, wondering what military business had brought "Mad" Anthony Wayne from West Point to Tappan. As soon as he entered the large room, a wonderful aroma drifted across to meet him, its origin the large oven against the back wall. Scrapple, and only as Amy could make it. He knew the recipe by heart. Indian corn mush, buckwheat flour, pig's heart, liver, and rib scrapings, dusted with sage, salt, and pepper. It was then cooked to the texture of mashed potatoes, placed in molds and when set, baked in the oven and served with maple syrup and stewed apples. It was a far better meal than he could expect from the headquarters mess this evening. He advanced upon the oven and cracked the door, allowing a wave of delicious aroma to swirl into his nostrils.

"No you don't!" Amy entered the room, hurrying toward him. Shoving him aside, she removed the large pan from the oven and placed it on the bleached wood table. She began cutting the steaming contents into generous portions, placing them onto four earthenware plates.

"Mmmmm," Joshua murmured appreciatively. He was hoping to return to her good graces after last night. "No one would believe you're not from Philadelphia."

"Pennsylvanians aren't the only ones who can make scrapple," she countered. "We've made it in New York for years, and we make it better. Now get out of the way," she said, balancing the four plates with both arms, "while I serve your superiors."

Her voice was cool, but at least she had spoken to him. Joshua pulled a stool up to the table and cut himself a portion from the pan. As he raised his spoon, he hesitated, then brought down another plate and cut a second portion, this one for Amy. He wanted to start the evening off well, with an apology. By promising to take over his duty officer tour, Joshua had arranged to exchange rooms for the night with a friend who enjoyed a room of his own. If he and Amy could spend the night together, it might heal any injury their argument had caused. They had never really argued before, and it had upset him more than he expected. If he could persuade her, he vowed not to become involved in any discussions or actions which might ruin a romantic mood.

Amy re-entered the kitchen, carrying two brimming pewter mugs of cider. It was a good sign. It seemed as though she might be willing to overlook last night.

They ate in silence, enjoying the contrasting flavors of the food, washed down by the crisp, fresh cider. When his plate was empty, Joshua broke the silence. "Amy, I'm sorry about last night."

She had not yet finished her food, and it was a moment before she spoke. "I am, too. I...I said some provoking things." She sighed and shook her head. "It's this trial. How I wish it were over, and it has only begun."

He reached out and grasped her hand. "We mustn't let it come between us, Amy."

"I know," she said, but she still sounded dispirited. It was time to change the subject.

"I saw General Wayne at table with the others. Would you know why he's here?"

"He wants to see Major André." She was as eager as he to turn the conversation elsewhere.

"André?" Joshua's voice registered his surprise. "Why?"

"It seems that he's written a very unflattering poem about General Wayne, which has been recently published in the New York Royal Gazette. The general is here to meet with him."

Joshua was now even more surprised. "Meet with him? To what purpose?"

Amy shrugged. "I have no idea. But judging from the general's mood, it's not to praise his literary skills."

"Has Washington allowed this?"

"General Wayne only just arrived this afternoon, and Washington is on an inspection tour. General Greene has refused Wayne permission to see him without Washington's authority. Wayne is going to ride out before dawn to find Washington. Colonel Hamilton, who is sitting with John André tonight, was able to find a copy of the newspaper at headquarters, and he brought it over late this afternoon. When I brought Major André an early supper they were laughing over it."

"Hamilton and André?"

"Yes." Sensing his disapproval, she added. "It's a very funny poem, Josh. He has titled it *The Cow Chace*, and it ridicules General Wayne's most recent action at a place called Bull's Ferry."

Joshua was aware of the Bull's Ferry affair. Wayne had been given the mission of destroying a blockhouse occupied by a small

British force established to protect some wood-cutters for the British Army and a neighboring Loyalist community. He was also ordered to seize all cattle and horses within the area, and drive them within American lines. Wayne sent a cavalry detachment to capture the livestock, while he attacked the blockhouse with a force supported by light artillery. His cannon proved too small to damage the stout walls of the blockhouse, and an assault upon the building was repulsed with heavy losses. The mission's only success was in driving off the cattle, and burning a few boats.

"I imagine that one of the things that General Wayne is upset about," Amy continued, "is that the poem makes reference to him as a tanner and a 'warrior-drover.'" Before the revolution, Wayne had owned a successful tannery in his hometown in Pennsylvania.

"That's typical of British officers," Joshua said. "They've always shown contempt for American officers, as far back as the French and Indian War. It's based solely on the fact that we are not members of an aristocracy. In their view, an officer must be of noble birth, and have enough money to purchase his commission. That a tanner, like Wayne, an apothecary, like Arnold, or a Virginia planter, like Washington is capable of leading men in battle is a concept they refuse to accept. Do you know that at the beginning of the war, when sending correspondence to Washington, the British command referred to him as 'Mr. Washington,' refusing to afford him the title of 'general,' yielding only when he returned their letters unopened? Personally, I think it's far better to have officers come from an honest profession rather than simply be the product of an effete society. I'd much rather be led by a warrior-drover than a warrior-poet."

Amy put down her spoon. "I don't see how the ability to write poetry conflicts with being a capable officer."

By her tone, he knew that he had gone too far. He was in danger of ruining the evening after all the preparations he had made. He backtracked. "I didn't mean to imply that." Thinking quickly, he asked, "Do you think you could borrow the *Gazette* from Hamilton? I'd like to read the poem myself." She gave him a sharp, penetrating glance, looking for any sign of sarcasm. He responded with his most ingenuous and conciliatory expression.

Apparently satisfied, she rose, left the room, and soon returned with the newspaper. "While you're reading, I'll go tend to my guests."

Sighing with relief, Joshua opened the paper. He discovered that the poem was evidently divided into three cantos, the third and final one appearing here. The others, the paper announced, had been published in previous editions. The current canto, heavy with mischievous satire, described how Wayne, unable to capture the blockhouse, made war on the cattle instead, losing his horse in the process.

> His horse that carried all his prog
> His military speeches,
> His cornstalk whisky for his grog,
> Blue stockings, and brown breeches.

But it was the final stanza that most caught Joshua's eye.

> And now, I've clos'd my epic strain,
> I tremble as I shew it,
> Lest this same warriordrover Wayne,
> Should ever catch the poet.

In the public room, the generals had now left, and Amy returned, carrying a tray with the empty dishes and two refilled mugs. Quickly washing the dishes in the sink, she brought the mugs to the table. Joshua thanked her and took a long drink. "Beer this time," he smiled appreciatively. "You are truly a witch."

"I know you, that's all." She nodded toward the paper. "Well, what do you think?"

Anxious to avoid a confrontational discussion, Joshua held up the paper. "Did you note the publication date of the newspaper, September 23rd, the same day that André was captured?" It did not seem to register with Amy. "Don't you find that ironic, in light of his final stanza?" Puzzled, she took the paper from him and read it again. Joshua explained. "André pretends to tremble over publishing his poem, fearing what might happen if Wayne ever caught him. Well, in effect, Wayne *has* caught him, and he is here right now, about to confront him."

Her expression registered a mild alarm. "You don't think Washington will allow that, do you? What would be gained?"

"My answer to both questions is, I have no idea, but Mad Anthony is not the type to accept riding all this way in vain."

After thinking about this for a moment, Amy returned to her original question. "What do you think of the poem?" She was not going to let him off the hook.

"It's well done," he replied cautiously, "and he does have an ear for rhyme. What comes across most strongly is André's amusement that a tanner should 'pretend' to be a general, which reinforces my earlier point about the conceit of British officers."

"But?" She had sensed his reserve.

"I would enjoy the humor more if I were on the other side, which makes me wonder why Hamilton found it so comical."

"Perhaps it's because Colonel Hamilton is able to appreciate a talented work, regardless of its target. After all, Major André was only poking a little fun at General Wayne."

Joshua knew that he was again approaching dangerous ground, but it irritated him that Amy was so defensive wherever André was concerned. "Poking fun at one of our generals is not something I would expect Hamilton to laugh at, especially in the presence of the enemy. André also refers to our soldiers as 'dung-born tribes.' Is that something humorous also?"

"I think he was probably referring to their appearance. You only have to look at our army on the march, uniforms in tatters, many with no shoes—"

"Which, of course, is their fault." He felt his anger rising.

"I'm not saying it's their fault." She was becoming equally irate.

"It would seem to me there is a considerable difference between describing an army as ragged and calling it dung-born—"

"Enough!" Amy rose, her anger flaring. "I'm tired. I'm going to bed."

Joshua rose quickly, reaching for her arm. "Amy, I'm sorry. Let's not fight. Willie Aiken has let me use his room tonight. We could—"

She turned, and he could see there were now tears in her eyes. "Oh, Josh, Josh, this trial is poisoning our relationship."

"But we need not let it." He had never before seen her cry, and it shook him. Please come with me. Let's talk about it."

She shook her head. "It's no use. It seems that every time we're together now, we argue."

"But—"

"I don't want to talk any more tonight. I'm going to sleep at Mary's."

After she had gone, Joshua sat back down and put his head in his hands. He had done it again.

# CHAPTER TWENTY-SIX

*The Manse, Tappan, New York*
*Saturday, October 7, 1780*

AS SOON AS the court settled in, Edwards called Brigadier General Henry Knox to the stand.

Knox was big—in all directions. More than six feet tall, and weighing over three hundred pounds, his broad shoulders helped disguise the fact that he was considerably overweight. Although possessed of the geniality attributed to the portly, Knox had none of the fat man's languor. He was known as an energetic and active officer. This was the man who had brought the cannons of Ticonderoga to Dorchester Heights. Moving overland almost 320 miles in the dead of winter, using sleds to carry the big guns down snow-packed roads and across frozen rivers, his feat forced the British to abandon the city of Boston. Ever since then, Knox had been the commander of American artillery, appointed to the position at the age of twenty-six. Knox had been a member of the court during Benedict Arnold's previous trial, and he and his wife were known to be on friendly terms with both the Arnolds.

After being sworn, Edwards led Knox through his receipt of the packet of documents from Lieutenant Colonel Jameson, his delivery of them to Washington, and Arnold's subsequent arrest. He then turned to Washington's order to Knox to proceed to West point and evaluate the situation there.

"General Washington's main concern was that, due to the conspiracy, an attack upon the fortress might be imminent," Knox stated, "and he wished the garrison to be brought to the highest state of alert. Of almost equal importance was to determine whether the plot had penetrated any deeper into the ranks of the command. When I landed at Fort Arnold....I'm sorry, Fort Clinton...I was met by Colonel Lamb, the resident commander. Without mentioning the conspiracy, I only informed him we had reason to believe the British were planning an immediate attack. His surprise and alarm seemed genuine. He at once ordered the drumming of a call to arms, and the garrison fell out in quick order and assumed their appointed stations. He and I then began a detailed inspection of the works, which took the remainder of the day."

"During this inspection, did you note any deficiencies or weaknesses in the fort's defenses?" Edwards asked.

Knox's expression turned thoughtful before he answered. "The fortress was not as prepared as I expected it should be. The complement was not at full strength. There were ammunition shortages, both for musketry and artillery. Food stores were low, and of mediocre quality. And there were places where the walls needed repair, although Colonel Lamb assured me repair was under way."

"Did you conclude that any of these weaknesses were part of a deliberate plan?"

"No, rather, they seemed to be the same deficiencies which have bedeviled our forces since the beginning of this war."

"General," Edwards pressed, "are you stating for the record that these deficiencies could not have been part of a plan to deliberately weaken the fortress?"

"No, I cannot make such a statement. It just seemed to me that my first judgment was more likely."

"Then it's possible that the fortress could have been deliberately weakened."

Knox hesitated a moment before replying. "Yes, it's possible."

Satisfied, Edwards turned to a different subject. "What was your conclusion as to the extent of the conspiracy?"

"Some time that afternoon, after questioning many individuals, and having seen no indication of treachery on the part of any member of the garrison, I informed Colonel Lamb and his officers of the situation. They were as truly shocked and disbelieving as the rest of us were when we first heard the news. I was convinced then the plot had gone no further, and I remain so."

"Thank you, General. I have nothing further." As Edwards resumed his seat, Joshua saw Knox and Arnold exchange glances. An unspoken message seemed to pass between them as Arnold rose.

"General Knox, do you remember an evening in August—the date escapes me—when you and I dined alone in the headquarters mess?"

Knox nodded. "I do, it was near to the middle of the month."

"That would be about right, since I just taken command of the Highlands Department. Do you remember a conversation we had about West Point?"

"I do."

"Will you please tell the court the substance of that conversation."

"You expressed shock at the poor condition of the fort's defenses, and that such an important post had been allowed to deteriorate in such a manner." Knox paused and his gaze shifted momentarily to Major General Robert Howe, who was sitting on the court. Arnold had taken over command of West Point from Howe. "You mentioned that the garrison was almost 50 per cent under strength, and that you had requested reinforcements from Governor Clinton. You also said that some of the outlying forts and redoubts were in need of repair, and complained about shortages in everything from rations to ammunition."

"Did I say that I was doing anything about this?"

"You did. You said you had made an urgent request to the Quartermaster General for emergency issue, and that you had started immediately rebuilding and repairing the walls and breastworks."

Arnold paused a moment to let the answer sink in. "I ask you, sir, does that sound like the action of someone set upon weakening the fortress?"

"On the contrary, I was convinced you were doing your best to strengthen it."

"Thank you, general, I have nothing further."

As Knox left the room, Joshua reflected on his testimony. Arnold had again turned the testimony of a prosecution witness to his own advantage. But the fact that Arnold had to pry it out of him showed that even his friends were distancing themselves from him.

Thomas Edwards was in a quandary. His next witness was to be John Lamb, the commander of West Point, but he pondered whether or not to call him. Lamb was an old friend of Arnold's, going back to the Canadian campaign, and Edwards had no way of knowing how he would react as a prosecution witness. However, he had an important piece of testimony to relate, and Edwards could see no way around calling him. Arnold's success in turning prosecution witnesses to his advantage had come as a surprise. Even though Arnold had vowed that was exactly what he would do, Edwards had considered it an empty threat. He now knew better. Yet, it was possible that this situation was different. Lamb might be less willing to support Arnold, since in doing so he, as the commander of the fort, must accept responsibility for any of its deficiencies. Edwards decided to go ahead.

There was an unusual stillness as Lamb entered the room and took his seat. Those who did not know him were shocked by the grievous wound, which had torn away part of his face, to include his left eye. Taken prisoner at Quebec, months of imprisonment without proper medical attention had not been kind to the mending wound. Adding a thatch of unruly gray hair gave the old artilleryman an angry, Cyclopean stare.

Under Edwards's questioning, Lamb confirmed the conditions existing at the fort as stated by Knox. He was also careful to point out that he had inherited these conditions, and tried his best to correct them. "But I was realistic," he stated. "These were the same conditions we have all faced all along. Shortages have always existed in this army, ever since the beginning. I could not expect a static, rear area command to have priority while the active divisions starved, even one as important as West Point."

"Did conditions improve after General Arnold took command?" By this line of questioning Edwards wanted to foreclose any advantage to Arnold's questioning of Lamb, and perhaps even dissuade him from doing so.

"He got us more troops, which helped in repairing the works, and increased our security. As for the rest, he was no more successful than any of us had been, but it was out of his control."

"Did he do anything, which, in your view, would weaken the ability of the garrison?"

Lamb seemed reluctant to speak, but finally did so. "There were several requirements upon manpower directed by General Arnold which weakened the garrison unnecessarily. We had dispatched two hundred men from the Massachusetts brigade to serve as guards at Fishkill. I couldn't understand the need for such a guard at that place, and told the general so. I was then told to furnish two hundred more men to the deputy quartermaster general to cut firewood for the different posts. On top of that, I had to send guards to escort prisoners of war to Tappan. On a daily basis, our force was reduced by four to five hundred men performing these duties, and I complained about it to General Arnold." Here, he glanced quickly at Arnold, whose expression did not change from that of attentive listener.

"Also, I felt we needed more artillery," Lamb continued. "At our first meeting, I told him we needed more guns to repel a heavy enemy assault. I said we needed more twelve-pounders, at least ten more six-pounders, plus assorted small bores, and a dozen howitzers. In the past he'd always listened to me, but this time, as far as I know, he didn't."

"Could you construe that as an attempt to weaken the fortress?"

For a long moment Lamb did not answer. "In every other way he was trying to make it stronger. Like I said, he increased the garrison, although, as I said, I was vexed by his subtractions from our effective strength, and he tried his best to increase our stores of all kinds."

Edwards, ignoring that Lamb had not really answered his

question, now moved on to another subject. "I believe you were dining at General Arnold's headquarters on September 17th last, when he received a letter from Colonel Beverly Robinson, commander of the Loyal Americans?"

"That's right."

"Please describe what occurred at that time."

"While we were at dinner, General Arnold received a letter forwarded under a flag of truce from the British ship *Vulture*. He informed his guests that the letter was from Colonel Beverly Robinson, the owner of the very house we were dining in, who was seeking a meeting with him to discuss the possible return of some of his property. I warned General Arnold that such a meeting wasn't wise, and any such request should be made to the governor of the state, rather than to a military commander. I suggested he seek the advice of General Washington, whom he was to see later that day. The general agreed to do so, and the matter was dropped."

"Did you actually see the letter?"

"I did not. General Arnold read the letter to himself, and announced its contents to us. He then put the letter in his coat pocket."

By having Lamb bring up the letter, Edwards had achieved his purpose. He felt certain he would use that letter later. He saw no way that Arnold could benefit from cross examining Lamb, and announced he had nothing further. He felt there was a good chance Arnold would not cross examine.

But Arnold rose. "Colonel Lamb, Please think back to February, 1777, when you were released from prisoner of war status. What was your first official act?"

"I began raising a new artillery battalion."

"And what was the result?"

"I was able to raise the men, but Congress couldn't come up with the money to pay 'em or buy new guns. It was frustrating, because there was a real shortage of artillery in the line."

"Has there ever been a time when there was *not* a shortage of artillery?"

"Not to my knowledge."

"So, assuming the shortage still existed when I took command of West Point, would it be unreasonable for me to conclude that I would have more success requesting men, ammunition, and stores, rather than expensive guns already in short supply?"

Lamb shifted uncomfortably in his chair. "It wouldn't have hurt to ask." He was not about to give in.

"But what good would it have done to have more guns only to have them stand useless for lack of shot and shell?"

It was a rhetorical question, and Lamb was obviously not willing to engage in an argument with his former commander. Arnold did not push him, turning as if to go back to his seat. But he stopped and addressed Lamb once more.

"Oh, by the way, how did your efforts go to raise the battalion."

"I raised it, thanks to a thousand pound loan from you, which I regret I have not yet been able to repay."

"Don't worry, John," Arnold's voice softened. "With your gallant action at Ridgefield, helping me to send the British reeling back to their ships, you repaid it tenfold." As Arnold limped back to his chair, and Lamb rose to leave, Joshua thought he saw a tear roll from the old artilleryman's lone eye.

Edwards next called Lieutenant Colonel Richard Varick, Arnold's secretary. A tall, 22-year-old law student when the war began, Varick was commissioned a captain in a line regiment. He soon became military secretary to General Philip Schuyler, and it was in this capacity that he first met Arnold, who was at the time building the American fleet on Lake Champlain. Varick earned Arnold's praise by his untiring efforts to seek and provide the supplies and materials necessary for the ship construction. Temporarily detached from Schuyler, Varick served as Arnold's aide at Saratoga, and was able to report Arnold's heroic actions in that battle to Schuyler. He left the Army in 1778 to resume his law studies.

"Colonel Varick," Edwards began, "How long have you been General Arnold's secretary?"

"I assumed those duties on August 13th last." Rather than end his answer here, Varick chose to elaborate. He knew he and Major Franks, Arnold's aide, were both under suspicion of involvement in the Arnold affair. In fact, he had been told so by Washington himself, and he wanted to bring his side of the events to light. "The general had sent me a letter on August 5th, asking if I would consider working for him again. He informed me that my duties would allow me ample time to continue my law studies. Naturally, I was honored to be able to serve an officer of his character and reputation again. At the time, I had a very high opinion of General Arnold."

"And what caused you to change that opinion?"

The witness shifted in his chair, glancing briefly at Arnold. "Shortly after arriving at his headquarters, I found that General Arnold had changed. He seemed not to wish to take me into his confidence or seek my advice. He wanted to do everything himself. He appeared secretive about much of his correspondence, and even maintained an inner office where he kept most of his files, and to which I was denied access. From our previous association, I knew that General Arnold has an almost compulsive desire to keep all correspondence relating to him, even the most mundane. As his secretary I was surprised and affronted that I saw almost none of it."

"But surely, Colonel Varick, this matter alone could not have caused you to change your opinion of him so drastically."

"You are correct," Varick replied. "It was his actions that were much more disturbing to me. Shortly after I arrived, I discovered that General Arnold was drawing large amounts of stores from the commissary, supposedly for his own use, and then selling them. I spoke to Franks about it, who told me it had been going on for some time, and he had expressed his disapproval to the general, to no avail. Over the next weeks, Franks and I watched helplessly as barrels of rum and pork, sacks of grain, and dozens of hams were regularly moved from West Point to the other side of the river and stored at Robinson's House. No amount of remonstrating with the general would prevent him from selling these stores to willing merchants and ship captains who came to the house or called at the landing. He claimed Congress owed him thousands of rations, and he was only taking a portion of what was due him."

"Did it occur to you that this might be a deliberate plan to weaken the fortress by making it less able to withstand a siege?"

"I have to admit that it did not. I felt that he was unjustly profiteering from his official position, but treason was the furthest thing from my mind."

Edwards now shifted direction. "Colonel, are you familiar with a man named Joshua Hett Smith?"

The distaste in Varick's expression was obvious. "I am."

"Describe, please, the circumstances of your acquaintance, and the nature of your dealings with him."

"I became acquainted with him because of his association with General Arnold, an association which was viewed with alarm by Major Franks, several other officers of his staff, and ultimately myself."

"What was the cause of this alarm?"

"Smith is viewed as a man of questionable loyalty. His brother is William Smith, the Loyalist Chief Justice of New York, and Joshua Smith is strongly suspected of dealing with both sides. At dinner one evening at Robinson's House, he even suggested that the visit of the Carlisle Commission had given us a lost opportunity to make an honorable peace with Great Britain."

Joshua allowed himself a wry smile. He wondered how those in the room would react to the knowledge that he shared almost the same sentiments.

"Major Franks and I urged General Arnold to end his relationship with Smith," Varick continued, "but he refused. Finally, the situation exploded. At dinner at Robinson's House on September 23, at which Mrs. Arnold was present, the supply of butter ran out. General Arnold produced some olive oil in its place, which he said had cost him eighty dollars. Smith arrogantly proclaimed that in reality it was only eighty pence, since the Continental dollar was only worth a penny. I took affront at this maligning of our currency and told him so. One remark led to another, and soon there was a shouting match at the table. With Mrs. Arnold almost in tears, begging us to stop, I left and went to my room.

"Later on that evening, General Arnold confronted both Franks and myself, accusing us of insulting his guest. He told us that if he invited the Devil himself to dine with him, he expected the gentlemen of his official family to be civil to him. Franks replied that despite his nearly three years of loyal service, General Arnold had become prejudiced against him. He asked to be relieved of assignment as his aide, and left the room. The general and I continued to have words after Franks left. I believe I was somewhat intemperate, calling Smith a scoundrel and a spy. The general ended the conversation by saying that he was always willing to be advised by his official family, but he would not be dictated to by them. About an hour later, after serious consideration, I went to General Arnold and tendered my resignation. But the general, in a conciliatory mood now, said that he had been thinking matters over, and assured me he would end his relationship with Smith. I returned to my room, and spent the following day in bed. For some days I had been ill with fever and the flux, and it was worse that Sunday. On Monday I felt no better, but events drove me from my room. It was the day of General Arnold's arrest."

"I have no more questions for Colonel Varick," Edwards said.

Before Arnold could stand, Joshua rose quickly. "Sir, I request a short recess to speak privately with General Arnold."

Greene, appearing annoyed, looked at his watch. "Twenty minutes," he announced.

"Sir," Joshua began, after they were seated in the small side room, "I know you wish to do so, but I advise you against questioning either Colonel Varick or Major Franks. It appears you are on poor terms with both of them, and they can only do you damage."

Arnold shook his head. "I cannot simply sit here and let their statements damn me."

"Better that than to be twice damned by their answers to your questions. There are some questions that should not be asked. The answers only pound home the points made by the trial counsel. Can you present proof to deny their charges of corruption?"

"It is not corruption. I have done no more than many others in my position."

"Sir, that is not a defense."

Visibly annoyed, Arnold still managed to keep his voice calm. "Major Thorne, I know you are trying to be helpful, but I still believe that I know best what is in the interest of my defense and what is not. There are matters I must bring out with Colonel Varick. Major Franks may be a different matter. We will see. For now, I shall question Varick." He stood, indicating the conversation was over, and they returned to the courtroom.

"Colonel Varick," Arnold began, "You are aware, are you not, that I have not received my pay for more than five years, and only rarely received the special allowances due me?" For the first time since the trial began, Arnold remained seated, rather than rise to address the witness. Joshua wondered if the rain, which had started again after clear skies the day before, was having a painful affect upon his wound, or was this a deliberate attempt by Arnold to show contempt for the witness.

"I believe that is correct," Varick replied.

"And you are aware that I am due thousands of rations never drawn?"

"So you have told me."

Arnold appeared undisturbed by the tone of the reply. "In the matter of the rations you noted that I drew from the commissary, you stated that you saw some of these stores sold by me, is that correct?"

"I saw a great deal of them sold," Varick answered, staring directly at Arnold. Joshua closed his eyes in frustration. It was going exactly as he had warned. Any favorable feelings Varick might have previously held for his former chief were obviously gone.

"Did you ever see stores like salt pork and flour exchanged, say, for fresh produce, such as vegetables, fresh meat, eggs, and milk?"

"Yes, that did occur," Varick admitted.

"Tell me, do you find anything wrong with exchanging one form of ration for another?"

"I also saw them exchanged for gold and silver."

Joshua closed his eyes again.

"But if the gold and silver were then used to purchase fresh produce, it would still count as an exchange of rations, would it not?"

"I cannot say. It all seems devious to me."

"Colonel Varick, considering that I have received virtually no pay, allowances, or rations, what amount of stores do you think would compensate me for my years of service? How much is the victory of Saratoga worth to the nation? The British naval check at Valcour Island? The relief of Fort Stanwix? The defeat of the British at Bridgeport...."

"General Arnold," Greene interrupted, "these are rhetorical questions which the witness has no way of answering. We are all aware of your achievements, sir. There is no need to recite them here in this manner. Please turn to another line of questioning."

Arnold bowed slightly from his sitting position. He was happy to do so. He felt he had made his point. Every officer on the court was owed many months of back pay, and he was sure at least some of them had taken actions similar to his own. He knew Howe had.

"Now, sir, let us turn to Joshua Hett Smith. You have stated that he is suspected of dealing with both sides, and have called him a scoundrel and a spy. Is that correct?"

"I am not the only one with those opinions," Varick replied.

"Are you aware that Squire Smith was recommended to me by General Howe, the previous commander of West Point and the Highlands, who told me that Smith had proved useful to him, and would doubtless prove the same to me?"

"I...no...I was not aware of that." With Howe sitting on the court, not contradicting Arnold, Varick was obviously flustered.

"What if I told you that Squire Smith acted as a special agent for General Howe, that he supervised a spy network for him? Would that explain some of what you refer to as his suspicious activity?"

"If that is indeed the case...." Varick shifted his glance to Howe, as if trying to gain confirmation of Arnold's statement. Howe, however, simply stared back at him, his expression non-committal. "If that is true, I suppose...yes, it might explain it."

"What if I told you that Smith was acting as my agent in a similar capacity? Would that explain my anger at your ill treatment of him?"

By now, Varick seemed overwhelmed, drowning in information previously unknown to him.

"It...it would explain it, yes."

Arnold then changed the subject, but not the momentum of his questioning.

"Do you recall my mentioning to you that I was in secret communication with an American agent in New York, whose fictitious name was John Anderson?"

"I remember you told me that, yes."

"Did I not dictate a letter to you, addressed to him?"

"You did."

"Yet, you stated here earlier that when you came back into my employ, I had changed, that I no longer took you into my confidence."

"Well...."

"When I received a letter from Colonel Robinson, commander of the Loyal Americans, and drafted a reply, I showed it to you. You said you thought the letter's tone entirely too friendly, and urged me to revise it, which I did. Is that not so?"

"Yes, it is."

"Yet, you complained here that I no longer took your advice." Arnold had not asked a question, for which Varick was grateful. He would not have known how to answer one.

"I have nothing further for this witness," Arnold announced. He turned toward Joshua, with a "see-I-told-you-so" smile of satisfaction. Joshua nodded in acknowledgment. Rather than doing harm to himself, Arnold had succeeded in damaging Varick's testimony. Once again, he had proved Joshua Thorne's advice to be wrong.

Edwards then called Major David Franks, Arnold's senior aide. Joshua knew little about Franks, only that he was the son of a rich merchant, whose ties to the governor of Quebec made the son suspect among some officers of the headquarters. The fact that Franks had at first served Arnold without pay led the most suspicious of them to speculate that the family was playing safe by having connections on both sides of the fence. Yet there had never been any hint of impropriety in any of Franks' actions, and when Arnold became military commander of Philadelphia, he was able to secure him a major's commission in the Continental Army.

Edwards took Franks through the same questions he had asked Varick. Franks corroborated the details of the misuse of rations. He claimed, however, that the dislike and suspicion of Joshua Hett Smith originated with Varick, who took every opportunity to malign or provoke Smith. Arnold, satisfied with his rebuttal of Varick's testimony, declined to question him. Franks first appeared surprised by this decision, then crestfallen that his former chief did not consider him worth cross-examining.

As yet there had been no reply from General Clinton regarding André testifying. Edwards had reached the apex of his case, and lacking André, he was about to call his most crucial witness. He no longer felt the total optimism with which he had embraced his assignment. Arnold had been unexpectedly successful in cross-examining prosecution witnesses, and Edwards had no reason to hope he would be less successful with this one. Joshua Hett Smith was either a co-conspirator with Arnold or a gullible dupe. Whichever he was, his first-hand participation in the affair made him a strong witness. But not strong enough, Edwards feared.

*He needed André.*

# CHAPTER TWENTY-SEVEN

"I CALL JOSHUA Hett Smith," Edwards announced.

There was a stir on the court as two military guards entered the room, escorting a man in civilian clothes. Under any other circumstances, Joshua Smith would have appeared to be what he was, a rural lawyer, successful in his small arena, and with some influence in his community. He resided in a fine stone home, known locally as Belmont, where he had entertained such prominent figures as Washington, Howe, Lafayette, and other high-ranking officers of the Continental Army. Now, however, after more than a week in close arrest, and under suspicion of being Arnold's accomplice in treason, he was a different man. The confident and easy manner he normally exhibited in such company was completely gone, fallen before the realization that he himself would soon face a similar trial, in which his life would be at stake.

After the witness was seated, Edwards established that Smith knew Arnold, and in fact, had a close relationship with him, which he was asked to describe. "I first met General Arnold sometime in the latter part of July last. I believe I had been favorably rec-ommended to him by General Howe." Smith glanced nervously at Howe before continuing. "General Arnold was interested in organizing his own sources for obtaining intelligence informa-tion, and asked me if I could assist him by providing names of agents he could trust. I informed him that I was happy to render him every aid in my power, and I feel that I soon established the same relationship with him as I had previously with General Howe."

"And what was that?"

"A confidential agent, primarily in procuring information of intelligence value. But I also started to enjoy a social relationship with the general. On her way to join her husband at West Point, Mrs. Arnold and her young child stopped at my home, where the general joined us for dinner and to spend the night. My wife and I also dined with the Arnolds at Robinson's House."

"Mr. Smith, please describe the events that you engaged in with General Arnold between Wednesday, the 20th of September and Saturday, the 23rd of September last."

Smith cleared his throat before proceeding. "Those events properly began on Sunday, the 17th, at Robinson's House. While we were at dinner, General Arnold received a letter from Colonel Beverly Robinson, requesting a meeting to discuss the possible return of some of his property. However, later on, after the other guests had left, the general took me aside, and in strict confidence informed me that Colonel Robinson's letter actually dealt with his desire to return his allegiance to the American cause, if he could secure the return of his lands and other property. He claimed he would be able to furnish information that would be of great value if his offer was accepted. General Arnold asked me if I would be willing to assist him in securing this result, and of course, I agreed. It appeared to me that I would be performing an important service to the nation. He then informed me that he intended to have a secret meeting with Colonel Robinson on Wednesday, the 20th, and asked that it take place at my house, to which I also agreed."

Smith paused to pour a glass of water. It was obvious that he was preparing his own case, using his appearance before this court as a rehearsal for his own. He had started out speaking in a nervous and hesitant manner, but as he went along, his confidence improved and his voice became more authoritative.

"Accordingly, the next morning I brought my family to visit friends at Fishkill, so that the house would be empty. I returned on

Wednesday by way of Robinson's House, where the general informed me that he wanted me to go by boat to a British warship anchored in Haverstraw Bay, and bring Colonel Robinson from the ship to my home for the meeting. He gave me a pass that would permit me to bring a Mr. John Anderson to my home. At the time, I assumed this was a cover name for Colonel Robinson."

Edwards then showed a document to Arnold, who scanned it briefly and nodded. He then showed the paper to Smith. "Is this that pass?"

> Headuarters Robinsons House,
> Sept. 20th 1780
>
> Permission is granted to Joshua Smith, Esquire,
> a Gentleman Mr. John Anderson, who is with him, and
> his two servants to pass and repass the Guards near
> King's Ferry at all times.
>
> B Arnold   MGenl

"Yes, it is."

"How did it come into my possession?"

"I surrendered it, along with other documents given to me by General Arnold, when I was being questioned regarding this matter."

Edwards then showed the document to Arnold, who, to Joshua's surprise, did not object to its introduction into evidence. He then turned once more to Smith.

"Sir, please continue with your testimony."

"General Arnold also gave me a requisition to draw a small boat from the quartermaster at Stony Point," Smith went on. 'I then rode south to King's Ferry, where I crossed to Stony Point, and presented my requisition to Major Kiers. The major informed me that there was no boat available, and he could do nothing for me. Thereupon I continued on to my house, where I sent a messenger to General Arnold, informing him of my lack of success in obtaining a boat.

Assuming that the general would have more success than I had, I then went about arranging for oarsmen for the boat, which the general had also directed I provide."

"Allow me to interrupt for a moment," Edwards said. "All this took place on the 20$^{th}$, the same day the meeting was to occur?"

"If I had been given a boat, I was to bring Colonel Robinson from the ship to my house that night. I assumed the meeting would take place the following morning."

"Was the fact that this was to be done at night due to the delay in securing the boat, or was that the original plan?"

"That was the original plan. General Arnold explained that the matter was highly secret, and must be accomplished under cover of dark to minimize detection by anyone, even our own patrols."

"But you left General Arnold still at Robinson's House. When would he arrive at yours?"

"It was my understanding that Colonel Robinson would spend the night at my house, and that General Arnold would arrive first thing in the morning."

Edwards nodded. "What happened then?"

"General Arnold arrived at my house some time after noon the following day. He also had no success securing a boat, and had sent his barge upriver to find one. It wasn't until early evening that a boat finally arrived. The only persons available as oarsmen were two of my tenant farmers, the Colquhoun brothers. I had approached them the previous day, but they had refused, claiming they were too tired from their daily farm labors to perform additional work at night. I thought it best to leave the matter for General Arnold to handle. At first he had no more success than I did, and only after many appeals to their patriotism, inducements such as whiskey and a large sack of flour, and finally the threat of arrest if they failed to help their country, did they reluctantly agree.

"Because the situation had changed, and we were a day behind plan, General Arnold accompanied me to the boat landing, and said he would have the meeting there, so that Robinson could return to his ship as soon as they had concluded the matter. The general then gave me a pass allowing myself and three men to be on the river should I be stopped by one of our own river patrols going or coming from the *Vulture*, and an open letter for Colonel Robinson."

Edwards gave Smith a document to read.

Headquarters Robinsons
House Sept. 21ˢᵗ. 1780

Permission is granted to Joshua
Smith Esqr to go to Dobb's ferry with three
Men and a Boy in a Boat with a Flag
To carry some Letters of a Private Nature
For Gentlemen in New York and to
Return immediately

B Arnold  MGenl

NB  He has permission
To go at such hours & times
As the tides & his business
Suites      B A

"Is this that pass?" Again, Arnold made no objection to the document.

"It is."

"Since the letter for Colonel Robinson was an open letter, I assume you knew what it contained?"

"I did. It introduced me to Colonel Robinson and stated that I would conduct him to a place of safety. General Arnold also gave me verbal instructions that I was to bring Robinson or Anderson ashore. He explained that Anderson was a New York businessman who was acting as an agent for Robinson. It was only then that I realized Robinson and Anderson were two different persons.

"It must have been close to midnight when we finally approached the *Vulture*, where we were met with surly words and deep suspicion by the officer of the deck. But after presenting the papers General Arnold had given me, I was taken below. In the captain's cabin I found Colonel Robinson, dressed in his Loyalist regimental green-and-red uniform, who greeted me and introduced me to the ship's captain, who was ill and lying in his berth. The colonel then excused himself to get Mr. Anderson, and soon returned and introduced me to him. They had apparently decided that Mr. Anderson would be the one to go ashore, and the colonel would remain behind."

"Didn't you find that unusual?"

"Not really. General Arnold had already prepared me for that possibility, and Colonel Robinson was well-known in the district, and might easily be recognized. Also, I had shown the colonel the pass I had received from General Arnold the previous day, for myself and Mr. Anderson. Colonel Robinson explained that since only Anderson was mentioned in the pass, it was best that he, Robinson, stay behind. As we shoved off, Robinson noted that we had only two oarsmen and offered us a tow part way ashore. I declined, fearing that it would be difficult to explain should we encounter any of our own river patrols.

"When we reached the landing, I climbed the embankment and found General Arnold waiting in a copse of fir trees. He asked that I bring Anderson to him, but when I had done so, he dismissed me, directing that I wait back at the boat. I must admit I was deeply disappointed. From my position with the general, my rank in life, and the trouble I had taken to effect the meeting, I had expected to attend the conference." For a moment, Smith fell silent, and it was obvious that the slight still rankled.

"I remained at the boat for several hours," he continued, "and when it started to grow light I felt it necessary to go back up the embankment and warn the general of the approaching dawn. A short time later, he and Anderson came down to the boat, and he asked me to return Anderson to the *Vulture*. I told him this was impractical, due to the distance involved and the fatigue of the oarsmen. I reminded him of his own desire that the operation be conducted under cover of dark, and that it would be light before we could reach the ship.

He then asked the Colquhouns, who declared themselves unable to do so through want of strength and the ebb tide being against them. The general then determined that it would be best if Anderson spent the day at my home, and returned to the *Vulture* that night under cover of dark. The general and Anderson then rode off, and the Colquhouns and I pulled the boat around Grassy Point and into the creek, when we heard cannon fire from the river. I knew what was happening. The previous day, before crossing at King's Ferry, I had stopped for a brief visit with my cousin, Colonel James Livingston, the commander of Fort Lafayette. He informed me at that time that he had obtained some artillery ammunition from Colonel Lamb at West Point, and intended to open fire on the *Vulture* the following morning."

This statement caused a stir in the courtroom, and Edwards interrupted the witness. "Sir, if you knew of this in advance, why did you not warn General Arnold?"

Smith only paused briefly before replying. "It did seem strange to me at first, but I was aware that this was secret business, and I might not have been taken into the general's full confidence. Further, it seemed inconceivable to me that General Arnold, the commander of the entire Highlands Department, would not be aware of such a significant event. I could only assume it was part of his plan."

It was clear that the members of the court were not satisfied with this response, and wanted to question Smith further, but procedure required that they defer any questions they had until the testimony of the witness and cross examination were complete.

"We beached the boat at Crom Island," Smith continued, "and I headed immediately for my house. When I arrived, the cannonade was still going on and both the general and Anderson were watching from the window. Anderson seemed particularly upset, pacing back and forth and exhibiting extreme nervousness. We could see that wind and tide were against the ship, but she eventually returned fire, and then her small boats put out and towed her out of range. I could see that this changed everything. It was now very doubtful that Anderson would be able to return to the *Vulture* that night, if at all. Also, now that I was able to get a good look at him in the light, I could see that Anderson was wearing a British uniform. When I mentioned this to General Arnold, he told me that Anderson had borrowed the coat from an officer in New York." Again, this statement drew a stir in court, but again, the questions would have to wait. Smith resumed his account.

"Now that his business was finished, General Arnold was anxious to return to his headquarters. He took me aside to discuss Anderson's return to New York. We both agreed that return by the river was now too dangerous."

Arnold suddenly straightened from his usual slouch, leaned forward and stared hard at Smith, something akin to both surprise and anger registering in his expression.

"However," Smith continued, not meeting Arnold's gaze, "because Mr. Anderson insisted on returning to the *Vulture*, the general gave me a pass to proceed with a boat and three men to Dobb's Ferry. But he also gave me two other passes, one authorizing me to pass the guards to White Plains, and one authorizing the same for Anderson. After—"

"That's a damned lie!" Arnold shouted, struggling to his feet.

Greene slammed down his gavel. "General Arnold, you are out of—"

"It's a damned lie and you know it!" Arnold's face was flushed with fury. Struggling with his leg, he appeared to be trying to get around the table and attack Smith.

"*Sit down, sir!*" Greene demanded, his voice as loud as Arnold's had been. "You are out of order!" It was only when Joshua rose and took him politely but firmly by the arm that Arnold returned reluctantly to his seat. "You will have an opportunity to confront the witness," Greene told him. "In the meantime, you will not interrupt his testimony."

Edwards handed Smith two documents. Appearing shocked and somewhat cowed, he identified them as two of the passes in question. "I would remind the court," Edwards said, "that the third pass, the one for John Anderson, was previously introduced as one of the documents taken from Major André." He attempted to show the documents to Arnold, who waved them away angrily.

"They are forgeries, damned forgeries."

Greene turned icily to Arnold. "Sir, if you interrupt these proceedings again, I will have you removed from court, and your defense will be conducted by Major Thorne." The threat worked. Arnold slouched back in his seat, glowering, but silent. Edwards then directed Smith to proceed with his testimony.

Smith cast a wary glance in Arnold's direction and then quickly looked away. "After giving me the passes, General Arnold said he would leave it to Anderson and I which to use, but it was clear to me that he expected us to use the land route. He then left."

"And what time was that?"

"Somewhere between nine and ten o'clock in the morning. Since we had all agreed that any movement by day would be too dangerous, whichever route we took, we would not start out until dark. It had also been decided that Anderson could not travel in a British uniform, and he would have to forego his scarlet regimental coat."

"You mean that Anderson willingly changed from his uniform to civilian clothes?"

"I must admit it was with much reluctance, and only after I insisted that we proceed by land. I pointed out that the river route was now impossible, in that we no longer had a boat or boatmen to row one. He was very upset with this information, refusing to believe that an officer in General Arnold's position couldn't arrange for something as simple as a small boat. He kept insisting that it had been settled that the way he came was also the way he was to return. I felt it useless to explain the difficulties we had obtaining the boat and then getting the Colquhoun brothers to serve as oarsmen, and Anderson spent a very disconsolate day at my house. He kept gazing out from the bedroom window toward the Tappan Zee, voicing his desire to be aboard the *Vulture*. In the absence of the general, I knew there was nothing I could do to induce the Colquhouns to make another trip. I tried to point out to him that because of the cannonade, the river would be alive with guard boats that might fire upon any vessel moving at night, before we could show our passes."

Joshua noted that Arnold was listening to Smith's account attentively, as if hearing it for the first time.

"As soon as darkness fell, we were on our way," Smith continued. "We passed over the ferry and through Peekskill without incident, and about four miles east of the town we were stopped by a patrol of Westchester militia. A captain Boyd examined our passes and warned me that bandits and raiders from both sides frequented the roads at night below the Croton River. He advised us to seek shelter for the night, rather than ride on. Although Anderson wanted to press on, I thought it best to accept the captain's suggestion, and we repaired to a nearby house he had recommended. We were off at first light the next morning. After being stopped at Crompond Corners and required to show our passes again, we halted for breakfast, after which I parted company with Anderson, just north of Pine's Bridge. I then returned to Robinson's House, where I reported to General Arnold. He seemed well pleased and invited me to stay for lunch. Afterward, I rode on to Fishkill, where I rejoined my family at the Hay home."

Smith then slumped back in his chair, seemingly relieved that his narration was over. The court stirred, and several members conferred in whispers. But Smith was not quite finished.

"The following day General Washington and his staff arrived in town, and I had the honor to be invited to join them for dinner. On Monday morning Washington and his staff left, and I spent the day on visitations and errands, retiring early. Late that night, or perhaps it was the early morning hours of Tuesday, my wife and I were rudely awakened in my bedchamber by soldiers with muskets and fixed bayonets. The officer in charge informed me that he had an order from the commander in chief for my arrest, and I have been in that state since that time. It was only later that day that I learned that General Arnold had gone over to the enemy."

"Squire Smith," Edwards reminded him, "General Arnold has been *charged* with treason; he has not been convicted of it. I have no more questions for you, sir." Edwards knew that Smith was awaiting a trial of his own, and felt anything further Smith had to say would best be reserved for that occasion. Besides, he still faced cross examination by Arnold and questions from the court.

Joshua then rose and addressed the court. "Sir, I request a short recess to confer with the accused." Greene granted thirty minutes, and Arnold and Joshua moved to the small room.

"That damned liar!" Arnold fumed. "What in God's name is he up to?"

"You did not write those last three passes?" Joshua asked.

"Of course not. They are false, just like the one taken from André." He slapped the side of his good leg with his hand in a gesture of irritation. "I had no idea Smith was part of the plot. I took him to be an ambitious, vain man, who would seek any means to enhance his own importance. But I did not expect such a depth of duplicity." He began slapping his leg again.

"Yet, it seems in character with the general suspicion of him as someone who played both sides. You know that he faces charges as a co-conspirator in this matter?"

"Yes, and I'm glad that he will now get what he deserves. We now have two of the plotters in our hands. We must find a way to make them tell what they know."

"I don't see how. We have no Star Chamber here."

"No, but at least I can cross examine Smith. By God, I'm going to tear him apart."

"Sir, you are overwrought. Wouldn't it be better if I questioned him?"

"No, you do not have the necessary information. I must do it."

Joshua nodded. He realized that Arnold was better qualified to deal with Smith than he would be. "May I only suggest, sir, that you conduct your examination with restraint and without inflammatory remarks, which will prejudice the court?" Arnold grunted in reply and they returned to the court room.

"Squire Smith," Arnold began, his voice under control, "you have stated that I sought your assistance in a matter that would produce information that would be of great value to our cause, is that correct?"

"It is, sir." It was clear that Smith now viewed his former commander with a mixture of suspicion and confusion, seasoned with a streak of fear. His eyes fixed on Arnold as he spoke.

"Will you please repeat what I told you regarding this matter?"

"You told me that Colonel Robinson was interested in returning his allegiance to the American cause if he could be pardoned and regain his property. In exchange, he was willing to provide information of great intelligence value."

"And what did I tell you about John Anderson?"

"You informed me that he was a New York merchant who was volunteering his services to Colonel Robinson as an intermediary, and that he was authorized to act in his stead."

"Now I want you to think carefully. The night that you brought John Anderson ashore, once I saw him, how did I react?"

Smith did not answer at once. "It looked as though you were disappointed," he said finally. "I thought perhaps you hoped Colonel Robinson would come ashore."

Arnold nodded. "Indeed I did. Now, did I ever say, or act as though, or did it ever occur to you independently, that rather than negotiating for Colonel Robinson's return, I was actually engaged in a secret conspiracy to surrender West Point to the enemy?" Joshua knew what the answer would be. Smith would have to protect Arnold in order to protect himself.

"Absolutely not." Smith stated firmly. "No such possibility occurred to me."

"You identified five passes here, which you stated I gave you. The first one, issued on September 20th I acknowledge. The second, issued on September 21st, I also acknowledge. Then you identified three passes, all issued on September 22nd, stating I gave them to you. Tell me, where did you really get them?"

Smith acted bewildered. "From you, sir."

"No, sir, you did not. There was no need for me to do so. The pass of the 20th allowed you and John Anderson to pass and *repass* the guards near King's Ferry *at all times*, and the pass of the 21st allows you, three men and a boy in a boat to go to Dobb's Ferry *at such hours and times as the tides and your business suits*. Both passes were still in effect. Why should you need others?

"We discussed the danger involved in going back to the ship and decided a land route would be better. Don't you remember?"

"I remember no such thing, and neither do you. There was never any intention on my part that John Anderson would go anywhere except directly back to the ship. Any *other* course would have been the dangerous one. Now, about those three passes, one of them allows you to pass the guards to White Plains, the other allows John Anderson to do the same thing. You claim I gave them to you because *we* decided that return to the *Vulture* would be too dangerous, is that correct?"

"Yes, sir."

"Then why would I give you the third pass, which allows you to be on the river with a boat and three hands, which would have allowed you to return to the ship?"

Smith was sweating now. "Well...er...In case—"

"In case? In case what?" Arnold's voice had risen considerably. "You said the issue had been *decided*. In case anything unusual came up, you already had two passes from me, either one of which would have allowed you and Anderson to return to the ship. Why would you need a third? I'll tell you why, because all three passes are forgeries, given to you to cover any eventualities which might come up in your scheme. When you met Anderson on board the *Vulture*, it was not for the first time, was it?"

Smith's eyes grew wide. "Of...of course it was."

"Then why were you not more concerned when you saw that he was in a British uniform?"

"But I was concerned, I—"

"You told us how unhappy he was when you learned from you that he was not to return to the ship. He expected to return to it. I expected him to return to it. Why did you insist he go by land?

Was it because you were furthering some plan of your own, one that neither Anderson nor I were aware of?"

Arnold's rapid-fire questions and accusations were having a disorienting affect on Smith. He was having difficulty deciding which to answer. "Plan of my own? I was following only one plan—yours."

"Then why did you disobey my instructions, and have Anderson go by land? When you reported to me later at Robinson's House, did you tell me that you had changed the plan?"

"There was no need—"

"Did you tell me that you had taken Anderson by land?" Arnold demanded.

Smith shook his head and tried to think. "As near...as near as I can remember, I told you that Anderson was safely on his way. You appeared satisf—"

"Why did you deliberately avoid telling me that you took Anderson by land?"

"General Arnold." It was Greene who spoke. "You are badgering the witness. You are asking him questions and not permitting him to answer. Please moderate your examination."

"That will not be necessary, sir," Arnold replied, staring contemptuously at Smith. "I am through with this...this...witness."

But Smith's ordeal was not over. Crusty John Stark, the victor of Bennington, who had once fought with Roger's Rangers, was the first court member to question Smith.

"You stated that you were under the impression that you were performing an important service for your country when you boarded the *Vulture* and brought John Anderson ashore."

"Yes, sir."

"Didn't it occur to you that the deck of a British warship was a strange place to be performing such a service?"

"When General Arnold explained about Colonel Robinson's desire, it didn't seem unreasonable that he might come upriver on a British ship. Besides that, we were operating under a flag of truce."

"A flag of truce? In the middle of the night? Flags do not operate at night, sir." Smith seemed taken aback by the news. "Furthermore, your pass authorized you to go to Dobb's Ferry with some letters and return immediately. Nowhere does it permit you to board a British ship of war and bring someone ashore."

"General Arnold explained that to protect Colonel Robinson's security, boarding the *Vulture* had to be done in utmost secrecy. That was the reason for doing so at night. The pass and the flag were to authorize us to be on the river, with passengers. I was unaware that the flag would not be valid at night."

"And if you were stopped by the river patrol?"

"We would say we were going or returning from Dobb's Ferry, as the case might be. We would not mention the *Vulture*."

"Then you're saying that General Arnold gave you a false pass, you knew it to be false, yet you operated under it."

Smith wiped at the sweat formed on his brow. "Sir, I would not call it a false pass. In undercover intelligence operations, unusual methods must sometimes be used."

Stark did not pursue the matter further, but he was obviously not satisfied. Jedediah Huntington then took over.

"When you were on board the *Vulture*, couldn't you tell that Anderson was in a British uniform?"

"No, sir. The gentleman wore a blue surtout which covered his upper body, and his nankeen breeches could serve either a military or a civilian purpose."

"But when you saw him in daylight in your home, there is no doubt that he was in such a uniform?"

"That is correct, sir."

"And you said that when you questioned General Arnold about this, he stated that Anderson had borrowed the coat from an officer in New York?"

"Yes, sir."

"Can you honestly claim that this seemed logical to you, that a British officer would lend his uniform coat to a civilian? What would he do then, go around half dressed?"

"Sir, it may have..." Smith was obviously becoming even more nervous, "...it may have seemed strange, but I had no reason to suspect General Arnold of anything nefarious. I thought perhaps there were portions of the operation he wished to keep secret from me, for good reasons of his own."

"So you admit that you believed that Anderson was a British officer, and you aided him to return to his own lines, yet you claim you were performing an important service for your country?"

"I...I believed it *possible* that he was a British officer, but I also believed that, even if he were, he could be part of the plan, and was assisting Colonel Robinson. After all, Robinson is also a British officer, and, according to General Arnold, he was trying to come over to us. Stranger things have happened in undercover intelligence, I assure you. And I swear before God to all you gentlemen that my sole purpose for involvement in any of this was that I thought I was assisting General Arnold in a matter of great importance to my country."

Joshua could see that other members of the court were debating whether to ask Smith questions. For his own part, he was not sure if Smith's turbulent cross examination had helped Arnold or damaged him. And Stark and Huntington had raised serious doubts about Smith's testimony. On balance, he felt that overall, it had been a plus for Arnold. How the court felt about it, however, might be a different matter.

In the end, no other court member decided to question Smith, and Greene excused him and adjourned the court until the following day. Although that was Sunday, there would be no observance of a day of rest until Arnold's trial was concluded. After the members of the court had cleared the room, the guards escorted Arnold out. As they were leaving the church, Edwards and Joshua met at the door.

"It seems as though your general is in good spirits," Edwards remarked.

"He's happy to be reunited with his family, and I think he's pleased with the way things went today."

"Is he? Well, let's see if he's as pleased the way things go tomorrow."

# CHAPTER TWENTY-EIGHT  ·

THE RAIN WAS beginning to slacken when Ebenezer Thatcher led his tired regiment into Tappan late that afternoon. It did not take long to discover that his commander, Anthony Wayne, had gone looking for General Washington, and it would be up to "Old Eb" to find a place to bivouac the troops. Although the main body of Wayne's brigade remained in the vicinity of West Point, it was his policy to have a reserve force under his control at all times. Thatcher's men had been designated to follow the brigade commander to Tappan. Outdistanced by their general, who had galloped ahead, they nevertheless had made good time, and were now eager to cook supper and bed down for the night. But tired or not, Thatcher was not about to straggle into the headquarters camp. Passing the order to bring the troops to shoulder arms, he instructed his six-man fife and drum corps to strike up a march. As the music sounded, the unit fell in step, shoulders squared and backs straightened—real soldiers, determined to impress these headquarters dandies. They swung almost jauntily into town to the tune of *Yankee Doodle*.

Had they been given time to converse, the marching men might have learned from the "headquarters dandies" that they were fortunate that General Washington was absent. It was well known at the headquarters that Washington disliked *Yankee Doodle*. Several reasons were advanced for this, one being that it had been used by the British to make fun of colonial troops ever since the French and Indian War, and even more so in the early days of the current struggle. The fact that American soldiers liked the tune and even the words, and quickly turned it from ridicule into their own rallying anthem, did not seem to extend to the commander in chief.

Another reason proffered was that, early in the war, during Washington's retreat from New York, British troops in pursuit had harried him by having bugles play over and over the first few bars of *Yankee Doodle* whenever they thought he was in earshot. But the most commonly accepted theory was that Washington was affronted by some of the verses of the song, at least two of which were unflattering to him personally. It did not help that they were American, not British, in origin. They both referred to Washington's well-known concern for the dignity of his office.

> *And there was Captain Washington*
> *And gentle folks about him*
> *They say he's grown so 'tarnal proud*
> *He will not ride without them*

Another verse, sung in lieu of the first, was also in the same vein.

> *There came Gen'ral Washington*
> *Upon a snow-white charger*
> *He looked as big as all outdoors*
> *And thought that he was larger*

These verses were rarely sung maliciously, and did not diminish the true affection felt for Washington by most of his officers and men. But no one was foolhardy enough to sing them in his presence.

Ebenezer Thatcher was one of the oldest colonels in the Continental Army, and one of the longest serving. A veteran of the French and Indian War, he had been with Braddock's army, along with George Washington, when it suffered its disastrous defeat near Fort Pitt. When the war ended, he had remained active in the Pennsylvania militia, and, at the outbreak of hostilities in 1775, he led his regiment into the Continental Army.

Checking in with General Greene, and learning that two regiments were located south and east of the town, Thatcher chose to place his men to the west, where a flat, harvested field bordered a wooded copse. He positioned his companies in depth along the edge of the woods, where they would have good fields of fire across the field. Although no threat was expected from this quarter, Thatcher had seen enough of surprise and ambush in his time, and he always settled his regiment in a defensive posture, with pickets well out and guards posted. And no member of Anthony Wayne's brigade would ever forget the "Paoli Massacre," when a British force, approaching silently at night and using only the bayonet, caught Wayne's men by surprise, killing more than 150, and sending the rest reeling in panic-stricken flight.

Moving among his men, who had begun preparing light defense positions, Thatcher eyed the woods on the other side of the field to their front. The trees were about 300 yards away, there would be a moon, and sentries on this side would quickly pick up any movement across the field. Sending pickets to those woods was probably unnecessary, and the men were tired. Yet, they needed to accept that even in a rear area situation, security was never taken for granted. Paoli had taught them that. He called for his regimental sergeant and two picket teams were soon sent grumbling on the way to the distant woods.

As his men divided the chores of cooking, Thatcher weighed whether to go into town for a meal at the headquarters mess. It had been a long day, he was off his horse, and his aging joints made him reluctant to remount. On the march, one of his companies had purchased two hogs, fortunately finding a rare farmer willing to accept the military scrip which promised payment at some future date. The smell of pork roasting on a spit just about made up his mind, and the generous amount of rum remaining in his flask—imported Barbados, not the stuff made in Boston—confirmed it. He would bed down tonight with his boys.

# CHAPTER TWENTY-NINE

THAT EVENING, JOSHUA Thorne invited John Lamb to an early dinner, repaying the colonel's hospitality during his visit to West Point. He invited him to Mabie's, hoping that by bringing a guest along, Amy would more likely be civil after their argument last night, and he might have a chance to make things up. But upon arrival Amy informed him coldly that she was taking advantage of the reduced patronage due to André's presence to tend to much needed cleaning and repair. She intended to close the bar and the kitchen early, warning them that the only food she could offer was an overdone beef joint the cook had prepared before leaving, served with boiled, unseasoned sweet potatoes.

"I've had worse," Lamb announced, obviously taken with Amy, and clearly preferring her presence to the dour servants at the headquarters mess. Amy served them the unappetizing plate then excused herself to her cleaning work. But she returned after they had finished the meal, to remove the plates and bring more wine. The choice was again Madeira, as Joshua had been offered by Lamb at West Point. But here, it was not only because of the expense and scarcity of port. General Washington's favorite wine was Madeira.

"I was telling Colonel Lamb that after the war I'm thinking of going west," Joshua told Amy, as she filled their glasses. He was hoping to engage her in friendly conversation."Do some lawyering and make Indian corn whiskey. I believe there's going to be good money in it."

"I told him he should take a fine, sturdy woman with him," Lamb said.

"What do you think of such a plan, Mistress Martin?" Joshua asked.

"The taste of the country seems to be for rum," Amy replied, not looking at him.

"Rum's too sweet for my taste, and for many others as well" Joshua said.

"Madeira's sweet," she answered, pouring the wine, "yet you manage to force it down."

"Yes, but I usually only drink it after dinner." His attempt to soften her feelings toward him was not working.

"Usually?"

"Come now, Mistress Martin, you know my taste runs to beer."

"Only because three-penny beer is cheaper than six-penny rum or eight-penny whiskey. Of course, when you don't pay at all, it's even cheaper."

Lamb grinned, enjoying the repartee between them. If Major Thorne wanted to pretend a more formal, if playful, acquaintance with the charming Mistress Martin, it was fine with him. But he knew what was going on here.

"But I will be making that very eight-penny whiskey," Joshua countered.

"That doesn't impress me."

"Why not? Indian corn is domestically grown. After the war, win or lose, Americans won't want to be at the mercy of the customs service or the British Navy by importing molasses to make rum. Corn whiskey will become the drink of our nation."

"You would starve."

"Starve? There will be a huge market for it here in all the colonies. How could I starve?"

"You'd drink up all the profits."

Both men laughed. "Not if I had someone to brew beer as well as you do," Joshua replied.

"There are many women who can brew good beer. As to finding

one who would accompany you, that would be another matter." She moved across the table to pour Lamb more wine. "I need to get started in the kitchen. There's more wine in the cupboard. Leave the empty bottles on the bar, so I'll know how much to charge you, not that I expect to see any ready money any time soon."

Trying to cover the minor embarrassment caused by Amy's attitude, Joshua turned to Lamb. "Well, what do you think of my plan?"

"I think anything you undertook with Mistress Martin at your side would be bound to succeed. Don't let her get away." They talked through several bottles of wine, mostly about the war and its currently bleak outlook. But the conversation kept coming back to Arnold and the trial. Lamb asked if Joshua had done anything about his warning about Peggy Arnold. Joshua explained that Washington had refused to allow them to examine her correspondence, and for chivalric reasons, would not allow her involvement in the trial. He then switched the subject from Peggy.

"I noticed that when Edwards asked you if you thought General Arnold deliberately weakened the fortress by not requesting more artillery, you didn't answer him." Joshua knew he had to take care not to violate court procedure in discussing the trial with Lamb. However, the colonel had already testified, and was not likely to be recalled.

Lamb took a pipe from his pocket and stuffed it with tobacco. He did not reply until it was lit, the smoke swirling from the bowl.

"Let's say that a commander plans to surrender a fortress to the enemy, for money or other advantage. If he increases the size of the garrison and the amount of stores, he increases its value to the enemy, who gains more prisoners and supplies. And, if he's short of artillery, there's less chance of the garrison defending itself."

It was a sobering comment, and it worried Joshua. "Do you think the court drew the same conclusion?"

"I gave 'em the information. I wasn't going to lay it out on a plate."

"Do you believe that's what happened?"

Lamb puffed hard on his pipe. "It's just speculation, and has no merit by itself without other evidence. Right now, I don't believe it, and don't want to believe it. But I'll tell you this. If he is guilty of this—I say *if*—they should cut off his wounded leg and bury it with honors at Saratoga. The rest of him should swing from a gibbet at the end of a slow rope."

The grim remark signaled the end of the evening. After seeing Lamb to his guest quarters, Joshua returned to Mabie's, hoping to find Amy still working. To his disappointment, she was asleep on the narrow cot in the storeroom. He thought about waking her, but finally decided against it. Better to wait until tomorrow night, when he would have no wine on his breath and a clearer head. He left in a hopeful mood, convincing himself that they had parted on reasonably good terms. Tomorrow he would make amends.

# CHAPTER THIRTY

*Tappan, New York*
*Sunday, October 8, 1780*

*4:05 A.M.*
THE RAIN HAD stopped, but the trees still dripped on the thirty-six men slipping silently through the woods. By direction of their commander, Captain Caleb Fowler, they proceeded Indian file, their moccasin-encased feet making no noise on the forest floor. With uniforms stripped of all accouterments that might produce a warning sound, and faces blackened, each man carried a tomahawk, a long knife, and a pistol. In addition, every second man brandished a musket, bayonet fixed. Six men carried rifles strapped firmly to their backs. All the firearms were unloaded, again upon the order of Captain Fowler. He would have no gunfire give away his presence, relying upon stealth to reach his objective. Once they had secured the house and taken charge of André, they would load their weapons and prepare to defend the position until the arrival of the dragoons.

Leading the single file of Rangers were two scouts, separated from their followers by about fifty paces. Twice they had come upon pickets, and twice they had approached them Indian-style, killing them silently with a quick stab of a knife. Emerging from the forest, the scouts saw what appeared to be the enemy lines. Signaling their comrades to take cover, and reinforced by two more men, they continued forward, crawling on their stomachs. Half an hour later they returned, five scalps dangling from their belts. Quickly and silently, the main body followed them safely through the American lines and into the outskirts of the town. Fowler now took over the lead, stopping once to get his bearings. The rain had stopped completely, and a gibbous moon was rising in the sky, providing enough light to make out the shape of some buildings. Nearby, a dog barked, and an early-rising householder cursed it into silence.

Satisfied that he had reached the main street of the small town, Fowler proceeded toward its far end, where the house was located, his men jogging behind him, still in Indian file. Moments later the house loomed in front of them. The tents of the guard detachment were just barely visible, pitched beside the house, no sound or stirring coming from them. Again scouts crept forward, reporting back that the front door of the house was unguarded. Fowler had expected at least two sentries at the door, but now he had to assume they were inside the building. Silently, he signaled his men forward, changing formation from file to double rank. When they were within ten feet of the porch, the door suddenly opened, light spilling from the entrance. Two armed men emerged from the doorway as Fowler and his Rangers froze in place.

After closing the door, the two men assumed a relaxed but watchful position on either side of the doorway. With their eyes not yet accustomed to the dark, they were unable to see Fowler's men, but their eyes would soon adjust. Before that could happen, the Rangers rushed forward, tomahawked the two sentries, and burst into the house. Two more guards rose from a table stumbling for their weapons, but were quickly overpowered. Another pair tried to rise from makeshift beds, but quickly gave up the idea when bayonets were shoved at their throats.

"Where is Major André?" Fowler demanded. One of the guards pointed toward a door at the end of the room. Fowler knew that André would have at least one officer with him as an additional guard, and he moved quickly toward the door, finding it locked from within.

"Major André," he shouted, "I am Captain Caleb Fowler of the

Loyal American Ranger Company. We are here to rescue you sir." His answer was a pistol ball, which blasted through the door, narrowly missing his head. As he was preparing to have his men break down the door, a voice shouted from inside the room.

"It's all right, Captain. We have them. I'm opening the door." Three Rangers, under command of a sergeant, had circled to the rear of the building and broken through the window of André's room, disarming Major Tallmadge, whose pistol was now empty. As the door opened, Tallmadge and André entered the room. Tallmadge was seized by two men, who proceeded to bind his hands behind his back.

"Please, gentlemen, do him no harm," André pleaded. "He has treated me most kindly, and I consider him a friend."

Realizing that he was still alive only by the grace of a few inches, Fowler was not as well disposed toward Tallmadge. "He will be bound hand and foot and placed behind the bar with the others. If he stirs from there, he's a dead man, friend or not."

Surprised by the shot through the door, the Rangers were on their guard, nervously loading their weapons as they prepared to search the rest of the house. Just as one of them turned the corner of the kitchen, he was suddenly confronted by a figure coming toward him in the darkened room. Instinctively, he fired his pistol at his would-be assailant. With a sharp cry, Amelia Martin crumpled to the floor, blood gushing from her chest.

*5:35 A.M.*

Beverly Robinson sat astride his horse, prepared to accompany the dragoons on their dash to rescue André. Although not a cavalryman, he prided himself on his horsemanship. Of all his acquaintances, he admitted to only one better horseman than himself—the former friend of his youth, George Washington. It had been a miserable night, rain pelting down on the marching troops, turning the road into a muddy mess for both horse and foot soldier. But the rain had aided the secrecy of the movement, keeping most possible observers indoors. Now it had finally stopped, and the first fringe of twilight began to appear in the east. He hoped it was a good omen.

With command of the holding attack in the capable hands of his son, Lieutenant Colonel Beverly Robinson, Jr., Robinson felt his place was with the most critical part of his mission. By now, the Rangers would have seized the house where André was held. Had they not done so, he would have heard the sound of gunfire from that direction. It was upon the action of the dragoons that the success of the operation depended, and it was there that Robinson would be.

Although the holding attack was a simple, straight-forward operation, the success of the dragoons depended upon the rebels believing it was a full-scale attack on their headquarters. Simply firing upon the rebel positions, was not enough. His battalions had to move aggressively, maneuvering as if they were part of a much larger force. The light artillery he had allowed to accompany them would need to masquerade as heavier caliber, more numerous guns. To accomplish this, his son planned to mass all the cannon in one sector, firing full bore against a narrow front, making up in concentrated barrages what he lacked in firepower. Every possible rebel soldier had to be drawn to the front lines, denuding the rear area of its defenses. Everything depended on the dragoons having a clear path for their dash to André.

A sudden crackling of musket fire to his right front caused his horse to shy, and told him that the holding attack had begun. He checked his watch. It would be at least thirty minutes before the rebels would be fully engaged. By that time the sun would be up. He settled back in the saddle to wait.

*5:40 A.M.*

It took half a minute for the firing to register through his sleep, but when it did, Joshua sprang from his bed, reaching quickly for his uniform. His post in the event of an attack upon the headquarters was at the DeWint house, prepared to act as liaison officer between the headquarters and the units engaged. He had no horse, one was supposed to be provided when he reported, so he ran the short distance. Occasional stray bullets were already whizzing by as he reached the headquarters, where General Greene had also just arrived. Greene stood outside the building, ear cocked toward the sound of the gunfire.

"It's from the east. That's Adcock's regiment," he determined "Get over there, find out what's going on, and report back at once. My orders are to hold all positions."

"Yes, sir." Joshua started to leave, but then stopped. "Sir, I have no horse..."

"Use mine," Greene replied at once, "but see that you bring him back. That horse and I have been through much together."

Joshua thought of the stray rounds, now more concerned for the horse than himself, but he raced out the door. The noise of battle had increased, as more American soldiers came on line and began to return fire. Several men were now running toward the command post.

"The bastards are tryin' to rescue Arnold!" one of them yelled as he ran by.

More likely André, Joshua suspected. Then he froze. André! Amy was at Mabie's! After a moment of panic, he relaxed. If this was an André rescue force, it was still a long way off, and with all the noise of battle, she would by now have taken herself to a safer location.

Not knowing precisely where he could find Colonel Adcock, Joshua used one of the most familiar principles of warfare and rode to the sound of the guns. He soon found what he was looking for. He intersected a narrow lane running almost due north half a mile from the eastern end of town. Here, partly sheltered behind a low rock wall, American soldiers had constructed light breastworks and firing positions. Some were firing, others were standing at the ready, but many sat or lay behind the wall, apparently awaiting instructions. Joshua was directed northward along the road, and in a few moments found Colonel Charles Adcock's command post. The colonel, exposed as much as any of his troops, directed Joshua to shelter his horse behind a farm shed and join him, which he did.

"They came out of those woods to their rear," Adcock informed him. He pointed to several bright red lines of men, about 300 yards away, moving slowly and deliberately, from one protected feature to another. As one group moved, another fired a volley, sending musket balls into the ground in front of the stone wall or whining overhead. "I'd say they're about two companies, with more coming on. They drove in my pickets, but they don't seem to be in any hurry, which probably means they're the advance of a large force, and they're waiting until the rest come up before they attack."

Joshua passed on Greene's order to hold position. Adcock merely nodded. "Tell Greene there's no artillery yet, unless it's lurking back in the woods. And so far I've had one killed and three wounded, all by curiosity—couldn't resist stickin' their heads up." Suddenly a loud burst of musket fire broke out to the southwest, rising in crescendo in only a few seconds. "That's from Peel's sector," Adcock shouted. "You'd better get over there and find out what's going on and get the word back to Greene."

"Where do I go?" Joshua shouted back.

"Straight back on the road you came up. You'll run right into 'em."

Joshua retrieved the horse, mounted and galloped back down the road, praying that a musket ball did not strike Greene's treasured animal. The road soon made a long curve to the west and then straightened. Within minutes he found himself at another defensive position almost identical to Adcock's. Major Simon Peel had just taken command of the regiment, following the death of its colonel, who had broken his neck falling from his horse. He was anxious to show his competence. When his pickets had opened fire and started to withdraw, he sent a company to reinforce them and another forward to reconnoiter. They were all now heavily engaged, but at a good distance from his main defense line along the road. There was too much smoke forward of his position to make any accurate assessment of enemy strength, but he estimated from the sound of things that he could be facing a battalion.

Joshua remounted, and raced back toward headquarters,

thanking his stars that the horse had survived. He had no sooner returned with the reports from the two regiments when Greene sent him north—on a different mount this time—with orders to a militia regiment encamped south of Kakiat. They were to march at once to reinforce Tappan.

When Ebenezer Thatcher heard the firing to the east, he brought his men to full alert. He had them quickly man the positions they had so hastily made the night before, but he prepared to move the regiment on short notice in case he was needed to reinforce the line somewhere. When additional firing broke out to the south, he sent an officer galloping to headquarters to furnish a status report and request instructions. Gazing at the woods to his front, he thought of recalling his pickets, which would help him move more quickly. He finally decided against it; he would wait hear what his returning officer had to say.

He allowed one man in four to build a small fire and make coffee for the rest, but there would be no preparing breakfast. Shortly after the start of the war, his men had replaced British tea with coffee, and it was now firmly entrenched in the regiment as a morning drink. Last night's roast pig was good and the rum even better. But the jolt of the sudden wakening this morning had upset his stomach. He was not sure he could keep the coffee down.

*6:10 A.M.*

The shock of shooting a woman had temporarily paralyzed the Rangers who had seized Mabie's. The soldier who had done the shooting stood mute over the fallen body, stunned by his action. Major André seemed particularly distraught, kneeling down by the woman, holding her hand helplessly. Only Fowler moved quickly. He ordered the unconscious woman moved to the cot in the storeroom. There, a Ranger trained to treat wounds applied compresses to staunch the bleeding. After a time, the bleeding lessened and then ceased. Fowler determined that the woman was still breathing, but there was not much else he could do. He had no doctor with him, and he was not about to poke around on a woman's chest to determine the extent of an injury he could do nothing for. He left her with André seated by her side, to be of assistance if she revived.

He had other things on his mind.

The shot fired through the door by Tallmadge had alerted the neighborhood, and a detachment of rebels now surrounded the house. Fowler held them at bay with musket and rifle fire, but he knew it was only a temporary standoff. He had a musket at every window, backed by riflemen posted to take aimed shots at selected targets. The rest, armed to the teeth, remained inside, ready for any eventuality. There was nothing to do now except wait.

*6:30 A.M.*

Robinson glanced at his watch. The sun had been up for half an hour, and from the sound of it, the rebel regiments to the south and east were fully engaged. Too much longer and they would begin to wonder why the British did not press the attack. It was time. He turned to the dragoon commander and gave the signal to advance. Forming a column of twos, the horsemen began a brisk trot through the light woods. In less than five minutes they would reach the open field which separated them from the final patch of trees before the road leading into town.

Before they were half-way to the clearing, a shot rang out, and a ball whined through the air. Robinson reined in. Picket or patrol? Picket, he concluded. A patrol would not have been in such a hurry to fire, especially from this distance. A patrol would be seeking information, not confrontation. A picket would be there to warn of his approach, and to temporarily check it. He knew now that he would face opposition. As he resumed the advance, now at a quicker pace, another shot came from his left, and this time a rider went down. On the opposite side of the field, Ebenezer Thatcher had just received an order from Greene to reinforce Major Peel's left flank. He was getting ready to issue a march order, when he heard the shots from his pickets.

When the firing first began, Colonel John Lamb was up and out in minutes, looking for something to do. Away from his own unit, and with no troops to command, he felt frustrated and useless. His guest quarters were across from Mabie's, and he soon noticed the soldiers surrounding the house. He found a young lieutenant in charge of the troops, obviously shaken by the failure of his men to protect the prisoner, the consequences certain to fall on his head. Apprising Lamb of the situation, he vowed, "They may have gotten in, but they're not gettin' out."

Lamb saw at once that an assault on the building would be difficult and bloody. Its stone walls were impervious to small arms fire, and the Americans would pay a high price for storming it. Right now both sides were keeping a low profile, maintaining their cover and withholding fire. Advising the lieutenant to maintain the status quo, Lamb rushed off. He returned with a six-pounder and its crew he had commandeered from the reserve being held in the artillery park, promising to keep it no more than thirty minutes. He signaled to the young lieutenant, who immediately ordered concentrated fire on the open windows. Under cover of this fusillade, Lamb ran the gun into a position aimed directly at the wooden door, then directed the crew to take cover. Directing the lieutenant to cease fire, he approached the house, waving a white hand kerchief. He stopped about thirty feet from the door, and a moment later Fowler came out and stood on the porch.

"I demand your surrender," Lamb announced. "You're surrounded, and resistance is futile."

Fowler, knowing the attack of the dragoons was imminent, shook his head. "I am not able to comply with your demand. My orders do not permit it."

Lamb gestured back toward his cannon. "Surely, you realize you cannot withstand artillery fire?"

Fowler shrugged, his ears straining for some sound of approaching horsemen. "We will do our best. But you should be aware that some of your own will suffer from such action. I am holding an officer and six of your men, two of whom are wounded. There is also a woman. She was taken with the house, and she is seriously injured."

Lamb blanched as he realized the woman could only be Mistress Martin. Recovering from the shock, he was not about to back down. "Surrender, or their fate will be upon your head, not ours."

"So be it, then." Fowler turned and strode back into the house. After reporting the conversation to his men, André took him aside.

"We must turn the woman loose. She is badly hurt and needs medical attention or she may well die."

Fowler shook his head. "The woman stays here. No matter what the rebels say, I believe their actions will be tempered by the knowledge that she's inside this building."

André's countenance darkened. "Captain, we cannot hide behind the skirts of an injured woman. I order you to release her at once."

"I'm sorry, sir, but you are not in my chain of command. I am not obliged to accept any order from you. However..." He now saw a way that might appease André and at the same time gain more time for the dragoons to arrive.

After Lamb left the conference with Fowler, he began preparations for storming the house. Assuming command from the young lieutenant, who was only too glad to release it, he explained his plan. The lieutenant's men would open a steady and sustained fire on all the windows on the two sides of the inn capable of aiming weapons at his cannon. With the enemy fire suppressed, Lamb would blast down the door to the inn with an iron ball, and follow that up with chain and grapeshot, which would create havoc inside the building. As he was about to give the signal to open fire, Lieutenant Colonel Edwards came running up.

"Sir, I beg you not to do so," he said, after hearing Lamb's plan. "I...we must have André alive."

"He's a dead man anyway," Lamb replied. "What difference does it make?"

"He is the main witness against General Arnold. Without his testimony, we may not have enough evidence to....to insure a fair trial for both sides."

"I thought he refused to testify?"

"He...we're still trying to convince him to change his mind."

Before Lamb had time to solve the dilemma he now faced, Captain Fowler reappeared on the inn's porch, waving a white kerchief.

After the second shot, Robinson knew beyond doubt that he had encountered pickets. His only chance was to hope they were from a small force that he could quickly override. Reaching the edge of the clearing, at his order the dragoons moved from column to line formation. Then, in four ranks, they drew sabers and began the gallop across the muddy field. Ebenezer Thatcher, moving to the edge of the woods where his men were now on full alert, squinted through the morning haze and saw them coming. A cavalry charge, several ranks deep, slowed by the muddy conditions, but coming on strong.

"Listen up, boys!" he shouted. "Muskets, form two ranks, volley fire on my command! Rifles, aim for the horses. We're going to bring these bastards down!"

Robinson, riding in the front rank of dragoons, saw a long white cloud billow from the tree line to his front. Seconds later he went flying over his horse's head as the animal collapsed beneath him. Almost the entire front rank of dragoons fell before a hail of bullet and ball. The second rank fared little better, crashing into their downed comrades, tripping and falling over those already on the ground. Screaming horses, disemboweled or broken-legged, lay writhing on the field, churning the earth into a bloody, red-brown froth. Those riders lucky enough to survive, fought to escape the melee, sometimes dragging wounded men with them.

The third and fourth ranks, their formation broken by riding through or around the mass of dead and injured horses and men, came gallantly on, hoping to ride down the enemy before they had time to reload. But Thatcher's regiment, well trained after years of fighting, quickly moved into cavalry defense formation, closing ranks and presenting a bristling wall of bayonets to the oncoming horsemen. Riflemen, whose weapons would not mount a bayonet, either retired behind a tree to reload, or stood with the second rank of bayonets, prepared to use their rifles as clubs.

"Steady, boys, steady!" Thatcher urged, standing immediately behind his first rank. It took steadfast soldiers to withstand a cavalry charge, even a weakened one such as this, but if they followed their training and pressed their bayonets home, their numbers would prevail.

As the dragoons reached Thatcher's line, despite the desperate urging of their riders, many of the horses shied away from the close-packed bayonets. Others were impaled, falling with as many as three or four bayonet wounds in their front or flanks, their riders stabbed on the ground before they could twist free of their dying mounts. Those who broke through, sabers slashing, faced more men armed with bayonets, pistols and clubs. Hindered by the trees and unable to reform, they were eventually surrounded individually or in small groups, and either cut down or forced to surrender.

*8:40 A.M.*

Robinson regained consciousness propped against a tree, a throbbing pain in his left shoulder. He had been carried to safety by two unhorsed dragoons, who were themselves wounded, but able to walk. As his vision cleared, he saw Captain Simon Kollock, the dragoon commander, limping toward him, uniform torn, his face smeared with dirt and sweat. A bloody bandage circled one thigh and another his right forearm.

"I have sounded recall, sir," he announced, "if there's anyone left to hear it."

Robinson gazed out onto the field, where a few able-bodied men searched for wounded among the dead. Others stumbled wearily back toward the woods, several leading a string of two or three riderless horses. All this took place under the silent guns of the rebels, who made no move to fire or otherwise interfere. Robinson sighed heavily as his eyes took in the pitiful remnant of what had been a fine squadron of dragoons. He looked back over the field again, staring at the heavily defended wood line. He had encountered a full regiment where none was supposed to be, and it almost seemed as though it had been waiting for him. He wondered if he had been betrayed.

Confirming Kollock's order to retreat with a gesture, Robinson struggled to his feet. A trooper offered him a horse, but with his shoulder throbbing and stiffening, it was too painful to try to mount. If the rebels had intended to pursue, he decided, they would have already done so. They probably felt it was not worth the effort. He wrote a message to his son, explaining what had happened, ordering him to break off contact and return to Fort Lee. He could do nothing for the Rangers. He ordered what was left of the dragoons to fall in, and joining Kollock, wearily led the men from the field, a few mounted, some leading a horse, most walking, like himself.

Across the field, squinting through his glass, Ebenezer Thatcher watched them go. He had given the order not to fire upon the retreating British dragoons, many of whom were helping injured comrades off the field. He could deduce what had happened. They had apparently reconnoitered the area earlier and found this flank open. Lowering the glass, he turned to his second in command, who stood beside him.

"I wonder what their mission was. A fast strike of some kind, but what? An attempt to kill Washington? Rescue Arnold? Rescue André?" He put his glass down. "Well, whatever it was, it failed, thanks to Mad Anthony Wayne."

"Thanks to Ebenezer Thatcher," his deputy countered with conviction.

Thatcher grunted and turned away. His regiment had not gotten off unscathed. He had lost eleven men killed and thirty-six wounded—a small price compared to what the British had suffered, but painful nonetheless. He had two dozen British prisoners, some of them severely wounded. He sat down and wrote a situation report to Greene, then turned to his sergeant. But there was no need to issue an order. Breakfast fires were already burning.

*9:05 A.M.*

Back at Greene's command post, with the Ranger's seizure of Mabie's and the arrival of Thatcher's report, the purpose of the British attack became clear. Fire from the enemy was already slackening, and Greene felt they would soon withdraw. He decided not to counterattack. There might be more surprises in store. At Mabie's, Doctor Thaddeus Stewart, the headquarters surgeon, had appeared in response to Fowler's offer to permit Amy to receive medical treatment. Fowler's concession was based not on chivalry, but to buy time for the dragoons to arrive. Stewart's patient was lying on a cot, conscious, but with the gray pallor common to those approaching shock. Her eyes seemed unfocused, and she was unresponsive to his questions. The injury was severe, but not life threatening. He did what he could, cleaning and debriding the wound, covering her with warm blankets, but she needed constant care and observation to prevent her from sinking further into shock. Yielding to Stewart's and André's entreaties, Fowler gave way and allowed Amy to be released in care of the doctor. He reasoned that the dragoons would be here at any moment, if they were coming at all.

After Amy had been removed, he moved around the room, insuring that everything was in readiness for the attack he felt sure would come. He had several heavy dining tables stacked against the door, turning the others on their sides to provide protection for his men to crouch behind. He placed six men in the storeroom where Amy had been, where they would be somewhat safe from small arms and even cannon fire. They were to be used as a contingency force. He tried his best to act cheerful and confident, two emotions he did not feel. The lessening of the sound of battle outside worried him. And the dragoons should have been here by now.

John Lamb debated his options. With the situation seemingly in hand, the artillery commander was not badgering him for return of his gun, but an assault would still be costly. He thought he saw a way to end the standoff without bloodshed. He left the force at Mabie's in the control of the lieutenant, and walked to Greene's headquarters. He quickly secured Greene's approval of his plan, and sat down to wait. Before long, a forlorn group of dragoons appeared, shuffling slowly down the road, under guard. Prisoners taken by Thatcher's regiment, they hardly seemed to require guarding. Uniforms spattered with mud—and often blood, they appeared dispirited and exhausted. Singling out an officer, a captain with his arm in a makeshift sling, Lamb led him back to Mabie's. Stopping behind the shed, he handed the officer his white hand kerchief.

"As I'm sure you know, that building is being held by a detachment of British troops. They were apparently waiting for you to ride to their assistance. We want them to surrender, without bloodshed, if possible. Their situation is hopeless. I think they'll be convinced of that, if you tell them what's happened."

For a long moment the officer stared at Lamb wordlessly. Then, without comment, he took the kerchief and walked toward Mabie's. Fifteen minutes later, the kerchief appeared again, this time in Captain Fowler's hand, as he stepped out onto the porch. The attempt to rescue André was over.

Before leaving the building, Fowler ordered tables and chairs returned to their original positions, and a general restoring of order to the premises. One of his men removed the basin used by the doctor to treat the injured woman. As he emptied it into the refuse container, he saw among the pieces of clothing, clotted blood, and bits of flesh, the unmistakable shape of a woman's nipple. Dropping the basin, he vomited on the floor.

*11:00 A.M.*

Joshua Thorne returned to the headquarters, reporting that the militia from Kakiat was on its way. Although their assistance was no longer needed, Greene decided to let them come.

"Ride over to Mabie's," Greene ordered Joshua. "Tell Major Tallmadge to position a full company around the building. We'll take no more chances with Major André."

"I don't understand, sir?" Joshua was still breathing hard from the ride.

Greene realized he had sent Joshua to Kakiat before he knew

about the Rangers. "Early this morning, a British unit seized the house, attempting to rescue Major André." Before Greene could say any more, Joshua whirled his horse around. "Wait!" Greene shouted, but Joshua was already galloping away.

As he approached Mabie's, Lamb waved him down, grabbing the reins of his horse. "She's not in there. She's been taken to the church. Stewart's using it as a hospital."

Joshua grew pale. "Is she all right?"

"She's been hurt. I don't know how badly."

Joshua turned and raced back toward the church.

It was five agonizingly long minutes before the hard-pressed Doctor Stewart was able to speak to him. Then, while he probed for a ball in the leg of a British dragoon, he told him that Amy had been taken to Mary Burns' house, where she was not to be disturbed. He had given her a sleeping draught, and he wanted her to rest. He waved Joshua to a bench, saying he would talk to him as soon as he could. Twenty more minutes crawled by before Stewart was able to break for a cup of hot tea, and let him know the extent of Amy's injury.

"The pistol was fired at close range, apparently just as she was turning the corner into the hallway," he told a stunned Joshua. "There was some burning from the powder, but, fortunately, most of this was absorbed by her clothing. The ball hit her left breast at about a 45-degree angle, and went on to crease her upper left arm. They are both surface wounds, but—".

"Is she all right? "She has lost a fair amount of blood, but she's a strong young woman. Unless an infection occurs, or putrefaction sets in, she should recover physically. The challenge will be how it affects her mentally. She has lost the front portion of her breast, the nipple and the aureole area."

"When may I see her?"

"Let her rest for now. I've given her a bottle of laudanum for the pain. Look in on her this evening, but don't press if she doesn't want to see you. She's still weak, and she needs to come to terms with her condition, and that may take some time."

Joshua left the church in a daze, trying to accept that he could not see Amy until evening. He wandered aimlessly toward the village green, wondering how he would get through the rest of this day.

Just after eleven o'clock, Washington galloped into town, his horse in a white lather, his Life Guards trailing behind, trying desperately to keep up with him. He was quickly briefed by Nathanael Greene, who satisfied him that the emergency was over. Washington's first act was to visit his units which had engaged the British that morning, to offer his commendation for a spirited defense. Upon reaching Ebenezer Thatcher's regiment, he spied Anthony Wayne, who, failing in his search to find Washington, had returned just a short time before the commander in chief. Advancing upon Wayne with his arms outstretched, Washington grasped him in an enthusiastic bear hug.

"Once again, your keen instincts and foresight have saved the day," he said. "Had it not been for your presence here, this action would have turned out much differently." Basking in the praise of his commander, Wayne saw no reason to mention the real purpose of his presence, and his grudge against André was forgotten. He was quick to point out the accomplishments of Thatcher, and Washington took sincere pleasure in congratulating an old comrade.

He then visited the wounded at the church, where he offered some kind words to a dying British dragoon. He also inquired about Mistress Martin, but was informed she was resting in her room and the doctor preferred she not be disturbed. Satisfied that the purpose of the attack had been to rescue André, not Arnold, he nevertheless doubled the guard on both men. Since Doctor Stewart had told him he would move all the wounded to better facilities in Orangetown the following day, Washington directed that the court-martial resume on Tuesday, the 10th, under heavy guard. He asked Greene whether they should terminate Arnold's unusual privilege of having his wife stay with him in his room of confinement. Since a guard always accompanied her any time she left the room, Greene did not see any risk involved in her remaining.

"I expect the matter will be concluded by the coming weekend," he said, and Washington acquiesced. He was in the process of moving his headquarters to the Dey mansion in Passaic County, across the border in New Jersey, but would delay his own departure from Tappan until the trial was over.

*4 P.M.*

When Joshua presented himself at Mary Burns' house, she met him at the door.

"She is still very weak, Joshua. She's really in no condition to have a visitor, even you."

"Just let me look in on her, Mary," he asked. "I promise not to disturb her if she's asleep."

But Mary Burns shook her head. "It wouldn't be fair. No woman wants to be seen unawares after something like she's been through. Come back tomorrow at this time. I'm sure she'll be better by then."

Frustrated, but helpless, Joshua pleaded, "You promise I can see her then?"

"Yes. I'll let her know you're coming."

Feeling helpless and alone, Joshua made his way toward the headquarters mess. Maybe he could find John Lamb and they could get drunk together. Anything to get through this, the longest day of his life.

# CHAPTER THIRTY-ONE

*Tappan*
*Monday, October 9, 1780*

THE CREAK OF wagons on Main Street reminded Joshua that the hospital was moving this morning, and that a long, sleepless night was finally over. He had not been able to find John Lamb last night, and had then gone to Mabie's, where the cook was gamely trying to fill in as bartender. The place was fuller than it had been since the start of the trial, and the cook was having trouble keeping up with the customers, all of them senior officers discussing the day's events. Joshua avoided joining their excited conversation. He had become increasingly aware of a coolness on the part of other officers in their contact with him, which he knew was because of his defense of Arnold, and he accepted it with resignation. Some dislike for the traitor was sure to rub off on his defender.

One problem was, he was no longer certain that Arnold was guilty. And the wounding of Amy had created a hatred for the British that he had not had before.He now easily understood how they could conspire to ruin Arnold's reputation. But he did not want to think about that or anything else. What he wanted was enough rum to insure he would sleep through the night. However, after downing only two glasses as quickly as they were brought to him, he became violently ill. He barely made it to the door, where he spent a long time vomiting what little was in his stomach. Weak and exhausted, he returned to his shared room, where he spent a miserable night, deprived of the one thing that could secure him oblivion.

Now, listening to the wagons, he realized he had another long day to fill before he could see Amy. It wasn't until he had his third cup of hot cider that he remembered he had stopped off to see General Arnold last evening before going to Mabie's, to try to set up a meeting for today to discuss his upcoming defense. It was also an attempt to fill the day, to get him through the long hours until he could see Amy. At first, Arnold had seemed reluctant, preferring to spend the unexpected free time with his family, but his wife had urged him to accept, saying she would be happy to take some time in the fresh air with their baby son. The appointment was scheduled for 10 A.M.

When he arrived at his former quarters, Peggy Arnold met Joshua at the door with a warm smile of greeting. He was once again impressed with her presence and her beauty. He could see at once why the general had been captivated. She ushered him to the table, where her husband was drinking a cup of tea, and she poured one for Joshua.

"Major Thorne, I sincerely appreciate the assistance you are giving my husband," she said. "I know it must not be easy to represent someone charged with such a dastardly crime. But you should take heart knowing that you are defending an innocent man from a despicable plot."

"I am simply doing my duty, madam," Joshua replied, feeling somewhat uncomfortable, yet also pleased.

"I sense that you are doing more," she replied. "And my husband tells me you have been of much help. I am most grateful."

Not knowing how to reply, Joshua merely nodded.

Peggy Arnold then excused herself, and bundling her child, she and the boy left the room.

"She is a wonderful woman," Arnold said, after she had gone. "I can't tell you how much it has meant to have her stand by me so faithfully through all of this."

"I can certainly understand your feelings, sir. I envy you."

Joshua quickly realized the incongruous nature of what he had just said. "Uh, what I meant was..."

Arnold laughed. "I understand what you meant major, and you are right. Where my wife is concerned, I am to be envied." He then informed Joshua that she would be gone for about two hours, indicating he wanted their business finished by then. Joshua tried to clear his head from the worry over Amy and focus on the work of the moment.

"General, I believe that Colonel Edwards has called his last witness. He will now attempt to introduce four letters purporting to be between you and Major André, offering your services to the British, including the surrender of West Point. Your defense, as you have previously informed me, is that these letters are forgeries, planted in your files by an unknown person. Is that correct?"

"Yes, major, it is." Arnold was watching Joshua closely.

"It's a reasonable defense, under the circumstances," Joshua said. "Edwards can show no corroboration for this correspondence except that it was found in your files. We must attack its validity by concentrating on the assumption of the unknown person."

Arnold regarded Joshua with a quizzical expression. "You know, major, I think I detect a new enthusiasm in your approach to my defense. Is there a reason for this change of heart?"

It was true, Joshua realized, and the grievous injury suffered by Amy, was part of that reason. The new anger he felt toward the British was still smoldering, making it easier to believe in a British plot against Arnold. But Arnold's examination of the witnesses during the trial, also created doubt in his mind about his guilt. And he thought he sensed that same feeling among members of the court.

"It's just that this is the weakest part of the government's case, and I feel that we should make the most of it," Joshua replied, not wishing to make further explanation.

Arnold suspected there was more, but he did not press. "I appreciate your attitude and advice."

They spent the remainder of the time discussing the letters and how best to attack them. When he had first examined them at the meeting with Laurance and Edwards, Joshua noted that three of the four had been from Arnold to André. Since they were intended for encoding, and would not be sent themselves, there was no signature, although they appeared to be in Arnold's handwriting. The fourth document was a decoded transcript of a letter from André to Arnold, again seemingly in Arnold's handwriting. Without the signatures of either party, and without André to identify them, Joshua felt he could create doubt of their validity. It all hinged upon whether the court would accept that the handwriting in the documents could be forged. Since a two-thirds vote of the court was required for conviction, if a reasonable doubt could be created in the minds of only five of the thirteen members of the court, Arnold would go free.

Their discussion was completed a few minutes before Peggy Arnold was due to return, and rather than go to the headquarters mess, Joshua headed for Mabie's. He had no appetite, especially for the heavy meal served at noon in the mess. If he ate anything at all, he would settle for whatever unappetizing dish the harassed cook could offer. Besides, he felt close to Amy at Mabie's. As he sat at the bar, a tall, slender man of about his own age entered from the common room. Since it was too early for service, Joshua judged that he must have come from André, whose place of confinement opened into that room. As Joshua was the only other person present, the stranger approached him.

"Excuse me, sir, is it possible to have a meal somewhere in town? They don't seem to be serving here."

"This is the only place. The cook will probably offer something soon, but I'm reluctant to call anything he prepares a meal, unless you're very hungry."

"I'll have to chance it," the man said, extending his hand. "My name is Pierre du Simitière, from Philadelphia."

Joshua introduced himself. "Did you just come from Major André's room?"

Du Simitière nodded. "A terrible business! He's a very old friend. I had petitioned to visit him several days ago. I was almost refused. It was only because I had letters of introduction from John Adams, and Benjamin Franklin, that General Washington allowed me the visit."

"You know Doctor Franklin?"

"Yes, I worked with him and Mr. Adams and Mr. Jefferson a few years ago." Although du Simitière spoke English well, he did so with an accent which Joshua could not identify. "If it wasn't for that," he continued, "my friend would have gone to his death without me seeing him one last time."

Joshua informed him of the attempt to rescue André the day before. "Ah, that explains much, then. I suppose I am lucky to have seen him at all."

"How did you come to know André," Joshua asked, curious now about this unusual relationship.

"I regard him as a countryman of mine," du Simitière said. "I am originally from Geneva, and, although he was born in London, André's family are of Geneva, and he was sent there very young to be educated. That's where we met. Our tastes were similar, and we both learned to draw under the same master." He was silent a moment, and then asked, "Are you acquainted with John André?"

Joshua explained that he was assisting Arnold in his defense.

"How interesting!" the young Swiss exclaimed. "I made a portrait sketch of General Arnold while he was military commander of Philadelphia." He paused a moment and then shook his head. "It seems impossible that a man such as General Arnold would betray his country. Did he really do such a terrible thing?"

"He claims that he is the victim of a British plot to discredit him, and he is making a good case for it." Joshua thought it astonishing that this stranger knew both principals in the West Point conspiracy, as well as Franklin, Adams, and Jefferson.

"I wish him well, then. But if he is guilty or not, it seems nothing will change the fate of my poor friend." He shook his head and sighed heavily. "I saw him often in Philadelphia—André, I mean. He never should have joined the army. He is a fine artist. He once showed me a wonderful journal he kept of all his travels and campaigns in America, in which he had drawn sketches of people, animals and plants, all in correct detail and proper colors. He really has a fine talent. I intend to open a museum someday, and was hoping he could contribute to it." He shook his head sadly. "Now that will no longer be possible."

As du Simitière went on about André, Joshua began to lose interest. Worry about Amy was crowding out the words, of which he only heard snatches. But when du Simitière mentioned that André was once billeted in Benjamin Franklin's house in Philadelphia, Joshua's attention revived.

"Yes," du Simitière confirmed. "I last visited him there as the British Army was evacuating the city, and I must say his conduct on that day was most shocking and disappointing to me."

Mary Burns lived in a small house which consisted of only two rooms and a lean-to kitchen. She had given up her bedroom to Amy, sleeping instead on a couch in the other room. She ushered Joshua in to see Amy just after 4 P.M. He was unnerved by what he saw. The figure in the bed managed a wan smile, but he found it difficult to believe it was Amy. The woman who stared back at him with sunken, lusterless eyes and an ashen complexion, was not the woman he knew.

"Do I look as bad as that?" Even her voice was weak and cracked.

"Not considering you've just been shot," he quipped, recovering. He moved quickly into the room and took her hand. It was as cold as ice and it transferred its temperature directly to his heart. He suddenly felt a deep fear he tried not to show. "You can't expect to be dancing yet. It will take a few more days." He smiled brightly, but she saw through it.

"It will...." she winced, as a pain coursed through her chest, "a long time yet before....." She relaxed and closed her eyes as the pain slowly ebbed, but did not bother to finish the sentence. Mary had placed a wooden chair beside the bed, and Joshua sat down, holding on to the cold hand.

"You're going to be fine, don't worry," he said, squeezing her hand. He thought he could detect a slight response. He continued to sit by her side, his fear growing. Was he about to lose her? How could he face that? He knew he should say something, offer comforting words, but his fear paralyzed both his mind and his tongue. He could only continue to sit beside her, one hand holding hers, the other stroking her arm, as if trying to coax some warmth into it. From time to time, she opened her eyes and looked at him, sometimes smiling slightly, more often simply closing her eyes again. Finally, she spoke, her eyes still closed.

"I'm very tired, Joshua. Please go now. Thank you for coming."

*Thank you for coming?* She made it sound like he had just attended a funeral. He sensed a finality in it that chilled him. "I'll be back soon," he promised. There was no response.

He expressed his concern to Mary Burns as he was leaving, anxious about any sign of infection or putrefaction. She assured him that so far there was none.

"I'll be changing the bandage every day, so I'll know." She was expecting him to ask for details about the wound itself.

He did not.

# CHAPTER THIRTY-TWO

*The Manse, Tappan, New York*
*Tuesday, October 10, 1780*

"I CALL MAJOR John André."

Edwards's announcement as the court opened caused a loud stir in the room, prompting Greene to rap his gavel. Joshua, although completely surprised, leaned quickly over to speak to Arnold. "You must let me handle this," he told him. "If you raise an objection, it will look as if you fear his testimony." Equally taken aback by Edwards' coup, the general nodded his assent. Joshua rose, anger beginning to replace his surprise. Had this been the plan all along? Had Edwards deliberately lulled him into a sense of false security, only to call André at the last moment?

"May I ask why the defense was not told earlier of the calling of this witness?"

"Major André is on the witness list," Edwards replied.

"But it is well known that he refused to testify."

"The witness has changed his mind," Edwards said, keeping a straight face.

"Would it be wrong to suspect that he has been offered an inducement for such a sudden change of heart, perhaps his life in exchange for his testimony?"

"I assure the court and my colleague at the defense table, that the witness has been offered no favor to himself to testify, nor is this event as sudden as Major Thorne implies. It is the result of an ongoing effort by the prosecution to secure the cooperation of the witness. It required the consent of General Sir Henry Clinton, which, due to recent events, was only early this morning received." Clinton had waited for the outcome of the rescue attempt before replying to André, hoping he would not be required to give his reluctant consent to the testimony. With the rescue mission a failure, he had given in, apparently hoping André's cooperation might in some way save his life.

"I would like to advise the court," Edwards continued, "that prior to the trial, Colonel Laurance approached General Washington about the possibility of offering Major André leniency in exchange for his testimony. The commander in chief firmly rejected any such approach, and prohibited us from making such an offer."

There was a brief discussion at the court's table as several officers leaned over to converse with Greene, who finally nodded.

"Major Thorne, the court finds nothing irregular in the prosecutor's calling of this witness, and he may now do so."

Joshua resumed his seat. He knew Greene was correct, but the knowledge did not dim his anger. Yesterday, after leaving Arnold, he had felt optimistic about the case. This new development changed everything. In the meantime, accompanied by two guards, André had entered the room. Before taking the witness chair, he bowed slightly to the court.

"We meet again, gentlemen."

"Thanks to your friends, we almost did not," Greene replied.

"I mean no disrespect, sir, when I say I wish we *had* not."

The remark brought good-natured laughter in the court. It was clear that its members had a genuine liking for the young major whom they had recently and reluctantly condemned to death.

"With the permission of the court," Edwards began, "I would like to recall Joshua Hett Smith, for purposes of identification." When Smith entered the room, Greene reminded him he was still under oath. "Squire Smith, can you identify the man in the witness chair?" Edwards asked.

Smith stared at André. "I can, sir. He is the man introduced to me by General Arnold as John Anderson."

"And this is the same man you rowed ashore from the *Vulture*, who had the meeting on shore with General Arnold, whom you then took to your house, and the following day escorted you through our lines to a point near Pine Bridge?" It was a flagrantly leading question, or series of questions, but Joshua let it pass. If he objected, Edwards would achieve the same object with point by point questioning.

"He is, yes, sir."

"Thank you, sir. That will be all." After Smith had left the room, Edwards turned his attention to André. "Sir, will you please state your name and position."

"I am Major John André, adjutant general to the British Army in North America."

"You have heard the questioning and brief testimony of the previous witness. Do you find anything in either that was not the truth?"

"No, sir."

"Then you admit that you are the 'John Anderson' he spoke of?"

"I do."

Edwards then had André review the documents which he had previously introduced, which had been taken from him at the time of his capture. One by one, he showed him the pass for John Anderson signed by Arnold, the document estimating the forces at Fortress West Point and its dependencies dated September 13th, the estimate of the men necessary to man the works at the fortress, the return of ordnance showing the number of artillery pieces at the fortress, the report showing details of the redoubts, and the copy of the council of war by General Washington of September 6th. André identified each by pointing out the creases and folds made in order to fit them in his boot. He seemed to expect something more, perhaps a further examination of the documents, but Edwards moved quickly to another subject.

"Since you have indirectly admitted that you had a meeting

227

with General Arnold, will you please tell this court how you came to be associated with him, and the purpose of this association?"

André took a deep breath and began. "On May 10th last year, Jonathan Odell, an acquaintance of mine, brought to my office a Mr. Joseph Stansbury, a crockery dealer who had just arrived from Philadelphia. He claimed to have a message for me from General Arnold. The message was—"

"Excuse me," Edwards interrupted. "You said May of *last* year. Did you not mean May of *this* year?"

"No sir, last year is correct." There was an immediate stir at the court table, and even Greene joined Edwards and Joshua in staring at André in astonishment.

"Do you mean to say that you have had dealings with General Arnold since May of 1779?"

"That's correct."

As members of the court turned to whisper among themselves, Arnold, his face flushed with anger, struggled to his feet. "I cannot sit here and listen to such a spurious accusation."

Greene appeared almost as angry as Arnold. "General, I have warned you before not to interrupt the proceedings of this court."

"But why should he be permitted to sit here and tell such a monstrous lie?"

"The veracity of the witness is for the court to decide. If, as you say, you cannot sit here and listen to him, you may be excused. But the court will hear him, and if you cause a further disturbance in this room, you will be ejected." Shaking his head, Arnold resumed his seat.

"The witness will continue with his testimony," Greene ordered. André, who had watched the incident with an air of calm detachment, proceeded as though there had been no interruption.

"The message that Mr. Stansbury brought me was that General Arnold had come to view the war between Britain and American as a mistake. He further stated that he felt the political separation of the colonies from Great Britain would be ruinous to both, and therefore wished to offer his services to the commander of British forces in any way that would restore the rightful government. He was willing to either immediately join the British Army, or cooperate with Sir Henry Clinton on some concerted plan. He wanted assurance that the British had no intention of giving up the war, and that he would receive appropriate consideration for his services."

Joshua rose from his seat and addressed Greene. "Sir, the views of General Arnold as told to Mr. Stansbury, and related by him to Major André, who now repeats them in this court are nothing but pure hearsay. I request that this testimony be stricken from the record, and that the witness not be permitted to continue in this vein."

Alexander and Howe both leaned over to speak to Greene in subdued voices, following which he nodded and turned to Edwards. "Could we perhaps hear this testimony from Mr. Stansbury himself?"

"Unfortunately, sir, Mr. Stansbury is not available. He has betaken himself behind British lines."

"The court will be closed," Greene announced.

"This will work to our advantage," Arnold said, after he and Joshua had relocated to the basement. "He has gone too far with his fantasy. No one will believe him now." Joshua, however, was far from certain. He had been as shaken as the rest of the court by André's assertion that Arnold had been furnishing information to the British a full year before previously thought. If this were true... "Do you think the court will uphold your objection?" Arnold asked, breaking into his thoughts.

"It's difficult to judge. The testimony is certainly hearsay, but you can be sure the court will want to hear everything André has to say, and they'll want to see that as much of it as possible gets into the record."

Within half an hour the court was called back in session, and Greene delivered his ruling. "The court takes due note that the previous testimony of Major André is hearsay, and will consider it so in its deliberations. The witness may continue his testimony."

"Sir," Joshua interrupted, "may I conclude that the testimony has been stricken from the record?"

"The testimony will remain in the record for now, but may be removed later in the proceedings."

"But sir—"

"The court has ruled, Major Thorne," Greene announced. "The witness may continue."

"Frankly," André began again, "I was astonished by Mr. Stansbury's message. One of my duties at headquarters was to oversee the command's intelligence program, and we had an interest in determining if there was any disaffection among rebel...uh...among American high ranking officers that we might...persuade to return to the Crown. Certain names were mentioned, but General Arnold was never even remotely considered. I was having difficulty believing the message was genuine, but I concluded that Mr. Stansbury had nothing to gain from duplicity. He was vouched for by Mr. Odell as a person loyal to the Crown, and he asked for nothing except a reply to General Arnold, and a safe conduct back to reb...American controlled territory.

"Asking the two gentlemen to wait in my office, I brought the matter to the immediate attention of General Clinton. Sir Henry at once agreed that I should reply to General Arnold accepting his offer. I then did so, including suggested ways that he could be of assistance to us. I also established a code system, as well as the use of invisible inks, so that future communications between us would be secure. Once I had written all this down, Mr. Stansbury agreed to be the intermediary between General Arnold and myself, and he transferred my letter into the new code. I then arranged for his transportation by water to a point beyond our lines."

"Can you be more specific about the suggestions you made as to how General Arnold might be of assistance to you?"

"Firstly, I assured him we had no intention of giving up the struggle until the rightful rule of Great Britain over its American colonies had been restored. I then let him know that he would be amply rewarded for any important services he provided, and compensated for any loss of property and position suffered by him should his regained allegiance to the Crown be discovered. As for suggestions, I naturally deferred to his own judgment, mentioning only the usual order of battle details."

Joshua rose again. "May I ask if the prosecution has any corroboration of this testimony, such as a copy of the letter in question, or are we to take the word of a convicted spy?"

The question drew an angry glance from Greene, but no comment, and Edwards accepted it calmly, but Joshua could see that his words had hit home with André, who was visibly affected.

"I have no supporting documents in this particular matter," Edwards replied, and turned his attention back to André, who was staring balefully at Joshua Thorne. "When was the next contact you had with General Arnold?"

"It was by a letter in late May, which began with General Arnold reaffirming that he believed the interests of America and Great Britain to be inseparable. He assured Sir Henry that he could depend upon his exertions and intelligence, and warned that it would be impossible to cooperate unless there was mutual confidence. He then provided some items of intelligence which were only of minor value to us."

When it was clear that André did not intend to continue, Edwards realized the major would not volunteer any information, nor reveal any more than he had to. It was almost as if he were protecting Arnold. That suited Edwards. If Arnold's claim of a British plot were true, André should be anxious to talk, eager to tell a story that would implicate Arnold deeply in it. He pushed on. "I assume you responded to this letter?"

"Not at once," André replied. "Our army moved against the Highland forts on May 31st." The British attack along the Hudson corridor had been sudden and successful, capturing Stony Point and also Fort Lafayette, across the river at Verplanck's Point. At the fort, André himself had taken the surrender of the garrison.

"I replied toward the middle of June," André continued, "offering suggestions, such as that he take command of a corps or larger force of five or six thousand men, and then arrange to be cut off, or otherwise forced to surrender. Since he, better than we, knew the vulnerabilities of the various American commands, I urged him to select an action which might, at one stroke, end the miseries of this war."

Joshua rose once more. "Am I to assume that this testimony also lacks the evidence of the written letter itself?" He was sniping now, and he knew it. He was doing no more than underlining the obvious, but his newly created anger at the British and his worry over Amy drove him to do as much as possible to discredit André's testimony. However, another withering glance from Greene made him realize that he was also irritating the president of the court, and that was not a good idea.

"I have no physical evidence to present," Edwards stated, "and when I have such, I assure my colleague and the court that I will introduce it." It was a mild slap, and Joshua decided to heed it.

As far as Edwards was concerned, he had no more realized than anyone else that the case against Arnold would go back so far. The information André was revealing was a treasure trove, providing the court believed his testimony. He was determined to mine as much of it as André could remember. He now led André to gradually reveal a burgeoning correspondence with Arnold. If André was to be believed, Arnold had disclosed an astonishing amount of intelligence about American forces between June 1979 and June 1980. It included troop strengths of the Continental Army brigades, operational plans, unit deployments, and the status of ammunition and other supplies. According to André, Arnold even imparted information about the infant American navy, to include the number of frigates, guns mounted, and their operating areas. If all of this proved true, it represented a staggering betrayal by Arnold of the cause he was sworn to defend.

Edwards then removed a document from his desk, showed it to Greene and then brought it to Arnold. It took the general a full two minutes to read it, punctuated with much head shaking and sighs of exasperation. Edwards then asked, "Sir, are you willing to stipulate that this document was found in your files by Lieutenant Colonel

Varick on September 25th, and turned over to General Washington on that date?"

"It is a damned lie from beginning to end," Arnold fumed. "And I was not there to see it taken."

"Sir, if I may have a moment?" Joshua asked, and Greene nodded. He turned to Arnold and spoke in a low voice. "Sir, we gain nothing by refusing to cooperate here. Edwards will simply call Varick to testify that he removed the document from your files."

"Let him do so, then," Arnold replied.

"That will only delay the proceedings to no purpose, and antagonize the court. The court will determine the validity of the evidence in any event. It's going well for us now. We must try to keep it so." After a moment of consideration, Arnold grumbled his assent, and Edwards approached André.

"I have here a letter taken from the files of General Arnold addressed to you, dated Fish-kill, 16th June, which contains information about the status of Fortress West Point. Do you recall receiving such a letter from General Arnold?"

"Yes, sir, I do."

Making a deliberate point of withholding the letter from André, Edwards asked, "Will you please summarize the information it contains."

"It began with General Arnold stating that he had called upon General Howe at West Point, which he had never visited before. He gave it that the fort was undermanned, but that reinforcements were expected. He said there were only ten days provisions on hand, but more were on the way. In his view, the fort had been greatly neglected, which he found surprising for a post of such importance." There were quick glances by members of the court toward Howe, who shifted uncomfortably in his chair.

"Although the works were well built," André continued, "they were 'wretchedly planned,'—General Arnold's words—for their purpose, which is to defend the area and bar passage of the river. And Rocky Hill, which commands all the other works, was so poorly defended, that a small force, supported by artillery, could seize it without much difficulty. He also gave it that the chain across the river to stop shipping could be broken by a large, heavily-loaded ship with a strong wind and tide."

Edwards nodded with satisfaction and handed the document to André. "Is this the letter to which you refer?"

André took a lot less time to read it than Arnold had. "It is."

"I request that this document be accepted into evidence," Edwards said, presenting it to Greene.

Arnold rose. "Sir, the technique used by Colonel Edwards to have the witness recite the contents of the letter without reading it is quite dramatic, but meaningless. If the witness is responsible for secreting the letters into my files, as I claim he is, he is certainly aware of what information they contain. There is nothing to indicate that I wrote this letter. There is no signature—"

"It is written in your hand," Edwards said.

"No more than the other forged documents which you introduced into evidence."

"Then I propose this letter be introduced with the same stipulation as the others, a letter found in General Arnold's files, purported to be in his hand."

"The letter will be so admitted," ordered Greene quickly, cutting off further argument from Arnold.

Edwards then introduced another letter from Arnold's files, dated July 15th, 1780, which André identified as having received in the same manner as the first. In it, Arnold offered to deliver West Point together with its garrison to the British for the sum of 20,000 pounds sterling, plus 10,000 pounds for loss of his property. He also requested a personal interview with a trusted officer to plan the details of the turnover.

Edwards introduced a third letter, this one from André, who acknowledged writing it, replying to Arnold's letter of July 15th, accepting his offer and agreeing to pay him the sum of 20,000 pounds for West Point, a garrison of 3,000 men and its artillery and stores. Regarding the compensation of 10,000 pounds for property losses, André wrote that no such guarantee could be made, pointing out that "Services *done* are the terms on which we promise rewards." However, he assured Arnold that if the enterprise for some reason failed or was discovered, he would not "be left a victim."

"What happened after you dispatched this last letter?" Edwards asked.

"General Arnold continued to provide us military intelligence, while we both worked upon arranging a meeting. It was eventually decided that it would take place on September 11th, at noon at Dobb's Ferry. I was there at the appointed time, but General Arnold failed to appear. I learned from him later that, as his barge was approaching Dobb's Ferry, it was fired upon and driven off by a British gunboat, at much danger to his person. Unfortunately, we had failed to communicate our plans to our navy." Here, the young major paused, seeming to reflect on the effect that failure had on his own fate.

"A second meeting was arranged, for the 20th. This time, an agent from General Arnold would meet me aboard the *Vulture*, and escort me to a secure location where the general would be waiting to have our discussion. But the agent failed to appear. Considering that some happenstance similar to that which had occurred at Dobb's Ferry might have interfered, I decided to remain aboard one more night, with the hope that the agent might yet present himself, which he did. I was then rowed ashore, and met General Arnold on the bank of the river, where our discussion took place."

It was evident that André was going to stop here, but Edwards was not about to let him. "And what, specifically, did you discuss?"

André took some time to frame his answer. "I believe my military oath prevents me from dealing in specifics, sir, but I will say that we discussed the means for the surrender of West Point, and the best time to do so."

"What date did you select?"

"Again, sir, that would reveal a proposed military plan, and I am not authorized to do so."

"Please abandon this line of questioning, Colonel Edwards," Greene ordered. "The witness is within his rights by refusing to answer."

"After your meeting on shore, you and General Arnold went to Squire Smith's house, where I assume you continued your planning, am I correct?"

"Yes."

"And it must have been here that General Arnold gave you the documents later found on your person, since you would not have been able to read them during your shoreline conversation, since it was not yet light."

"That's correct."

Under Edwards' prompting, André related the details of his journey from Smith's house until the time of his capture, which conformed to Smith's testimony.

Producing a new document, Edwards showed it to Arnold, who scanned it briefly, then nodded. Edwards then presented it to Greene, stating, "Sir, this is a letter from General Washington to General Arnold, dated September 14th last, and found in General Arnold's files." The letter was accepted into evidence without objection from Arnold. "The letter itself deals with two minor matters," Edwards continued, "but it is to the post script that I wish to call attention." He then read from the document.

> I shall be at Peekskill on Sunday evening on my way to Hartford to meet the French Admiral and General. You will be pleased to send down a guard of a Captain and 50 at that time, and direct the Quarter Master to endeavour to have a nights forage for about 40 Horses. You will keep this to yourself, as I want to make my journey a secret.

Edwards then presented two additional documents to Arnold, who bristled as soon as he started to read them. Face reddening, he began to struggle to his feet.

Joshua grabbed his arm, restraining him. "Sir, you must allow me to handle this," he said in a low, but firm whisper. "You must not alienate the court—not now. I promise you, I will make a strong objection on your behalf." Reluctantly, Arnold allowed himself to be drawn back down in his chair, but his fury was obvious. Joshua then rose and addressed Edwards.

"These documents refer to Specification 3 of the charge against General Arnold. May I ask the prosecution if it has any other evidence to produce in support of this specification?"

"None, other than to present them to the witness for identification and corroboration."

"Then I must most strenuously object to their introduction as evidence. Their sole purpose is to exert an inflammatory influence on the court. The documents are no more than scraps of paper—"

"They were found in General Arnold's files—"

"With no signature—"

"In his hand—"

"Give me the documents!" Greene demanded, his tone of voice silencing both dueling judge advocates. After reading the brief content, he turned to Joshua. "I see no reason why these documents should be treated differently from the others just introduced. The prosecution may proceed with the identification."

Edwards took the papers to Greene. "I would like to inform the court that these documents were found filed immediately next to the letter from General Washington, just introduced, in which he gave his future location to General Arnold." He then handed one of them to André. Irritated by the fervor of Joshua's objection, he decided to make another dramatic gesture.

"Major André, will you please read this document to the court?"

September 15th, 1780

To Major André

General Washington will be at King's Ferry Sunday evening next on his way to Hartford, where he is to meet the French Admiral and General. And will lodge at Peak's Kill.

When André finished, Joshua saw the gaze of most members of the court settle on Arnold. They were venomous. He would have to find some way to attack the document again.

"Can you identify that document, sir?" Edwards asked André.

"No, sir."

Edwards blinked. "You cannot identify it?"

"No, I've never seen it before."

"You did not receive such a letter from General Arnold?" Edwards sounded incredulous.

"No, sir, I did not."

Members of the court, expecting a pro forma identification, were nearly as surprised as Edwards. Joshua could hardly believe his ears. It was a windfall. One of the three charges against Arnold had suddenly dissolved. Edwards was now left standing with the second document in his hand, which was an encoded copy of the letter just read. He had wanted André to compare the two, and perhaps identify the code being used. Although it was doubtful if he would now succeed, he was unwilling to give up the attempt. He handed the coded letter to André.

"This is a coded reference, found with the letter you have just read. Will you please examine it and tell the court if you recognize it as one used to communicate with General Arnold?"

"No, sir!" Joshua jumped to his feet. "The witness has already stated that he has never seen the letter. Now the prosecutor wants him to decode it?"

"I merely ask that he—"

Greene slammed down his gavel. "The court will be closed!"

After the room had cleared, Greene turned to the members of the court. "How shall we treat this coded document?"

"I don't think we can accept it," Huntington said, "or the letter it refers to. André couldn't identify it."

"But he may be able to identify the code, without reference to the letter," Paterson pointed out.

John Glover shook his head. "All this business with code books and ciphers, invisible ink—it reeks of spy craft and secret dealings. It makes me think that a plot against Arnold might well be true. I am loathe to convict him on this type of evidence."

"I'm more inclined to believe André in this matter." It was McDougall. "He's been completely open, even to his own detriment. Why should he dissemble on this one?"

"Only if Arnold is telling the truth, and it is indeed a plot to discredit him," Huntington replied. "It all depends upon the believability of André."

"Are we to take the word of an enemy officer, a convicted spy, over that of one of our best generals?" It was Samuel Parsons, speaking for the first time. "Arnold's claim that these documents were planted is believable. It's his word against André's."

"But André's word has proven good before," McDougall countered. "At his inquiry he told the truth about not coming ashore under a flag, even though it condemned him."

"Damn it, this whole thing is far too confusing," Glover complained, throwing up his hands in disgust. "How can we possibly ferret the truth out of a mess like this?"

"Gentlemen," Greene interposed, "we are going far beyond the matter at hand. We are not at the deliberating point. We must decide now only how to treat these last two documents." After more discussion, it was determined that the letter and the coded paper would be accepted into evidence as "unsubstantiated documents found in General Arnold's files." The coded reference would not be shown to André. The court then reconvened, and its decision announced. Although not completely happy with the result, Joshua knew that without corroboration from André, Specification 3 would not stand. Edwards then announced he had nothing further for the witness. It was a tense moment in the court when Arnold rose to question André.

"Major André," Arnold began, "had we ever met before you stepped ashore at Haverstraw Bay?"

"No, sir."

"And the purpose of our meeting was to sever my allegiance to the American cause?"

"Well...yes...."

"And you offered me a large sum of money to surrender Fortress West Point?"

"That's correct."

"Thank you, sir, for your honest responses. I confirm that the statements you have just made are the truth." If Arnold's intent was to surprise and confuse the court, he succeeded. Even Joshua was not sure where he was going with this. "Since we have now established a foundation of truth, let us see if we can maintain it. Is it not also true that I rejected your offer?"

"No sir, it is not. That would have made no sense."

Arnold appeared perplexed by the answer. "Made no sense? Why not?"

"Because it was you who made the offer in the first place, and I was there to confirm our acceptance and work out the procedures for the surrender."

"I see. So you are determined to stand by your previous false statements."

"They are not false statements, sir."

Arnold sounded disappointed when he replied. "I see that we will achieve nothing by pursuing this line of questioning." He then changed the subject. "You said earlier that in determining which American officers who might be approached to return to the Crown, my name was not considered. Why was that?"

"Your reputation, sir. We considered you one of the rebellion's best generals, and fully committed to its cause."

"That would be a good reason to single me out for your special attention, would it not?"

André appeared puzzled. "What meaning does that statement have, sir?"

"Why, that you would mark me as a target for a plot, sir, the very plot that has now unraveled."

"On the contrary sir, it would single you out as someone impervious to any blandishments we might offer."

"You stated that I contacted you in May of last year, using the good offices of a Mr...uh...Mr..."

"Stansbury, sir."

"Ah, yes, the conveniently unavailable Mr. Stansbury. Although I would not have expected you to be aware of it, on April 3rd, Congress preferred court-martial charges against me on four counts. Between then and the time the court finally convened six months later, I had to prepare a defense to the charges. My wedding took place during this time, and I was deeply involved in the many problems and duties associated with being the military commander of Philadelphia. Yet in spite of all these conflicting demands on my time, and the fact that I was far removed from the active army, where intelligence can be best obtained, you maintain that I had time to engage in such intrigues."

"General Arnold, I am well aware of your previous court-martial and your problems with your Congress. Frankly, I am at a loss to understand a government that would treat its greatest military hero in such a manner. It is a tribute to your abilities that you were able to accomplish all these feats simultaneously."

Joshua was aware that Arnold was particularly susceptible to flattery, which might cause him to miss the irony in André's statement, if indeed that is what it was. Joshua had to remind himself that, in André's eyes, Arnold was doing the honorable thing, returning to his true allegiance and trying to end a tragic rebellion. In any event, André's comments had a predictable effect— intentional, he suspected. Arnold's tone became more muted and less confrontational.

"All this information you claim I furnished could have been obtained from other sources, could it not?"

"I'm sorry, sir, I cannot comment on operational capabilities of my command."

"And the so-called letters found in my files, they are well within the ability of a capable intelligence service to concoct, and surreptitiously place there, isn't that true?"

"Again, general, I am not permitted to comment."

"And the papers found on your person when you were taken, could they not also be concocted in the same manner?"

"They were in your hand, sir."

"Those papers are forgeries," Arnold declared. "I put it to you, sir, that I never gave you those papers. They were either obtained or manufactured by the elaborate intelligence apparatus under your control. The information contained in them could have been gotten by any of your field agents with access to West Point or its personnel. Your intent was to reveal them as evidence that I was negotiating to betray my country."

"If that were the case, sir, I could have done so without leaving New York. Why would I make a dangerous and unnecessary trip to meet you?"

"To prove that you *did* meet me, which would present the opportunity for the direct transfer of the papers from me to you. And you would have proof of the meeting, Squire Smith and the Colquhoun brothers."

"If I merely wished to establish that a meeting occurred, why would I bring the papers with me? That would certainly be an unnecessary risk, would it not?"

"Yes, it would," Arnold admitted, "and I don't know the answer to that question. But I am certain you had a very good reason, a plan that was probably aborted by the unexpected firing upon the *Vulture*. That plan no doubt included those documents falling into the hands of American authorities, thus implicating me. The irony is, sir, that they indeed did so, but in a manner quite unintended. Now, you have no choice but to play the hand through, even at your own peril."

"General Arnold, there is much I would do for my country, to include die for it if necessary. But I would not offer up *my* life in a charade designed to incriminate an innocent man and place him in danger of *his* life. To do so would be dishonorable, and you do me dishonor to suggest it. I am a man condemned to death. If what you say is true, would it not be wise for me to acknowledge that fact and thus spare an innocent man before I meet my God?"

"Not if you believe that in the eyes of your God your mission would be considered a higher calling. You do believe, don't you, major, that the colonies should return to the British Crown?"

"I do indeed, sir. The separation of America from Great Britain would be a tragedy of the greatest dimension."

"A tragedy you would do anything in your power to prevent, am I not correct?"

"Anything except traduce my honor, or bear false witness against an innocent man."

Once again, Arnold changed direction. "Major, one thing puzzles me regarding the circumstances of your capture. When you were stopped by the militiamen, why didn't you simply show the pass supposedly signed by me, instead of questioning them as to which party they represented? Had you done so, you would have been allowed to proceed. On the other hand, if they had been loyalists, upon seeing the pass, they would have arrested you and turned you over to the nearest British Army unit, thus achieving your purpose in either event."

"I'm afraid I just did not think of it. I was nearing the end of my journey, nervous and excited. I suppose I thought I was safe."

"Sir, you are the chief of undercover intelligence for the British Army in North America. You had the pass in your possession, and many hours to think about your course of action. You saw, that when riding with Squire Smith, whenever you were stopped and Smith presented the pass, it was accepted without question. Yet, you claim you did not think of it?"

André seemed to be groping for an answer. "We had been told that British irregulars were operating on the Tarry Town Road," he said, finally, "which is why I chose that route, rather than the direct route to White Plains, supposedly patrolled by their American counterparts. Also, the man who accosted me appeared to be wearing a cast-off British army coat."

"Even so, nothing is ever certain in war. Wouldn't presenting the pass still have been the foolproof thing to do?"

"In retrospect, sir, it certainly would have been. I shall regret not doing it until...." André stopped, and a slight, rueful smile crossed his face. "I was about to say, 'until my dying day,' which at least does not appear to make my period of regret overly long."

Arnold stared directly at André. "I sympathize with you, major, yet I still find your actions strange enough to suggest that there is something behind them that this court is not being told. It's almost as if you *wished* to be taken. And, of course, with your life already forfeit, you have nothing to lose by implicating me."

"Nothing to lose but my honor. I assure you sir, my life is already lost to me. In no way would I add my honor to the pot."

Joshua could see that Arnold did not want to leave it there, but there was nothing to be gained by further questioning of André, and Arnold seemed to recognize it also. After a long pause he announced he had nothing further for the witness.

"I have no more witnesses to call," Edwards then announced. "The prosecution rests its case."

Joshua rose. "Sir, I request an adjournment until tomorrow to confer with General Arnold on the presentation of the case for the defense."

Greene glanced impatiently at his watch. It was one o'clock. There was little chance the trial would end in the remaining three hours. "Very well, but before we do so, General Arnold, I would like to inform you of your rights regarding standing witness."

"I am aware of those rights, sir."

"Nevertheless, it is my duty to announce them to you. Firstly, you may stand sworn witness in your defense. If you do so, you may be questioned by the prosecution and the court regarding your testimony. Secondly, you may make an unsworn written statement to the court, upon which you may not be questioned. Finally, you may remain silent. If you do so, the court may make no presumption of guilt based upon your silence. The court will adjourn until tomorrow morning at ten o'clock."

# CHAPTER THIRTY-THREE

"I THINK IT would be a good idea to recall Colonel Varick."

Joshua had accompanied Arnold and his guards back to his room. Peggy Arnold had just returned from preparing tea at the home of the stable house owner, with whom she had become friendly. After pouring, she remained, listening to the discussion.

"Varick is the most logical person to have placed the documents in your file," Joshua continued, "and his remarks against Smith can be seen as an effort to deflect suspicion from himself. Further interrogation of him might yield valuable results."

Arnold did not seem convinced. "But could we prove anything by recalling him? Surely he will not implicate himself. Remember, Varick is reading for the law."

"We need merely create doubt in the minds of the court, which I believe we can do.

"You really think it is possible that Varick is the one? It is hard to believe. He has been a loyal patriot for so long."

"He had access, and could have acted in the confusion following your arrest. Also, he claimed to be ill at the time. Feigning illness would give him the freedom and the opportunity."

"I find it hard to accept that a member of my official family would do such a thing.

"Yet someone planted those documents," Joshua said. "Who else would have had the chance?"

"Franks, perhaps?"

"Major Franks was immediately and extensively questioned by Washington and his staff right after your arrest. He was not released until that evening."

Arnold shifted his injured leg, which he massaged with his open hand. He thought deeply before he finally spoke. "Recalling Varick will accomplish nothing. He will certainly admit to nothing, and if he is innocent we are casting suspicion on an innocent man."

Joshua was disappointed. He knew that Arnold was right, but he had wanted to give himself a role in the trial, regardless of how small. Now it would be smaller still.

"Our biggest problem is André," Joshua continued, accepting Arnold's decision. "At his inquiry André refused to lie in his own defense in the matter of whether or not he came ashore under the protection of a flag, and as a result, he's under sentence of death. There is a strong presumption that such a man is also telling the truth now. Throughout the trial, he's been careful to present himself as a man of honor, with considerable success, I'm afraid. But if we tarnish his honor, we reduce his credibility."

Arnold sensed the meaning behind Joshua's words. "You have a way of doing this?"

Joshua nodded. "I think so," and he told Arnold what it was.

Joshua then changed the subject. "In my judgment, there's nothing to be gained by you standing witness."

"Nevertheless, I prefer to do so."

"I fear, sir, it will be a grave mistake. You can achieve the same result by submitting an unsworn written statement."

"You are wrong. Should I fail to testify under oath it will be inferred that I am guilty and afraid of cross examination. I must defend myself and allow my accusers to question me. Only in that way can I assure the court of my innocence. My standing witness will be the key to destroying this plot against me."

"Do you really want to open yourself to cross examination?"

"I welcome it."

"Colonel Edwards is a skilled and clever interrogator. He will turn much of what you say to your disadvantage."

"You underestimate me, major."

"You underestimate *him*, sir. Frankly, I can think of nothing you can say that is worth the risk of cross examination."

"Nevertheless—"

"Major Thorne," Peggy Arnold interrupted. "Can you be sure my husband will be found not guilty if he does not testify?"

"I can't possibly be sure of that, madam. But I believe that reasonable doubt has been raised regarding the issues."

"If you were a gambling man, major," Arnold interposed, "what chance would you say I have of being acquitted of all charges?"

"Better than even, sir."

Arnold laughed, but there was no mirth in it. "So then I have almost half a chance of going to the gallows?" He shook his head. "No, major, that is not good enough. I must do everything in my power to improve those odds. I shall testify under oath. I assure you, that when you hear what I am about to say, you will be as convinced of my innocence as the court will be."

Joshua realized that further argument was useless, "May I suggest then, sir, that you relate your testimony to me exactly as you will do in court tomorrow?"

"I had fully intended to so." Arnold settled back in his chair and began to speak. As his story unfolded, Joshua's attitude slowly changed from skepticism to amazement. The story told by Arnold seemed not only believable, but logical, and he presented it with an eloquence and sincerity that had a strong ring of truth. For the first time, Joshua felt that reasonable doubt appeared not as a faint hope, but as a distinct possibility.

When Arnold finally fell silent, Joshua suggested that they go over Arnold's testimony once more. They began with an enactment of Arnold taking the stand and giving his explanation of the events, Joshua prompting with questions to make certain points or clarify specific details. Once satisfied that the testimony was complete and overlooked nothing favorable to Arnold's defense, they then gamed the cross examination by Edwards. Joshua introduced hypothetical questions designed to attack Arnold's version of events, and together, they brain-stormed possible answers until they were sure they found the best available. Through it all, Peggy Arnold listened, sometimes feeding or tending to her child, or busying herself with needlework, but always attentive to the discussion.

"Now that you have heard me out, major," Arnold said, after agreeing they had covered everything, "do you still think the odds against me are the same?"

"Frankly, general, I think they are somewhat improved."

"Then you no longer object to my standing witness."

"Let's just say I'm not as uneasy as I was. You're an excellent advocate for yourself, sir, but I still prefer the safety of a strong, unsworn closing statement instead."

"I appreciate your concern, Major Thorne, but standing witness is my best course."

Peggy Arnold placed her hand gently on her husband's shoulder. "Are you sure, my love?"

He covered her hand with his own, and met her gaze. "I am sure, my darling. Don't worry, tomorrow this will all be over."

Although he had not eaten since morning, Joshua had no appetite. All day he'd had difficulty concentrating completely on the trial, concern for Amy's condition paramount in his mind. Now, after leaving Arnold, rather than go to Mabie's or the headquarters mess, he walked quickly toward Mary Burns' small house. Ushered into her room, he was relieved to see that Amy seemed better. There were still circles under her eyes, but her skin was not quite as gray. Although she appeared more alert, there was a dullness in her eyes that frightened him more than her physical condition had frightened him the day before. He quickly sat down beside her on the same wooden chair and again took her hand. This time it did not seem as cold.

"You look better," he told her, relief flooding through him.

"I feel a little better," she said, her voice weak and subdued. "I had an earlier visitor."

"Oh? Who was it?"

"Mrs. Arnold." Seeing his surprise, she managed a bare hint of a smile. "She was very sweet. She wanted to apologize that her husband's trial was the cause of my injury, even if it was in such an indirect way. I thought it was very generous of her to come, especially considering what she's going through right now."

"She's a remarkable woman," he said. "Arnold is a lucky man." It was the same gaffe he had made to Arnold, and, as before, he had spoken without thinking. But Amy did not seem to notice. He saw her wince, and he reached for the laudanum at her bedside, but she shook her head.

"Only when I truly need it, mostly at night, so I can sleep. Doctor Stewart can't give me any more. His supplies are running low." She shifted her position slowly, wincing again as she did. "Tell me about the trial."

It gave him something to talk about other than her condition, for which he was grateful. It also showed she was taking an interest in things. He began by telling her of André's unexpected appearance, his revelations about his relationship with Arnold, and his surprising failure to identify the letter from Arnold giving away Washington's whereabouts. He then pointed out how much hinged on how the court felt about Arnold's claim that all the documents introduced against him were forgeries. Although he knew she would not be happy to hear it, he let her know that he felt that Arnold had a chance of going free.

"It takes two-thirds to convict, meaning nine members must believe he is guilty beyond a reasonable doubt. As confusing as some of this testimony is...." He let the sentence trail off.

"You seem to have done very well by him," Amy said.

"He handled most of his defense himself. Actually, I contributed very little." It was true, but she apparently chose not to believe it.

"If you could only direct such skill toward saving John André," she sighed. "I would give anything to see his life spared." Then her countenance brightened somewhat. "Joshua, if Arnold does go free, is there a chance that André would go free also?"

Joshua scowled slightly. It pained him that even in her desperate condition, she was still concerned about André. The major's situation would be altered, Joshua reasoned, but he could not see that it would be improved. He would still stand convicted on his own testimony of being a spy. Whether by suborning treason, as he admitted, or planning and executing a vicious plot against Arnold, as the general claimed, André would still hang. But, seeing how the injured woman clung to that hope, he would only say,

"Perhaps. We just have to wait and see."

There was more he wanted to say to her, much more. But she appeared tired out by his visit, and he needed to put his thoughts in order. It could wait until his next visit.

# CHAPTER THIRTY-FOUR

*The Manse, Tappan, New York*
*Wednesday, October 11, 1780*

BENEDICT ARNOLD AND Joshua Thorne were at the defense table early. Greene, the other members of the court and Edwards had not yet arrived. Arnold appeared resplendent in a freshly cleaned and pressed uniform, epaulets and gold sword knot polished and gleaming. He and Joshua were going over last minute details of Arnold's testimony when the general's expression turned somber, and he seemed to stare at something far away.

"You know," he said, his voice suddenly heavy with sadness, "convinced as I am that I will be found not guilty, I still will have lost everything. Because I kept all of this to myself, without notifying Washington, he will never trust me again. My days with the army are finished."

"That may be, sir," Joshua agreed, "but right now we must concentrate on the matter at hand, which is to gain your acquittal of these charges. I think your case as you will present it is plausible, and will raise enough question in the mind of the court that a two-thirds vote for conviction will be difficult to achieve. But you must be in full form and remain so. This is not only your final chance to influence the court, it's Edwards' final chance as well. You must be on your guard and not allow your mind to drift to speculating about the future."

"You are right, of course. Thank you."

The members of the court filed in, and Arnold and Joshua rose.

"The court will come to order," Greene ordered.

"All parties to the trial present when the court adjourned are again present," Edwards announced.

"Is the defense ready to proceed?"

"It is, sir," said Joshua.

"You may call your first witness."

"I call Pierre Eugene du Simitière," Joshua announced." Although several heads turned on the court, Joshua had informed Edwards and Greene the previous evening that he would call an unscheduled witness, and given them his reason for doing so. After being sworn, Joshua led du Simitière through the circumstances of his acquaintance with John Andre as he had related them at Mabie's. He then turned specific.

"Tell me, sir, did you have occasion to visit Major Andre in June of 1778, while the British Army was occupying Philadelphia?"

"Yes, I did."

"And where was Major Andre living at the time?"

"He was quartered in Benjamin Franklin's home on High Street."

"Was Doctor Franklin also in residence then?"

"No, he was serving as American emissary to France."

"When you visited Major André, what was he doing?"

"Doing?" Du Simitière shifted in the chair. Joshua could see he was stalling, avoiding the issue. He was an unwilling witness, testifying only because he was under subpoena to do so.

"What activity was he engaged in?"

"He was packing. The British Army was preparing to evacuate the city."

"Was there anything unusual about the nature of his packing?"

Du Simitière sighed heavily, obviously reluctant to answer, yet recognizing the requirement to do so. "He was removing some items, which...which belonged to Doctor Franklin."

"Sir, will you kindly be more specific?"

"He took some books...."

"Some books? How many?"

"Several packing cases."

Joshua was tired of the evasions. "In addition to many rare books from his library, what other items of the Doctor's personal property did you see André remove?"

Du Simitière realized there was no way to protect his friend. In his discussion with Joshua he had given a detailed accounting, and he knew Joshua was determined to make him repeat it. "I saw him packing some scientific instruments, several musical instruments, and a large portrait of Doctor Franklin. But I believe it's possible that...."

"In your view, are such actions those of a man of honor?"

Edwards rose. "The judgment of the witness as to Major André's honor has no bearing on this case."

"I believe it does," Joshua replied. "During this trial Major André has presented himself as a man of honor, and much of his testimony is based upon such. If his honor is in question, so is the truth of his testimony. However, I will not pursue the issue. I have no more questions for the witness."

Edwards declined to cross-examine du Simitière and as the witness left the stand, Joshua could see that several members of the court were viewing André in a new light. It was now time for the last act.

# CHAPTER THIRTY-FIVE

"I NOW WISH to call my second and final witness, Major General Benedict Arnold."

Arnold rose and walked toward a position facing Greene. Head held high, and trying to minimize his limp, he cut an awkward, yet dignified figure. He saluted the president of the court, was sworn, and then took his seat in the witness chair, his injured leg stretched out stiffly before him. The silence in the small church was total. Everyone in the room realized this would be the critical point in the trial.

"General Arnold," Joshua began, "You are present in this court today charged with three counts of treason against the United States of America. You have maintained throughout these proceedings that you are not guilty, and that you have been the victim of a plot by the enemy to destroy your reputation, and damage the cause of independence. You have agreed to testify under oath to explain to the court the full circumstances surrounding this plot and the ensuing charges against you. Please do so now."

Instead of leaning back in the chair, as might be expected in preparation for a long narration, Arnold leaned forward. It had the intended effect of making him seem eager to speak, to have his side of the story heard.

"First, let me say that attempting to unravel this enemy scheme on my own, without confiding in my commander, was a grave error. Yet I hope to explain to you why I was driven to do so. I realize that my actions in this matter leave much to be desired. Looking back, I can see that I have acted foolishly, and in some cases improperly. I have made mistakes and I accept responsibility for them. But the one thing I have *not* done is betray my country or my commander, and I hope that when my testimony is finished you will be convinced of the truth of these words." He paused temporarily, to let his words register.

"Early in the spring of 1779, I received a long letter from Colonel Beverly Robinson, the commander of the Loyal American Regiment, urging me to return to the allegiance of Great Britain and take command of all Loyalist forces. He pointed out the advantages to be gained by a return to the mother country under the terms offered by the Carlisle Commission the previous year. It was a well-reasoned approach, and flattering to me personally, but, of course, I gave it no consideration whatever. I did, however, respond out of courtesy, explaining that I was committed to the cause of independence for the United States."

Joshua then showed Arnold a two-page document. "Is this the letter from Colonel Robinson you are referring to?"

Arnold glanced at it briefly. "It is."

"Please explain how it came into my possession."

"I had no intention of keeping the letter, but, as I said, it contained some very flattering remarks about me. Because of this, my wife wished to have it as a keepsake, and I gave it to her. When she came to me here, she brought it with her, thinking it might be useful to me in my defense. I then gave it to you."

Joshua showed the letter to Edwards, who read it through and handed it back, nodding. Joshua then placed it before Greene, asking that it be accepted into evidence, which it was. He turned to Arnold. "Do you have a copy of your reply to Colonel Robinson?"

"I do not. Perhaps I might have made one if I did not have enemies so intent on bringing me down. I did not want any correspondence in my files to or from the British, especially anything soliciting me to commit treason. If my enemies got wind of such a communication, there would be no end to the mischief they could make, even though I rejected Robinson's approach."

During their conference the previous day, Joshua and Arnold had agreed that Joshua would ask penetrating questions, even potentially embarrassing ones. Better to raise them in the defense venue, Joshua reasoned, than allow Edwards to do so during a hostile cross examination.

"Thank you, general, please continue."

"I thought no more of the matter until a month ago, when I received another communication from Robinson. I was surprised to discover that, rather than another attempt to persuade me to change sides, he was now soliciting my help in assisting *him* to do so. Apparently, in the year and a half that had passed between our previous communication, he had come to believe this war would drag on until the British finally gave up the effort, and he was desirous of returning to our side and regaining his very large estate. He promised that he could deliver a wealth of important intelligence information, which would be of immense benefit to our cause."

"How was this letter delivered to you?"

"By a stranger who came to my headquarters and stated he was to give it to me personally, and to no one else. The letter suggested that, if agreeable to me, we could establish a two-way communication by the subterfuge that Robinson was seeking my assistance in regaining some items of personal property from his house."

"Am I to assume you did not keep this letter either?"

"I did not, not only for the reason I already cited, but also because Robinson asked me to destroy it, since it would be most damaging to him if its contents became known. In any event, I had much to think about. If the letter was genuine, and Robinson really wanted to change sides, it would be a great coup for us. Based upon his position, he most certainly was privy to information which would be of great value. He might even bring his regiment along with him, or if not, at least create dismay and discord in its ranks. On the other hand, I felt this could be a trap of some kind, either conceived by my sworn enemies or by the British to lure me into a compromising position. I had to proceed carefully, and, I felt, secretly. I could afford to take no one into my confidence. If this was a true attempt by Robinson to come over, and word of it got out, it would ruin everything, and put him in grave danger."

"Surely you could have taken General Washington into your confidence without fear of him violating it," Joshua stated. "Had you done so, you would not be here today."

"Of course I could have trusted General Washington, and in hindsight I realize that is what I should have done. However, at the time, knowing how he thinks, I feared he would refuse to allow me to continue the negotiations."

"And if he did so? It would simply be a matter of breaking off contact with Robinson, would it not?"

There was a significant pause before Arnold replied. "It would, except...." Here Arnold paused again, and when he resumed speaking, he turned to the court, an anguished expression in his eyes. "I must tell you now something which is painful for me to reveal, and I ask for your indulgence and understanding. In the letter, Robinson had indicated that I would not find him ungrateful if our plan succeeded. Robinson is a very rich man, possibly set to regain a vast estate, and I was desperate for money. I had not been paid in more than five years. Congress had still not approved my accounts from the Canadian campaign, now five years old. My allowances as military commander of Philadelphia would not support both my family and my governmental obligations. I was virtually bankrupt, and remain so. I admit that I saw an opportunity to profit and at the same time do a service to my country."

During their discussion the previous evening, Arnold and Joshua had agreed to pre-empt the prosecution by volunteering the information. "It is a damaging admission," Joshua had said "but if you offer it forthrightly it may lend an aura of truth to the rest of your testimony. In fact, I suggest we bring it up ourselves, rather than risk it appearing as though Edwards ferreted out a secret."

Arnold had fallen silent, and Joshua examined the members of the court closely, seeking some sign of how Arnold's admission had affected them. He was unable to reach any conclusions from the set faces, all staring at Arnold. Finally, he prompted Arnold to go on with his testimony.

"Once I decided to assist Robinson's offer to defect to us," Arnold continued, in a more subdued voice, "the first thing I needed to confirm was that I was actually dealing with Robinson and that his desire to change sides was genuine. The only way to do that was by a face-to-face meeting. For that, I needed the assistance of a trustworthy person who would be strictly under my control. I chose Squire Smith, who, as he correctly stated, had come recommended to me by General Howe. The rest of the story is pretty much as stated in the *truthful* parts of his testimony.

"My first attempt to meet Robinson at Dobbs Ferry nearly ended in me being killed, when, as André stated, my barge was chased and fired upon by a British gunboat. The second attempt, foiled by lack of a boat, failed also. It succeeded on the following night, because Robinson decided to try again by staying over on the *Vulture*. However, to my surprise and disappointment, instead of Robinson, a British officer came ashore."

"You had made out a pass for Joshua Smith and John Anderson. Will you explain that?"

"Robinson and I had agreed that he would assume the name of John Anderson in our correspondence. Obviously, it was impossible for me to issue a pass to Beverly Robinson, who is well known as the commander of the Loyal Americans. I assumed he would have some identification showing him to be John Anderson, and issued the pass in that name."

"Major André testified that was the cover name he used in his correspondence with you."

"He's lying. I never had any correspondence with Major André, or even heard of him, until he stepped ashore from the *Vulture* in place of Colonel Robinson."

"What happened after André came ashore?"

"I asked him who he was and why Robinson had not come. He identified himself as a British officer, but withheld his name. He apologized for Robinson, claiming the colonel had decided at the last minute that he was too well known in the valley to risk exposure. He then produced a letter signed by Robinson stating the same thing. I explained to him that the whole purpose of this meeting was for me to be assured I was dealing with Robinson, that although the signature was the same one I had seen on his letters to me, there was now no way I could know if the signature was genuine, and therefore the purpose of the meeting could not be achieved. Furthermore, I told him, I found it highly suspicious that a British officer would be assisting a fellow officer to desert to the enemy.

"He then made an astounding revelation. He admitted to me that the entire matter of Robinson wanting to change sides was a hoax, a subterfuge to enable this meeting with me. He introduced himself as Major John André, adjutant general to the British Army, and informed me the purpose of the meeting was of far greater import than that originally proposed. He began by telling me that he was intimately aware of the details of my military career, and stated that, except for Washington, I was viewed by the British as the finest general on the American side. He mentioned my performance in the Canadian campaign, which he said had even come to the attention of Lord Germain, British secretary of state for the colonies, who remarked to General Burgoyne that he felt that I was 'the most enterprising man among the rebels.' He went on in a complimentary fashion about my actions at Valcour Island, Ridgefield, and Fort Stanwix, culminating with my actions at Bemis Heights, which, according to Burgoyne, forced his surrender at Saratoga."

There was nothing new to the court here, except that, according to Arnold, it was supposedly coming from a British officer. But, in addition to explaining the purpose of André's visit, it gave Arnold another opportunity to summarize his achievements. Joshua again scrutinized the court members, trying to determine the effect Arnold's testimony was having, but other than noting that they seemed to be concentrating on every word, again, he could tell nothing.

"Although this was all very complimentary," Arnold continued, "I informed André that it did not explain the purpose of his visit. He asked for my patience, and then said that he and many others in the British Army were mystified by the way my government had rewarded my service. He was aware that I had been passed over for promotion by Congress. He knew of what he referred to as my 'persecution' by the Council of Pennsylvania, and said he could scarcely believe the news when he heard of my first court-martial. To be subject to such a draconian measure for such trivial charges would be unheard of in the British Army, he claimed. And Washington's reprimand of one of his finest field commanders he felt was unnecessarily harsh. To my embarrassment, he even knew of my financial difficulties.

"André then changed direction," Arnold continued. "He began to speak of what he called 'the evils of the rebellion,' the turning of brother against brother, friend against friend. It was time to end the bloodshed, he said. Although Britain would never acquiesce to complete American independence, she would grant every other demand of the colonies, to include full self-government. United, Britain and America would rule the world. No nation could ever match us in military or economic power. Why destroy such a partnership?"

As Arnold paused, there was not a sound in the room. All eyes were focused on him, waiting for him to continue. Whether or not the members of the court believed the testimony, Joshua still could not tell, but there was no doubt they were spellbound by the story.

"André then finally came to the heart of the matter," Arnold resumed. "He told me he had come to the conclusion that I was the one person who could end the war and bring about the reconciliation of the colonies and the mother country. By changing sides, I would serve clear notice that a most illustrious American general was convinced that the war could not be won and to continue the destruction and killing was wrong and useless. To insure that the switching of sides would be devastating, he said it must be accompanied by a momentous military blow to the rebellion, something which would make its continuation impossible. He suggested that as commander of the Highlands, I could arrange the surrender of Fortress West Point, which would sever the New England colonies from the rest of the country. He did not seem to see the irony in the fact that this was the very result that I had prevented at Saratoga. He promised I would be handsomely rewarded for this service, compensated for any loss of property I might sustain, and be accepted into the British Army with the same rank I now held. In this connection, he assured me that I would not be required to fight against my former comrades unless I chose to do so. I could be of valuable service to General Clinton in other ways, by being a rallying symbol for all Loyalist forces, and by providing him sound military advice.

"Well, there it was," Arnold continued after another pause, "finally out in the open. Aware of the fact that I needed money, André hoped that I would yield to the temptations he had dangled in front of me. I must admit that I spent several minutes frantically scouring my memory, trying to recall any act of mine which would have led him to assume I was capable of such treachery. Why else would he have taken the risk to come here? But, finding nothing, I realized he assumed that what he saw as the unjust acts of my government would have caused sufficient disaffection on my part to entertain his proposal. I quickly and forcefully rejected his overture. I pointed out, that although I might have been treated unfairly at times, I remained a firm patriot, dedicated to the cause of American independence, and that no amount of money would sway my loyalty."

At the conclusion of this statement, Arnold seemed to sink deep into thought, and he paused so long that Joshua felt it necessary to prompt him. "What happened then, sir?"

"We continued the discussion for some time," Arnold said, rousing himself. "André tried to change my mind. He pointed out other probable benefits once the war was over, a knighthood, lifetime pensions for myself and my family, even a grant of a large tract of land in the west, upon which I could settle my own tenants and collect rents. It was an alluring prospect, but one which I obviously could not accept. Eventually, Smith came up to remind us that daylight was approaching. We had been so focused on the discussion that we had let the passage of time escape us, and I now realized that André would not be able to return to the ship until dark that night.

Accordingly, we made our way to Smith's house, where André could safely wait out the day.

"On the way, my thoughts turned on what to do about André. I seriously thought about taking him prisoner for suborning treason, but then I realized that he was here at my invitation to ostensibly discuss a secret plan which I had revealed to no one. His presence as a prisoner, and subsequent interrogation, would raise matters difficult to explain and cause me great embarrassment. I decided it was best to simply let him return to his ship, his plan a failure.

"It was then that the firing upon the *Vulture* began. I was caught totally by surprise, not having ordered such an act. I later learned that Colonel Livingston, irritated by the presence of the vessel so close to his command, had requested ammunition from Colonel Lamb at West Point to take the ship under fire. As we watched the action, André expressed concern, especially when the ship appeared to take several hits. When it became apparent that it was being towed downstream, he became distraught. I assured him that the vessel would not leave without him, and shortly thereafter the action broke off. My trip having ended in a goose chase, I now wanted to be off as soon as possible.

"When Smith arrived, I issued him instructions that André was to be taken to the ship that night without fail, and I left. When he reported to me the next day that André was safely on his way, I thought the matter closed. I was seriously disabused of that notion when General Washington placed me under arrest the following Monday. I was absolutely speechless. I had no knowledge of any documents in André's possession—no pass, no documents concerning Fortress West Point. As far as I knew, he had returned to the ship and I was rid of him."

"If the account you have just given us is true, how do you explain André's actions after he left you?"

"The only possible explanation is that there was an alternate plan. André came to me to try to induce my defection. If I refused, he would somehow see that those documents fell into American hands, falsely implicating me in a plot to commit treason, probably with the assistance of Smith. He had witnesses to the fact that he had met with me—Smith and the Colquhoun brothers. For some reason the plot went awry, and he wound up a prisoner with the papers still in his possession."

Joshua had one more point to clear up before he surrendered Arnold to cross examination. "General, why did you refuse the command of the left wing of the Army, a position of high honor, and instead request command of the Highlands and West Point?"

"There were several reasons," Arnold replied. "First, my leg was still causing me a great deal of trouble. I was in almost constant pain, and long periods on horseback would have aggravated that. I could not mount or dismount without assistance, a condition embarrassing to me personally, and a danger to others on the battlefield. I had recently married, and for the first time in many years I was enjoying the comforts and attentions of a beautiful woman. I felt that I had given enough to my country to earn a respite from lonely and arduous field duty. But I fully intended to return to active service as soon as I was fit to do so."

"Sir, I have no more questions. Do you have anything you wish to say in conclusion?"

Arnold reflected for a moment. "In judging my actions, I ask the court to consider only the case before it. As I mentioned at the beginning of my testimony, I am aware of having failed to notify my commander of my actions, and will stand trial for that if I must. But I plead with you not to let that influence your judgment of my guilt or innocence of the present charges against me. To do so would play in the hands of the enemy, who is hoping that this foul plot will succeed."

As Joshua sat down, Edwards rose. "General Arnold," he began, "your defense in this case is to claim that you are victim of a plot hatched by Major André to discredit you, is that correct?"

"It is not a claim, it is the truth."

"And all these documents—the letters discovered in your files, the passes carried by Smith, and the documents found on André when he was taken prisoner—all are forgeries?"

"Except for the ones I have acknowledged, yes."

"It must follow then that both Smith and André have lied under oath in their statements to this court."

"They obviously have done so."

"Tell me, general, what could Major André possibly gain by lying at this time?"

"Frankly, colonel, I wish I knew. Why did he not simply admit that he tried to turn me, failed, and was on his way home? Why was he carrying those forged West Point documents? Why did he not return to the *Vulture*, as he was supposed to? I don't know the answers to any of these questions."

"I'll give you an answer, sir. It is that Major André is telling truth, and you are not. He did not lie to save his life at his hearing. Why should he do so now?"

"For the reasons I have already explained. Something went wrong with his plan, poor execution or bad luck. Being dealt a bad hand, he is making the best of it. He tried to turn me, but failing, now hopes to convince this court that I am a traitor to my country."

"Forgive me, sir, but I have to say that I find his statement much more believable than yours."

"If you wish to take the word of a convicted spy over a general officer in the Continental Army...." Arnold let the sentence trail off, and Edwards did not pursue it.

"Regarding the letter you received from Colonel Robinson while at dinner on September 17th, Colonel Lamb stated that he advised you against meeting with him, and suggested you take the matter up with General Washington. Did you do so?"

"I did."

"And what was the result?"

Arnold was aware that Edwards knew the answer to the question. "He suggested that I... not meet with him."

"Suggested, or ordered, sir?"

Shifting uncomfortably, Arnold realized he had little choice in his answer. "I suppose it could have been considered an order."

"An order which you violated by going ahead with the meeting.

So at the very least, you are guilty of disobeying your commanding officer."

Arnold struggled for a reply. "If so, I shall answer for it later. But the matter has no place here."

"Except to wonder how many steps it is from disobeying an order to committing treason."

Joshua rose quickly, hoping to intercept the wrath he saw gathering in Arnold's expression. "Sir, the prosecutor is out of order."

"So you are, Colonel Edwards," Greene agreed. "The court has no need for your personal conjecture. The remark will be removed from the record."

Undaunted, Edwards continued without pause. "You testified that you did not keep a copy of Colonel Robinson's letter because he requested that you destroy it. While that was most considerate of you—especially since Robinson is an enemy officer—would it not have been wiser to keep a copy, to justify your actions?"

"I also destroyed it because it could easily be seen as an incriminating document, which, if you think on it, is why those other documents you found in my files could not possibly be genuine. Why would I have destroyed the letter from Robinson, but left far more incriminating documents in my files?"

"I can think of a good reason. Because they are the most important of all. They show your offer to surrender West Point and the British acceptance of your terms. You would want to keep them as proof of the bargain if there should be any question later about the payment offered."

"And they are exactly what would be planted in my files by a carefully engineered scheme, to show 'proof' of offer and acceptance. And my enemies would have made much mischief with that letter, much as you are trying to do now."

"You know, general, I find myself intrigued by the number of enemies you have claimed to have during this trial. I know of no other officer in the service who can match your record. Can you enlighten us on why you should have so many hands raised against you?" It was an unexpected question, concerning a relatively minor matter. In Joshua's view, it was designed to throw Arnold off balance. Arnold, however, seemed to take it in stride.

"I don't believe that I have had more than my share of men who dislike me. I have made many stout friends, and I have been told that I am held in high regard among the rank and file. My misfortune has been that those few who wish me ill are so energetic and persistent in their hatred. Much of it, I think, has to do with the difficult assignments I have been required to perform. As far back as Ticonderoga, I have had to contend with unruly men who resented discipline, such as those under Ethan Allen, and dishonest and avaricious officers such as Easton, Brown and Mott. Later, on the march to Quebec, struggling with nature, weather, and starvation, I was again bedeviled by Brown and Easton, and obliged to prefer charges against them for plundering the baggage of British officer prisoners of war. In addition, I was plagued with a new curse, Moses Hazen, whom I had to court-martial for neglect and theft of our vital stores. It is easy to understand why these men would think ill of me."

He paused here, but it was apparent that he was not finished, just gathering his thoughts. Edwards let him do so, and Joshua soon realized why. "I have already shown that I have enemies in Congress," Arnold continued. "Who, why, or how many there are, I have no idea. But their existence is proven by the many acts of disfavor that body has shown toward me." It may have been a valid complaint, but Joshua knew that Arnold was doing himself no good by voicing it. Rather, he was painting a scene which gave him good reason for disaffection. He tried to get the general's attention, but Arnold did not seem aware of the danger.

"And Joseph Reed, Timothy Matlack, and the other members of the Council of Pennsylvania have been implacable foes ever since my appointment as military commander of Philadelphia. They hounded me for traveling by coach-and-four instead of horseback, although my leg makes riding painful and almost impossible. They accused me of providing 'splendid entertainments,' and of an ostentatious lifestyle unbecoming my position. They charged me with courting Loyalists, and showing favoritism toward them, even to the point of criticizing my marriage. But, by far, the worst damage they did me was to work tirelessly for months to amass a series of baseless charges against me, and constantly agitate Congress for disciplinary action. I think it fair to state that, in the end, forced to decide between threats by the powerful state of Pennsylvania to withdraw its support for the cause, or take action against one general officer with no political influence, Congress chose the latter."

At this point, Joshua finally caught Arnold's eye. The general had gone too far, and Joshua hoped that by his expression, and the faint shake of his head, he would send that message. It seemed to work, and Arnold changed course.

"Considering all I have just said, I was convinced I had to proceed with utmost secrecy every step of the way, lest I expose myself to someone eager to do me ill. It was even possible that one or more of my enemies had engineered the whole plot, in an attempt to brand me a traitor. To me, it is not far-fetched that Colonel Hazen, for example, might have been in collusion with Major André. There would be a pretended 'capture' of André in which the papers were 'found,' and then he would make his 'escape.' That's why it was so important that I meet face to face with Robinson, to establish that the approach was genuine."

"Speaking of Philadelphia," Edwards said, shifting the direction again, "I have examined the allowances for your duties as military commander of the city. They seemed quite adequate."

"They were barely adequate for official requirements. They were not adequate at all when my military salary was withheld, and, in addition, I was required to support my family from them."

"Yet you managed to purchase Mount Pleasant, a fine Philadelphia home on an estate of 96 acres."

"With a large mortgage, and which was on lease to the Spanish Ambassador because I could not afford to live there."

Edwards then picked up a paper from his desk and showed it to Arnold. "Sir, will you please identify this document for the court?"

Glancing briefly at the paper, Arnold's expression turned grim. "It is a copy of General Orders of April 6th, 1780."

"Are you willing to stipulate that this document was found in your files?"

After a quick glance at Joshua, Arnold nodded. "I am."

"For the benefit of the court," Edwards announced, turning toward its members, "the subject of this document is the court-martial of General Benedict Arnold, which took place at Morristown from the 23rd of December to the 26th of January last. The Order ends with the reprimand from the commander in chief as directed by the sentence of the court. I would like to read that reprimand."

Joshua rose. "Sir, the reprimand given at General Arnold's previous trial has no place here."

"If the court will indulge me for a moment," Edwards responded, "I will show its relevance." Greene ruled that he could proceed, and he began to read.

> The Commander in Chief would have been much happier in an occasion of bestowing commendations on an officer who has rendered such distinguished services to his Country as Major General Arnold; but in the present case a sense of duty and a regard to candor oblige him to declare, that he considers his conduct in the instance of the permit as peculiarly reprehensible, both in a civil and military view, and in the affair of the wagons as Imprudent and improper.

"Written into the margin beside this paragraph," Edwards continued, "is penned the Latin phrase, '*E tu, Brute*?'" He then walked back to Arnold. "Did you write this phrase, sir, or do you claim it is another forgery?"

It was moment before Arnold spoke. "I wrote it," he admitted.

"So it is safe to say you felt betrayed by General Washington?"

"At the time I did. I had expected to be acquitted with honor of all charges. When I was convicted of two of them and sentenced to be reprimanded I was shocked, yet, in light of my rank and service to the nation I expected the reprimand to be a mild one. The severity of it, when it finally came, cast me into a severe depression. I felt as if my last friend had turned from me. However, General Washington sent me a private letter, written the same day, but received later. In it, he was much friendlier, even apologetic, in explaining the reprimand. He urged me, and I can quote verbatim, to 'exhibit anew those noble qualities which have placed you on the list of our most valued commanders. I will myself furnish you, as far as it may be in my power, with opportunities of regaining the esteem of your country.'"

Arnold then turned to the court. "I have that letter in my possession," he added. "It was another which my wife had wished to keep, and she brought it here with her. I had not intended to introduce it, since it bears on my last trial, not this one. I can do so now, to attest to what I have said."

"The prosecution has no objection to its introduction, if General Arnold so wishes," Edwards informed the court, "however, rather than delay these proceedings to produce the letter, I am willing to stipulate that its contents are as stated by him."

Arnold accepted the stipulation, adding, "And as you know, gentlemen, General Washington kept his word as stated in that letter by appointing me to command the left wing of the Army on August 1st."

"An honor which you declined to accept."

"For reasons which I have already explained."

Edwards went on to a new subject. "Now, sir, if I may turn to the matter of Fortress West Point. We heard Colonel Lamb complain that you weakened the garrison by sending two hundred woodcutters to Fishkill."

"True, but I gave orders for the detachments at Fishkill and Kings Ferry to move to West Point at first alarm, so as to increase the number of defenders."

"To increase the number of defenders, or to increase the bag of prisoners which would be taken?"

"According to you, if I send the woodcutters out, I am weakening the garrison. If I keep them in, I am increasing the bag of prisoners. I sent a blizzard of requisitions to the quartermaster general for supplies of all kinds. By your reasoning, I was increasing the booty for the enemy to capture. Had I failed to do so, you would accuse me of deliberately starving the defense of the fort. I appealed to both Governor Clinton and Quartermaster General Pickering, seeking to repair the river chain, which was sinking due to the logs floating it becoming water-soaked. If I pulled it up for repair, its absence would aid the enemy. If I did nothing, its deterioration would accomplish the same thing. You cannot have it both ways, colonel. Which is it to be?"

It was a brilliant counter-attack, Joshua thought. Arnold at his best. He had taken the initiative from Edwards and scored decisive points in his defense. With a thrill of anticipation, he now felt that Arnold almost surely would go free. This was finally a case he was going to win!

Edwards, however, seemed unperturbed and again shifted direction. "I would like to go over with you once more the documents Major André claimed he received from you, and which were taken from his person."

Joshua could see no benefit to the prosecution in this line of questioning. Why was Edwards going back over this? It would only give Arnold another opportunity to deny the documents and brand them forgeries. He must be rattled by Arnold's reply, trying to think of a way to regain control of his cross examination. It could also mean that Edwards had reached the end of his rope, and was stalling for time, trying to think of a new approach. Joshua's confidence surged.

"First, there is the pass issued to John Anderson and signed by you," Edwards began. "You have claimed you did not issue it. How, then, could Major André have come into possession of such a pass?"

"Easily. As I have said before, as spymaster for General Clinton he certainly possessed the necessary assets to produce such a forgery."

"I see. But how about the estimate of the forces at West Point, and also the number of men required to man the works? Wouldn't they require knowledge not available to Major André in New York?"

"Such information was common knowledge among the officers and sergeants at West Point. It could have been obtained from an agent within the fortress and passed to André."

"A fairly high-placed agent, wouldn't you say?"

"Not necessarily. Strength figures are known to many in the command, and are required in many reports, and for requesting rations and ammunition."

"But then we have the description of the condition of the fortress and its redoubts, to include pointing out weaknesses—"

"I can tell you where that came from," Arnold interrupted. "Two weeks ago, General Washington asked me for such a report, which I furnished to him. Someone either had access to his files or to mine."

"So now you are suggesting that Major André had an agent on General Washington's staff?"

"It is possible. Such things are not unheard of." Arnold was clearly becoming irritated by the exchange, and Joshua was perplexed. Edwards' questions were unusual and uncharacteristic. He seemed to be encouraging Arnold to speak, offering him the opportunity to attack each document once more. It was an action which clearly favored the defense, and Joshua could not understand why Edwards was pursuing it.

"Then there is the inventory of artillery, sir."

"The number of guns in inventory was known to many, and available to others, for requisition and training purposes."

"And the Artillery Orders?"

"Again, also available to many. Every unit commander in the fortress needs to know the disposition of the artillery in the event of an alarm. And the artillery units themselves must know where their postings are."

Edwards, who had been referring to his notes, looked up and stared at Arnold. Joshua saw that his eyes had narrowed and his expression had changed. But his voice retained the same almost friendly tone.

"Artillery orders are published frequently, and typically deal with many diverse subjects, routine and otherwise, do they not?

"That is correct."

"Well, then, sir, how did you know that the particular order found in Major André's possession dealt with the disposition of the corps in event of an alarm?"

"I read it at the beginning of the trial, of course, when you introduced it with the others."

Edwards let Arnold's answer hang for a long moment before he spoke.

"I'm sorry to contradict you, sir, but that is impossible."

Arnold blinked, an expression of confusion in his eyes. Edwards walked quickly to the court table, picked up a sheaf of documents and brought them to where Arnold was sitting. Joshua felt as though the blood had turned to ice water in his veins. He now knew why Edwards had encouraged the general to talk about the André papers, and his heart sank.

"Sir," Edwards announced, "these are the documents I have introduced at this trial as found on Major André's person when he was taken." Then, one by one, he laid them in front of Arnold, naming each as he did so. "The pass allowing John Anderson movement between the lines, the estimate of actual strength of forces manning West Point, the estimate of manpower required to man the works, the inventory of artillery at West Point, the report concerning construction and condition of the redoubts, and finally, the extract of General Washington's council of war of September 6th, 1780."

Slowly, Edwards held up a seventh document. "This is Artillery Orders for September 5th, 1780, which you just described, but which I did *not* introduce." The quiet in the courtroom was the silence of the tomb. "Oh, you are correct, sir," Edwards continued. "The document is exactly what you say it is, and it was found on the person of Major André, along with the others. However, I never showed it in this court room, nor made any reference to it. I introduce it now, however, since you have yourself identified it." In the dead silence that engulfed the room, Edwards laid the document before Greene.

"General Arnold," Edwards said, turning to Arnold once more, "since I never showed you this document, nor was it mentioned anytime in these proceedings, the only possible way you could have known that this particular artillery order was in Major André's possession is that you gave it to him."

A barely audible collective sigh seemed to come from the court. It was over. Everyone in the room knew it, including Arnold. Nathanael Greene slowly put his head in his hands. Baron von Steuben slumped heavily back in his chair, and several others appeared dazed. The suddenness of the end stunned them all. Finally, Edwards broke the silence.

"I have nothing further," he said, and walked slowly to his desk and sat down.

"Does the defense have anything further?" Greene asked, looking directly at Arnold. But Arnold said nothing, staring straight ahead, motionless as a statue. Finally, Joshua rose.

"The defense has nothing further," he said, his voice cracking.

"Does the prosecution wish to offer closing argument?"

"The prosecution does not," replied Edwards.

"Does the defense wish to offer closing argument?"

Arnold remained silent, immobile.

"The defense does not," Joshua responded.

Greene rapped his gavel. "The court will be closed."

While the court deliberated, Joshua and Arnold waited in the now empty witness waiting room across the hall, the general totally withdrawn into a world of his own, and Joshua too much in shock to try to make conversation. The court reopened thirty minutes later to announce a finding of guilty of Specifications 1 and 2, and a finding of not proven of Specification 3, which charged that Arnold had attempted to betray Washington.

"The court will hear any citations which the prosecution or the defense may wish to present," Greene announced. The court was now inviting legal instructions and matters in mitigation.

"I have two citations to refer to the court," Edwards stated. "First, the Continental Congress Resolution of 1776, which provides the sentence of death for conviction of the charge of treason against America. Second, Article 19, Section XIII of the Articles of War, which states that 'whosoever shall be convicted of holding correspondence with, or giving intelligence to the enemy, either directly or indirectly, shall suffer death, or such other punishment as by a court martial may be inflicted.'"

Greene then turned to Joshua. "Does the defense have any citations to present?"

Joshua glanced at Arnold, who still maintained his stone-like silence. "I would only ask the court to consider General Arnold's long and distinguished service to this nation, and the slights and injustices he perceived, which most certainly have been the primary cause of his actions."

The court closed again, and reopened twenty minutes later. Arnold and Joshua rose to face Greene for the last time.

"General Arnold, it is my sad duty to inform you that the court has sentenced you to death by hanging for the offense of treason against the United States of America."

Now, Arnold finally broke his silence. "By taking up arms against the British Crown, everyone in this room has committed treason."

"If that is the case, sir," Greene responded," then you have committed it twice. Do you have anything else you wish to say at this time?"

When Arnold spoke, it was as if he were a different person than the one who had so forcefully proclaimed his innocence such a short time ago. His voice rang with the same conviction with which he had so fervently defended himself.

"History will show that the real traitors are those who have condemned me," he said. "Your cause is doomed, gentlemen. Look around you. Regiments mutiny, desertions grow, and corruption prevails, while Congress vacillates helplessly. Your so-called French ally provides you little. In returning to the loyalty we all owe to the crown of England, I have no regrets, save that I left it in the first place. Murder me on your gallows, gentlemen. Although you do me injustice, you also do me honor, for I shall rise like the phoenix from the ashes of your failed revolution, a true hero of the times, while you, sirs, will go to those same gallows, but in ignominious disgrace."

A gloomy quiet settled over the court room as Arnold finished. Finally, General Greene spoke. "Does anyone have anything further?" No voice broke the silence. "Guards, return the prisoner to his place of confinement. This court is now adjourned."

As the grim-faced court members rose and left the room, General Jedediah Huntington was heard to mutter, "The bastard may be right. Things have never looked worse."

# CHAPTER THIRTY-SIX

"IT HAS ALL happened so quickly," Amy said, after Joshua had related the day's events. "I always felt that he was guilty, but you had made it sound as though it was going to be hard to prove. Now, suddenly, it's over." Physically, she seemed somewhat better. Color had returned to her cheeks, but her entire left side appeared grasped in a vise of sore stiffness, and any attempt to lift her arm still met with pain. It was her mental outlook that worried Joshua. Her voice was still lifeless, her eyes stricken. Joshua was grateful that she seemed to express an interest in the trial.

"Washington has moved with equal speed," he informed her. "Two hours after the court closed, he approved the sentence and set Saturday noon for the hanging. An express rider is already en route to Philadelphia to get the consent of Congress." He, too, had difficulty adjusting to events. Having almost convinced himself of Arnold's innocence, the unexpected proof of his guilt had been a blow. No small part of that was the knowledge that Arnold, through lies and consummate acting skills, had betrayed him into believing his story.

"This whole drama has played out like a Shakespearean tragedy," he said. "Washington, acting too late in offering Arnold the command of the left wing of the army, which would have erased all the humiliation of his previous court-martial and the slights of Congress, and given a clear indication to all of the commander in chief's confidence in him."

"Why didn't he accept it, then?"

"By then he'd gone too far."

"He could have simply stopped, or called it off."

Joshua shook his head. "No, I think that by then he'd lost faith in the revolution. He believed the war was lost, and being who he was, he wanted to be on the winning side."

Amy was silent for a moment, and when she spoke, it was on a new subject. "With Arnold's conviction, there's no hope for John André." Her voice mirrored her inner despair.

"I'm surprised you still care what happens to him, after...after your injury at the hands of the British. Right now I wish I were in the line. I'd shoot every damned redcoat I could find."

"It was an accident, Josh. No one deliberately tried to shoot me. I should have made myself known, instead of tip-toeing in the dark."

"Well, this is certainly an unusual twist. Here I am faulting the British and you're defending them."

"I'm not defending them, I'm just not blaming them. I might just as reasonably blame Benedict Arnold. If not for his actions, the British wouldn't have been in Mabie's that morning." She sighed heavily and sank back on her pillow. "Oh, how I wish John André had gotten away."

Joshua felt it was time to change the subject. "You know, ever since that...accident, I've been thinking how uncertain life can be. I know I don't have much to offer as a husband...." He noted the pained expression in her eyes, and stopped.

Amy hoped he could not see how her heart ached as she heard those words. If only they had reached this point earlier, and under different circumstances. As much as she wanted him, she would not inflict a maimed woman on him. But was she going to be strong enough to let him go?

"We've never spoken of marriage," she said, after a long pause.

"I know. I've felt the times were too unsettled. But there may be many years of unsettled times ahead. Your injury has made me realize that I don't want to lose you along the way."

"How could I marry now?" she asked, her voice a dull monotone. "I'm disfigured."

"You must never think of yourself that way."

"How else *can* I think of myself?" she persisted. "People will view me as deformed." She was deliberately exaggerating her feelings, trying to turn him away.

"Just some padding under your bodice, and no one will ever know."

"You will."

"I promise to tell no one."

"No man will have me now." She was beginning to panic, reaching for straws as he refused to be swayed.

"I'm a man. At least I was the last time I noticed." He was hoping his light manner would cheer her, but he could see it was having the opposite effect.

She shook her head and tears welled in her eyes. "It's no use, Joshua. I can't marry. Not now, not ever." It was going to be harder than she thought, much harder.

"Nonsense, there's no reason—"

"How could I ever undress again before you...let you see..." Her grief choked off further words. He bent down and tried to kiss her, but she turned away. "Please go now, Joshua. I don't want to talk anymore."

"But—"

"*Please!*" The desperation in her voice told Joshua he had no choice. Feeling leaden, he reluctantly left her crying on the bed.

# CHAPTER THIRTY-SEVEN

*Headquarters Mess, Tappan, New York*
*Thursday, October 12, 1780*

"YOU'RE GOOD, THOMAS. You are very good." Joshua and Thomas Edwards were finishing a shared breakfast of slapjacks, washed down with hot cider.

"I only presented the facts."

"You set a trap for him."

"He trapped himself."

"What would you have done if Arnold noticed the omission of the artillery order early on in the trial, when you first introduced the papers?"

"He wasn't the only one who didn't pick up the omission. The members of the court all saw the documents at André's inquiry, including Greene, but none of them seemed to notice my omission of the artillery order."

"André did."

"Ah, you saw that," Edwards smiled. "Good for you. But he probably saw no reason to mention it. And Arnold could hardly have called attention to it. How would he have known about it except by giving it to André?"

"But he could have remembered when you mentioned it later, when he was testifying, and played dumb."

"Possibly, but it was a gamble I had to take. The larger gamble was that Arnold would choose not to testify, but knowing him, I felt fairly certain he would."

"And knowing *you*, if he hadn't, you'd have found something else."

"Tell me, Josh, would you have had it any other way? A traitor has been fairly tried and truly convicted, and by his own words."

Joshua sighed. "You're right. I became his partisan. After getting to know him, and seeing him as a mistreated hero, I wanted him innocent, and therefore believed him to be. I allowed 'reasonable doubt' to obscure the facts which pointed to his guilt."

"I don't blame you. A cloud of reasonable doubt was starting to form over the whole case. But toward the end of the trial, wasn't there something that should have made you suspicious?"

It took Joshua only a few seconds to respond. "It was when André stated he had never seen Arnold's letter giving away Washington's location."

"Exactly. If André could identify the other letters, but not that one, he could not have arranged to have it planted in Arnold's files. Therefore, it must have been originated by Arnold."

"Unless you look at it in a very Machiavellian way. André arranges to have it planted in the files, then denies all knowledge of it, so that the only explanation is that Arnold wrote it."

Edwards frowned. "I'm not sure I follow."

"Don't bother. The letter was almost certainly sent by Arnold," Joshua agreed. "But why didn't André receive it?"

"It may have been lost somewhere along the way. Then again, perhaps he did receive it." Seeing Joshua's perplexed expression, Edwards continued, "Did you notice the way Arnold reacted when André failed to identify the letter? It was only momentary, but he seemed as surprised as anyone else in the court room." It took Joshua a long moment to make the connection Edwards was trying to make.

"You mean...."

"Perhaps this was a gift from André to Arnold, who was already charged with providing intelligence to the enemy and attempting to surrender West Point. He would spare him the added ignominy of betraying his commander."

"But why?"

"Who can tell? A favor from one gentleman to another? We'll never know what sort of personal relationship there was between Arnold and André. But it's probable, that to André, Arnold was a hero, trying to return to his true allegiance at great risk to himself."

Joshua nodded, then changed the subject. "How did you persuade André to testify?"

"By playing on his feelings for Peggy Arnold. I led him to believe that unless I had him as a witness, I would need to introduce a certain letter establishing a relationship between him and Mrs. Arnold."

"A letter which Washington had prohibited you from using."

Edwards smiled and shrugged. "André had no way of knowing that. Now let me ask *you* a question. I compliment you on your attack on André's honor. I'm certain it had an influence on the court. How did you find du Simitière?"

Joshua explained du Simitière's coincidental visit. "He had once worked with Franklin and was incensed that André would steal the great man's possessions. But he also strongly suspected—and André did not deny, that the loot was being collected at the direction of General Grey, André's superior officer at the time, and with whom he shared Franklin's house." Joshua then added, "But I saw no need to bring that up."

"Ah, so that's why you cut off his testimony." Edwards smiled again. "It seems, Josh, our tactics are not so different, after all."

Later in the morning, Joshua called on Amy. He found her dressed and sitting in a chair, her left arm in a sling. Her dress revealed no lack of form in her bosom, due to the padded bandage still in place underneath. She looked better. Only her eyes betrayed her inner feelings. She had gotten out of bed to dress, she told him, managing the feat with the help of Mary Burns. She wanted to walk, she said. Her back was stiff from sleeping in the unaccustomed position forced by her injury, and she wanted to work out the stiffness. With his help, they walked slowly a short distance down the lane leading to Main Street, then returned. She asked him to bring chairs outside, so that they could enjoy the fresh air and the warmth of the noonday sun. She asked if he would read to her, since it was difficult for her to hold a book and turn pages with only one hand free. The book she handed to him was *Le Mort D' Arthur*, whether by accident or design, although he suspected it was her way of getting him to read it. By late afternoon, when the chill forced them inside, he agreed with her, it was a fine, if almost unending, story.

Several times during the day he tried to bring up marriage again, but she rebuffed all his attempts. Finally, as she was getting ready for bed, she raised the issue herself.

"Why are you suddenly interested in marriage?"

"I told you why yesterday. The accident made me realize...well... that I love you, and want you—not just in bed, but by my side... always." The words came with difficulty, and only poorly expressed what he felt. To him, they sounded hollow, insincere. He wished he had made his proposal earlier, before her injury. He did not want her to think he was doing so out of pity for her condition, but he could not frame the words to say so.

"You never brought it up before," she said quietly.

"I've never felt so close to losing you before." At least that sounded right. But he could sense the feeling behind her words. She *was* afraid that his proposal was based on pity.

"Joshua, I can't think about marriage now. Perhaps not for a long time. There is much I have to reconcile myself to. You must understand that."

"The only thing I understand is the longer we wait, the more time we rob from ourselves." Involuntarily, his thoughts returned to the room where Benedict and Peggy Arnold shared the remaining time the sands of the hour glass allowed them. What advice would the young wife, soon to be a widow, give to Amelia Martin? But he would not bring the grief of one household into another. He and Amy would have to cope with their own demons alone, as Arnold and his wife must be doing. He decided to say no more about it this evening. As Mary Burns came in to help Amy prepare for bed, he left.

"Do you love him?" Mary Burns fluffed two pillows and propped them at the head of the bed.

"I don't know," Amy said, leaning back and closing her eyes. What she did know was that she wanted Josh more than ever, but she was determined not to inflict a maimed wife upon him.

"Of course you know. You wouldn't have stayed with him all this time if you didn't. Accept him and be done with it."

"I can't. He'll think I'm coming to him because of my injury, because no one else will have me now." Tears welled in her eyes, then rolled down her cheeks.

Mary Burns was having none of it. "Nonsense. Do you think he has stuck by you out of pity?"

"Perhaps."

"More nonsense. It's because he loves you and wants you for wife, and one less tit isn't going to change that. If that were the case, he would have cleared off by now."

"I won't marry him if he thinks I am coming to him out of desperation or gratitude."

"Of course not. Marry him because he loves you and you love him, and be done with all this self pity."

# CHAPTER THIRTY-EIGHT

*DeWint House, Tappan, New York*
*Friday, October 13, 1780*

THERE WERE TWO things Joshua needed to do on this day, and he had no enthusiasm for either. His appointment with George Washington was for 10 A.M. Although he had told her nothing about it, he was making this visit for Amy. Arriving promptly, he was ushered into the commander in chief's office by Alexander Hamilton.

"Major Thorne, I have agreed to see you as a formality," Washington informed him, "as I am sure your visit must be. But I must tell you that no appeal you can make will change General Arnold's fate."

"Your Excellency, I am not here to appeal for General Arnold, but for Major André."

A momentary flash of surprise flashed in the commander in chief's eyes. "Then, sir, your visit is equally pointless. I have been besieged by appellants on his behalf." He glanced sternly at Hamilton, who quickly stared up at the ceiling. "What makes you think you will be more eloquent or successful than they?"

"Sir, I have little confidence in my eloquence, especially since the gentlemen of your official family, men far more eloquent than I, have pleaded his case. I will not bore you with similar entreaties attesting to Major André's noble character and his unfortunate and unintended circumstance. However, your Excellency may wish to consider that there will come a time when our country and Great Britain are no longer at war. It is not unreasonable to assume that friendly relations will one day resume between the mother country and its former colony. Our two nations, united in history, culture, and language, shall certainly once more forge bonds of friendship and cooperation, and stand together against our common enemies."

Joshua thought he might have detected a momentary flicker in the steel-gray eyes that were staring so intently at him. Without pause, he continued. "How much better it would be for those relations, sir, if Major André were still alive as a prisoner, and could at some future date, in a gesture of friendship and mercy, be pardoned, rather than nothing remain but the bitter memory of a patriot who had been martyred for his country. I plead not for André's life, sir, but to permit the future I have portrayed."

Joshua stepped back and made a slight bow. "Thank you for hearing me, sir."

Washington studied him a moment before he spoke. "You are more eloquent than you give yourself credit for, Major Thorne, but in this matter, eloquence must yield to necessity." He nodded, indicating the interview was at an end.

As Hamilton led him out, he informed Joshua that Congress had approved Arnold's death sentence. Since Washington could act in the André case on his own authority, he had signed both death warrants that morning. Joshua felt himself sweating, despite the autumn chill. "It appears as though André is doomed," Joshua said, "and I have wasted my time."

Hamilton shrugged. "We have moved mountains trying to save him and have not prevailed. I'm afraid his mind is made up. I know he feels deeply for the young man, and is unhappy about his fate, but he will not yield the principle based on sympathy for him. He feels that to spare André would set a dangerous precedent, and he is determined to see them both men hang, if only to insure that such treachery will not happen again. But I thank you sincerely for your effort."

Joshua's second call was in many respects more difficult. Although he had been nervous about seeing Washington, he dreaded the meeting with Arnold. He was unsure how he would react when confronting for the last time the man who had misled him so badly. As he lingered over the heavy afternoon dinner in the headquarters mess, he thought of all Arnold's playacting, his opening statement, the performances with Smith and André, and his final one on the witness stand. Almost everything Arnold had told him had been a lie, yet the anger he should have felt was not there. After all, he never had a proper lawyer-client relationship with Arnold, and an accused could not be faulted for falsifying information to escape the hangman's noose. And, despite everything, he still confessed to himself a lingering admiration for the man. He had fought for his life with the same skill and daring as he had fought for his country before he betrayed her.

When he arrived at Arnold's room, he found that the guard had been increased. A sentry checked his identity before he could enter the grounds, two more did the same at the entry to the stable, and he had to pass an officer and a guard at the door to Arnold's room. As he entered, he could not help speculating whether he would get his old quarters back, and how he would feel about moving into them again. Arnold was standing at the barred window, staring outside. Mrs. Arnold was not in attendance, and Joshua assumed she was with the mistress of the house. When Arnold made no acknowledgment of his presence, he cleared his throat. Arnold turned.

"Ah, Major Thorne. Come to make your goodbye, I presume."

Surprisingly, Joshua felt his throat tighten. Sorrow was the one emotion he had not anticipated. "I...I am sorry it turned out this way, sir."

"I suppose it was inevitable. They were determined I should hang."

The remark jolted Joshua. Arnold seemed to be denying any responsibility. "You said yourself that you deserved it, sir," Joshua reminded him. Arnold seemed not to understand. "In your opening statement you told the court that if you were guilty of treason you should be hanged from the highest scaffold in the land."

Arnold accepted the remark in silence. When he finally spoke, it was if he had not heard it. "We started out with such high hopes," he mused. "We could have been a shining example, a beacon to the world, but it was all lost to weakness, corruption, and inefficiency. It finally became obvious to me that our democratic experiment would never measure up to the order, security, and prosperity of the British system." Joshua realized that Arnold had moved to another dimension. From attempting to prove his innocence, he had now turned seamlessly to justifying his treason. "Once I realized that, my path was clear. I knew I had to end this war, this unnecessary and evil bleeding of life and treasure on both sides. And I would have done so, except for the interference of three ruffians bent on robbery."

"Three, who as General Greene noted, probably saved the country," Joshua countered.

"They have saved nothing!" Arnold's voice rose and his countenance darkened. "They have merely delayed the inevitable, at a cost of more blood and destruction. The army has just endured a winter more disastrous than Valley Forge, and it is now penniless, starving, and disintegrating. Yet Congress is helpless, as individual states squabble among themselves and scramble for power. It is no wonder that the people turn away, and yearn for their former peace and well being."

There was no point in arguing with him, Joshua knew. Most of what he said was true, times had never been worse. Moreover, Arnold was beyond argument. He was no longer Benedict Arnold, patriot of the American cause. He was Benedict Arnold, restorer of the British Empire. He now saw himself as a savior of the nation, thwarted in his mission by evil men. That belief, Jonathan knew, sustained him in these last hours before the gallows, and he would not deprive him of that.

"You almost convinced me of your innocence." When Arnold made no reply, Joshua went on. "Tell me, what would you have done if you had been found not guilty?"

For the first time, Arnold's expression assumed an air of interest. "What would I have done?" he repeated, turning the question over in his mind. "I would have made my way to the British and placed myself at their disposal. After all, General Clinton had given assurances that I would claim my same rank in his service. I would become a rallying point for all those who realize this war is lost and who want to return to the Crown. With my example, the rebellion would soon collapse, and I would take the lead in reuniting America and Britain in one great commonwealth, the like of which the world has never seen." He felt silent then, sobered by the realization that if and when this scenario came to be, he would not be there to see it. Finally, he approached Joshua and held out his hand.

"I thank you for your efforts on my behalf. Now if you will excuse me, I wish to spend these last few hours with my family."

Feeling lower than he could remember, Joshua made for Mabie's. When he arrived, he found it closed and closely guarded, just as Arnold's room had been. Discouraged and adrift, he crossed to the village common, where, finding a small wooden bench, he sat down heavily. His mind kept dwelling on the room he had just left, where a former war hero, his beautiful young wife, and his baby son were spending their final hours together. Please, God, he prayed silently, spare me from knowing in advance when my time comes.

He could not overcome a dread which haunted him. If Arnold was right, that the American cause was about to collapse, then they were hanging a hero tomorrow. In the aftermath of a failed revolt, would Washington, Jefferson, Adams and all the rest be hanged as traitors? How would the returning British authority view the members of the court who had condemned Arnold? Would he, Joshua Thorne, escape retribution because he had defended him?

But there was a greater consideration than personal safety. Washington, the officers and men of the Continental Army, and the Congress, had chosen to risk their lives and their fortunes to create a new form of government unique in today's world. A government where citizens ruled themselves, free of kings, emperors, and other potentates. Arnold was right. If it succeeded, it would be a shining light, a beacon to the world. But that light was now no more than the sputtering flame of a candle about to be extinguished by a cold, unfriendly wind.

He shook his head, trying to clear it of his depressing thoughts. He yearned for Amy's company, but realized that his talk of marriage only seemed to upset her. Yet, he had nowhere else to go, and nowhere else he wanted to be. He rose, and made his way slowly down the small lane off Main Street. As he approached Mary Burns' house he could see Amy standing in the doorway. When she caught sight of him, she raised her good arm in a wave.

"Josh, Josh," she called, starting toward him. It seemed to him that if she could have run, she would have done so. Alarmed, he rushed toward her. As soon as they were close enough, she grasped his hand. Her eyes were shining above a radiant smile.

"Josh, you saved John André's life!"

His shoulders sagged. "No, Amy. I tried, but it was no use."

But her smile only widened. "You don't understand. Colonel Hamilton was just here looking for you. He said that an hour before you spoke to him, General Washington had signed André's death warrant, and thirty minutes after you left, he tore it up! You saved him, Josh. *You* saved him. Everyone else tried and failed. *You* succeeded."

"But that can't be." He was too surprised to think clearly. "His mind was made up...."

"You must go at once to the headquarters mess. There's a party going on. Colonel Hamilton said to be sure to tell you."

"But I came to see you...." He was not sure he wanted to face a party with the mixed emotions that were now spinning through his brain.

She turned him toward the mess and pushed gently. "Go, Josh. They're waiting for you."

"Gentlemen, I give you the greatest advocate of us all!"

There had been a great cheer when Joshua entered the headquarters mess. About twenty officers were present, and they had all pressed forward, congratulating him with handshakes, hugs, and pats on the back. It was Hamilton who proposed the toast, which was followed by a rousing chorus of 'Hear! Hear!" Laurance and Edwards were there too, and seemed especially proud that one of their own had "moved Mount Olympus," as Hamilton christened the event. After he had accepted, but not yet downed several celebratory drinks, Joshua was able to ask Hamilton exactly what had happened.

"Washington has reduced the recommended death sentence to life in confinement, and made it clear that André is to be treated as a spy, not a prisoner of war. It's to be prison, not parole for André, nor is any exchange likely. But you can rest assured, it will be just as you proposed. He'll not languish long in jail after hostilities cease."

As the circle of admirers around Joshua gradually thinned, Laurance and Edwards approached him. "Well, this has been a great day for you," Laurance said. Joshua, his emotions still in turmoil from a tumultuous day, smiled, but said nothing. "You may have lost the battle to save Arnold," Laurance went on, "but you won a far more difficult one today. And a far more popular one, as is obvious," Laurance added, gesturing toward the crowd.

"Joshua didn't lose that battle," Edwards said. "Arnold lost it for himself."

As several more drinks were pressed upon him, Joshua found himself nursing them. For some reason, the rum failed to have its usual appeal. He put it down to his concern for Amy. He declined supper, explaining his desire to be with her. Those still present, aware of the situation, lined up to shake his hand again, and wish Amy well. Returning to the Burns house, he found Mary cleaning up in the small, lean-to kitchen. She informed him they had finished a light supper, and Amy had now taken to bed. She made no objection when Joshua knocked lightly and entered the bedroom. Amy was sitting up in the bed, trying to read with one arm by the dim light of a single candle. She smiled as she saw him.

"I didn't expect you to come back tonight," she said.

"I have something important to say." His throat tightened as he looked into her questioning gaze, wishing now that he had consumed the full number of rum flips he had been offered. Amy continued to eye him warily, but said nothing. "Do you remember the other night, you said that you would give anything if André's life could be spared?" She nodded, still suspicious. "Well, I'm asking you to honor that pledge by giving me your hand in marriage."

She took time to study him before replying. "You're serious, aren't you?"

"I've never been more serious in my life."

"You'd tie yourself for life to a disfigured woman?"

"You are not disfigured. I told you that you must never think of yourself that way."

"I'm not sure I can think of myself any other way, and I don't want to inflict myself upon someone I...upon any man in such a condition."

"You're not inflicting yourself on me. I am the suitor."

"It doesn't matter." He could see she was becoming upset again. "There is so much to consider. Have you thought about children?"

"You only need one breast to nurture our children."

She shook her head. "It's not that simple. Please, Joshua, let's not discuss it anymore."

He did not want to cause her more anxiety, but he could not leave it there. Too much was at stake. "Just let me say one final thing, and I promise to say no more." She closed her eyes, but did not object. He took a deep breath.

"Your injury, if it does anything, will always remind me how fortunate I was that you were not taken from me by it. There's no question of 'inflicting yourself' upon me. If anything, the incident has made me realize how much I love you, and how much I want us to share our lives together. I know I should have spoken sooner, but there was an incident in my earlier life that made me hesitate. And, you have to admit that I have few of the attributes of a good husband, and a goodly portion of the bad, which alone would make me reluctant to speak." It was not coming out well, he felt. It was too formal, too much like a speech, something a lawyer would deliver. And the hard part was coming now. "Turning me down because of my deficiencies is something I can understand and will have to live with. And I wouldn't blame you. But rejecting our marriage because of your injury and because you want to spare me is something I *could not* live with."

Her eyes remained closed as he kissed her and left the house. As he walked toward his billet, the gloom he felt when he left Arnold closed around him once more. He thought about returning to Mabie's and accepting its hospitality. But he knew that this time the rum and the beer would not help.

# CHAPTER THIRTY-NINE

*Tappan, New York*
*Saturday, October 14, 1780*

THE MORNING DAWNED gray and cold. The sun appeared as a hazy circle of dim light, providing no warmth. As the creaking wheels of the small wagon came to a stop outside the stable, the officer driving the single horse stepped down from the seat, and spoke to the sentries in a low voice. Two of them climbed the stairs, returning shortly with a small amount of luggage and a bassinet, which they placed carefully in the covered part of the wagon. The officer, Major David Franks, blew on his hands as he waited in the cold air for Peggy Arnold. Only a month ago he had brought her to her husband from her parent's house in Philadelphia. Now, on General Washington's instructions, he would take her back.

The lady wanted her departure unannounced and unnoticed, no painful goodbyes or curious stares, hence, the early hour. It wasn't long before Peggy Arnold made her appearance. She was alone, the couple having decided to make their farewells in the privacy of the upstairs room. Silently, Franks helped her into the wagon. Although her face was covered by a light veil, he could tell that she was crying. A moment later the creaking began again, fading slowly, until the town was silent once more. A short time later, under a slightly warmer sun and thirty-five miles to the north, Major General Benedict Arnold's

Life Guards struck their encampment at Robinson's House, and marched home to Connecticut.

As the sun rose higher, the morning warmed, but the sky remained gray. At nine o'clock General Greene and a small delegation appeared in Arnold's room to read him the General Order of the Day, which stripped him of his rank and cashiered him from the Continental Army. He would go to the gallows as a disgraced civilian. His uniform coat and accouterments were taken from him, but it was decided that he could retain his boots and breeches, and his white muslin shirt. He was provided a plain green coat for warmth. By ten o'clock a crowd started to gather, spacing itself along the route from the stable to the small hill where the gallows had been erected. They were mostly curiosity seekers, but there was a surly element that wanted to see the traitor get his due, and ready to hurl insults as he passed.

At eleven, soldiers of the Continental line began to form on both sides of the route, facing outward, so that their backs would be turned to Arnold as he passed. Mounted on horseback, forming the last part of the route, were the generals who had been on the court, as well as Wayne, Knox, and Lafayette. Every general in the headquarters was present except one, who remained behind the tightly drawn curtains of the DeWint house. At eleven-thirty, Lieutenant Colonel Alexander Hamilton and Major Benjamin Tallmadge knocked on Benedict Arnold's door.

Accompanied by the two officers, Arnold slowly descended the stairs, assisting himself with his cane. Waiting for him was a wagon, a guard of six soldiers, and a small fife and drum band. When Arnold saw the wagon, his expression turned grim.

"I will walk to my death, gentlemen. I will not be carted to it like a common criminal."

Hamilton and Tallmadge exchanged glances. "But, your leg, sir," Hamilton said.

"Damn my leg! I will walk."

After a brief hesitation, Hamilton nodded, and Tallmadge ordered the wagon away. The order of march was arranged quickly.

Two guards fell in behind the band, then Arnold, with one of the officers on each side, then four guards bringing up the rear. Upon a signal from Hamilton, the band stepped out and struck up the *Rogue's March*. Arnold registered distaste at the tune, but said nothing. As the procession moved forward, there were shouts of excitement as the crowd surged against the barrier of troops, trying to get a good view of the traitor. But as Arnold came into view, head held high and staring straight ahead, limping resolutely on his injured leg, the shouts died down, and soon stopped. In the figure approaching them, those assembled saw not only the traitor, but also the soldier who had fought so valiantly for his country, and had been wounded so severely in its service. Even those who had come prepared to throw more than insults, allowed eggs and overripe fruit to drop to the ground.

As the procession reached the line of generals, Arnold turned and made a slight nod to the left and then to the right. The only one who returned the gesture was General Greene. The band now started the slow dirge of the *Death March*. Joshua and Amy stood nearby, a location to which his uniform and position during the trial gave him access. She had insisted on witnessing the event, and they had taken a cart to the foot of the small hill where the gallows stood. Leaning heavily on Joshua, Amy had then slowly made her way up the hill. They watched as Arnold, now visibly in pain, struggled slowly up the scaffold steps, assisted by his two escorts. Amy, who had no love for Arnold, tightened her grip on Joshua's arm as she witnessed the scene. The silence of the crowd was now complete. Once on the platform, the hangman quickly bound Arnold's hands behind his back, led him over the trap, and placed the heavy noose around his neck. He then stood aside.

"General Arnold," Hamilton said, granting for one final time the title Arnold no longer held, "if you wish to say something, you may speak, for you have but a few moments to live."

Arnold took time to gaze out over the crowd, and then raised his voice.

"I stand here today convicted of the crime of treason. But my true treason is not that for which I die, but the earlier act in which I repudiated my king and my country. I have but one regret, and that is that I took up arms in a rebellion against a government more just and more benevolent than any other upon this earth. I have but one wish, and that is to see my country united once more, to see these colonies return to their rightful place as part of the British Empire, and to see peace, harmony and prosperity restored to their people. God save the King!"

The hangman then came forward with a blindfold, but Arnold shook his head in refusal. The hangman stepped back, reached for the lever and sprung the trap. Arnold's body fell, jerked to a brutal stop, and hung motionless. Then, suddenly, like a corpse returning to life, the body started to writhe and twist. The drop had not achieved its purpose; the noose had failed to break Arnold's neck. Amy buried her eyes against Joshua's shoulder rather than witness the long strangulation. Finally, the body ceased its struggle, and began turning limply in a slow circle. Benedict Arnold had died as his old friend John Lamb had wished him to—at the end of a slow rope.

As the crowd began to disperse, the mounted generals closed around the body as it was lowered from the gibbet, protecting their former comrade from the stares of the morbidly curious.

"It is an ignominious death," Greene said, breaking the somber silence, "but in his eyes, it is a glorious one. In the end, he chose the side he felt would win. Whether he is a martyred hero or an infamous traitor, the outcome of this war will decide."

As Joshua and Amy prepared to leave, several acquaintances, including Edwards, who had not seen Amy since the accident came over to greet her. As she became engaged in conversation with some of her women friends, Edwards approached Joshua.

"Another should have mounted the scaffold with Arnold today," he said to him.

"You mean André."

"I wasn't thinking of André."

Joshua raise his eyebrows. "So you think Mrs. Arnold was involved? But, surely, you wouldn't want to see a woman hanged?"

"I want to see whoever is guilty punished, and the beautiful and scheming Peggy Shippen Arnold is as guilty as her husband, perhaps more so. Her family are Loyalists, she had a previous personal relationship with André, and, through him, access to the British high command. I refuse to accept as coincidence that her husband just happened to deal with André on the turnover of West Point. And André can talk all he wants about his honor, but he testified to protect Peggy Arnold. I'm sure of it. I believe she, not her husband, was the architect of the treason."

"My nomination for that title is Joseph Reed and the Council of Pennsylvania," Joshua said. "An organization of vindictive, self-anointed patriots determined to destroy him. I believe they are as guilty of fomenting this treason as Arnold."

"The trial has been a watershed," said Edwards as they parted. "It has established the need for an 'adversarial' defense of the accused. Laurance has decided that henceforth all general courts will have separate officers representing the government and the accused, and Washington has approved a large increase in the size of our department." He broke into a smile, "Joshua, you'll go down in history as our first military defense counsel."

"That's probably exactly where I will go in history," Joshua agreed. "Down."

As Joshua and Amy made their slow return to the cart, they were passed by an old couple helping each other down the narrow path.

Stopping to watch them, Joshua remarked, "Benjamin Franklin says that there are three faithful friends, an old wife, an old dog, and ready money. If you would marry me, I would someday have at least one of them." When she remained silent, he turned and started down again. He had only taken a few steps when he heard her voice.

"I think we should get a dog," she said. "Then you will at least have two of them."

Her answer made his eyes burn, so that he dared not look at her.

"But if you go through with the plan you explained to Colonel Lamb," she continued, "I despair of us ever having ready money. The corn whiskey you make will never see the market."

He finally managed to get control of his voice. "If you continue to make excellent beer, I promise not to touch the whiskey." He reached for her hand, and she grasped it tightly. Together, they followed the old couple slowly down the hill.

Back at the small house, they found themselves alone. Feeling tired from the relatively long walk, Amy lay down on the bed, requesting that Joshua read more of *Le Morte d'Arthur* to her. He was not much into it before she fell asleep. He left her and took a chair in the next room, prepared to continue reading. But his mind was too full of the day's events, and he could not concentrate. Overriding all was the quiet joy of knowing that he and Amy would share their lives. But the Arnold tragedy would not go away. If only Arnold had accepted Washington's offer of command of the left wing, he thought, how different things would have been. After the war the honor and fame he craved all along would have been his. The financial success he always sought would have been achieved, when a grateful nation showered him with land grants, public office, and business opportunities. Of course, that was assuming their cause would prevail, which, Joshua knew, was a rash assumption to make at this time.

When Mary Burns returned, she found them both asleep, Joshua in the chair, Amy still in bed. Seeing them there, she somehow sensed what had passed between them, and nodded in satisfaction. Humming to herself, she went to the kitchen. As was usual on any occasion that brought people together, even an execution, a small market had formed afterward, consisting of farmers and tradesmen from the surrounding area. There had been no time for a proper dinner that afternoon, so an early, more substantial supper than usual was called for. Some of the various items she had been able to buy at a good price, including oysters, sturgeon, and Irish potatoes, would make a fine seafood hotchpot. The aroma of cooking eventually roused the sleepers, and the three sat down to a long leisurely meal, washed down by an especially good cider Mary had found, which came from an orchard in the Catskills.

"My friends told me today that more and more people are

coming to believe that divine intervention was involved in foiling Arnold's plot," Amy said, as they were finishing up.

"Oh?" The heavy meal at the end of the day, plus the excellent cider, had given Joshua a comfortable, mildly soporific feeling. He was content to listen.

"Think about it," Amy continued. "Washington choosing that particular time to visit West Point, the messenger to Washington arriving before the messenger to Arnold, Colonel Livingston choosing that particular moment to bombard the *Vulture*, André running into three irregulars who just happened to be there, the arrival of Wayne's reserve just in time to foil the André rescue attempt, all this suggests to many people that an unseen hand was looking out for us."

"Well, if that's the case," Joshua replied, "I wish that same unseen hand would find food, clothing, and pay for our army, forage for the animals, powder for our guns, and, most of all, administer a good kick in the arse to the Continental Congress."

"There was a sadness at the market today," Mary Burns noted. "A feeling that, although a traitor had gotten his due, a great patriot had been turned from the cause. However, there was also something else. I sensed a new mood. Folks are more serious, more determined. It's as if this whole treason thing has made us realize that if we want to succeed, we've got to pull together, get it done. It's a welcome change from the usual gloom and doom."

Later, after Mary had gone to visit a friend, Joshua told Amy about the conversation he had with Edwards, and the relative responsibilities of Peggy Arnold and Joseph Reed in the matter.

"No one is responsible except Arnold himself, Josh," Amy said, "neither Peggy Arnold nor Joseph Reed. The choice was Arnold's to make. No one forced him."

"Perhaps not, but Reed gave him a mighty push."

"Which he could have resisted. That he didn't, reveals his character. We are well rid of him."

"On the contrary, our army will sorely miss a leader of his energy and daring."

She cocked her head and gave him a quizzical smile. "Josh, are we always going to disagree like this?"

"Probably," he answered, kissing her. "It will keep our lives interesting."

They sat in silence for a while, happy simply to be together and sobered by the change in their lives over the last week. The sky had cleared, turning red as the sun lowered. They went outside to watch what promised to be a fine sunset. He realized that he had not told her what André's new sentence was, and was surprised she hadn't asked.

"I haven't thought about him at all since yesterday," she said, after he informed her. She reached across and took his hand, smiling. "Thanks to you, I'll never have to think about John André again." But then her expression changed. "It won't be as easy to forget Benedict Arnold. I must admit his last words chill me yet." She pulled her shawl closer around her shoulders. "He died convinced that our cause is lost."

As he watched the deep orange sun slowly disappear, Joshua Thorne felt that he had finally come to the end of a long, twisting path, and at last knew where he stood. He hugged Amelia Martin close to his side.

"Then we shall have to prove him wrong."

# EPILOGUE

THIRTEEN MONTHS AFTER Benedict Arnold's treason, British General Charles Cornwallis surrendered his army to a combined American and French force at Yorktown, Virginia, effectively ending the fighting in the Revolutionary War.

Instrumental in this victory were the actions of Major General Nathanael Greene, now in command of the Continental Southern Army, who forced Cornwallis northward into Virginia, the Marquis de Lafayette, who harassed Cornwallis' march across Virginia to the Chesapeake and blocked his escape once he reached Yorktown, and of Colonel John Lamb, whose artillery brigade pounded the British fortifications incessantly and accurately during the siege. Lafayette's division was given the honor of storming one of two critical British redoubts protecting the main defense walls, and Alexander Hamilton, finally freed from his staff duties, personally led the assault which carried the position.

On the morning of the surrender, the bandmaster of the Continental Army requested that General Washington select the music to be played during the ceremony. At noon on October 19, 1781 the Continental Army of the United States of America marched onto the field of victory to the tune of *Yankee Doodle.*

## WHERE DID THEY GO FROM HERE?

### THE AMERICANS

**George Washington** resigned his commission as commander in chief of the Continental Army on December 23, 1783. He was unanimously elected as the first president of the United States in 1789, stepping down after serving two terms. He died at Mount Vernon, Virginia in December 1799, mourned by the nation as "First in war, first in peace, and first in the hearts of his countrymen."

**Benedict Arnold**, contrary to this story, made his escape from Robinson's House to *HMS Vulture*, just moments before Washington's arrival. He was commissioned a brigadier general in the British army, where he fought against his former comrades in raids on Richmond and Portsmouth in Virginia, and led a particularly brutal attack upon New London, in his home state of Connecticut. Following Cornwallis' surrender at Yorktown, he sailed for London, where, despite his efforts, he was unsuccessful in obtaining any position in the active army, and was forced to accept retirement at half pay. Over the years, he engaged in various mercantile adventures, which included a four-year stint in New Brunswick, Canada, where he had been awarded a large tract of land for his service to the British Crown. Failing in his attempts to achieve either military or commercial success, he died heavily in debt in 1801, at age 60.

**Margaret (Peggy) Arnold**, after a short stay with her family in Philadelphia, joined her husband in New York. She accompanied him to London and later to New Brunswick. She bore him four more children, three sons and his only daughter. By most accounts it was she who held the family together during financial adversity and long separations. Through it all, she remained a devoted wife and a loving mother. When Arnold died, she eventually paid off his debts and provided for her family, assisted by pensions awarded her and her children by the British government. She died in 1804, surviving her husband by three years. She was only forty-four. Early historians believed Margaret Arnold innocent of any knowledge of her husband's attempt to surrender West Point. Most modern historians, using more recently discovered files, accept that she was aware of her husband's plans, probably assisted him, and perhaps even initiated the treachery. Whether or not she betrayed her country, she remained loyal to her husband and her family all of her life.

**Nathanael Greene** was appointed commander of Continental Army forces in the south by Washington less than a month after Benedict Arnold's treason. He reorganized the defeated and dispirited American units, and within a year had forced the British to give up all the territory they had taken in Georgia and South Carolina. At the end of the war, he returned to the south, to a plantation near Savannah, which had been given to him by the state of Georgia in appreciation for his military service. In despair at being unable to discharge heavy debts which he acquired while in the army, and worn out by his wartime efforts, he died in 1786 at the age of forty-four.

**Marquis de Lafayette** returned to France following the victory at Yorktown, where he was received with acclaim. He returned to America for a visit in 1784, to a hero's welcome, and which included a long visit to Washington at Mount Vernon. Initially a leader of the French Revolution, he was later denounced, and imprisoned from 1792 to 1797. Released by Napoleon, he retired to the life of a gentleman farmer. At the invitation of President Monroe, he returned to the United States a second time in 1824, receiving a triumphal reception throughout the nation, which he toured for more than a year. He died in 1834, the last surviving general of the Continental Army.

**Henry Knox** was promoted to major general following the outstanding performance of his artillery at Yorktown. When

Washington left the army, he appointed Knox to succeed him. He became the nation's first Secretary of War, serving six years in Washington's cabinet, then retired to his wife's large estate in Maine. Always a lover of food and fine eating, he died unexpectedly at fifty-six as a result of swallowing a chicken bone.

**John Lamb** received a brevet promotion to brigadier general following the siege of Yorktown. After the war, he returned to New York City and later served in the state legislature. In 1789 President Washington appointed him federal customs collector of New York. When his chief clerk embezzled a huge sum of money, Lamb sold all his own property to make good the loss, and died in poverty several years later. One of the true heroes of the revolution, he deserved better.

**John Laurance** left the army in 1782 and went on to a distinguished career in New York, where he served first in the state senate, and was then elected for two terms as a representative to Congress. He was appointed United States Judge of the District Court of New York by President Washington, a position he held until elected to the United States Senate.

**Thomas Edwards** succeeded John Laurance as Judge Advocate General of the Continental Army. Promoted to colonel, he served in that position until the end of the war. Returning to his home state of Massachusetts, he vanished from the pages of history.

**Alexander Hamilton** returned to New York and through his chief authorship of *The Federalist Papers* (along with James Madison) successfully advocated the adoption of the Constitution. Selected by Washington as the first Secretary of the Treasury, he created the Bank of the United States and established the nation's credit at home and abroad by insisting upon funding the national debt at full value, to include assumption of debts incurred by the states during the Revolution. After leaving the cabinet, Hamilton became head of the

Federalist Party, and continued to wield considerable influence in government affairs. He was killed in a duel with Aaron Burr in 1804 at age forty-nine.

**Phillip Schuyler** continued to hold important positions at the state and national scene following the war. He was a strong supporter of the Federal Constitution, and together with his son-in-law, Alexander Hamilton, worked to secure its ratification in New York. He represented New York in the first Senate of the United States.

**Richard Varick**, absolved of any connection to Arnold's treason, became George Washington's recording secretary in 1781 and spent almost four years cataloging and transcribing his confidential papers written between 1775 and 1783. His work is now part of the Washington papers in the Library of Congress, and known as the Varick Transcripts. After the war he returned to New York, where he became attorney general of the state, mayor of New York City, and founder and president of the American Bible Society.

**Joshua Hett Smith** was tried by a military court-martial, despite his civilian status, and was found not guilty. Rather than being freed, he was turned over to the civil authority of New York State and imprisoned without trial. Finally, eight months after his arrest, he escaped to his relatives in New York City. In 1784, he fled to London in advance of the returning American Army, where he practiced law. In 1808 he published a book giving his version of the Arnold-André affair, and sometime after that he returned to America to spend his final days in New York City. Historians remain divided over his true role in the Arnold conspiracy.

**Pierre Eugene du Simitière**, appointed as an artist and consultant to the committee to design the Great Seal of the United States, offered the phrase *E pluribus unum*, which was accepted as the nation's motto. His portrait of Benedict Arnold is the only one known taken from life. He opened his museum in Philadelphia in

1794, which featured the flora, fauna, and natural history of America, but nothing from John André.

**John Paulding, David Williams, and Isaac Van Wart** received medals from Congress and lifetime pensions for their capture of Major John André.

## THE BRITISH

**Sir Henry Clinton** resigned his post as commander in chief in North America in 1781, and returned to England to a cool reception. He found himself blamed for the disaster at Yorktown, primarily because Cornwallis had arrived several months before, and presented his own version of events. Out of favor, he never held another military command. Near the end of his life he was appointed governor of Gibraltar, but died before he was able to assume the post.

**Beverly Robinson** never recovered his confiscated estates in America. At the war's end he took most of his family to England, where he spent the rest of his life in unhappy retirement. The British government eventually granted him 17,000 pounds as a partial reimbursement for his lost property.

**John André** was hanged as spy on October 2, 1780, nine days after his capture. His appeal to Washington to die as a soldier, before a firing squad, was denied. He was buried on the site. In 1821 his body was disinterred and taken to a place of honor in Westminster Abbey. A small monument remains at his execution site. The British attempt to rescue André as described in this book is fiction. There is a rumor that, although they remained friends and worked together for many years, Alexander Hamilton never forgave George Washington for not sparing John André's life.

# THE COURT-MARTIAL OF BENEDICT ARNOLD

## THE ACTORS

**Joshua Thorne** achieved his dual ambition of practicing law and making whiskey. Moving west after the war, he used his legal fees to establish a distillery. Since so much of his spare time was spent improving his product, his friends never understood why he never drank any of it, although he was known to enjoy his beer and cider. He became a judge, and served on the bench until he died at age 72, respected as much for the quality of his whiskey as the soundness of his justice. The distillery remained in the family until the1840's when it combined with another, to eventually become one of the largest whiskey producers in Bourbon County, Kentucky.

**Amelia Martin Thorne** survived her husband by 14 years and became the matriarch of the family. She gave birth to seven children, five of whom survived to adulthood. Initially resuming her career as a teacher, she was later appointed supervisor of schools for the county, and eventually established an academy funded by the distillery to educate young women to teach school.

**Ebenezer Thatcher** continued to lead his regiment until the end of the Revolutionary War. He attended Washington's emotional farewell to his officers at Fraunces Tavern in New York City on December 4, 1783, and died in his sleep that night.

**Dr. Thaddeus Stewart, Charles Adcock,** and **Mary Burns** have my thanks for their brief performances.

## THE PLACES

**West Point** is now the home of the United States Military Academy. It is the oldest continuously occupied military post in the United States.

**Mabie's House** still exists, and is now known as The Old '76 House, doing business as a restaurant and bar.

**Robinson's House,** Arnold's headquarters and residence, burned down in 1892. A historical marker stands on the site in Garrison, New York.

**DeWint House,** which served as Washington's headquarters on four separate occasions (including during André's trial and subsequent execution), still stands as a memorial to the first president. It is open to the public.

**The Old Dutch Reformed Church**, in which the André inquiry was held, no longer exists. A historical marker on the side of the present church, built on the site in 1835, marks the event.

**The Manse** still exists, continuing to serve as the parsonage for the present Dutch Reformed Church. Much of its original structure remains.

**Belmont,** Joshua Hett Smith's home, where Arnold and André conferred regarding the surrender of West Point, was demolished in 1929. The site is now within the grounds of the New York State Rehabilitation Hospital. A historical marker identifies the location.

**The Franklin Portrait**, removed from his house by Major John André, was returned to the United States by a descendant of General Charles Grey on the 200th anniversary of Franklin's birth. It now hangs in the White House.

**Saratoga National Historical Park.** On this historic battlefield stands a monument with the following description:

*In Memory of the most brilliant soldier of the Continental Army, who was desperately wounded on this spot, the sally port,*

*Burgoyne's Great Western Redoubt, 7th October, 1777, winning for his countrymen the decisive battle of the American Revolution and for himself the rank of Major General.*

There is no name on the memorial, nor is there a statue of a military officer striking a heroic pose. Instead, carved in stone in life size, the monument bears the image of a booted left leg.

# ACKNOWLEDGMENTS

I would like to express my appreciation to the following folks who provided valuable and cheerful assistance during my research in the town of Tappan, New York:

> Mary Cardenas: Orangetown Town Historian, and Director, Orangetown Museum and Archives,
> Carol LaValle: President, Tappantown Historical Society,
> Donald J. Hoover: Pastor, Dutch Reformed Church,
> Jules Loh, Local author and historian.

My thanks also to Jose Ramirez of Pedernales Publishing for his excellent work in formatting the book, creating a dynamic cover, catching errors, and willingly assuming other tasks above and beyond expectations.

PREVIEW

# THE DARK SIDE OF GLORY

By

RICHARD MCMAHON

## MYSTERY—SUSPENSE—LOVE—AND WAR

In this mystery/suspense novel set during the Korean War, Matthew Clark, the biographer of a respected and highly decorated Army general, learns that there is a hidden side to his life, involving a brutal, covered-up murder, a secret mistress, and an abandoned illegitimate daughter. As he delves deeper, Matthew discovers an intriguing mystery and a tragic love, in a world of surprises where nothing is at it seems.

Tracing the general's earlier career during the occupation of Japan and through the beginning days of the Korean War, Matthew follows the lives of four principle characters: Philip Coursen, who appears to be the perfect Army officer, but with a disturbing dark side, Miriam Coursen, equally perfect Army wife, who may hide a secret agenda, Calvin Carter, an idealistic young West Pointer, beset with guilt as a result of his clandestine affair with another officer's wife, and Samantha Winstead, the beautiful, vivacious cause of Calvin Carter's discomfort. The biography takes a personal turn for

Matthew, as he finds himself drawn into the story when he falls in love with the young woman who claims to be Coursen's daughter.

**PRAISE FOR *THE DARK SIDE OF GLORY***

AWARDED THE 2014 GOLD MEDAL FOR HIS-
TORICAL FICTION BY THE MILITARY WRITERS
SOCIETY OF AMERICA

The Dark Side of Glory by Richard McMahon ranks right beside David Baldacci's bestselling novels when it comes to plot twists and turns and jaw-dropping surprises. Just when you think you've figured out what happens next, McMahon throws a ten-pound sledgehammer through your preconceptions. It's an edge-of-your-seat thriller by a top-flight talent. Truly, The Dark Side of Glory is a stunning triumph!—**Dwight Jon Zimmerman, award-winning military historian and #1 New York Times bestselling author. President, Military Writers Society of America.**

In this page-turning suspense novel, Richard McMahon expertly switches between two settings and time periods, the earlier being the Korean War, and the current a who-done-it mystery. McMahon's novel is ranked up there with some of the most renowned mystery writers of our time. You will stay up late reading it all the way to the very end, when the final secret is revealed.—**Michael Christy, Editor, *Dispatches,* official member publication, Together We Served.**

Fans of "M.A.S.H." (and who isn't?) will enjoy this tale of sexual and military intrigue during the Korean War. Winner of a gold medal for historical fiction by the Military Writers Society of America, the novel jumps about in time from a young woman's murder in 1950s Tokyo to a burial in Punchbowl in 1969. The Honolulu author's suspenseful plot is nicely carried by sparse, clean prose.—**Honolulu Star-Advertiser.**

# PROLOGUE

*Setagaya-ku, Tokyo, Japan, February 9th, 1953.*

THE BODY LAY NAKED on its side in the middle of the room, the knees drawn slightly toward the chest. She was young and still very beautiful, even in death. Her arms, tied together at the wrists, were extended above her head. Her legs were also tied together at the ankles. A white silk scarf was tied across her mouth, apparently to act as a gag. Her long black hair spilled over her shoulders and onto the tatami-mat floor. There was a head wound to the rear of her left ear, apparently caused either by a blunt instrument or a fall. Other than that, she was unmarked in any way.

Inspector Shimizu gazed impassively at the body as the medical examiner crouched over the nude form. Whatever he was thinking, nothing could be construed from his expression.

"She has been dead for some time," said the examiner. "At least 12 hours. I cannot be more precise until I have examined the body more fully."

Shimizu turned his attention to the woman's clothing, folded neatly on top of a tiny bureau standing against the wall. There was no sign that it had been removed hastily or roughly. He picked up the top garment, a pink blouse. His body stiffened as he saw the cloth object that lay beneath it.

"We must leave here at once," he said.

The medical examiner stopped what he was doing and turned to stare at him, incomprehension in his eyes.

"We must leave," Shimizu repeated. "We have no authority here."

# CHAPTER 1

## THE FUNERAL
## SIXTEEN YEARS LATER

*National Memorial Cemetery of the Pacific, Honolulu, Hawaii, June 6, 1969.*

I SOMETIMES THINK that had I known what lay ahead, I would not have agreed to write the life story of General Philip Sheridan Coursen. But, then, when I'm being honest with myself, I admit I probably would have done so in spite of everything. Somewhere deep inside most of us lies a taste for mystery and violence. "Sex and violence," my writing professor used to say, "is the secret of a commercially successful novel." And through the lifeless eyes of General Coursen I was destined to encounter plenty of both.

It began the day of his funeral. The American flag snapped against a clear blue sky as the trade winds coursed across the Punchbowl. The service was just about over, and my gaze took in this final resting place for more than 12,000 veterans of America's wars. No rows of white crosses here. Stone plaques, flush with the ground, were all that marked the graves. Occasionally a small flag or a bouquet of flowers rose above the sea of green, but no heroic equestrian statues or ornate headstones called attention to the high and the mighty, as they did at Arlington. Here, all were equal in the arms of death.

I had never written about a dead man before. I call myself a novelist, but the novels I write don't sell well, or don't sell at all. You won't find the name Matthew Clark on any best-seller list. To keep the wolf from the door I often do biographies, usually for successful executives who want their dull lives immortalized in prose. And I sometimes write histories of organizations for the same purpose. Writing about a man I could not interview would involve a lot more research than usual, but I was suffering from a long bout of bank account anemia. That, plus a free trip to Hawaii, were two good reasons to take on the job.

My gaze came to rest on the general's widow, the lady who had hired me. She'd gotten my name from a mutual friend who worked for the *Honolulu Star-Bulletin* and called me when it became known that the general was terminally ill and near death. Ever since his retirement, she had wanted him to write his autobiography, but he had refused, nor would he allow a biography written by someone else. She was now determined that his life story be told. We settled fees and procedures, and I was on my way.

Miriam Coursen possessed the calm dignity I had come to associate with the wives of senior military officers. Her tanned, smooth complexion showed no emotion as she listened to several speakers extol her husband's virtues and mourn his departure. Her blonde hair, pulled gently back to form a brief bun, could have been bleached, but it could very well be natural. On her, it didn't seem to matter. I knew that she was nearly fifty, but I would have accepted mid- thirties had I not known otherwise. Miriam Coursen had obviously been a striking beauty as a young woman, and she was still a beautiful woman today.

It was then that I noticed someone else. Under a large banyan tree, about a hundred feet away and slightly uphill, a young woman stood alone, obviously attentive to the ceremony. My eyes narrowed as I tried to see her Asian features more closely. Why was she standing removed from the rest of the mourners? Did the general's widow know she was there? My eyes returned to that lady. If she knew, it didn't show.

The speeches were over, and the chaplain stepped back from the flag-draped coffin. A young officer in dress blues issued a series of commands, and seven rifles rose in unison. Three sharp volleys echoed from the crater walls. Then the sad, proud notes of "Taps" brought the first hint of tears to the eyes of the general's widow. I could understand that. I was affected myself and I didn't even know the man. "Taps" has a way of doing that.

The bugler lowered his instrument, and the honor guard marched away. Normally the service would have ended here, but instead, six men detached themselves from the group of mourners and gathered directly at the open grave, around the casket. They were older men, probably in their sixties, and each one put on a military-type overseas cap bearing a patch I was too far away to identify. One of them produced a bottle of champagne and six glasses. Then, hesitatingly, and slightly off key, they began to sing.

> Old soldiers never die,
> Never die, never die.
> Old soldiers never die,
> They just fade away.

I had not heard that song since the days following General Douglas MacArthur's farewell speech to Congress when it poured out over the air waves. As emotional as it had been at that time, it paled compared to the effect of these six men, their voices small and wavering, singing in the stillness of this huge memorial. For the second time I felt my throat constrict, and this time my eyes stung as well. When the song ended, they raised their glasses in a toast over the casket and drank. Then, one at a time, each man laid his glass on top of the casket and stepped back into the group of mourners.

The service was over. People began to disperse slowly to waiting cars, some of them stopping to talk to the widow on the way. I wondered if I would interview any of them in the succeeding weeks. I would not know until I had my first talk with Miriam Coursen tomorrow. Grief or not, she was determined to get the project started. As I turned toward my rented Datsun 240Z, I saw that the young woman who had been standing under the banyan tree was gone.

# CHAPTER 2

## THE ALERT

*Camp George Armstrong Custer, Kokura, Japan, home of the Tenth Armored Cavalry Reconnaissance Battalion, United States Army, 0350 hours, 16 January 1950.*

THE LONE JEEP GROUND slowly up the winding dirt road, feeling its way around ruts and potholes, blackout lights its only illumination in the pre-dawn darkness. Its sole occupants were the driver and one passenger in the front seat. Radio equipment filled the rear, where the back seat should have been. The gate of what was obviously a military reservation gradually took shape in the gloom, but instead of proceeding toward it, the jeep veered off the road and climbed to a small knoll overlooking the camp. If the guard in the sentry box saw the blacked-out vehicle he gave no sign, and no challenge was issued as the jeep came to a stop.

The officer beside the driver drew a flashlight with a subdued beam from his pocket and consulted a notebook. The dim light from the flashlight barely revealed the silver leaves of a lieutenant colonel on his shoulder and the printing "Coursen" on his name tag. He turned to the radio and flicked the dial. The driver revved the engine and then switched off the ignition. Only the steady hiss of the radio disturbed the stillness. The passenger faced forward again and looked at his watch. Five minutes to four. Five minutes to go.

# RICHARD MCMAHON

\* \* \* \*

## AMAZON FIVE-STAR REVIEW EXCERPTS

Great Book, I could not put it down, and what an ending!—**Helga G. Minderjahn**

I don't often write reviews, but this book deserves one. It's terrific; one of those that you are sorry to see end. The plot is more than engaging and the characters eminently believable. Additionally, it's realistic. I served in the military for 30+ years and the author captures the culture entirely. I also served several times in Japan and again he does that justice. I probably read at least a book a week and likely more. So far this is the best novel I've read in a year. Well done.—**Neil**

I loved this book! Mr. McMahon brings his characters to life through his extensive knowledge of history, the US Military and martial conflict. The twists and turns this book takes, keep you guessing as you experience this wonderful love story filled with military action, mystery and intrigue.—**caligirl**

This is a great book. Do not start reading with a hot cup of coffee, because next time you take a sip it will be cold. This book is extremely well written and will hold your attention from front page to last. It has a surprise ending, one you will not expect. It excels when covering the Korean conflict and other military details. Excellent value, great read!!—**Jay Feldman**

Richard McMahon does a fantastic job writing truly believable and mesmerizing fiction. I sat in a chair, in my jammies, from morning to night reading till the surprising end. This book is that kind of read.—**Amazon Customer**

First I don't normally read "war stories" unless I'm researching my father's time as a POW in WWII. That being said I'm really glad that I read this one. The book is well written and I quickly became invested in the characters, I mourned when a character was lost to the brutalities of war and cheered when they survived that said war. The intrigues will surprise you and keep you reading til the end. Out of the ashes of the broken lives of the characters rises a rebirth called love. —**trekker**

It was a pleasure to read & I hated to see it end. I hope for more novels from McMahon! It had the true ring of authenticity, and gave me an insight into Army life I didn't have.—**Jim Haas**

Excellent writing. I enjoyed the story line and especially the fact that I did not "guess" the outcome. I will look for other books written by Richard McMahon.—**Sandy Speed**

This work has an unusual and interesting plot. It was an "I can't lay this down until I find out what happens next" type of work. Very good writing style—**bigbaddoc**

Richard McMahon's The Dark Side of Glory is a classic, probably the best insight into the pre-Korean War US Army, and the war, itself, ever written. As an Army brat in the 1950's, and an active duty Naval officer from 1959 - '65, I have only praise for his accuracy and skill in portraying military life and warfare. His battle scenes are devastatingly brought to life, as a framework to a complex and irresistible plot, peopled by believable characters. The Dark Side of Glory is, at the same time a subtle and multi-faceted mystery that captivates as seduces the reader until the last page.—**William F**

AVAILABLE NOW IN EBOOK AND PRINT EDITIONS FROM AMAZON, BARNES & NOBLE, AND OTHER BOOK SELLERS.

## JUST PUBLISHED

### ALSO BY RICHARD MCMAHON

When Michelle Iverson disappears after posting a provocative message on an Internet bulletin board devoted to BDSM practices, her father hires Mason Grant to find her. Mason teams up with the missing woman's stepsister, Tracy, and the pair delves into the dark side of cyber space, seeking clues to Michelle's disappearance. The journey leads Mason and Tracy into a love affair, down false trails, and finally to a confrontation with a sadistic abductor, who is obsessed with seeking a woman who will be a willing partner in his sexual fantasies. Mason's search results in a shocking revelation, which turns his world on end.

# A WEB OF EVIL

There is no evil from which some good does not result, and consequently men should do evil as much as it suits them, since it is merely one more way of doing good.

— Voltaire, *Zadig*, Chapter 18,
quoted at the beginning of *Justine.*

Once my grave has been filled in, it will be seeded with acorns, so that the dirt of said grave will eventually hold vegetation, and once the thicket has grown back to its original state, the traces of my grave will disappear from the face of the earth, just as I hope that my memory will be erased from the minds of men....

— Last will and testament,
Donatien Alphonse Francois,
Marquis de Sade

# 1

*URL: http://www.darkchateau.com/bb*

*FROM: MichelleIverson@lava.net*

*Hello Members of the Dark Chateau,*

*My name is Michelle. I am 21 years old, blond, with blue eyes. I am 5 ft 6 inches tall, weigh 118 pounds, and my measurements are 36-22-34. I am shaved everywhere and pierced everywhere. I need a harsh, cruel master to put me through intense humiliation, degradation and pain. You can do anything to me: hurt me, beat me, humiliate me, treat me like a dog—I mean ANYTHING. Send me email describing what you will do to me. Make me be your slave!*

MASON GRANT handed the computer printout back to Frederick Iverson. "How long has your daughter been missing?"

"It's been two days." Iverson's bloodshot eyes stared vacantly out the large picture window of his home high on Tantalus. The view encompassed almost the whole of Honolulu, from the mountains to the sea, but Iverson didn't appear to notice.

The note had been posted two weeks ago, Grant noted. Enough time for the weirdos and kooks to respond, and perhaps do more. "I think this is a matter for the police," he said.

Iverson exhaled deeply and walked away from the window, his

slippered feet making no sound on the highly polished koa planks. Grant's own shoes had been left at the door, Japanese style, a custom that most people followed in Hawaii. When Iverson finally spoke, his voice sounded despondent but emphatic.

"You read that damn thing. I could not possibly let something like this become public. It would ruin my business."

"Your daughter's life may be in danger," Grant replied. "Don't you think that's more important than a threat to your business? Besides, I think you may be exaggerating the consequences of this becoming public. In today's social environment—"

"Mr. Grant, I am the financial manager of some of the largest fortunes here in Hawaii and on the West Coast. This is old money. I am sure you know what that means."

Grant did. Old families, rich for generations, living on inherited wealth, shying from publicity of any kind, conservative to a fault.

"I am entrusted with virtually complete authority over these funds," Iverson continued. "Mine is a business where trust and reputation are paramount." He paused for a moment, running his fingers nervously through his uncombed hair. Grant sensed that Iverson was trying to find a convincing argument, for himself as well as his listener. "To my clients," Iverson went on, "trust and conservative behavior are synonymous. Their morals tend to be old-fashioned, and they look closely at the family as well as the firm. If it became known that one of my daughters was dabbling in..." He struggled to find the words, "kinky sex...well, I could lose everything. This entire matter must be handled in the strictest confidence, investigated privately."

"I'm not a private investigator," Grant reminded him.

"I know that, but General Talbot recommended you very highly. I am confident that you will be discreet. You're one of us."

Grant wasn't, but he let it pass. The wealthy always assumed that because he was financially independent he was a member of their society. He wondered what some of them might think if they knew that he had grown up in one of the poorest sections of New York City, with a widowed mother struggling to raise three children on a combination of welfare, and support from the men who came and went in her life.

Grant walked over to the place at the large window that Iverson had vacated, mulling over what he had heard. It seemed clear to him that further attempts to persuade Iverson to turn this matter over to the authorities would prove fruitless. Although he seemed obviously worried about Michelle, Iverson's concern for his business appeared to override that worry. Grant also thought he detected a certain anger, a resentment on the father's part toward his daughter for putting him in this predicament. If that were indeed the case, such resentment might be reinforcing Iverson's decision not to call in the authorities. Grant turned back toward his host.

"Is there anyone beside yourself who knows about this?"

"My other daughter, Tracy. It was she who found—that." Iverson grimaced toward the printout, which he had replaced on his desk.

"Did Tracy find anything else? How about Michelle's email, have you checked that?"

Iverson shook his head. "We cannot get into Michelle's account. It is password protected. And there is nothing else in writing. Tracy has been through all her things."

"Have you tried to find the password, things like birthdays, significant dates, familiar names?"

"Tracy is trying all of that. So far nothing has worked. Can you help with that?"

Grant was no computer geek, but he had friends who were. "I may know someone who can help," he said.

Iverson nodded, his eyes returning once more to the printout, and he picked it up again. "Pierced everywhere! What the hell does that mean?"

Grant did not answer. He didn't think it was really a question. Instead, he posed one of his own, deciding to be direct rather than delicate with his approach. "Mr. Iverson, did you have any reason to suspect earlier that Michelle had masochistic fantasies?"

Iverson winced, but did not hesitate in his reply. "Absolutely not. And I'm not sure that she does have them. Tracy pointed out that lots of people post that sort of thing on computer bulletin boards just to…well, for titillation. And she thinks Michelle may have done the same thing. She has always been rather impish. But she is not like that. I cannot believe that she wanted…really meant those things. I'm sure it was a lark, some new way to be far out, to push the limits. Maybe she enjoys doing that."

"Mr. Iverson, unless we can get into Michelle's email, we may never know what happened to her."

Iverson sighed. "I am aware of that."

Grant decided to try one more time. "And you still don't want to go to the police? HPD is a good police department. They might find her quickly."

"There is no assurance that she is in the city, or even in the state, for that matter."

"Missing Persons Bureaus cooperate with each other, exchange information, and have access to federal government files."

Iverson dismissed Grant's remarks with a wave. "Missing persons are the lowest priority of police departments everywhere." Grant felt that all depended on who the missing person was, but he didn't interrupt. "Besides," Iverson continued, "it's just not possible. I cannot risk this… this obscenity becoming known."

"Informing the police doesn't necessarily mean publicity. The case might be handled in confidence."

Iverson grunted. "Do you really believe that? Well, I do not. There are just too many opportunities for a leak, for the media to find out. Can you imagine what the press would do with a story like this?"

Grant tried one last tack. "How does your wife feel about keeping this away from the police?" Grant asked.

"My wife died years ago."

Grant was now convinced it was useless to pursue the matter. Above all, Iverson seemed determined to conceal what he obviously considered would be a fatal embarrassment to his business and his social standing. Grant watched him turn to the printout again. He seemed unable to let it go.

"The Dark Chateau," Iverson read aloud. "What has that got to do with what she…what is described here—humiliation, beating, piercing…?"

From the heading of the printout, Grant surmised that *darkchateau.com* was a web site for those interested in unusual sexual practices, a place where they could communicate with each other by bulletin board postings, and perhaps obtain other services. Again, Iverson was not really asking a question, so Grant said nothing. Finally, Iverson dropped the printout back on the coffee table and turned toward him.

"Well, where are we then? Are you willing to help me and keep the police out of it?"

Grant knew that Frederick Iverson had pretty much said all he wanted to say. "I'm willing to try, although I don't know how much help I can be."

In spite of the weakness of Grant's answer, Iverson seemed satisfied. They spent some time settling financial and other details, and Grant prepared to leave.

"Is there a time when I can talk to Tracy?"

"Right now, if you wish," Iverson replied. "She's out by the pool. She's waiting for you."

11647537R00207

Made in the USA
San Bernardino, CA
06 December 2018